French
Lessons

E-book ISBN: 978-1-957081-27-4

Paperback ISBN: 978-1-957081-28-1

Hardcover ISBN: 978-1-957081-29-8

KAREN HEENAN

French Lessons

Also by Karen Heenan

The Tudor Court:
Songbird
A Wider World
Lady, in Waiting
The Son in Shadow
The Tudor Court (ebook only omnibus)

Ava & Claire:
Coming Apart
Coming Closer
Coming Together
Coming Home (ebook only omnibus)

Alternate Endings (anthology)

Toto, I have the feeling we're not in Kansas anymore.
Dorothy Gale

Contents

Prologue – April 1947

I lock the trunk, put the key in my bag, and take a final look around. The room in which I have spent the last twelve months—the most eventful, meaningful year of my life—has slowly emptied. Now all that remains is the furniture.

The things I have purchased to make it feel more like home are either given away or packed in the trunk, cushioned by my winter clothes. My notebooks, of which there are too many, are tied with ribbon and stowed into an empty spot in my suitcase.

I turn out my handbag, to make sure I am carrying nothing that should be discarded. A small square of blue paper falls on the bedspread and I smile. Before tucking it away for safekeeping, I unfold it and read it one last time.

This trip is long overdue. We both know that. It isn't easy to let go, because you're my little girl. But it's time. Mama

Believe in yourself, kid. Dr. Max

I'll miss you. Dan

Go to every show you can afford and tell me about them, even though I know you won't be able to describe the dancing properly. Thelma

Have a good trip. Toby

Have a good trip. George

Have lots of adventures and write them all down. You're already a great writer. Just think what Paris will do. Grace

I remember a pond with sailboats. Send me a postcard when you find it. Teddy

At long last! I hope Paris treats you well. Claire

April 1946

All my life, I've been a good girl. As the eldest daughter, I helped my mother with my siblings and my siblings with their schoolwork. When I was done with that, I helped Mama with her dressmaking business. My grades were excellent. I got a scholarship, went to college, and became a teacher, and then I helped my students.

I am exhausted by my own virtue.

"Do you want anything?" I ask, shifting in my seat. "I'm thirsty."

My companion shakes her head, not raising her eyes from the book on her lap.

Leaving my book behind, I take my bag and make my way down the corridor to the connecting door to the dining car. The train sways and my toes curl inside my shoes, as if that will help me keep my balance. I take a window seat and watch the scenery fly past. On the other side of the rain-spotted glass, it is April, cool and showery, but the train is as stuffy as an old person's parlor. The dry heat makes my eyes burn, and I squeeze them shut for a moment, letting the constantly threatening tears serve a purpose beyond embarrassment.

"Menu, miss?" the waiter asks, proffering a card.

"Just tea, thank you." As I pull a quarter from my coin purse, my fingertips encounter something unfamiliar: a small square of blue paper, not much bigger than a postage stamp.

I unfold the paper, pressing it flat against the white linen, and read what my family has written to send me off into the unknown. Only Grace, my youngest sister, could have run down all three of my brothers and made them write a single word.

It is ridiculous to be on the verge of tears again. I've been away from my family before, though never for more than a few weeks. And Paris has been a dream almost as long as I've wanted to be a writer.

I scan their messages once more, then exchange it for the letter I started earlier in the day, reading it over again. It conveys the right tone: guilt-inducing without revealing the depth of my hurt feelings.

April 3, 1946

Dear Hazel,

I'm writing this from the train, where I thought we would be sitting together, about to embark on our grand adventure. But you chose a different adventure. I understand, I do. I only wish you'd chosen sooner so I could have prepared to be alone.

I'm not alone now. Sofie is with me for the voyage, but once we land in France, she'll travel straight on to Berlin in the hopes of finding her family. (According to Uncle Harry, the ones who weren't Jews were Nazis, so it's not likely she'll find anyone, but I pray that she does.).

I shouldn't gossip. You know how fierce Sofie can be. Her family is her business. And were we so brave at nineteen that we would cross the world to look for people who are almost certainly dead? Especially when Aunt Claire and Teddy need her at home?

But Uncle Harry knew she would want this, the same way I wanted Paris, so he put money aside for both of us. No one can object because they're all sad that he's gone. So am I. You know that. I'm just wasting paper at this point, trying to find ways to say how much I'll miss you.

Truthfully, I'm also a little bit scared, though I've been dreaming of this trip for ten years.

Love to you and your (surprise!) husband.

Pearl

I can't address the letter until we reach New York. My address book is deep in my suitcase, and for the life of me, I can't remember my friend's new last name. Trust Hazel to completely prepare for our trip—including commissioning a few pieces from Mama and a whirlwind shopping spree that cleaned out at least two dress shops—only to appear at the train station this morning, not with her suitcases, but with the man she'd married yesterday in Maryland.

During the darkest days of the war, when it felt like Europe would never be free, Hazel and I had planned where we would go when it was finally over. We sat on the bed with my illustrated guidebook, picking out destinations. Hers was the top of the Eiffel Tower, preferably with a handsome Frenchman; I wanted to walk along the Seine and breathe it all in. When the city was liberated in 1944, we drank champagne in Uncle Harry's living room and sang *La Marseillaise* until even Thelma abandoned us. And my sister never leaves a room if there's an opportunity for her to make a spectacle of herself.

At that point, it was all a pipedream. While Hazel has her own money, every cent of my paycheck went to my family or to pay back what I borrowed for college. It would be years before I could afford such a trip. Then Uncle Harry died, right before Christmas. When his will was read, it contained bequests for everyone, but mine came with the stipulation that the money had to be spent on a year in Paris.

When she heard the news, Hazel postponed her plan to join her father's law practice to come with me. The days since were spent in a frenzy of preparation.

And yet here I am, on a train bound for New York, with no one but Sofie, who, absorbed in her weighty German tome, doesn't even notice that I've returned. Though she is fluent, ten years in Philadelphia with my aunt and uncle have erased every bit of her accent, and ever since she decided to go back, she's been immersing herself in her first language.

I've studied French since 1934, though it's done me no good until now. Four years of high school and again in college, despite being an English major who intended to be a writer.

But writers need to eat, so practicality made me become a teacher. For the last few years, I've taught a combined class whose fathers were fighting and whose mothers were working for the war effort down at the Navy Yard. I enjoyed teaching, and because my students were young,

I could complete my grading over supper and write in the evenings, regularly sending out stories to all the magazines which might be willing to print them. So far, I've had pieces published in *Colliers*, *Scribners*, and *The Ladies Home Journal*. I was still banging on the door of the *Saturday Evening Post*—almost literally, since their offices are in Philadelphia.

"You sigh any harder, you'll blow my hat off." Sofie regards me, rectangular lenses glinting in the light from the window. "What is wrong, is it that Hazel abandoned you?"

"Isn't that enough?" I try for a light tone, but I'm blindsided. "Jilted me for a soldier."

Hazel and Press had been on-again, off-again since 1942, but when he came home from the Pacific in his ill-fitting lieutenant's uniform, gaunt and twitching from shell shock, they'd had a huge fight, and she called off their engagement. It was as our trip got closer that she began to regret her decision.

"I should make up with him," she said last week. "Maybe a year apart is what we need."

"You were apart for almost three years," I pointed out. "Neither of you like to write letters. How will separation fix anything?"

"Hmm." She scrunched up her freckled face and stuck her tongue out at me. "You may be right."

It's my fault: I made her think about it. Now she's Mrs. Preston Something-or-Other and tomorrow I'll be on a ship bound for Paris, all by myself.

Pennsylvania Station is as high-ceilinged as a cathedral and as loud as a boxing match. I keep a tight hold on my handbag and the small case containing Mona, my precious Royal Arrow typewriter. The rest of my luggage was checked onto the train in Philadelphia and I have no idea now where to find it. Uncle Harry would have known how to retrieve our bags and find a taxi to the hotel.

"Pearl!" Sofie's voice, impatient. "Where are your tickets?"

"My tickets?" I look around again at the swarming crowds and feel light-headed.

She brandishes a handful of cards. "For your things. The porter will send them on to the hotel. I want some air. Come along."

Put in my place by a girl barely out of high school, I fish the tickets out of my pocket and hand them to the porter, watching as Sofie gives him first the name of our hotel and then a handful of coins.

"What was that?"

"A tip." She pushes her glasses up and straightens her hat. Other than her slenderness, she is as unlike Aunt Claire as it is possible to be. Dark-haired, dark-eyed, severe. She abhors ruffles and flounces and the only flowers she approves of reside in vases. "You are a sheltered goose. You can't stumble around Paris like this. You are asking to be taken advantage of."

"Yes, Mother." I follow her through the packed humanity and out onto the street, just as crowded, but with swiftly moving, purposeful New Yorkers. My few trips to the city have been with Aunt Claire, wrapped in comfort at every step. This is very different—and yet Sofie, raised in my aunt's household, is completely at ease.

She pauses on the corner until the light changes, one finger held up as if to test the wind. "This way, Pearl. Come along."

Our hotel reservations were taken care of by Aunt Claire. I'm surprised—and very glad, considering my unsettled state of mind—that we're not staying at the Waldorf Astoria. I see Sofie's hand in that. While she is accustomed to her guardians' wealth, she does not squander money. We will share a room tonight, as well as a stateroom for the next ten days. I wonder how I will manage almost two weeks with Sofie aboard ship. She can be hard going at times.

Once through the doors, she marches up to the desk. Despite looking no older than fourteen, her authoritative manner makes the clerk treat her as if she were Renate Steiner, Aunt Claire's opera singer friend. Sofie signs the register and gestures for me to do the same.

"Our trunks will be sent straight on to the ship," she says, "and our cases will arrive soon. Please have them brought up so we can change for dinner."

My family never changes for dinner, nor do we go to the sort of restaurants that require special clothes. Whenever I dressed up for dates in high school and college, I ended up wearing my best dress to a diner or drugstore because the boy's money had run out after he paid for movie tickets.

The elevator opens on the sixth floor, and we follow discreet signs to room 614. The spacious room has two beds, two dressers, and a small desk tucked into one corner. I make a beeline for its familiar shape while Sofie investigates the bathroom.

A soft knock reveals a pimply young man in a dark green jacket and cap. I step back and direct him to set the bags down at the foot of each bed, letting Sofie have the one nearest the window. When he lingers, I guess wildly and hand him a quarter.

Sofie comes out as the door closes. "Good. Now we can unpack."

"We're here for one night." It is pointless to unpack only to pack it up again in the morning. "I'm not taking out anything but my nightgown."

"Are you going to spend the rest of today and tonight in your traveling clothes?" She can convey skepticism in the slightest lift of her brow. "If you take them off now, the hotel will press them."

Defeated—and educated—I open my suitcase and begin piling clothes on the bed.

April 5, 1946

It was too much to hope there would be a library on the ship. I'm glad I brought Sense & Sensibility *to tide me over. Dear Jane Austen, she's always so comforting.*

I need all the comfort I can get right now. Our cabin is like a closet, with five of us crammed into two sets of bunk beds, with a cot in the center of the floor. Because we all have knees and elbows, it's very cramped. None of us spend any time there if we can help it. Our suitcases are shoved under the beds. There's nowhere to set up my typewriter, so Mona's under the bed for the duration, as well.

I'm not writing anything anyway, other than here. I hope I'm gathering experiences and sensations that will make me a better writer. I don't want to go through all this to come out on the other side the same old Pearl Mary Kimber I was when I began. That's why I told the family not to come to New York to see us off. I couldn't bear watching them on the pier, waving up at me, without wanting to run back down the gangplank.

Amazingly, Sofie has made friends. That makes me feel even more backward. They're a Jewish couple, also traveling to Germany to see what, if anything, remains of their former lives. She's arranged to travel with them as far as Berlin. She's halfway gone already, and we won't dock at LeHavre for more than a week.

I spend most of my time on deck, wrapped in my heavy coat because the ocean breeze is constant and COLD. There are deck chairs (one thing I expected that came true) but no steamer rugs. I bring the blanket from my bunk, which means I have to keep track of it and can't go to the dining room without dashing back to put it away.

I made a promise to myself that I won't hide with my nose in a book and waste the experience of an Atlantic crossing. My cousin is not the only one who can make friends. It just feels like she is.

Even though I knew this would be nothing like Aunt Claire's luxury voyage on the *Normandie*, the *S.S. Oregon* is a continual surprise. It's a cargo ship, for one thing, but these days, it also carries passengers. The French Line and Cunard ships, if they've been released from military service, are busy ferrying servicemen home; try as he might, Dr. Max couldn't get us a place on one of them as they returned to Europe.

All the cabins are as crowded as ours. Even married people are sharing with other couples. War tourists, they call us, but from what I can see, most of the passengers are desperate to get to England, France, or Germany for reasons other than curiosity.

I don't imagine a cargo ship is ever attractive, but the *Oregon*'s public areas are downright shabby. There is adequate seating in the dining room, though the tables and chairs, along with the dishes, are functional rather than pretty. That's fine by me: Aunt's stories of the *Normandie* were fascinating, but even she said it was too much by the end. It would likely be too much for me in the beginning.

The other women in our room are:

Mrs. Zelda Morgen, a fortyish widow from New Jersey. She recently received word that her brother was located in a DP camp after having been freed from Dachau. She is traveling to see if he is well enough to come home with her. She doesn't talk much.

Miss Maud Culver (thirty) is going to England to visit family. She's a bit full of herself, talking about yearly pre-war trips to her cousins' house in the country, but she's not sure what's ahead because the place was taken over by the army and her relatives are living in something called a dower house, which is apparently a small house on the same estate. At least they have a house.

Miss Anne Painter is Sofie's age. She got out of France right ahead of the invasion and left a friend behind when her papers were questioned. Her friend is living in the outskirts of Marseille, so they will be reunited.

So many stories. If there are a hundred passengers on this ship, there are a hundred compelling reasons that they are here.

Why can't I think how to write about them?

Sofie has the upper bunk, but she is dressed and gone before I am out of bed. It's not that I oversleep, only that the ship doesn't go quiet until late, and I stay up to enjoy the silence and the lack of people. Sitting swaddled in my blanket, I can finally hear my thoughts in a way that I can't indoors. Snatches of dialogue. Questions without answers. Eventually, these thoughts will lead somewhere.

I stay up late in the hopes of having an idea, but also to think about my family. I try to calculate what time it is at home and what they're doing.

It is Friday, so they will have eaten supper at Aunt Claire's house, a tradition that started when we first moved to the city. After the table is cleared, they'll move to the living room to talk and listen to records. In addition to her love of classical music, Aunt has developed a taste for Glenn Miller. Dan and I taught her how to swing dance when Uncle Harry was sick and she needed distracting.

My eyes fill as I remember Mama and Dr. Max following along, laughing until they were breathless. I blot my tears with a corner of the blanket, thinking how silly it is to get weepy over happy memories. I can't be more homesick in Paris than I am on this ship. I'm not used to being alone, much less surrounded and alone at the same time.

I'd better get used to it. I'll be staying with a friend of Aunt's until I find a place to live, but after that, I'm on my own. Alone, in a strange city, a strange country, where my accent will mark me as an outsider.

That, too, is what I need. I have this because my uncle remembered my long-ago disappointment and put money aside for me—enough so I can rent a room, walk the streets and sit in the cafés and *write* until I finally write something good enough that I can call myself a writer.

But Paris isn't just about becoming a writer. Having never been on a path of my own choosing, I finally feel, for all my loneliness, a little bit free. The weight of the past, the long years of war, the lingering grief at my father's death, the responsibilities placed on me from a too-young age—even the joyous shackles of my job can't reach me across the ocean.

Will I be able to manage? I would hate beyond anything to give up and return home early, crammed into another tiny cabin filled with strangers, none of whom would care that I had failed.

That means I can't fail. I sit up straight, letting Mama's strength seep into my spine, and give a final enormous sniff.

"Are you all right, miss?" It is one of the many stewards tasked with keeping the crowded ship functioning. "Only you've been out here every night."

"I'm fine." I pull the blanket around my shoulders, surprised that anyone has noticed. "I like the fresh air—and the lack of people."

He grins at me. "You think you're cramped, miss. We're packed in like sardines in a can." Looking down at the blanket, he says, "It's getting cold out here. Why don't you come in and I'll find you a cup of tea."

I follow him to the lounge, a room I have mostly avoided as it is occupied by male passengers alleviating their boredom with endless games of cards. A single table of players remains, the air above them heavy with smoke.

"Sit here, miss." He directs me to the table farthest from them. "I'll fetch the tea. How do you take it?"

"Two sugars, if you have it." I give my blanket its own chair, then settle in to wait. Before long he returns with two steaming mugs.

"Sorry," he says, placing one in front of me. "I can sit someplace else if you want to be alone. It's just that I'm off duty now..."

"Sit," I say. "I've had enough of my own company for one day."

He raises his mug. "It's already tomorrow, miss."

"Is it that late?" The tea is strong and sweet, the way I like it. Growing up, we didn't often have sugar; when we did, it went to Daddy or Dan. "I should go."

"Stay a little." He nods at the gamblers. "They usually leave about now—they'll go back and drink themselves to sleep—and then it's just us, cleaning up and having our own good time."

"I'm Pearl," I offer, before I change my mind. "Pearl Kimber."

"Pat." He dredges from somewhere an Irish accent and kisses my hand like a gentleman. "Patrick O'Shaughnessy at your service."

The card players leave shortly after and another uniformed young man comes to clear the table. He looks over and Pat O'Shaughnessy raises a finger. "Go ahead, Cal," he calls. "She's one of us."

"Am I?"

"You're not one of *them*. That's all that matters."

Cal disappears with a tray of glasses and overflowing ashtrays. In a moment, music filters into the room. The tables rapidly fill, stewards and waiters and young men in smoke-and-grease-stained clothes, each one curled over a mug.

"From the engine room," Pat confides. "They come up late to get some air and a hot cuppa."

"I can't blame them." They look like the men I grew up with: hunched shoulders, squinting eyes, vivid smiles of pleasure at a sugared tea and the unexpected sight of a girl.

The tempo increases. I swing my foot along with Count Basie, stopping when I catch Pat's eyes on my leg.

"Dance?" He holds out his hand. "Come on, Miss Pearl, cut loose. There's not another dame on this tub who would come in here."

That's what I am afraid of, abruptly. It is after midnight, on a sleeping ship, and I'm alone with a dozen strange men. I close my eyes, and like a kaleidoscope, the picture shifts and changes. These men, likely every one of them, have been through the war. Have survived and deserve a bit of fun.

And so do I.

I do not want to be bad, only a little less good. Looking back over my shoulder, I say, "If my blanket disappears, you're going to have to find me another one."

It is well after two when I slip barefoot into the darkened cabin and retreat to the bathroom to brush my teeth. The flushed face in the mirror is almost unrecognizable. I look—and feel—more alive than I have in years.

I danced not only with Pat but with another steward, then Cal and two more waiters—brothers—named Jimmy and Bill. Frankie, one of the young men from the engine room, proved the most adept, spinning me dizzily around and sliding me between his legs to great cheering from the others.

It was fun. Sheer, uncomplicated fun. If I can remember how to do this, the next year might prove very interesting indeed.

April 12, 1946

Despite loving the idea of travel, there is little about the actual process of traveling that is enjoyable. If that sounds negative, then so be it. After nine days, I've had more than enough of cramped quarters and bad manners brought on by discomfort and impatience. And I'm tired of hearing people snore! I've shared a room almost my entire life, but five grown women is four too many, even if one of them is Sofie.

The *Oregon*'s crew is more intent than usual, busy with last-minute duties to ensure our smooth arrival. Nevertheless, when I pass a steward in the passage on the way to dinner, he whispers that the lounge will be "hopping" later, and I should come along if I want a proper send-off.

Sofie is already packed and settled on her bunk with another German book. "You will have to pack in the morning," she says, looking me up and down with narrowed eyes. "Unless you plan to travel in your red flowers."

"Then I will pack in the morning." I fold the blanket over my arm and tuck my room key into my brassiere. "I'm going out."

"Wherever *do* you go?" There is no actual curiosity in Maud Culver's tone; she is too uninterested to do more than ask insinuating questions.

It will be two hours before the lounge is cleared, but I'm afraid that if I stay inside, I might fall asleep and miss the final night. Instead, I stand at the rail and stare out at the vast black ocean. If I ever needed a reminder of my relative unimportance in the universe, looking out at the Atlantic is just the ticket.

Somewhere out there is France. I strain to see harbor lights but there is nothing but the flickering of moonlight on the waves. I am ready. Almost ready. These nights in the lounge, talking and dancing with the crew, have done more to ease my anxiety than any conversation with my fellow passengers would have done. I'm scared to speak French to actual French people, but I will cross that bridge when I come to it. At least I will have already crossed the ocean.

I'll be sad to leave Pat O'Shaughnessy behind. When we're not dancing, he makes me weep with laughter by mimicking the passengers—including the snooty Miss Culver. We've also found time to talk. He knows my plans and made me promise to send him one of my stories. In return, he told me about his family back in Minneapolis and his dream of transferring to a proper passenger liner once they're reconditioned and running again.

Not long before midnight, the doors open. Pat's brogue reaches the deck chair where I have established myself. "You'd better have your dancing shoes on, miss."

"Don't you worry about that." I duck under his arm into the brightly lit passage. "You try to keep up with Frankie this time."

His laughter follows me to the lounge, already crowded with familiar faces and more than a few new ones, including three women who give me tentative smiles. Also present is what appears to be the entire crew from below decks, cleaned up for the final night in bright white undershirts, their hair slicked back with water.

"Ready?" Pat catches my hand and spins me into the center of the floor, where I am caught by someone else. There are hoots and applause and so much music. I dance until I lose myself.

The morning light is misty and uncertain when we gather to present our passports for inspection. Only after that will we be permitted to disembark. Over the rail comes the bustle of the port—the creak and groan of machinery, the twin smells of smoke and exhaust, shouts in every language. It is rather like listening to a pot come to a boil.

Once our passports are checked, we make our way toward the gangplank. The crew lines up to see us off. I smile at the men I've danced with and try not to notice that Pat's shaky grin has tears behind it.

"You get into the *Saturday Evening Post*, you'd better send me a copy," he murmurs, his lips barely moving.

The gangplank lurches under my feet the way the deck did ten days ago. The ground isn't any better. I put down my hastily packed bags and pull my coat closed, buttoning it over my crumpled red dress, letting the crowd flow around me. My eyes burn and my feet hurt, but I am tingling with life.

A line snakes slowly into an echoing, barnlike building where we make our way through customs. There are police everywhere and not nearly enough agents to accommodate the passengers. While my papers are glanced over and handed back immediately, Sofie's are scrutinized for such a long time that I begin to fear they won't permit her to enter the country. Finally, after a muttered consultation between several uniformed men, her passport is returned and we join the jostling crowd outside, where four rumbling, pre-war buses wait to take us into the city.

I rub the dust from the window with my handkerchief and look out at the port. Shattered buildings cling to the edge of the harbor: even the jetty alongside which the *Oregon* docked is pitted with holes, stretches of its surface missing entirely. It is enough to drive the events of last night out of my head, at least temporarily.

"It didn't seem real until now," I whisper to Sofie. When we emerged from the customs building, she climbed directly onto the bus, standing to one side so I could take the window seat.

"It did to me." Her glasses are folded in her gloved hand; she does not wish to see, not yet.

The Normandy beaches, where thousands of men died less than two years ago, are barely a hundred miles from LeHavre. France is still raw, as are its people; I will have to keep that in mind.

APRIL 14, 1946
ARRIVED FRANCE. PARIS TOMORROW. LETTER FOLLOWS. PEARL.

The train to Paris is crowded and slow, stopping frequently for no reason at all, rocking violently from side-to-side as it maneuvers over mended tracks. I am tucked into a window seat, my typewriter case on my knees, noting the vivid scars of war in the green countryside.

Sofie left on an earlier train, accompanied by the couple from the ship. My fear of being alone has resurrected itself and I made sure to give her my temporary address in Paris, begging her to let me know how she got on with her search.

"I will likely know nothing for some time." She tucked the slip of paper into her bag. "It will not be easy. It may even not be possible."

"I want you to find your family, but I'm more concerned about you," I said. "Please write, Sofie."

"Cheap sentiment," she scoffed, but she was smiling for the first time since we'd touched French soil. She spent the night pacing our hotel room like a caged beast, impatient to get to Berlin, no matter what she found. I would have preferred that she abuse me for staying out all night, but my behavior was no longer important enough to warrant a lecture. "I will write when I have something to say."

It was the best I would get from her. I lay back against the pillow, defeated, and closed my eyes. Then, my sleep had been dreamless, but now, on the hypnotically rocking train, my mind returns inevitably to the final night celebration and its unconventional end.

"Enough!" I said to Pat when he threw himself into the seat beside me. "I can't dance any more, I'm dizzy with spinning."

"Me, either. And we need to be on duty in a few hours." He tried to hide a yawn. "I'll walk you back."

"You don't have to." The ship was always deserted when I crept from the lounge. "You must be exhausted."

He laced his fingers through mine, pulling me to my feet. "Last nights can be different. Let me walk you."

The feeling of his rough fingers sent a shiver through my body, settling somewhere in the vicinity of my belly. Interesting. I'd never found Pat attractive in that way; he'd felt almost like a brother, except I was no longer feeling sisterly.

"Can we stop?" I paused at the rail. "The moon is so pretty."

"So are girls in the moonlight." Pat leaned beside me. "I'll get thrown off the ship if they catch me out here with you."

"What about the lounge?" I turned to face him. "All the dancing? Wouldn't that get you in trouble, too?"

"It would." The breeze was quickening. He brushed a stray hair from my face, his fingertips leaving a trail of goosebumps. "But that's in public, you see. Taking a girl out in the moonlight makes it look like I have bad intentions."

"And do you?" I hadn't meant to say it out loud.

"Well." He laughed with surprised delight. "I wouldn't be normal if I didn't, out here with a pretty girl who's let me dance the legs off her for the past week." Squeezing my hand again, he said, "But I also know a nice girl when I see one. Otherwise, I'd work up the nerve to kiss you goodnight."

Two days before I left, Mama had come to my room and sat down with me in all the chaos of my packing. "I don't know what you got up to with Cliff," she said with her customary directness. "I know you missed out on a lot because of the war and work and doing your best to take care of everyone. But this next year, Pearl—that's for you. Don't deny yourself an experience because the girl you've always been wouldn't do it. And don't you dare worry about how I would react."

Mama wasn't comfortable talking about intimacy, but that never kept her from telling us what we needed to know: at the appropriate ages, my sisters and I all had the facts of life thoroughly explained. She'd never come this close to talking about having sex, though, not even when I was dating Cliff. Which was fine, because his ideas about such things were very traditional. After a year of keeping company, we'd progressed no further than necking in the front seat of his car, even though I was not only curious but willing. There was time enough for that, he said, when we got married.

"I'm saying you've been very good," she said with a sigh. "And that if you meet a man and... want to experience something new, you shouldn't automatically say no."

My mouth fell right open. I'd never anticipated my mother telling me to go out and take a lover. "Mama!"

"I know. I should be the last one to encourage you, but if it hadn't been for the war, there's a good chance you'd be married by now. You deserve a little fun." Pausing for a long moment, she added, "One thing, Pearl. Make sure he's careful, for your sake if not for his. Make sure he wears a rubber. Telling you he loves you too much to wait, or that it feels better without, that's just selfishness. A man who won't protect you isn't worthy of your time, much less your body."

"What about my heart?"

Mama took my hand, holding it on the rough candlewick bedspread. "That either, my girl. But sometimes the heart and the body are on different schedules."

I thought those words as I leaned forward to kiss Pat O'Shaughnessy full on the mouth. His lips parted with shock, then with intent. The dizzying feeling of need was even better than dancing.

When I climb down at Gare Saint-Lazare, along with seemingly every other passenger on the train, the platform is seething with people and all the conversation is in French. My head pounds. I close my eyes for a moment, holding tight to my things, then take a deep breath and push my way through the crowd. Eventually I catch sight of a red-faced man holding a card with my name on it. I breathe a sigh of relief: he will be able to deal with my trunk and get me to Miss Gold's apartment, where I can collapse in a soft bed and catch up on the sleep I am sorely lacking.

"I'm Mademoiselle Kimber."

"Welcome to Paris, mademoiselle. I am Gaston. Miss Gold has sent me to retrieve you." He holds out his hand for my baggage tickets, finds a porter, then escorts me outside to wait in the car—which, as it turns out, is a gleaming, dark blue Rolls Royce with a winged silver lady on the front.

The door shuts on the outside world and I tip my head back against the buttery soft leather seat, tuck an actual silk cushion behind my back, and do my best to relax and enjoy the silence while Gaston loads the car.

When we start to move, I notice the tiny liquor cabinet built into the seat back in front of me. The brown contents of the glass bottles, marked with the RR logo, slosh from side to side when Gaston turns corners.

The streets fly past. Because I've studied Paris like I was working toward a degree, everything is *almost* familiar. The tall, pale, foreign-looking buildings with their slate or tin or tile roofs; the iron balconies; the cafés with tables spread across the sidewalk. I can't wait to throw myself into it—after a nap.

Miss Gold's apartment building is as impressive as her automobile. Gaston surrenders me to the concierge in the marble-floored entry, and I am directed toward a pair of gated elevators with massive flower arrangements on either side.

Four floors up and the elevator stops. The uniformed boy pulls back the gate and I step out into a plush carpeted hall. There are two doors, one on either side. "A droit," the boy says, and shuts the gate. To the right.

Before I can knock, the door is opened by a young woman in a black dress and apron. "Mademoiselle Kimber!" she says with an appearance of relief. "Please come in. Miss Gold is dressing. Allow me to show you to your room. I am Nina."

It is three in the afternoon; I pause to wonder whether Miss Gold is rising from her bed or if she's changing for an afternoon social obligation.

"Pardon." Gaston eases past with my trunk.

Nina raises her shoulders with a smile. "Now," she says, "we will attempt your room."

The room has a tall window opening onto a narrow balcony and its very own bathroom. Yards of silk in my aunt's favorite ice blue are swagged and draped over everything. I remain at the window, looking down over the street, until Gaston has delivered the rest of my things.

"Would you like me to unpack?" Nina hoists my case onto a rack at the foot of the bed. "Or I could run you a bath."

"A bath, please." I had one last night at the port hotel, but I am stiff and feel slightly grubby. "If Miss Gold wouldn't mind."

Another impish smile. "Miss Gold approves of pleasure."

Well, then. She disappears into the bathroom. Water thunders into the tub. I wearily open the suitcase, glad I won't have to see it again for a week, if I'm lucky. My visit is of uncertain duration—as long as it takes, her letter said blithely—but I can't imagine living here for long. I want to experience Paris, not an enhanced version of Aunt Claire's life. Several items of clothing need cleaning, and I put them aside to ask how they should be dealt with. The rest of my things are swiftly folded into drawers and hung in the wardrobe, and when the maid emerges to tell me the water is ready, I am already setting up my typewriter.

"You are very quick," she says. "I hope you like lilac bath salts."

"Lilac is my favorite scent." I gather my bathrobe and toiletries. Before I can ask, she has already picked up the clothes in need of freshening.

The water is hot, sweetly scented bubbles rising to my chin. My shoulders relax for the first time since I left home. This foray with Miss Gold will be like Aunt's trip on the *Normandie*—far too luxurious for my tastes, but I will enjoy it while it lasts, as I enjoyed my final night aboard ship.

When the bells rang five, Pat bolted from the floor, rapidly resuming his scattered uniform. "Do you need help getting dressed?" he asked. "We shouldn't be seen leaving together."

"No, I don't imagine so." I hid a smile as I reached for my slip, hung over a mop handle in the closet we had claimed as desire claimed us. "I'll find my way back."

He whipped a knot into his tie and buttoned his jacket, then reached around me to retrieve his shoes. "I wish I could stay," he said, bending to kiss me.

I accepted the kiss, but the mad burning of the night before had already flickered out, leaving him once again the sweet, friendly young man who had made my voyage so pleasurable. "I'll say my goodbyes now. I don't imagine there'll be time later."

"I suppose not." His face fell, and he reached out to touch my hair. "This was special, Pearl. I do this run twice a month, but I've never—"

"Well, now we both have." I twisted to close the side zip on my dress. It fought back, because I refused to wriggle into my girdle in front of him; I'd skinned out of it in the dark and tucked it under the blanket, where it pressed uncomfortably into my back for the duration of our relations. "I won't forget you."

"I won't forget you, either." His eyes brightened. "I hope you find what you're looking for in Paris."

Sofie and the others were already dressed when I returned. The weight of their judgment told me all I needed to know about my appearance; defiantly, I packed my nightgown and didn't bother to change into my traveling clothes.

When I kissed Pat, I hadn't intended to end up in a closet off a service passage, but I also hadn't *not* intended to end up there. I have no adolescent fantasy that this year will change everything, but if I wanted to make changes, it seemed best to make them before I even arrived.

I have come to Paris to make something of myself beyond what has always been expected of me. My relationship with Cliff ended because we wanted such different things. Being a musician himself, he was supportive of my writing—until he wasn't.

"It's a good career for a woman," he told me in all seriousness. "You can write while our babies are napping, or whenever you have a spare moment."

No one who has ever been around an infant could believe it was possible to get anything done in the brief moments of their napping. Or rather, too many things needed to be done in those moments. My writing would be the first thing sacrificed.

I said that and he disagreed, then came around to, "Well, it wouldn't be forever. Once they were in school—"

"How many is *they*?" I asked. "Even if it's one, that means I defer everything for six years, unless you intend to come home every night and cook dinner and do laundry and play with them while I work."

"Well, actually," he said, flushing, "I've been asked to go on tour. You could come with me—I know you want to travel. Wouldn't it be wonderful to get married before I leave?"

It would not. I hadn't even finished college. And though I was fond of Cliff, I didn't love him so much that it clouded my thinking. We parted, not quite amicably, and after that, I devoted myself to my education and then to teaching. My writing was relegated to evenings and weekends. When the war came, Hazel and I went to the canteen and danced the night away with untold numbers of boys on leave. Unlike Hazel, who sent every one off to war with a few sweet memories and a photo tucked into his pocket, I'd never been tempted.

But now I had checked one thing off my list that I hadn't been brave enough to write down. I don't know if losing my virginity is a positive change, but it is a change, and one long overdue. Most of my friends are already married, and I'm fairly certain that Thelma, for all her dedication to dance, has also given in to one of her many boyfriends. I was envious. And curious.

Now that curiosity has been satisfied. I am not as satisfied, but Mama said it took time to get the hang of these things. Both Pat and I were nervous and awkward, but I'd appreciated it when he pulled a rubber from his wallet without being asked. What we did wasn't unpleasant, by any means, and the debilitating pain that Hazel described had been momentary, almost lost in the kissing.

What do I care if Sofie and the others judge me? I will never see those women again and my cousin looks at everyone that way. She has her own mission, and it is not the same as the expansion of my small world. Tipping my head back on the broad porcelain rim, careful to keep my hair dry, I close my eyes and wish them all well.

It's my turn now.

APRIL 15, 1946

DARLING CLAIRE, YOUR NIECE ARRIVED THIS AFTERNOON. PARIS AND I WILL DO OUR BEST TO EDUCATE HER WITHOUT CHANGING HER TOO MUCH. SHE'LL HAVE HER BEARINGS BEFORE I LEAVE. THE BANK IS AWARE OF HER ARRIVAL. MJG

April 16, 1946

Dear Mama (and Dr. Max),

I'm sorry for the short telegram. I wanted to let you know I'd arrived as soon as I could. Now I can write a proper letter.

Aunt's friend is lovely, and her apartment is as fancy as a hotel and as big as a house. I'm glad I won't be here long. Not only am I looking forward to setting up on my own and getting to know the city as myself (not as the guest of a rich American), but Miss Gold is leaving soon because she's having a house built on the Riviera.

A house on the Riviera sounds even fancier than a Paris apartment. Beach pajamas and Fitzgeralds and money.

Sofie and I stayed overnight at LeHavre. As expected, she took charge of the next stage of both our journeys. She's very good with concierges and train

tickets. Timetables, which look to me like algebra problems, speak plain English to her.

I'd hoped we could spend a little time together, but she was on the first train to Berlin. I can't blame her for being impatient. If I'd lost you all, I'd be frantic to know what had happened.

On Monday, I will be meeting Mr. Julian St. John Armitage from the bank. I had a letter from him the other day. He promised to explain how Uncle Harry's trust works and offered to take me around to look at apartments until I found something suitable. It seems like an imposition, but perhaps a banker will not wish to spend Uncle Harry's money as quickly as Miss Gold, who suggested I take over her *apartment once she left!*

She makes Aunt Claire look like the patron saint of thrift.

For the next five days at least, I am in her hands. She is giving a small party on Friday to introduce me to people. My French might not be good enough, but I know my clothes will be. Thank you, Mama, for all your hard work. I know you didn't want me to go, but I have to fly before I forget that I ever wanted to.

All my love to everyone, with a kiss for Dr. Max, a tug on Grace's pigtail, and my special love to Dan. And of course, everything to you, Mama.

Pearl

"These shortages are such a bore," Miss Gold says as the butler delivers a tray of fragrant roast lamb to the luncheon table. "You have no idea how difficult it is to get decent food."

"I didn't realize it was so bad." It's hard to know what Paris is like outside this cushioned apartment; ordinary Parisians can't possibly eat this well. "What kind of shortages?"

"Food. Wine. Coal, if you can believe it." Shrugging, she adds, "I should have sent you to the *mairie* to get your ration cards when you first arrived, but you might as well do that when you find a permanent roost. You'll only have to go to a different office and change your address anyway."

It hadn't occurred to me that I would need a ration book. At home, most rationing had ended with the war.

"If you're set on staying in a hotel instead of taking an apartment and hiring someone to do all the tiresome standing around," she says, "you'll likely turn over your ration books to them anyway, as they'll be supplying your meals."

I help myself to a slice of lamb, then a second one, just because. Wherever I end up, I won't be eating like this, so I intend to enjoy Miss Gold's excellent cook while I can.

"Would you be able to amuse yourself tonight?" she asks suddenly. "My friend Liliane called while you were in the bath. Her husband's left her and she's desperate for a chat."

"I'm so sorry." I'm more than happy to be left alone with my diary and my letters, but I feel rude saying that; she's trying so hard to entertain me.

"No, no," she says. "It happens all the time—he leaves her, or she leaves him. It's as tiresome as rationing. But if I don't cheer her up, she won't come tomorrow evening."

Miss Gold sails into my room in a cloud of Chanel. She wears an abundance of diamonds and a bias-cut red satin gown the color of dried blood. "Our guests will be arriving soon. You should change."

I slip off the bed and stand before her, smoothing the skirt of my good blue dress. At lunch, she had called the gathering informal. "I'm sorry, I didn't realize—"

"Of course!" She slaps her forehead. "I should have been clearer. In my set, dress is always formal, even when it's *in*formal. The French never gave up on fashion, even during the war, and now that the Germans are gone, they are as elegant as ever. We have to make an effort, considering that we are the liberators and have all the money."

I want to remind Miss Gold that the money I have is not mine, but she is already striding across the carpet and flinging open the wide Art Deco wardrobe. Sorting rapidly through the hangers, she pulls out my green crepe gown and tosses it on the bed. "That will do," she says with obvious relief that I have something suitable. "Do you have jewelry?"

"Aunt Claire gave me a string of pearls for graduation." I am almost embarrassed to wear them in the company of the diamonds at Miss Gold's ears, neck, and wrists.

"Pearls will make you look like a shrinking virgin, and you are a young woman on the verge of a great adventure."

I may no longer be a virgin, but I'm definitely shrinking at the prospect of her grand salon filled with elegant people who might judge Mama's efforts and find them wanting. I will not tolerate any pointed glances about my evening dress, which we had toiled over for long evenings before my departure.

"You'll want to buy something new," she said as we stitched. "Once you get there. And you should. But this will hold you until you see what they're wearing in Paris and learn where to buy it."

She was right. She usually is. And a part of me is excited by the thought of buying a Parisian gown. In Paris.

"Get changed. I'll go and root through my jewel case and find something for you to wear." She pauses, hands on sleek hips. "Your hair…"

"I'll fix it." I had a permanent wave a week before leaving and I can almost always get my hair to cooperate now, although my fingers never could manage a proper victory roll.

The dark green crepe fits like a dream, with a draped bodice and a skirt full enough to swirl around my ankles. As I pin up my hair, anchoring it with a set of gold combs, also from Aunt Claire, Miss Gold returns with a flat velvet case.

She looks at me appreciatively. "Very nice. Claire had a few gowns made by your mother. She's very good."

Her praise of Mama warms me. "It's easy to dress Aunt Claire."

"That's true enough. She's built like a mannequin." Opening the case, she holds it out for my inspection. "What do you think of this?"

I take a step back, stunned at the piece nestled in the case's white satin interior: a deceptively simple collar of woven gold ribbons with a diamond at the center. It is not Aunt Claire's style—she favors more delicate pieces—and I'm not at all sure it's my style, either, but I let Miss Gold clasp it around my neck.

"There," she says with satisfaction. "That's better." Another thought, and a panicked look. "You do have gloves?"

As if the women of my family would send me out into the world without proper accessories! I pull them on and prepare to follow her.

"No, no, Pearl. You are my special guest. The etoile—the star—of my gathering. I will send Nina to fetch you when the others have arrived."

I sit carefully on the edge of the bed and resist the temptation to remove the gloves so I can bite my nails. Despite my gown, my well-behaved hair, and Miss Gold's necklace, I already know how the evening will go. In a room full of native speakers, my French will desert me. Fear of looking foolish will make me sweat, and my girdle will become sticky and uncomfortable. The other guests will look questioningly at Miss Gold, wondering why she has introduced them to such an inept, wordless ninny.

My heart beats fast. I close my eyes and think of Mama. Over the space of five years, she transformed from a miner's wife to a dressmaker with a thriving business to the wife of a doctor. She must have been terrified, but we never saw it.

"You are Ava Kimber's daughter," I murmur. "You are as good as any of these people."

On the other side of the door, people begin to arrive and voices—speaking rapid-fire French—become audible. Eventually Nina comes for me, peeking around the door with her gentle smile. "It is time, mademoiselle."

The grand salon, a lofty room decorated in shades of sage and cream, is filled with a muted buzz of conversation. People stand in small knots, heads down, glasses held lightly in their fingers.

Miss Gold flits from group to group like a sleek, satin moth. She sees me immediately and raises her hand in summons. "Pearl! Come here."

I make my way over to her, smiling at the few people who bother to look at me.

"Here she is!" she says gaily to the others. "Pearl Kimber, the niece of my very good friend Claire Warriner, here to spend a year in Paris."

They offer greetings of varying levels of enthusiasm, only one man bothering to look into my face and see me. He is tall and lean, dressed in immaculate evening clothes.

"Mademoiselle," he says gravely, leaning in to kiss my cheek. "May I bring you a glass of champagne?"

"Please." Then I will have something to do with my hands. "And thank you."

Miss Gold raises an eyebrow. "The man you sent to do your bidding is the Vicomte Luc Reynaud. The others"—her arms spread to encompass them—"are Monsieur and Madame Clermont and Mademoiselle Violette Trouville."

"Pleased to meet you," I say in English. I stop and then repeat myself in French. My accent sounds thick and clumsy.

The vicomte returns with a shivering coupe of champagne. "Mademoiselle Kimber." It sounds like Keem-bear in his silky voice.

"Merci." I accept the glass and take a healthy swallow, resisting the urge to sneeze as I am attacked by bubbles. "I apologize. I should have waited for someone to bring it."

"Nonsense." He smiles easily, dimples flickering in a thin, tanned face. His eyes are brown and bright, with thick lashes and nearly straight brows above. He touches his glass to mine with a crystal chime. "I never do anything I do not wish to do."

When I fail to respond to such polished masculinity, he drifts away. Bewildered, I turn to the window and quickly drain my champagne. Perhaps it will give me courage—or improve my French.

A quiet step wakes me. When Nina throws open the curtains, I put my arm across my face.

"Good morning, mademoiselle." Placing a tray on the bedside table, she smiles slyly at me. "You had a good time?"

I sit up, shoving a pillow behind my back. My nose twitches at the scent of coffee. "Yes—oh, my head aches."

"There is aspirin next to the coffee," Nina says. "Mademoiselle Gold claims that orange juice and three aspirin will cure even the worst hangover, but I brought coffee as well."

Reaching for the pills, I wonder if it is possible for my head to tumble off my neck from its own weight. Why do people drink? I've suffered from headaches since I was a girl, but they are generally eyestrain or exhaustion; a hangover headache is very different and much worse. "Is Miss Gold awake?"

She dissolves into giggles. "We will not see her until noon!"

I drink the coffee—slowly, the way I should have drunk the champagne—and when the pounding in my temples recedes, I venture forth to sit in the bath until I feel more like myself.

The space occupied by my headache is now filled with colorful fragments of the previous evening. These memories come not in single spies, but in battalions, until I want to jump back in bed and bury myself beneath the covers. Had I truly drunk so much that I found my missing French and told Monsieur Delacroix to remove his hand from my bottom? And had the vicomte flirted with me, or was that memory also the product of excessive champagne?

No one like Luc Reynaud has ever looked twice at me. And I have never seen anyone who looked like him except on a movie screen. Even thinking of him now makes me shiver. I swiftly dry off with one of Miss Gold's enormous white towels and don the silk dressing gown that has been left for me.

How much champagne had I drunk? I retrieve my diary from its drawer and sit there, the fountain pen idle in my fingers. Four glasses? Five? As nervy as I'd been about being presented to Miss Gold's guests, when had I last bothered to eat?

I was lucky I hadn't passed out or been sick on someone's expensive shoes. The thought of vomiting on the exceptional vicomte makes my headache return.

No more champagne, I write slowly. *No more vicomtes. No more rich people.*

A light knock warns me of Nina's return. She smiles to see me upright and functioning. "You look much better." Reaching into her apron, she produces a telegram. "This came for you while you were in the bath."

The trustee assigned to watch over my interests will arrive at ten tomorrow morning. Once we have discussed the trust, I will ask for his assistance in finding a place to live. Every time I have suggested doing that, Miss Gold offers to take me to lunch or to do some sightseeing, and we never end up coming close to my plan for the day. She's heard from the decorator working on her house in the south; it is nearing completion and soon she will wish to leave Paris.

I will meet with this Mr. Armitage. Together, we will find a place for me. If I must have a minder for the next twelve months, he might as well make himself useful.

April 21, 1946

Dear Dan,

It's strange here. I wrote to Mama, which I guess you know. Please don't show this letter to her. I want them to think everything is perfect.

And it is, or it will be, as soon as I get over my nervousness about speaking French and navigating a city that is beautiful and terrifying and so scarred by the war.

When you left us that summer, were you ever scared? You thought you were going with Tommy, and I thought I was going to have Hazel, but we both ended up going solo. It's a good thing Mama raised us to take care of ourselves. If I was anyone else's daughter, I'd be afraid to leave the house.

I wish you could see Paris. Through your camera, I think I would understand it better.

I love you, my other half.

P

"I'm sorry, darling, I must dash. So much to get done before I leave." Miss Gold pauses long enough to study her reflection in the mirror, adjusting the tilt of her hat a fraction of an inch. "I feel bad that I won't be here to meet your banker."

We are in the apartment's second salon. It is smaller, with pale peach silk on the walls and layers of filmy nothingness over the windows. There is a tufted velvet sofa and two pretty armchairs, along with a vivid Monet painting of a garden that makes my heart squeeze every time I look at it.

If I had money, I would buy art. Books and art. And nice shoes.

"It's not necessary," I assure her. "He'll probably be a dried-up old stick who will treat me like his granddaughter. You would bowl him over." She is absolutely dashing in a fitted black suit and a severe hat with a long pheasant feather. "Think of his heart."

"You are a darling!" she exclaims. "I should have handed you a bottle of Veuve Clicquot when you were fresh off the boat, it's turned you into a whole different girl."

My head throbs faintly at the memory. "I'm glad you did not."

Her laugh trills. "I wish I had a photo of Pierre's face when you told him—so politely—to remove his hand before you broke it. Claire said you had brothers. Now I believe it."

"I can't believe I said that." Shame heats my cheeks. I feel no older than my sister Grace, who would easily have said those same words and then followed through.

"Dear girl, it was perfection." She kisses my cheeks and pats my hair, which will never be as perfect as hers, no matter what I pay to have done to it. "The vicomte was most impressed."

"When did he say that?" There is a tingling in my belly at the thought of the vicomte.

"I spoke to him yesterday," she says breezily, picking up her handbag and checking for her cigarettes. "He called to thank me for the introduction."

"Why?" I summoned the nerve to speak to him later in the evening, but the details of our conversation elude me. The feeling—warm, intimate, and desperately uncomfortable—remains.

Miss Gold gives me her bright, brittle smile. "Because he is weary of French girls and you are, he says, *très charmante*. As you are." She puts on her gloves, straightening their seams with focused attention. "Now you must charm your banker. I want to hear all about it over dinner. It will be just the two of us, I promise."

Promptly at ten, Mr. Armitage rings the bell. I watch from inside the salon as Nina lets him in, wanting to get a sense of the man before my initial reaction is skewed by conversation.

He could not, I think, be anything but English. Medium-tall—a few inches taller than me—with a tidy mustache and beautifully tailored pre-war tweeds. His silk tie is a muted stripe and the felt hat in his hand is the same rich brown as his hair.

"Mr. Armitage." I step into the hall, offering my hand. "I'm Pearl Kimber."

"Julian Armitage." His hand is warm and dry, his grip firm. "I'm sorry for the loss of your uncle. Rest assured that I will do my best to carry out his wishes."

"Thank you." I turn toward the arched doorway to the large salon: I might as well see what he is made of when faced with the excesses of Miss Gold's decor. "Can I offer you coffee or tea?"

"Coffee, please." He smiles faintly at my surprise. "I prefer tea, but coffee is in short supply at home. It makes for a change."

We settle on one of the intimate seating arrangements scattered throughout the room. I had been introduced to Liliane Barbier, the abandoned wife, in one of these chairs, and watched in fascination over the evening as she imbibed more and more champagne and became less and less depressed about her situation.

My life strikes me as increasingly strange.

Mr. Armitage speaks of his long trip from London, his regret that the boat train has not yet resumed service, and his opinion of the eighth arrondissement, where Miss Gold's apartment is located. "Pleasant, but I think not what you are looking for?"

"Not at all!" I shudder at the thought of spending the next year separated from everything real. "I want something far more modest."

Nina brings a tray with a silver pot and two tiny, almost translucent cups and slides it onto the table between us. She pours the coffee and leaves.

"I had someone in the Paris office prepare a list of suitable lodgings," he says, stirring in a spoonful of sugar. "I have no other appointments today, so we can look at them after we're done here, if you like."

"I'd appreciate that." I drink my coffee black, having grown accustomed to the taste during the war. "Miss Gold left her car at our disposal."

"That was very kind of her." He sets his cup down precisely in its saucer, making no sound, and produces a folded sheet from an inside pocket. Smoothing it open on the table, he says, "These are the flats I thought we could look at."

Despite the eighth being too staid and luxurious, the list contains one address there and another in the similarly upper class eleventh. I dismiss both options out of hand. There are two addresses in the third, which I know from my years of studying maps is the Marais—a Jewish neighborhood. Are there many vacancies, I wonder, or have the occupants returned?

"I'm here to experience Paris," I tell him. "I don't want to take up housekeeping, so I don't need an apartment."

As if on cue, Nina comes in to clear the table.

"You could—"

"I don't want a maid, either." Why does everyone think I want to live like a rich woman? "How much money did my uncle leave, anyway?"

He tells me and I fall silent. Because I am my mother's daughter, my first thought, whenever I want something, is, "Can I afford it?" Uncle

Harry's generosity means that, if I want, I *could* have an apartment, along with a maid to stand in line at the butcher, and all the conveniences to cushion me from the discomforts of post-war Paris.

"Well, that's too much." I hear Mama in my voice. "I want a small hotel, something inexpensive. Preferably near the Sorbonne."

He receives this disruption to his plans with a placid expression. "Do you intend to take classes?"

"No, but that's the atmosphere I want." It would be too easy to slip into complacency, to write a bit, wander the streets looking at art, and wake up one day to realize that the year is over and I haven't done any substantial work. Being surrounded by students will keep me on the right path, without attending a single class.

"Then this is of little use." Mr. Armitage crumples his list. "We're fortunate your friend left her car. It may take longer to find something that meets your needs."

"You don't have to waste your time," I say hastily, not wanting to spend the day with someone judging me. "Tell me what I need to know about the trust, and I'll find my own lodgings."

"You will not." His tone brooks no argument. "My instructions were to see you settled, and that I will do. I have no control over your choice, Miss Kimber. I am here to assist you."

"Fine." It feels ungrateful to give him trouble over the matter. "Why don't we leave now, and you can explain everything to me as we drive?"

April 22, 1946

Little sister,

Have you moved into my bedroom yet and left Grace to her mess and her moods? Remember how you were at that age, wanting your own way and not wanting to hear a word from anyone? Be nice to her. She'll be better in a few years, I promise.

Paris is magical. I wish you could see it. You would break into pirouettes at the sight of the Eiffel Tower, so romantic at night, or the way the light sparkles on the spray of the fountains, like sequins on one of Aunt's dresses.

I have found a place to live, assisted by a very proper gentleman from Uncle's bank. His name is Julian St. John (pronounced Sinjin for some mysterious British reason) Armitage and he appeared a week after my arrival, armed with a list of suitable apartments in suitable neighborhoods at suitable prices.

I shouldn't poke fun. He was very kind, and went far beyond his instructions, I am sure. I am also sure that he was shocked when Miss Gold's bonne *opened the door and led him into her silk-wallpapered entry with the gold framed mirrors and absolute masses of lilies. (He might represent a bank, but I don't* think *he's used to dealing with people as rich as her.)*

But then, most people aren't as rich as Miss Gold. Aunt told me she's absolutely rolling in it and the people I met while staying with her seemed that way, too—screamingly expensive clothes and jewels and that odd, clenched way of speaking.

Anyway, I have rented a room in a small, residential hotel on the Place Dauphine in the very center of Paris. Staying in a hotel sounds fancy but it's not. At least not this hotel.

Mr. Armitage wanted me to choose something more respectable. I wanted something Bohemian—like Mimi in her garret—but after we drove around for several hours in Miss Gold's car, visiting various rundown establishments, I chose the Grand Hôtel Dauphine, which is not grand at all. I suspect it will be plenty Bohemian, though, and the location couldn't be better. I can walk to Notre Dame in minutes, and even though my board includes breakfast and dinner with the other residents, there are an abundance of cafés and small restaurants called bistros nearby which are within my budget.

I will close now because I must pack my suitcase and trunk again so they can be ferried across the city tomorrow and up the stairs to my room. (I will be very happy to pay someone to do that because my room is at the very top of the house. I was offered a room on the third floor with a view over the tiny square below, but the upstairs room is larger, with a window where, if I lean out very far, I can see not only the square, but two inches of the Seine.

Please write. I miss you all so, so much.

Big sister

I beg Miss Gold to call a taxi, but she tells me they are almost non-existent due to gasoline shortages; every time I have left the apartment, other than to go to the boulangerie down the street, I have been driven by Gaston. She will not trust me and all my worldly goods to a vélo-taxi, whatever that may be, and insists on having me delivered. "If Claire's niece is going to slum it in Paris, she will arrive at her slum in style!"

We stop outside the hotel, Gaston easing the big car along the curb. Madame is in her chair inside the door, but when she sees the midnight blue Rolls Royce Phantom, she leans so far to the left that she nearly topples over. I wait patiently to be released. On two previous occasions, I let myself out of the car and had to contend with Gaston's sad-hound expression. I turn away when he realizes that his employer—and good manners—will require him to carry my trunk up six flights of stairs.

"Let me carry the suitcase," I say, as he unloads my things into a tidy pile, maneuvering them between the evenly spaced bollards that prevent cars from parking on the sidewalk.

"As you wish, mademoiselle." He shoulders the trunk and tilts his head back to cast a mournful gaze at the building. "Allez!"

I greet Madame, and say, apropos of Gaston, "I have been staying with my aunt's friend."

Her fiercely plucked eyebrows draw together. "I keep a good house, but you are a fool to leave her."

"I want to experience the real Paris, not live in such a way that I could be anywhere—"

Madame cuts me off. "You are a silly, romantic child. If you'd come here a year ago, you would sing a different song."

Considering the privations of the war are still being felt, she is right, but the level of Miss Gold's luxury makes me uncomfortable. She and Aunt Claire first met at an art gallery, when Aunt was buying the painting that hangs over the fireplace at home and which I have spent countless hours staring at, wishing I could transport myself into its rainy Parisian streets. I tried asking Miss Gold about Paris then, but she doesn't talk about the past, not even the pleasant bits.

I pick up my suitcase and Mona and start up after Gaston. He is well ahead of me, but his panting echoes down the stairwell. I feel guilty; he is too old to be carrying trunks.

When I reach my open door, the trunk is centered on the worn carpet. Gaston leans on it with both hands, puffing like a steam engine.

"Are you well?" I ask. "Can I get you a drink?"

He wipes his red face with a handkerchief and straightens his cap. "You'll have legs for the Folies Bergère if you climb these steps every day."

Madame waits for us at the foot of the stairs, a small glass in one hand. She speaks to Gaston, her words so rapid that I fail to grasp a single one. He breaks into a broad smile, takes the glass, and throws back the contents. A shudder runs through him, and he hands it back with a crisp nod. His step, as he walks around the car, is almost jaunty.

"Thank you for your kindness," I say to Madame. "I shall unpack now."

"I will need your ration book," she says, wiping her finger around the rim of the glass. "Dinner is at seven."

"I don't have one yet," I admit, embarrassed. "May I get it tomorrow? I will not be in this evening." Mr. Armitage made me promise to have dinner with him before he returned to London. I wish to be left alone to settle in—but if I had not accepted, I would have to face a dining room full of strangers. I am no more ready for that particular terror than I am to have dinner with my trustee, but at least we have met before.

"Tomorrow morning you will go to the *mairie*. Leave your key at the desk when you go out."

"What if I'm late?"

"My son-in-law will be here." Her tone does not conceive of a world where he would be anywhere other than where he was told.

"And if I want to take a bath?" The bathroom had been pointed out on my brief tour, but the door was locked.

"You bathe on Tuesdays. There is a sink in your room."

I come down early to investigate the dining room. Tables fill rapidly as the clock strikes seven, but there appears to be no assigned seating. My dinner companion, wearing a double-breasted gray suit, arrives with the soup.

"Miss Kimber," he said, offering his arm. "You look very nice."

"Thank you." I wasn't certain what one wore to dinner with a banker, and so I settled on the chic black suit Mama made for me, with white spotted blouse and my black heels. They will be challenging on the uneven sidewalks, but I must learn to deal with them.

"Do you mind walking?" he asks. "The restaurant is across the bridge in St. Michel."

"I intend to walk everywhere."

Out on the street, the weather is glorious. Two boys throw a ball in the park, shouting and kicking up grit. Their dog, some sort of terrier, is enjoying itself immensely, yapping and bouncing. I would like to forget my grown-up propriety and play with them.

We cross the Pont Neuf to the Left Bank—the Rive Gauche, at last!—and as we walk, he asks, "Are you unpacked?"

"I've barely started," I tell him, stepping up on the high curb. "Miss Gold had me driven down after lunch."

"I'm sorry." He steps in, his grip on my elbow tightening as a bicycle cuts close to us. "Perhaps tonight was inconvenient."

"Unless my uncle's instructions specifically said, 'take my niece to dinner and make sure that she's settled,' you needn't have done this."

"His instructions were detailed, but dinner wasn't part of them." Mr. Armitage looks younger when he laughs. "We had an awkward time the other day, finding your lodgings. I wanted to start fresh."

As we walk, my eyes dart from a fragrant café-tabac to a boulangerie—closed for the night—to small balconies groaning with potted flowers. I try to take it all in so I can find my way back. "Look at all the bookshops!"

"The Sorbonne is close by," he says. "And there are bookstalls along the river, as well. That will give you a pleasant afternoon or two."

"I know about those," I say, intending to reward myself with a browse if I survive my morning trip to the *mairie*. "I will have to be careful not to waste all my money on books. Are there limits on my spending?"

"None at all." Mr. Armitage stops at the corner to make his point. "Miss Kimber, while I am nominally in charge of the trust, I'm not your guardian. Spend whatever you wish, on whatever you wish. If you require more funds, you have only to ask."

Despite his kind manners, the arrangement makes me feel like a child. Why could the money simply not have been put into an account for me to draw from? Or is France not so different from the United States, unwilling to let a woman handle her own affairs?

We reach the restaurant before I can ask. A sagging striped awning casts a shadow over a cluster of rattan chairs and small tables, most of which are occupied. Mr. Armitage opens the door and stands back to allow me to enter. A few quiet words to the maître d' and we are led to a table at the open front window.

The restaurant is like most of Paris I've seen so far: grand but run down, like an old woman whose once-elegant wardrobe has begun to show its age. The gold and burgundy wallpaper is dimmed by decades of smoke, the lace curtains are clean and starched, but mended.

The war, again.

I unfold the thick linen napkin, wondering if it is correct to do so before the food arrives. Although I've eaten at fancy restaurants before, I don't completely trust myself not to make mistakes in this strange new world.

Without asking, Mr. Armitage orders two champagne cocktails. When they arrive, we open our menus and lapse into silence.

"Do you like seafood?" he asks. "They make a very fine Dover sole. Or they did, before the war."

I meet his gaze over the stiff card. "You could say that about almost anything. Before the war."

The waiter, a tall man in a long black apron, returns to take our orders. After a moment's hesitation, I order the sole, hoping I know how to eat it.

"Something to start?" the waiter asks. "If mademoiselle is unfamiliar with French cuisine, I would recommend the onion soup gratinée."

"Two of those," Mr. Armitage says crisply. "And I'll have the sole, as well." He orders white wine to go with the fish. When the waiter departs, he turns to me. "I hope you don't mind about the soup?"

"No. I've had it before, at a restaurant in New York with my aunt."

"Do you like New York?" He takes a sip of his drink.

I haven't tried mine yet. Mama never encouraged alcohol at home, because her father was a drinker. In my week with Miss Gold, I came to understand that drinking here is not only socially acceptable; it's expected. I would be seen as provincial, she said, if I avoided drinking.

"It's very loud and fast compared to Philadelphia," I tell him. "I want to like it more than I do."

"I like it, though I haven't been since the war. I've never visited your Philadelphia."

"It's not my Philadelphia." I taste the cocktail and smile at how good it is. "It's like New York, just smaller and older and not as"—I search for the right word—"brash."

"Your uncle said you were a writer. I can tell."

It is odd that this stranger knows something so personal about me. "You knew my uncle?"

"Oh, yes." His smile is almost shy. "There was quite an age difference, so I wouldn't say we were close friends, but whenever he was in London, we would have a meal and take in a concert. When he knew his time was limited, he shared his intentions for you with me."

My eyes fill at the thought of Uncle Harry speaking to him about my future. I sniff and take another drink.

"I'm sorry if I've distressed you." Mr. Armitage's forehead creases. "According to your uncle, your trip to Paris had been delayed."

"Did he tell you why?"

"Other than the war? No."

His hair is silver at the temples, reminding me of Aunt's muskrat coat. I drop my eyes before he catches me staring. "He and my aunt spent a year here, in 1935. They invited me to come with them, but my mother wouldn't let me go." After a decade, I keenly remember the pain of being left behind. "I'd only started high school, you see."

"A wise decision."

"At the time, I was inconsolable." I play with the stem of my glass. "You know how overwrought fifteen-year-old girls can be. Nothing in the history of the world had ever been as bad."

Fully half that year had been spent avoiding my mother, even as it broke my heart to turn from her when she needed my support.

"I don't have much experience with fifteen-year-old girls," Mr. Armitage says, "so I will have to take your word for it. I hope Paris in its current state lives up to your expectations."

"It's Paris," I say. "How could it not?"

The waiter arrives with a bottle of wine, followed by two steaming, cheese-encrusted bowls. Mr. Armitage looks relieved at the interruption.

"Consider it part of the service, if it makes you more comfortable, but I would genuinely like to hear how you get on. Mr. Warriner also said that you were a teacher?"

I tell him about the mixed second and third grade class I left behind, forty children crammed into one room because of wartime overcrowding. When will we be able to stop using the war to qualify everything? The world is divided into before and after, but at some point, after should become normal.

"You do understand," he says, testing his trustee capabilities, "that your uncle left funds sufficient to pay for far more pleasant accommodations than those you have chosen?"

"But I like where I'm living." I'm not certain I do, but I understand, more or less, how to find new lodgings if once-weekly baths become intolerable.

"All right." His expression is gracious, but I sense a stubbornness behind it. "It was merely a suggestion. My superior thought I should point out that you might be happier in a more luxurious setting."

I laugh in his face. "Mr. Armitage, you know very little about me. I grew up sharing a bedroom with all five of my brothers and sisters, and often my parents. As a child, I would have thought the Grand Hôtel Dauphine was a palace."

"I'm sorry." The lines around his mouth and eyes could come from smiling, which he does easily. "I wasn't aware of that. I must sound terribly condescending."

"Just a bit."

Mr. Armitage is far more human when he's uncomfortable. And he has my uncle's blessing, which is no small thing; Uncle Harry had excellent instincts about people. As reticent as I am with discussing personal matters with a near-stranger, it's unlikely I'll be making friends here anytime soon, and a part of me needs connection.

It's taken longer than it should to figure out what's wrong. I'm not homesick, precisely, but I've never been away from my family for a long stretch of time. As a college student, I lived at home. When I began teaching, my parents' house was close to the subway, convenient for work. I've never *not* had a family member or a friend close by if I needed to talk.

"I miss my family." I take a gulp of wine to cover my embarrassment, trusting that he will get me safely back to the hotel if I overindulge.

"That's perfectly understandable," he says calmly. "If you're close, it will take time to adjust."

"Do you think so?" I can't imagine a year with this hole in my chest.

He blinks and says, "I was sent away to school when I was seven. I cried myself sick for the first weeks, and then one morning I woke up looking forward to football that afternoon and..." His expression tells me he's not used to revealing himself, either. "It got better."

I see a small, serious boy in a sea of boisterous children and my heart hurts for him. But it is also an opening. "Does telling me that mean I can ask you questions?"

Mr. Armitage strokes his mustache with one finger. "What would you like to know?"

"I'm not sure. But since you're in charge of doling out my allowance, I feel like I should know something about you."

"I was born in 1910, which makes me thirty-six. I grew up in Norfolk and was educated at Cambridge. After university, I entered the bank. I had no particular plans, and my father worked there." His face tightens. "And then the war came, and plans became meaningless."

"What did you do in the war?"

He looks uncomfortable again, fiddling with his glass. "Various things," he says at last. "When it was over, I returned to the bank."

"And your life." Most people who spoke about the war had something they wanted to come back to: wives or jobs or gardens.

"Not so much. My wife was killed in the Blitz. My parents, too. I'm not close to my brother and sister."

For the first time, I notice the plain gold band on his left hand. "I'm sorry. I shouldn't pry."

He scrapes his spoon around the edge of the bowl to capture the scraps of melted cheese, giving me permission to do the same. "It was almost six years ago."

"That doesn't make it any less terrible."

"No." There is something different in his smile now, as if I've broken through to the man inside. "But I've come to terms with it."

April 23, 1946

It isn't just Miss Gold and her friends. Paris stays up late.

After dinner, we walked to the Île Saint-Louis for ice cream. I had vanilla and cassis, on his recommendation, since the sole was so good. It was hard to believe I was walking through Paris at night with a man, even a man like Mr. Armitage who, while very nice, is no hero of romance.

The shop is run by a large and argumentative family. Listening to them reminded me of dinners when we were young, when Toby and George would squabble until Mama had to threaten them with a wooden spoon. I told Mr. Armitage about them, and he said his family never shouted, except at the races, and that my life is a different world. Isn't that we travel, to learn about different worlds?

We sat outside at a small table on the cobblestones, and over his shoulder I could see the miracle that is Notre Dame. The sky was going purple and against it, his profile looked like one of those old-fashioned silhouette pictures. A high forehead, a straight nose, an unexceptional chin. The sort of face that would pass unnoticed in a crowd; I should know, having a similar face.

Eventually I caught him trying to check his watch and said we should go. I've taken up more than enough of his time. A part of me would have been happy to stare at Notre Dame until sunrise, despite my exhaustion, to prove that it is real. I am in Paris. These places exist, and soon I will exist in them.

It was after ten when we reached the hotel. Madame had gone to her rest, and so Mr. Armitage escorted me upstairs to the reception area. Philippe yawned and handed over my key. He is pale and stoop-shouldered, and his clothes hang on him. Duty done, he sank back into his chair and closed his eyes.

Mr. Armitage asked if I would have dinner with him the next time he was in Paris. There is a telephone at the hotel and Madame had already told him she would take a message from my "guardian." He said he already feels as old as the hills, and she made him sound like a grandfather.

I assured him that he was no one's grandfather. After all our conversation, Mr. Armitage feels almost like a friend, despite his serious demeanor. And like Sofie and Miss Gold, he is now gone.

The next friends I make must be French, so I don't lose them.

The alarm rings at six-thirty. I wash and dress quickly and put on careful makeup. I might be scared, but I can pretend to be brave. Other than meeting my fellow residents and somehow obtaining a ration book, I have no plans for the day. At this point, those tasks feel insurmountable.

When I open the door, the stairwell is filled with the scent of fresh bread. My stomach rumbles; despite the excellent meal the night before,

I am ravenous. I smooth my hair one last time, take a deep breath, and start down.

It is early enough that only one table in the yellow dining room is occupied. I murmur bonjour to the old couple seated there, then daringly take a seat at the large table in front of the window.

A woman brings a small coffee pot and a plate with a foot-long stick of bread, a pat of butter, and a small bowl of jam. This is, apparently, the hotel's standard breakfast. I think longingly of bacon and eggs, then remind myself that I am in a different country, with different customs. I pour the coffee and discover that while the liquid in the pot is brown and pungent, it isn't coffee. Nor is it tea. I take a tentative sip and wrinkle my nose.

The bread is more appealing: warm from the oven, with a thin, hard crust. I look surreptitiously at the couple and see how the woman has spread butter and jam on the split loaf and copy her, resisting the urge to eat it all at once.

Laughter from the hall announces more arrivals. A second couple, along with two girls close to my age. They join me at the window table, their eyes widening when I say good morning.

"American?"

"Yes." Do I sound so American, after all these years of French lessons?

"Bien! I love Americans."

"Especially American men," the second girl says. She has short-cropped black curls, while her American-loving friend is blonde with gold-rimmed spectacles. Both are dressed in plain skirts and blouses with heavy-soled wedge shoes. "Cécile welcomed the liberation."

Cécile fails to look embarrassed. "After four years of Germans and grandfathers, who would not like a healthy American boy?"

"You like his chocolate and nylon stockings." She turns to me with an impish smile. "I am Remy Aubert, and this is my best friend, Cécile Ménard."

"My name is Pearl," I tell her. "Pearl Kimber."

Their breakfasts arrive and Remy downs her brown liquid in a single gulp. "Why have you come to Paris, Mademoiselle Kimber? We are not at our best, as you can see."

Put on the spot, I stammer something about having wanted to visit since I was a girl. "And now I am here," I conclude. "At last."

"At the Grand Hôtel Dauphine." Cécile looks on the verge of giggles. "Why this place?"

"You live here," I point out. "Why not?"

"We are poor midinettes—seamstresses," Remy explains. "We have no money."

"My mother is a seamstress," I tell them. "And I"—I hear Miss Gold's voice, *begin as you intend to continue*—"I am a writer. But I am a poor writer."

There is no reaction; France is a country of artists and writers, after all. Why shouldn't there be a writer in their hotel?

"Do you know where to get a ration book?" It is less frightening to ask these girls than to face Madame.

"Yes," Remy says, "but we can't go with you. Madeleine will tell you how to find it."

"Madeleine?"

"Madame's daughter." Remy points to the woman clearing the elderly couple's table. "She'll take you if she has time."

Looking at Madeleine's haggard posture, I know she doesn't have a spare moment. "I'll find it," I say with more courage than I feel.

"Come, Remy." Cécile pushes back her chair. "We will be late again."

Remy bounces up, straightening her hat—a ridiculous straw confection covered in cherries—before giving me a broad smile. "We will see you this evening, Miss Kimber."

As I leave, I greet Madame and offer my fingertips to her dog. He yawns, not deigning to raise his head, and I walk past them both into the bright morning.

"Cross the Pont Neuf and turn left at Samaritaine, down the small street to the Place du Louvre until you reach Saint-Germain-l'Auxerrois. The *mairie* looks like part of the church, but it is on the other side of the belfry."

Madeleine's instructions are clear enough, but I feel like I am floating, untethered, over a map that doesn't make sense. My stomach is in knots, though that also could be the bitter chicory. If I'd had my wits about me last night, I should have asked Mr. Armitage to have the bank handle this chore. Instead, here I am, about to attempt bureaucracy in a foreign language.

Samaritaine, it turns out, is a department store. I will investigate later, if I have any strength left after dealing with the town hall. The church is also easily found, another pale, beautiful building glowing in the morning sun. It is separated from a similar building by a tall belfry. As I crane my neck to look at it, the carillon rings out and I am struck by wonder. When the bells stop, I take a deep breath and approach the doors.

Philadelphia's City Hall is a French-inspired wedding cake, but its halls, offices, and courtrooms are drab and functional, and the building smells like a school. The first arrondissement's town hall is impressive inside and out. Beyond the grand vestibule is a lofty hall with an elaborate staircase. Columns and statues and swags of carved plaster make it feel more like a museum than a civic building.

I pause, hoping for a helpful sign or someone to direct me, but no one comes to my rescue. Moving to one side, I pretend to study a map of the district. Reflected in the glass, my eyes are wide, blue irises surrounded by white. A scared little rabbit.

I whirl around, accosting the first person I see. "Bonjour, monsieur. Pardon, but do you know where to apply for a ration card?"

With a smile, he tells me the office is to be found on the first floor, up the stairs and to the right. I follow his directions and encounter a line of people, mostly women, waiting outside a closed door.

"Is this the place for rations?" I wonder at the number of people on a weekday morning. The woman ahead of me is holding a baby. Three children not much larger hang on her skirt. Surely there are not that many new arrivals in the city?

"Yes. We have been waiting already one hour."

Her accent is French, but not, I think, Parisian—she doesn't sound like Madame or Madeleine, or even Miss Gold's servants. Perhaps she's come from the countryside, looking for work.

Eventually the door opens. One by one, we filter into the office, where a single middle-aged woman takes down my information, scrutinizing my passport and the receipt from the Grand Hôtel Dauphine which proves my residence. In my purse I have two hundred francs, suggested by Madeleine in the event that the proceedings need lubrication. But all appears to be well. Boxes are checked, lines are signed upon, stamps are stamped, and finally I am presented with cards for food, clothing, and coal, along with an unexpected smile.

"Welcome to Paris."

May 1946

May 1, 1946

Dear Hazel,

I thought I would write and tell you about my room, which is not anything like the room we would have had if you'd come with me. Get out your map, the one you should have given me if you weren't going to use it. I had to buy my own.

Unfold it. Find the Île de la Cité, right in the center. Then find Notre Dame. Walk your fingers to the left but stop before you get to the little triangular park at the end of the island. That is the Place Dauphine.

I'm telling you this first because I already know you will disapprove. The gentleman from Uncle Harry's bank certainly did. I chose this hotel because it is ten minutes from Notre Dame, with the river on all sides and the flower market and cafés and everything that means Paris to me.

The Grand Hôtel Dauphine is a cross between a rooming house and a cheap hotel. And it's old. As in built in the 1600s old. And that's how old I feel after climbing up to my room on the top floor, up and up and up these crazy circular stairs that go on forever. There's a skylight in the roof, which is good because the French are thrifty and the lights in the stairwell turn themselves off if you don't move quickly enough. It turns out I'm not very fast.

Anyway, back out to the Place Dauphine, a little sand-covered triangle filled with pigeons and benches and very peculiarly shaped trees. They're almost square. You leave the park and cross the narrow street to the black-painted front door. To one side is a shield-shaped sign on an iron bracket. The door is unlocked, and when you go inside, there's a space, no bigger than a closet, where Madame, the concierge, sits with her dog and watches the world go by. You greet her—woe if you do not say bonjour quickly enough—and climb one straight flight to the reception area, which has a desk and a half dozen armchairs that were old before the last war. Through an archway is the dining room, with a window overlooking the park. The view is better than the food (soups and stews, heavy on vegetables and light on meat), so I try to sit there every day.

Up and up and up to the sixth floor, where there are two rooms and a toilet. The toilet is reached by a door that opens onto a balcony over an airshaft. There is a bathtub (downstairs), but it must be reserved, and Madame requires five francs for the privilege of a once-a-week soak in three inches of water. Madeleine, her daughter, recommends the local public baths, where I can have all the hot water I want for fifty francs.

So. My room is not too big or too small. It faces the street, with the same view as the dining room, just higher up. There is an iron railing outside, so I call it a balcony. There is a bed (lumpy), a long bolster (also lumpy), and a wardrobe big enough to hold a family of four which doesn't like to stay closed. I wonder how they got it all the way up here.

There is a white enamel sink with a shelf for my toiletries. An armchair like the ones downstairs, but plum-colored velvet and the stuffing is leaking out only along one seam. There's a crucifix over the bed and a Dürer print that is both grim and water-stained. I've heard about a street market that sells antiques and the sort of second-hand junk I like. I'll go there soon and find something to replace it.

But... best of all, Hazel, there's a desk! Okay, it's a table but there's a chair too, and I dragged it over to the window so I can write and look out over Paris. Madeleine didn't think much of that, because I stirred up dust from the time when Madame was a frisky young widow back in 1918. Possibly since Henri IV himself laid out the park in 1600-and-something.

Now you can imagine where I am when you read my letters. Write back and tell me all about married life, where you're living, and how disgustingly happy you are. At least all your shopping for Paris means you have an amazing trousseau.

Pearl

Hazel would call the hotel's conditions primitive, yet in some ways I am less homesick because of them. I don't mind that the hotel is run down; it's painfully clean, despite its age, and my door locks. If I leave the breakfast table early enough, I will catch Madame putting away her bucket and mop in the little closet behind her chair. Although Madeleine cleans the rooms, her mother does the cooking, as well as washing the entryway and front step every morning, a proud housewife for all that she's running a hotel. While she works, her small dog, Pepe, sits either on the chair or just beyond the door, patiently waiting to resume his spot at his mistress's feet.

When I planned this year, I'd somehow never gone so far as to imagine what my days would be like. After having spent my life either at school or at work, having no schedule at all is disorienting. I've never had this much free time and so few people to share it with. The two midinettes are good company, but they are a closed circle and I have not yet found my way inside.

Gradually, I acquaint myself with the streets around the hotel: the Quai de l'Horloge with its enormous clock; the Conciergerie, where Marie Antoinette was held; the flower and bird markets; the soaring beauty of Notre Dame; the pigeons, everywhere. I revisit the Île Saint-Louis, where I went with Mr. Armitage, wandering with deep joy through the narrow streets, pausing on the bridges to stare at the river or at buildings familiar from a decade of dreaming.

After a week, I expand my territory, crossing the Pont Neuf and walking along the Quai des Grand Augustins to browse the bouquiniste stalls and down the cobbled ramp to the promenade at the river's edge. I find a small café, tucked between two shabby art galleries, where I can watch the constant parade of people and hear the river traffic and the bells from the nearby churches. It has a worn interior and a half dozen rattan tables and chairs outside. The proprietor, who never comes out from behind the zinc bar, is short, fat, and dour, while the sole waiter is tall, gaunt, and similarly weighted down by life.

In my imagined Parisian existence, over and over I had pictured myself at a table at the Café de Flor or Les Deux Magots, a pensive expression on my face, writing slowly and deliberately in a notebook. There would be a tiny cup of coffee and perhaps an ashtray at my side—I hadn't yet decided whether smoking would make me look more grown up. The waiters would tiptoe around me, understanding the seriousness of my purpose, and the café's other patrons—writers and artists all—would accept me as a member of their exclusive fraternity.

In reality, the cafés around Saint-Germain are crowded and over-priced, and they tend to save their coffee, if they can get it, for regular patrons, not young women with stars in their eyes and delusions of a literary life.

I go to the Café des Augustins at every opportunity, knowing how easy it would be to choose a café within a block of my hotel and end up with a life that extends no farther than the boundaries of the Île de la Cité, leaving unexplored the rest of the city's wonders. The café quickly becomes my office, though I do little actual writing beyond a stream of letters home and keeping up with my diary. I don't remember when my love of stories became a desire to write them, but I knew I had nothing to write about, so I started to keep a record of my life, in case it ever amounted to anything. Those old diaries are at home on my bookshelf; they would have taken up valuable trunk space, and some of them are no more than scraps of paper shoved into the leather-bound diaries Aunt Claire gives me every Christmas.

The words will come when they are ready. Paris has been such a disruption that they can't find their way out. I content myself with vivid descriptions of my surroundings, and documenting my thoughts and daily interactions so they will not disappear upon my return home.

May 2, 1946

Dear Miss Kimber,
I am writing to ascertain that you are comfortable and content in your eccentric hotel. As explained, the trust has been deposited into your account,

and a portion will be released on the first of each month to cover your rent and any other expenses.

On my own behalf, I wish to thank you for being such a pleasant dinner companion. I'm sure you would have preferred to spend that time settling in and getting acquainted with your fellow residents, so your sacrifice was much appreciated.

If you have any questions or require at any time an advance upon the remainder of the trust, you have only to write to me. Please note that I have included my telephone number and home address at the top of this letter. If it is a matter of urgency, you should feel encouraged to use them rather than wait until business hours.

I told you that I wished to hear about your progress. I meant every word. Best wishes for an interesting, educational year.

Regards,
Julian St. John Armitage

It is a somewhat formal message, but Mr. Armitage is a somewhat formal man, and his concern—albeit on my uncle's behalf—warms me, as I've yet had no letters from home. I was told that mail to Europe was slow, but I hadn't expected the better part of three weeks would go by without a single letter.

I drop the note on my desk where it shows crisp and white against the dark wood. That is another thing I need: some sort of case in which to keep my letters. At home I would have liberated a cigar box from Dr. Max or Uncle, but I haven't smelled a cigar since I left Miss Gold's apartment. I will have to find something.

It is another reason to visit the Marché aux Puces in Saint-Ouen. It feels a bit beyond my scope to venture that far from the hotel. My French is adequate to speaking to my fellow lodgers and ordering in cafés, but markets involve negotiating and conversation beyond daily politesse. Will I be able to conduct myself properly and come home with the items I require?

There is one way to find out. I mention the errand to Remy in the morning and she wrinkles her nose.

"I spent two years working a market stall while my uncles were in hiding." She purses her lips; a memory not to be shared with such a new acquaintance. "Thank you, but no."

When Cécile joins us, she too looks appalled. "I hate a date on Saturday," she says, fluttering a hand up to her golden hair, pinned into two elaborate rolls. "Madeleine has promised me the tub at noon, while Madame is visiting her sister."

An illicit bath is not to be missed, I understand that much.

May 3, 1946

Dear Aunt Claire,

Every day when I return to the hotel, I hope to find letters from you and the others, and every day I am disappointed. You did warn me! I am grateful, because without that knowledge I would feel abandoned, despite the magic of this city.

I dreamed of Paris full of color, coming out of my ordinary life like Dorothy waking up in Oz. Instead, it is the reverse. Paris is suffering the after-effects of years of war and occupation. There are food shortages, coal shortages and power cuts.

While I wouldn't trade this experience for anything, sometimes it's hard to make the two versions of Paris I have in my mind come together. There's the Paris of books and movies and the stories you told me, all chestnut blossoms and champagne cocktails, patisseries filled with every kind of pastry, well-dressed men and women in couture dresses and pretty shoes.

Then there's the city that exists outside my door. They are not the same. And yet they are. It is a black-and-white world, often grim but very beautiful nonetheless. I have found places to call my own, a café, a particular flower seller, the tiny park at the foot of the Île de la Cité, mere steps from my hotel.

No one talks about the war, not to an outsider. There are jokes about the black market and grumbling about food prices and rationing, but the war goes unmentioned. From another resident, I have learned that Madame's son died in some sort of German prison camp, but this news was conveyed quietly. Madame does not speak of it.

How are you and Teddy? I think of you often and try to imagine how different it must have been when you were here with Uncle. Please write

*and tell me your news, and what Teddy is doing. He's growing up so
quickly, he'll be a young man by the time I get home.*

*If it's not too personal, I would love it if you would tell me about one
place in Paris that means a lot to you. Not anywhere famous, necessarily,
just somewhere that made you exhale and say, "Yes, this is why I'm here."*

I love you,

Pearl

On Saturday, I catch an early morning train to Porte de Clignancourt
with Antoine and Sita Trier, the younger of the two couples living at
the hotel. Sita overheard me talking to Remy and offered to accompany
me, then offered her husband to carry our purchases.

I have barely spoken to the Triers before this; they are newlyweds,
rarely speaking to anyone. After breakfast, they sprint from the building
to go to their jobs, kissing passionately on the front step to Madame's
disdain. He is a clerk in an office, Remy told me, and she works in a
nearby shop. But today I am included and grateful for their company.

"Do you seek anything particular?" Sita is dressed for the day out in
a light floral dress. It is obviously pre-war, as the hem is unfashionably
long, and it pulls over her bust. Perhaps I could suggest an alteration in
return for this trip into the unknown.

"Some things to make my room more comfortable." I think of my
love for the flower market. "A vase, so I stop bothering Madeleine."

"She calls you petit fleur." Antoine smiles beneath his mustache. "She
keeps one close by for when you stagger in burdened with blooms."

My face heats. "I do not wish to put her to any inconvenience." I will
leave it for the next tenant when my year is up. "Also, I would like a
picture. The one that is there is terrible."

The Dürer is so depressing that I have turned it against the wall. I
don't know what I want in its place. Something with color would be
helpful.

The streets here are shabbier than in the parts of the city I've explored, with cracked curbs and the occasional cobble missing from the
sidewalk. Houses and shops are packed close together, but many of the
businesses are shuttered and the houses have an air of cramped poverty
that reminds me of my childhood.

A group of barefoot boys run straight at us. Antoine Trier swears at them and they run off, jeering. We walk on, rattled by the encounter, and within ten minutes the market comes into sight.

When I see it, all I can think is how much Mama would enjoy this trek. For the most part, she cares little for material objects—we were too poor for too long for her to ever buy anything simply because it appealed—but the goods laid out on blankets, under tents and awnings or on cleverly built stalls run the gamut from the utterly frivolous to the deeply useful. I wish I could transport her here. I will have to settle for yet another letter.

Sita and I browse a table packed with millinery trimmings. She buys a clutch of pink rosebuds for her hat, while I consider a small bunch of silk violets, but put them back, wanting to save my money for things I need.

I stumble upon a table manned by an elderly woman in black. Among the many objects she has for sale is a flat, embossed leather case with an intricate clasp. I want it immediately.

"Bonjour, madame. Combien ça coûte?"

She stirs from her stool. I can almost hear her ancient bones cracking. "Dix francs," she says, her lips barely moving. "It is leather."

"May I?" I inspect it more closely. She expects me to haggle, but the price she has given me is ridiculously low for a case of such quality. I already know I will buy it, but what decides me is the discreet monogram pressed into one corner. *A*. It is as if Mama were here beside me.

"I like this very much," I tell her. "Do you have any paper to wrap it?" I have brought a basket with me, supplied by the patient Madeleine.

"Oui. Vous-ete Americaine?" Her tone says that only an American would pay such an inflated price, while I think that only a Frenchwoman in desperate need of money would sell such a treasure for so little.

"Oui. When I return home, I will give this to my mother." I point to the monogram. "Her name is Ava."

Her face breaks into a rusty smile. "This belonged to my mother. Her name was Annelise."

While I conduct my business, Antoine and Sita wander along the row, side by side, their fingers touching. I catch up to them, glowing with success at my transaction and the contact made with the elderly woman.

"I think I am all right," I tell them. "If you would like to go off on your own, perhaps there is a café where we can meet later?"

"You have found your feet," Sita says. "There is a café two streets farther along, on the corner. We will meet you there in two hours?"

That should give me enough time to acquire more treasures. "I will try not to buy anything too heavy, so that Monsieur Trier does not strain his back."

"I am stronger than I appear," he boasts. "Tell her, cherie."

Alone, I browse table after table, making up lives for the objects I see. Damask napkins and tablecloths for twenty-foot tables. Full sets of china, as if household after household has ceased to sit down to elaborate meals. There is an equal amount of silver, elaborate and plain, candlesticks, centerpieces—all the accoutrements of homes shattered by the war.

I find a small porcelain bird for Aunt Claire, who loves breakable ornaments, and a glass bowl the color of plums for Mama. She will fuss, but it was too beautiful to leave behind. She can put it on the dining table and fill it with fruit.

My favorite stalls are the ones where everything coexists in a messy tangle. I sort through knickknacks and statues, costume jewelry, linens, and scarves. Treasure can hide at the bottom of the most disorganized jumble.

In due course, I add a silk scarf and a pair of blue gloves to my basket. The gloves are still on their cardboard forms, but the scarf has lost its hem. As Mama always delegated rolled hems to me, it will be good as new in less than an hour.

I haven't yet found a vase or a picture, but when the bells chime ten, my stomach growls along with them; hunger declares that my journey is over. While I would kill for a cup of coffee and a turkey sandwich, I will accept the inevitable chicory, soup and bread. I rearrange the items in my basket, straighten my hat, and turn toward the café.

And it is right there, my picture, leaning against the leg of a table. The painting depicts a young woman in a blue jacket holding a letter in her hands. Light from an unseen window pours over her like honey, so beautifully rendered I can almost feel its warmth.

I have spent years visiting the Philadelphia Museum of Art and gone twice with my aunt to the Metropolitan Museum in New York. The painting before me is not a real Vermeer, but it is a very skilled copy.

Two men stand behind the table, bickering amicably. Their speech is rapid, but I believe they are arguing about a girl.

"Pardon?" They look up in unison. "What is the price on this painting?" I nod to where it sits at my feet.

The younger of the two comes forward, smiling. A missing front tooth is balanced by snapping brown eyes. "For such a beautiful woman," he says in English, "two hundred francs."

The other man, older, slightly heavier, interrupts. "Two-fifty, brother. The frame."

"The frame is wood, and very plain," I point out, braver after my previous successes. "I can buy a better frame and you may keep this one."

They exchange glances and the stocky man sighs and steps back.

"One hundred eighty," the younger man says. "Because you are beautiful."

"One hundred seventy-five," I counter, "because you are a liar and a flatterer."

They burst into laughter and the grumpy one reaches under the table for newspaper. The younger one, still smiling, wraps the painting and ties the parcel with twine. He looks at my basket, shaking his head.

"I will manage," I tell him, tucking it under my arm. "I am meeting a friend at the café"—I point to the building just ahead—"and he will carry it for me."

He claps his hand over his heart. "Je suis désolé," he proclaims. "Did you hear? She has a man already."

"This is why you are unmarried!" his brother says, clapping him on the back. "You can't tell when they're taken."

When I reach the café, Sita and Antoine are coming from the other direction. I wave to them and find a table. They sit, and I say, "Please let me buy you an early lunch. Having you here with me has made me brave."

"I love Americans," Antoine says. "They're so rich."

His wife slaps his arm. "Don't be rude, Antoine."

"I'm not rich," I say for what feels like the hundredth time. "My uncle left some money for this year. He would want me to spend it on people who are kind to me."

The hotel wakes later on Sundays. Madame goes to early mass, so that she misses nothing, but the rest of us, if we attend at all, go later in the day. When I get up at seven, the sun is slanting through my small window, and the sky unrolls like blue silk beyond the iron railing. I lean out the window and breathe in the sweet spring air.

Remy and Cécile are at the table when I come down. Cécile is by far the prettier of the midinettes, with a bright complexion and thick, fair hair fixed in a roll above her forehead and rippling down her back. Remy is as gamine and boyish as her name; her only feminine affectation is the hideous cherry-strewn hat she wears every day.

"Hats were a form of resistance," she tells me with a grin. "Fabric was rationed, but hats were not. And they kept our spirits up, you see—you could put anything on a hat. When one material ran out, we used something else. It was a finger in the eye of the Nazis, who wanted to see us ground down and starving."

We go to Notre Dame for mass. I cannot get over the fact that the ancient cathedral is an active church. It somehow means more to pray in a building saturated with centuries of faith. After church, we separate. The girls are going to Aubervilliers to visit Cécile's grandmother, and I plan to spend the afternoon at the café, which means I have to retrieve my notebook.

"All those stairs for a notebook!" Remy teases. "You should buy a smaller one with all your American money, so you can keep it in your bag."

I don't mind the extra effort. The steps, like the cafés, like my new friends, are a fact of my Parisian life. Gaston would be proud, I think, of how easily I take the steps, even if I have no intention of joining the Folies Bergère.

"Bonjour, Madame."

When I descend, clutching my notebook and two sharpened pencils, she raises her brows. "You have too much energy, Miss Kimber." From beneath her chair, Pepe barks once in agreement.

"I am going out," I tell them both, "and I will not return until I have written something worth reading."

Her lips twitch. "Should I tell Madeleine you will not be in for dinner?"

Even her jaundiced humor cannot touch me on such a day, and I set off for the Pont Neuf with a song in my heart.

Pascal, the sad waiter, recognizes me now. If I have not already taken a seat, he will theatrically produce a cloth and flourish it over the table he knows to be my favorite. Today he sees me coming and within moments a tiny cup of chicory is placed at my side. I've grown used to it and take a slow sip, open my notebook, and disappear.

"Pascal! Pascal, mon ami!"

A loud American voice tears me from my work. The man is speaking French, or almost French, but his nationality is obvious. Embarrassed for both of us, I return to the page, where I am trying unsuccessfully to describe the light inside Sainte-Chapelle, which I visited earlier in the week and am still trying to believe is real.

At the next table, a chair is pulled out and a body thuds heavily into it.

I raise my eyes. The American is tall and solid, with curling reddish-brown hair. He wears flannel trousers and a plain shirt, but his coat is an olive drab tunic with sergeant's stripes on the sleeve.

Pascal, rather than being annoyed, bustles up to the table with a glass of red wine. "Monsieur Rafferty!" he says enthusiastically. "You have not been here for ages!"

I've been coming here for three weeks, and I've never seen this man before.

"I've been away," he says easily, standing to kiss Pascal's cheeks. "But you can't get rid of me that easily."

"Non, and who would wish to?" the waiter asks. "You are always welcome. You"— he looks quickly at me—"and all other Americans."

I focus hard on my words, trying to be invisible, but the pencil marks swim before my eyes. They weren't very good words even when they were clear, but I resent the interruption. I thought Pascal and the owner were nice because they liked me, but it's just being American again. One of the liberators. I take another sip of chicory and realize that my cup is empty.

The sergeant has propped one foot on the chair across from him and is removing, with great industry, a collection of papers from a battered leather satchel. A fountain pen follows, which he uncaps and proceeds to turn through his fingers like a magician's trick. Finally, he sighs loudly, tucks his chin, and begins to write.

Once he is occupied, I discreetly let Pascal know that I need another drink. My work no longer satisfies me, and instead I tear a page from my notebook and begin a letter to my mother.

May 5, 1946

Dear Mama,

Paris is beginning to feel like something more than PARIS, the place I have dreamed of. It's beginning (just) to feel like where I live. I have a routine: get up, have breakfast, go to a café to write, have lunch, explore (someplace new every day if I have time and am feeling brave), then come back to my room to write some more.

Dinner is at seven. Because it stays light very late, I often walk in the evenings, either around the island or across the bridge to St. Michel, where there are student cafés and jazz clubs and so much life. It's fascinating to see it all, and to try to take it down.

I've made a couple of friends, which helps. Cécile and Remy work for the couturier Lucien Lelong. Aunt has at least two dresses with his label. They ask questions about your business and in return I make them tell me what it's like to work for a couture house. It almost sounds like they do piecework, because neither of them ever gets to see finished garments, just the bits and pieces that they work on.

I'm not the only American in Paris, that's for sure. There's a very loud one at the next table and it makes me cringe to be associated with him, even by nationality. But they are patient with us, because Americans liberated the city. Though I think there's also a sense of obligation there, and we both know that feeling obligated to someone doesn't always end well.

How are you and Dr. Max? Do you have any trips to the shore planned, or are you going to play it by ear and let him whisk you away one day, leaving everyone behind?

I was thinking the other day about Granny, and how far she came from Ireland, to land in such a bleak place as Scovill Run. Could she even imagine the lives we have now?

I miss you,

Pearl

On Tuesday, I return to the café and find my usual table occupied by the American. I stop short, then sit at the next table, discomfited by what feels like a deliberate attempt to inconvenience me.

"Good morning!" he says brightly. He's in shirtsleeves in the soft air, his uniform jacket slung over the chair back. "I hope you don't mind. It's where I always sit."

"Oh." Apparently, I've claimed *his* favorite spot. "It's all right."

He angles his chair toward me. "Pascal says you're a writer, too."

I've never told Pascal that; has he been reading over my shoulder, or did he assume, because the city is full of writers?

"I'm trying to be," I say shortly, and nod toward his pile of paper. "And you?"

"I'm a reporter. Or I was, before the war. Currently, I'm writing a novel." He sticks his hand out abruptly. "Michael Rafferty, formerly of the *Newark Star-Ledger*. More recently of the third army, and currently a citizen of the world. More specifically the eleventh arrondissement."

"Pearl Kimber." I retrieve my hand, flexing my fingers under the edge of the table. "Formerly of Philadelphia. Currently a resident of the first arrondissement."

Sergeant Rafferty leans forward, paper crackling under his elbows. "Why are you here, Miss Kimber?" he asks with deep interest. "Why Paris? Why now?"

His eyes are hazel, intense and alert. Resisting the urge to squirm under their scrutiny, I say, "Because I've always wanted to, and now that the war is over, I finally can."

"Did you always want to come *here*," he asks, sitting back, "or did you just want to escape Philadelphia?"

"I like Philadelphia." Pascal arrives with my chicory, and I break off to thank him. "Did you leave to escape... Newark, was it?"

"I left because the army came calling." He raises his cup. "And I'm here now because I don't want to go back to Newark."

My brothers hadn't waited to be drafted. Toby enlisted right after Pearl Harbor. George wasn't old enough, but he lied about his age and got in anyway. Wherever one went, the other always followed. The Navy made Toby an aviation mechanic and sent fierce George straight into the Pacific. He didn't turn eighteen until after he'd been through the Battle of Midway. Dan was classified as 4F because of his bad hand. He got a job as a welder down at the Navy Yard. It made him feel that he was doing his bit and gave me one less brother to worry about.

I push thoughts of my brothers aside; this is a passing conversation, nothing worth rendering judgment.

"What's wrong with Newark? And what about your job?" The hard times of my childhood are too close to imagine abandoning a job, especially one at a newspaper.

"They weren't going to hold it. The guys who got home early, they took all the best jobs." He shrugs. "And it was a golden opportunity, you know, to stay on here and see what I can make of myself."

I understand that well enough, but I'm not ready to discuss my dreams with a stranger. "Well," I say, "perhaps we should both get some work done."

May 10, 1946

On my way back from the café, I saw Cécile coming up from the Métro, unsteady and white in the face. She said she gets headaches at her time of the month. Today it was so bad they sent her home.

When we walked into the hotel, Madame took one look at her and told me to get her into a chair while she made a tisane. The brew must have worked, because the color started coming back into her cheeks. She said she would nap until Remy came in, so I helped her upstairs.

Their room is larger than mine, with one bed and two very distinct personalities. Remy is all order, few clothes, no books, while Cécile has things strewn everywhere—stockings and lipsticks and scarves. I thought it was impossible to get stockings, but she manages somehow.

I sat with her for a while, listening as she worried about not being well enough for her date tomorrow. She attracts men the way Hazel always did, except Cécile is movie star pretty and Hazel would be the first to say she was a walking freckle. I think it has to do with liking men. They sense it.

When she asked if I was seeing anybody, I laughed. The only men I've had any conversation with since leaving home, besides waiters (and Pat, who's tucked away in a box in my memory), are Julian Armitage and the annoying sergeant from the café, neither of whom Cécile would class as boyfriend material.

I told her hadn't come to France to meet someone. And then she said it. "You'll feel different when you meet the right man."

I've heard variations of that all my life, ever since I told people I didn't want kids. Mama understood. She said it was likely her fault for giving me so much responsibility while she had to work. And that's part of it, but it's not like she had a choice.

I do. I don't want to be a mother. Maybe that makes me selfish, but I don't want to spend my life worrying about keeping a small, helpless, totally reliant being alive.

Knowing that about myself made it hard to date after Cliff. For all that girls are supposed to be the ones who want to settle down, almost every boy I've ever known has a long-range plan that involves a job, a car, a wife and kids. Maybe a white picket fence for good measure. They don't want to know about my aspirations, only their own. That limits the number of men who would want me.

Even before I open my eyes, the knowledge is there: I am twenty-six. Far from home, surrounded by strangers who neither know nor care that it's my birthday. While my family doesn't go all out, some observance would have been made. A cake or a small gift. If Aunt was involved, a bigger cake and a bigger gift.

I roll over and thump my uncooperative pillow, then make a decision. After breakfast, I'll take myself out and do something special, something I haven't done yet. The Eiffel Tower, maybe? An hour or two at the Louvre? No, from the breeze stirring the curtains, it's too fine a day to spend inside a museum, even one such as that. The Mona Lisa can offer nothing on a day like this.

I take my notebook when I set out; it won't do to find myself at a café table, assailed by an idea with no way to write it down.

Although the Métro can get me anywhere within minutes, I take advantage of the day and go on foot. It will take an hour to cross the city and reach the tower, but I'm in no hurry. If something catches my attention, I want to be able to stop without feeling constrained by my original plan.

Before I head west, I run to the flower market and return with an armload of lilacs. Since I haven't managed to purchase a vase, the flower seller let me have a tall metal bucket with handles for a few francs. I turn its dented side to the wall and inhale their fragrance. I will not live extravagantly, no matter the size of my bank balance, but I will fill my room with my favorite flowers while they are in season.

The sky is a clear blue with pale streaks of cloud; the trees are in leaf, their color still tender and new, unlike the deeper green of summer. A plethora of scents reach me as I walk: bread, flowers, real coffee. My mouth waters at the thought, and I wonder where in this city I could find coffee. Probably in the fancy hotels, the George V or the Ritz, where I'd gone with Miss Gold for a memorable lunch—which means I will do without. I don't have the nerve to go into such a place by myself. I can manage cafés or even a bistro, but not a grand hotel. It's not Paris; I wouldn't feel comfortable in such a place at home, either.

I enter a street of small shops and amuse myself by window-shopping. Most businesses are still recovering and their stocks are either sadly pre-war, fetched from some dingy storeroom, or fashionable and unattainably priced. For the French, at least.

A milliner's sign draws me across the street. I've always loved hats, but all of mine are practical: serviceable colors, felts or straws that can be improved with a change of trimming. In my closet at home is Mama's old cloche from the thirties; my first grown-up hat, though I wouldn't wear it nowadays.

The window display is more appetizing than the coffee I can't get out of my mind. Six mannequin heads, each wearing an enviable confection, gaze blankly toward the street. Berets and cartwheels, turbans and veiled pillboxes, half-hats that are nothing but enormous ribbon bows or clutches of artificial flowers, in an assortment of delicious spring colors.

I want one. I want all of them, but I will keep it to one. In all my life, I've never bought more than one hat per year. My good black felt was purchased special for this trip. It was pricey, as hats are taxed as luxury items, but it will stand me in good stead for years to come.

This hat will not be like that. It will be frivolous and pretty and impractical.

A bell jangles musically when I open the door. "Bonjour," I call to the invisible saleswoman, and turn to inspect the models displayed on stands and shelves.

It is like a patisserie, with hats instead of sweets. I reach a tentative finger toward a blowsy pink silk rose ornamenting a simple ivory band. The petals are so skillfully colored that they appear real.

"Bonjour, mademoiselle." A young woman comes from behind an awning-striped curtain. "How may I help you?"

"I need a hat."

She nods, slipping out from behind the counter. "For an occasion?"

"No." I take a breath, squelch the butterflies. "It is a gift for myself."

"You are American." Her eyes drift toward the hats in the window; I likely have more to spend than her typical customer.

"I am a woman in need of a hat." There is a Mama-like edge to my voice. I won't be fooled into paying more than I should, no matter how badly I want one of these beauties.

"Of course." Her expression adjusts to the reality of our situation. "A particular color?"

"Blue, I think. May I try that one?" I point to a slate blue pillbox with a spotted veil. Something in me yearns to decorate it with a tiny bunch of daisies.

As the hat is fetched from its stand, I sit in front of the mirror, remove my hat, and reset the tortoiseshell combs holding back my curls. In this setting, my hat—new two summers ago—feels like an antique from another century. I watch as the shop assistant settles the pillbox on my head, then tweaks it to one side to follow my part. She arranges the veil and steps back.

"Well?"

"It's perfect."

It makes me look not older but more sophisticated, and the blue straw brings out the color of my eyes and the lighter streaks in my dark blonde hair. I can walk around Paris in this hat and blend in, instead of feeling like there is a blinking neon sign over my head that reads 'American'.

"I'd like to wear it," I tell her, and continue to admire my reflection as she puts my old hat in a tidy gold-and-white box. On my way to the counter to pay, I see a sleek charcoal beret on a stand and completely lose my grip on frugality. "That one, too, please."

She nods. "It will look well on you."

Hats old and new tucked into the box and an uncomfortable number of francs surrendered, I continue on to the Eiffel Tower. There are, I believe, restaurants on its upper levels, but they are likely out of my budget, especially after such extravagance. After I have completed my journey to the top—something to tell Hazel about in my next letter—I will find a bistro in the neighborhood and treat myself to lunch. Perhaps they will even have coffee.

When I return to the hotel in the late afternoon, Madame greets me with a smile. The expression is so unlike her that I nearly forget my bonjour.

"Philippe has letters for you," she says. "I know you have been waiting."

Her news is the best present I could wish for. I dash up the stairs and he produces a tidy bundle of mail from under the counter. "All for you," he says, with a flourish.

I take the letters and kiss him on both cheeks. "Thank you!"

Spreading them across the table, I glory in the sheer number of messages. There are three envelopes in my mother's handwriting, two from my aunt, one from Hazel, and an envelope from the Sisters of St. Joseph: a rare communique from my friend Peggy, who found an abrupt vocation in 1942 and entered the convent.

Nothing from my siblings, unless they are enclosed in my mother's letters. This is to be expected, but I'd hoped for a letter from Dan.

"Will you read them all at once?" Philippe's voice startles me; I have forgotten he is even in the room.

"One at a time," I tell him. "So they last longer. If the mail is this unreliable, I don't know how long I'll have to wait for the next batch."

I organize them by postmark, oldest to most recent, and am pleased to see the first letter is from Mama, written to Miss Gold's address and forwarded on. The portico clock on the sideboard says I have an hour before anyone comes in from work. I put the rest of the letters in my bag and curl up in an armchair with the single letter I will allow myself today.

April 10, 1946

Dear Pearl,

I always knew you'd leave home, but if I'm honest, I'm glad the war and your job kept you with us as long as it did. I miss having another woman around, and not only because you always had the coffee on when I came down in the morning. The house feels empty without you.

Enough of that. Life has gone on here the way it will. I'm keeping busy at the shop. More customers are coming back now that things are returning to normal. Max has talked Claire into expanding the clinic and taking on another full-time doctor. He can always wind her around his finger. When they get started with their plans, I close my eyes and think about whatever dress I'm working on and put it together in my head. I've solved a lot of fit issues while nodding and looking attentive.

The kids are doing well. Not that they're kids but you know what I mean. Dan is working steadily but also taking pictures again, which makes me happy. The boys are who they are. They could have come from another planet, they're so different from the rest of you. Maybe that's my biggest failure as a mother, not understanding how to make them fit into the family. But other than a few instances, they never seemed to need us.

Thelma is waiting tables and going to dance classes and auditions. She had a small role in the chorus at the Forrest Theatre. The show closed in a week but she's not giving up.

Grace is doing well in school but has no particular favorite subject. Out of the lot of you, she's the only one without a passion for something. You had your books and as soon as Thelma's legs were strong enough, we couldn't keep her still. Dan has his pictures, Toby his motors, and George has the firehouse. I sometimes wonder if Grace never needed an escape the way the rest of you did, because her life has been easier. But she's a happy child, and that is what matters.

Teddy has been a pillar for Claire. He's even managed to forge a relationship with Irene. I can't believe that old bat outlived her son. I've had words with God about it, but he hasn't seen fit to respond.

Claire is improving. She's thrown herself into a variety of projects to take her mind off things. I try to spend time with her and be easy, but it doesn't always work out. You know how it is. No one knows you like a sister, and that's both good and bad.

I will close now. We were happy to have your telegram and your first letter. I hope this year is everything you hope for. In case I haven't made it clear, I'm proud of you. And while your daddy wouldn't know what to make of who his princess Pearl has become, he wouldn't be at all surprised.

Mama

"Go to the public baths," Madeleine said when I first moved in. "You'll get all the hot water you want there."

When she gave that advice, I hadn't yet tried the hotel tub which, while clean, is as high and uncomfortable as a shipping crate. The addition of lilac soap and a clean towel did little to make the scant inches of tepid water more appealing. After my first experience, I took to washing at the sink in my room, but I missed submerging, and I missed truly hot water. I wasn't sure I could face the public baths.

Just how public were they? I wondered as I dressed, sniffing discreetly at my armpits. I smelled of soap and powder and perfume, but in my imagination, I was unfit to be in polite society—even if polite society also bathed in ankle-deep water.

Remy explained that the nearest baths were in the fifth arrondissement, not far beyond the Pont St. Michel. "It serves the Sorbonne students," she said, "so it's cheaper than the others, but clean."

There are separate bathing hours for men and women, which is a small comfort. I agree to go with the midinettes at two o'clock slot on Saturday afternoon. As usual, Cécile has a date and wants to look her best.

"What about you," I ask Remy. "Do you have a boyfriend?"

Cécile has a different one each week; I have no idea how she meets them, working such long hours.

"No," Remy says placidly. "I live through her. It is more than enough."

The baths are located in a broad stone building with a faintly Moorish aspect. We hand over the fee in exchange for soap and towels, and follow the signs to an echoing tiled room, filled with bathtubs, which smells pleasantly of disinfectant. It is a strange sight. There are, I note with deep discomfort, no barriers around the tubs. The only possible privacy is a half wall, with a bench to hold the bather's clothing. Once in the tub, I'll be invisible, but I will first have to undress to my skin in a room full of strangers.

There are two tubs side by side. Remy pushes me toward one. "Go ahead," she says.

"What about you?" I don't want to take off my clothes while my friends stand there and watch.

"I'll take the one next to you," Cécile says airily. "Remy always rushes, so she can be last."

Placing her towel on the bench, she turns on the water and steps out of her shoes and socks; her stockings are saved for evenings out. The rest of her things are shed while I'm still figuring out how best to leap from the bench into the tub without being gawked at.

I turn the faucet and hold my hand under it to test the temperature. The water gushes out boiling hot, something I haven't felt since I left home. Maybe I *can* do this.

Turning toward the bench, I catch a full view of Cécile as she steps into the tub. She is unexpectedly rich in flesh for a girl who has suffered through years of deprivation. Her boyfriends must feed her well, I think, before I drop my eyes.

I strip rapidly, not bothering to fold my clothes as I remove them—years of Mama's training out the window. She would understand, as she is very conscious of her body and would likely stick with washing at the sink rather than disrobe in public.

Cécile is submerged now, head resting on the edge of the tub, her hair carefully wrapped in a scarf. Remy is pacing, none too tactfully, next to a tub whose occupant is taking her time.

No one is looking at me. I unclasp my brassiere and step out of my pants, diving into the tub before I lose my nerve. The hot water hits me like a wall and all my anxiety drains away. No one is looking at me. No one is looking at anyone.

"Finally!" Remy's voice echoes in the tiled chamber. A worker comes to quickly clean the tub. While Remy waits, she drops her things on the bench and looks around the room. "Does anybody have a cigarette?"

Cécile's eyes flutter open. "In my bag, if you're that desperate."

She comes around the wall to rummage in her friend's purse. "Oh, it's not worth it. You didn't carry this much when you fled Paris."

My eyes are closed, as well, but I open them when Remy's bare feet pass my tub. She is thinner than Cécile, with no curves to speak of and tiny breasts above protruding ribs. Embarrassed to have been caught looking, I slip under the water to wash my hair.

"You are not comfortable with your body," Remy says as we make our way back to the hotel. "Tu as de jolis seins."

The word is unfamiliar, but I believe she's referring to my breasts. I take a breath. "I'm not comfortable being naked in public," I respond, raising a hand to the back of my neck, where a trickle of water is making its way from my damp hair toward my collar. "We have a bathroom at home. With a door."

"Ooh la la!" Cécile splays a hand on her chest. "Such wealth."

"Not wealth, just privacy." When we lived in Scovill Run, we bathed in a tin tub in the kitchen, one after another. Once a child was old enough to be safely left alone, the door was closed. Public baths are the norm in France; even people with money don't have elaborate facilities for bathing; if Cécile thinks I come from wealth, Mary Jayne Gold's apartment with its marble bathrooms would stun her into silence.

May 12, 1946

Hello darling,

You asked what place will always mean Paris to me, and while there are many, the Leda and the Swan fountain in the Jardin de Luxembourg is the only one for which that would be wholly true.

The first time I saw Paris was my honeymoon trip with Harry, the year after the last war ended. Everything was amazing to me. You must remember that I'd gone from Scovill Run to Scranton to Philadelphia in the space of a year, and now I was in Paris! I didn't have the sense God gave a rabbit, as your grandmother would have said, but I knew how lucky I was to have found Harry.

We were living at the Hôtel Lutetia and generally all our time was spent together, but one morning Harry stayed behind to deal with some business. I crept timidly out of the hotel and stood trembling on the sidewalk, won-

dering where to go. I didn't speak the language except to read menus or ask prices, and people speaking French at me scared me stiff. Remember that rabbit?

The gardens were close by, so I decided to go there. They couldn't possibly be crowded and if a stranger spoke to me, I could run away.

I walked and walked and eventually found the Italian fountain. I'm sure you've seen it, but have you seen the small fountain behind it? It's nothing special. Most people don't even know it's there. But I found it. As I stood there, I wept at how out of place I was, not only in Paris but in my life. I felt as alien as Leda must have felt from her swan.

Then, all of a sudden, my fears drained away. Calm wrapped me like a blanket. I knew that if I could keep that feeling, I could learn how to be a good wife to that very good man.

That is a very long-winded answer to your question and has made me cry again, but happy tears, dear Pearl, because I think I did learn.

Teddy sends his love.

Claire

June 1946

I alter my routine, writing in my room after breakfast and not going to the café until an hour before lunch, leaving myself less time with Sergeant Rafferty. It is wrong to allow myself to be driven away by someone so pleasant, but it is also impossible to concentrate with him there. He never stops talking, whether to me or Pascal or himself, and his mess of papers migrates from his table to mine, as if his ideas are too large to be contained.

When I arrive, Pascal brings my chicory and leaves me alone to work. At noon, when the bells ring, I tuck my notebook into my bag and produce a novel, which signals to him that it is time for lunch. I rarely look at the menu; he will bring the best of what they have, usually an omelet or a bowl of soup with crusty bread.

Today's special is an omelet with chopped herbs, which I consume while keeping my eyes fixed on the copy of *Gone with the Wind* that I'd found at a bookstall last week. Having seen the film first, I will never be able to envision Rhett Butler as anyone but Clark Gable. Leslie Howard, on the other hand, is *not* my idea of Ashley Wilkes. His character wasn't—in my opinion—adequately explored in the movie. On the page, I understood why Scarlett wanted him; on screen, I wanted to pelt them both with turnips for risking their marriages for a totally unsuitable attraction.

The story holds my interest, though, even as I think—again—that I could do as well, if I were given the chance.

A pelting rain, which had kept me tucked far back beneath the awning, has blown over. Once I have finished eating, I take the weather as a directive to continue along the quai and browse the green-painted bookstalls. The bouquinistes are a rare aspect of Paris that matched my aunt's descriptions and my expectations. The small shelf in my room has begun to sag beneath the weight of the treasures I've accumulated.

The first stall is a trove of richly scented antique books. Most are sadly out of my price range. I continue on, stopping to rummage through a box of old fashion prints, choosing four to take home for Mama; Dan can frame them to hang in her shop.

"That doesn't look much like literature." A grinning Sergeant Rafferty points at the prints in my hand.

"They're a gift." I pay for my purchase and wait as the bookseller wraps them in paper. "My mother is a dressmaker."

He steps back so I can move away from the stall. "She must be pretty successful, if you're living in Paris."

I'm so tired of explaining my existence to people who automatically assume I'm rich. Tucking the prints into my bag, I say, "My uncle died in January. He left money for this trip in his will."

"Nice uncle." His eyebrows raise. "My most successful relative ran a taproom, and he wouldn't have sent me to the corner for beer."

"I have a few uncles like that." I think of my mother's brothers who haven't been seen in years and are not missed.

"I suppose everyone does." Sergeant Rafferty falls into step beside me. "I haven't seen you at our café recently."

Our café?

"I've been working at home," I tell him. "Don't you enjoy not having to fight for your table?"

He bumps my shoulder. "We could always share."

"I suppose." Walking with him is pleasant; people step out of my way when I am with a man in a way that never happens if I'm alone or walking with the midinettes.

"I'm going there now." He stops, and I continue on. "If you come with me, I'll buy you a cup of that terrible chicory you seem to like."

That was interesting—he noticed what I drank. "I can't," I say. "I've just finished, and I have errands."

"I'm not used to being turned down by pretty girls." The words are lightly said, but his expression shows that he means it. "Maybe tomorrow?"

"Maybe." It wouldn't be the end of the world to share a table, so long as he kept his papers to himself. "So long as you let me work."

He strikes a dramatic pose, hand over heart. Several passersby stop to look at him. "I solemnly swear," he says. "We can egg each other on and both succeed."

I like the sound of that: someone to hold me accountable, who will elbow me if I'm writing letters instead of stories. "Deal," I say, and hold out my hand.

"American!" he says scornfully, before kissing me on both cheeks.

Working with Sergeant Rafferty is better than I expected. He talks too much, but I've learned to tune him out, and when I'm finished for the day, he is lively company, full of colorful stories about his time in the army or his concierge, who is cut from the same cloth as Madame.

He is inconsistent, though, coming and going as he pleases; the absence that coincided with my arrival in Paris happens again the week after we begin to work together. Gone a few days this time, he returns to the café with his usual fanfare and falls into the chair next to mine, slinging his bag up on the table and bumping my cup. Liquid sloshes onto the table, narrowly missing my notebook.

I glance up in annoyance. "Where have you been?"

Instead of answering, he says, "I brought the magazine."

For a moment, I don't know what he's talking about, then I remember. "Your *Harper's* article?"

"You said you wanted to read it." He slides a magazine from an envelope.

Unlike *Time* or *Life*, the unadorned black and white cover shows the seriousness of its content; the stark title *"Germany's Deformed Con-*

science" dominates, with two columns of text beneath. It makes the *Saturday Evening Post* look like a comic book.

"Is that your article?" I try to read the byline, but he won't hold still, riffling the magazine's pages and jigging in his seat.

"I wish." He pushes the magazine across the table. "I'm way inside."

Picking it up with tentative fingers, I ask, "Can I take it home to read?"

"Nope." A lock of reddish hair falls forward when he shakes his head. "It's my last copy. You'll have to read it here."

I hate watching someone read my work and assumed he was the same, but apparently not. My other concern is understanding what he's written; being unaware of world affairs would be impossible with Dr. Max and Uncle in my life, but I don't read the sort of articles that *Harper's* publishes.

"All right." I bite my lip. "I wanted to get some work done this morning."

"It won't take long, they cut half of it." He takes the magazine back and opens it, presenting me with a page titled *"Isolationism for a New World,"* by Michael S. Rafferty.

Before Pearl Harbor, America had looked at the war in Europe through the lens of isolationism. That lens was shattered in the attack, and though we were late to join the war, we made up for it with vigor, men, and equipment. Isolationism, I had thought, was dead.

Pascal slips a fresh cup of chicory onto the table. I nod my thanks, my eyes already racing over the lines of crowded text and equally crowded thoughts.

The guns are silent at last, but an insidious enemy lingers, haunting our dreams and our waking hours alike. It is the specter of economic uncertainty.

While soldiers fought overseas, a different battle raged on the home front. Industries were converted to war production and workers rose to meet the demands of global conflict. Now, in a time of apparent peace, we face a similarly daunting challenge: how to transition our economy back to civilian production without plunging the nation into economic ruin.

Millions of young men, having risked all for their country, return to a nation struggling to give them employment. It is our solemn duty to ensure that our heroes are not forgotten, and that their sacrifices are rewarded with opportunities, not empty promises.

The article makes the case for a new form of isolationism brought about by war weariness, defense of the national economy, and fear of communism. The money spent on the occupation and rebuilding of Germany, he argues, would be better spent at home or in support of our allies, who will be in worse shape than our vanquished enemy if we keep to our present course.

His words are incisive and convincing, yet I'm not convinced. It is a far more cynical view of the world. I also think it's somewhat selfish to keep the excellence of America penned up inside its borders, rather than allowing democracy to spread across the globe by example. Isn't that partly why we fought the war?

The Truman administration persists in its attempts to rebuild a country shattered by its own evil as surely as by any bomb dropped by a Liberator or a Flying Fortress.

Not all Germans were Nazis; however, a certain collective guilt must be assumed. Individual citizens are not culpable for crimes committed in their name, but should a nation not bear some responsibility for its leaders? Any assistance given by the United States should be measured and conditional. Let us harness the same spirit that carried us through the darkest hours of war and apply it to the task of rebuilding our nation first.

I finish reading and place the magazine on the table, taking a careful sip of chicory while I corral my unruly thoughts.

"Well?" He slips it back into his bag. "What do you think?"

"You're an excellent writer." His journalist's brevity is evident in every line, and even the opinions with which I disagree are set out so cogently it is hard to find the words to explain why they are wrongheaded.

"Tell that to their editorial board," he grumbles. "Them and *The Atlantic*. I submit to them regularly, and have I even had a nibble?"

He wasn't going to ask for my thoughts; my praise was sufficient. The tension in my shoulders relaxes and I'm able to raise my eyes to the river, where a low-riding barge is plodding past.

"This is from January," I point out. "*Harper's* most likely doesn't publish the same writers all the time, unless they're on staff."

"Don't give me logic when I'm wallowing. It's not helpful."

"I just told you that you were an excellent writer," I remind him. "Don't tell me you've gone from preening to self-pity that quickly."

His face brightens. "You look like butter wouldn't melt," he says wonderingly, "but you've got a mouth on you."

As would anyone raised in a family like mine, with a mother like mine. I learned at her knee that words are often the most effective weapon.

Dear darling Pearl in the wide, wide world,

You probably figured this out when the check fell out of the envelope, but YOU SOLD A STORY TO THE POST!!!!!!

I know the teacher in you is gasping at all that punctuation, but you'll have to forgive me.

When you gave me your stories and that long list of magazines to send them to, I was scared spitless that I would mess up. You know I can't keep my head on straight half the time, but I did this for you. FOR YOU. So you'd better have an extra special present for your baby sister when you get home. You have a whole extra FIFTY DOLLARS to spend on me. Can you believe it??

Grace

P.S. Mama and Pop are good, Thelma went to New York for an audition without telling anyone (the shouting!!), G&T are who they are, and Dan said to tell you he loves you.

P.P.S. Tommy is back. I haven't seen Dan smile like that since Pearl Harbor.

P.P.P.S. Why have I never realized that the war started in a place named for you? I'm going to call you Pearl Harbor from here on out. Pearl Harbor The Author.

Love you!

Grace's exuberance bursts from the page but I can't get past the first paragraph. "I sold a story to the *Post*?" I whisper. "The *Saturday Evening Post*?"

I pick up the check and attached note that has fluttered from the envelope and under the bed. Fifty dollars payable to Pearl M. Kimber, for the story *Believe in Me*, to be published in the July 13 edition.

What do I do with a check in American dollars? I suppose I can take it to Julian's bank and let them cash it for me; that's what banks are for. I feel like a child at Christmas, ripping paper off a box to find inside exactly the gift that was most desired. My heart is racing and for a moment the room swims behind a film of happy years.

I sold a story to the *Post*. At last.

Holding tight to the edge of the desk, I grin at the letter, tears leaking from the corners of my eyes. I will indeed have to find a special present for Grace so she realizes how much I appreciate what she's done.

When Hazel and I decided to go to France, Mama had been the one to ask how I was going to keep up with trying to publish my stories. Surprisingly, my little sister volunteered to take on the task, sitting patiently as I explained my system of sending out a story, marking its inevitable return and rejection, and then sending it to the next magazine on the list until it was either accepted or had been rejected by them all. I bought envelopes and stamps so she wouldn't be tempted to spend my money on candy, kissed her soundly, and told her she was my good luck charm.

And now she was. *Believe in Me* had been turned down seven times already. I'd completely rewritten it the week before I left, having woken up in the middle of the night knowing exactly what was wrong with it. The *Post* had rejected it last November, but rewritten, neatly typed, and with a new title, I thought it deserved a second chance and they agreed.

It is early afternoon. No one will be home for hours, and who in this place will even understand why I'm so excited? Remy and Cécile are always up for a celebration, but they won't truly know what it means. Madeleine? She's become used to talking to me, enough that she's admitted to not having read anything since she was at school. Miss Gold would open a bottle of champagne, but she has moved to Gassin so I can't turn up on her doorstep. Julian Armitage would understand, I think, but I don't want to sit down and write a letter—I want to dance and sing and tell the world what I've finally managed to do. There is no one. Unless—

Looking at my watch, I pull on a light sweater and hurry down the stairs, tossing my key to Philippe on my way out.

He's there! Crossing the bridge, I gain the curb and see him at the far table, his leather satchel gaping open, one foot propped, as always, on the chair opposite.

"Sergeant Rafferty!" I call, skidding to a stop. My bag is clutched against my chest, and I realize I'm still holding the check.

He has a way of blinking, then raising his eyelids slowly, as if just waking up, and looking around with surprised delight. "I thought you weren't coming today."

"I have news!" I gulp air and proffer the check with shaking hands. "I sold a story."

He takes it from me, scrutinizing it thoroughly. "Curtis Publishing, hmm? Which magazine?"

"*Saturday Evening Post.*" I sink into the empty chair, all my energy abruptly draining away. "I've been trying to sell a story to them for two years."

"Congratulations." His smile is blazing. "That's wonderful, Miss Kimber." He frowns. "If I'm going to buy you a glass of wine to celebrate your achievement, I can't possibly keep calling you Miss Kimber."

"Then call me Pearl." He wants to celebrate with me! I'd been afraid that, despite being a writer himself, he wouldn't understand how special this was. "And you're... Michael?"

He stops in the midst of hailing Pascal. "Mick to my friends."

Pascal arrives with a half bottle of red wine and two glasses. "There is good news?" he asks.

"Pearl has sold a story," Mick tells him. "To a very important magazine."

The waiter inclines his head respectfully. "Felicitations, mademoiselle."

"Pour one for yourself, Pascal." Mick hands me a glass. "This is a big day."

As we touch glasses, my heart is beating hard enough to fly out of my chest. I take a sip, shudder involuntarily at its vinegar taste. Nothing can spoil this moment.

"How long does it take for the *Post* to arrive in Paris?"

Mick knocks back his drink as if it were ambrosia. "Magazines are two weeks behind, sometimes three." His eyes glint. "Let's finish our drinks and find a kiosk, see how old the latest issue is."

"All right." I take another sip. This stuff is even worse than what Madame serves with dinner.

"This is your celebration," he says, refilling both our glasses. "Drink up."

Our mission takes us to three newsstands, a bookstore, and another café in the fifth that Mick likes. More harsh wine, but I am developing a taste for it now—or possibly growing numb to its flavor.

"I have to go home for dinner," I say regretfully as the bells chime six-thirty. Madame will not care about my good news; if I don't appear for dinner, there will be a lecture at breakfast. "My landlady doesn't like to waste food."

"Who does, these days?" He shrugs, and his hand curls possessively around my arm. "Tomorrow, you'll meet me at the café at nine and we'll work until noon, then break for lunch and go for another hour, like Sartre and Beauvoir at the Café de Flore."

It isn't an invitation but an assumption, and I am happy to agree. I am a writer who has sold a story to the most important magazine I can think of; I need to work. Being in the company of someone who pushes me can only help. We exchange cheek kisses and I cross the Pont St. Michel. When I look back, he has disappeared.

I read Grace's letter again before bed. The glow of my achievement and my tumultuous afternoon with Mick Rafferty has left me in a pleasant state of exhaustion. Curling up in the velvet armchair, I skim the lines, hearing them in my sister's headlong style, with a gasp for breath at the end of each long sentence.

One phrase in particular stops me.

Tommy is back.

Tommy Marinelli was my brother's best friend and my first boyfriend. We'd kissed a few times, but it wasn't until Dan returned from his hobo summer that I realized why our relationship had never gone further.

Very few people know Dan well. He's private to begin with, and being different, as far as girls are concerned, makes him more so. Mama didn't even know for the longest time how he was. When she did find out, she said there was nothing to forgive. Loving as he does makes his life more complicated, but he's never expected easy. None of us have.

Dan worked in the shipyard during the war, long shifts, sometimes sleeping there, as if to make up for his inability to serve. He lost a finger in a mine accident when he was ten and he has nerve damage in that hand, which we didn't know about until he tried to enlist anyway and was sent home.

I think he felt lost. I know I did. While I spent the war waiting for my life to start, Dan waited for Tommy to come home. I don't know for certain how Tommy feels. They're still best friends. Whether there's more to it than that is nobody's business but theirs. Until Tommy joined up, they shared a room at a boarding house near Baldwin Locomotive, where they worked, passing as cousins. I guess that's all the answer I need.

Tommy hasn't been home since 1941. I know they write but considering Dan's letters are ten words at best, they'll have a lot of catching up to do.

I'm yawning and my eyes are gritty with tiredness, but instead of going to bed, I move to the desk. First, I'll write to my brother. Then I'll sleep. I have a writing date in the morning.

June 4, 1946

Dan,

Grace told me your news. I don't need to tell you how happy I am. I hope you'll write and tell me how happy YOU are. Will you? Only time will tell.

I feel like I've started to settle in here. I've made some friends. They're seamstresses, wouldn't you know? I can't get away from sewing even by crossing an ocean. I've also met a man. More about him later, if there's anything worth telling. (I'm not sure there is). He's a writer, too, so we have something in common. But I don't want to distract myself from the reason I'm here, which is to write and write and write and build a future for myself.

You'll have heard about the story I sold to the Post. *While I'd like to write a novel, I'm also trying to figure out exactly what I did with that story that got my foot in the door, because maybe if I find the formula, I'll be able to do it again. A girl can dream, anyway.*

Write to me, brother. I miss you.

Pearl

When the alarm jerks me awake at six-thirty, I spring out of bed to take possession of the toilet before anyone else. Back in my room, I unpin my hair and brush it into a semblance of the style I had in mind. My blue dress is pressed and waiting, to make up for sprinting to the café in trousers and a sweater yesterday. I squint at the mirror, weaving to avoid the patches where the silvering has worn away, and draw on a brave red mouth.

Mick wants to write together! The thought has circled my brain during the long night. I can make nothing of it except that he wants to spend time with me.

I started out resenting his takeover of the café, but my feelings have gradually changed to curiosity and more than a bit of attraction. His cocky manner is appealing; it speaks of a confidence I lack. If I'm lucky, it will be contagious, like measles.

After sharing a swift breakfast with Remy and Cécile, I go upstairs for my notebook and pencils, then stand, torn, looking into the hulking wardrobe, which now sports a blue bow on its handle to hold it shut. Jacket? Sweater? Perhaps just the dress, with my watch and a gold bangle. I jam on the bracelet, scraping my wrist, and run back down the steps.

Our table—our table!—is empty. I take the seat facing the river, then reconsider and move the other chair next to mine so it's not as obvious that I've stolen his seat. Pascal glides up with a cup of chicory and a croissant on a small white plate.

At my startled glance, he says, "The boulangerie had extra."

"Thank you."

He moves smoothly away. I wonder if the croissant, delicious and tasting of butter, is because my story was accepted or because I have been accepted. It doesn't matter. Despite Madame's bread and jam and a delicious cup of black market coffee, I find space for it. By the time Mick ambles along the Seine, there is not a flake of pastry to be seen.

He drops down beside me. "Took the best spot, eh?"

"To the early bird go the spoils." I raise my brows. "You said nine, didn't you?"

"When did you get here, eight?" Mick leans close to kiss my cheek and I catch a whiff of something spicy on his skin. Warmth blooms in my belly. "Did Pascal give you my croissant?"

"Croissant?" I look at him with the innocent gaze of someone adept in the art of dodging guilt. "He brought my chicory and that was it. Do you get croissants?"

"Once in a while." Raising a hand to Pascal, he drags another chair across the terracotta tiles and swings his foot up on it. "Your presence will have to be sweetness enough."

I look down at my notebook so he doesn't see my red face.

We work quietly for two hours. Mick's papers spread gradually until they are fluttering off the side of the table. Finally, I shove the whole un-tidy pile into his lap. He looks up, clearly unaware of what has happened.

"If this blows into the Seine," I say firmly, "it will be your fault."

"Understood." He shuffles them into a semi-neat stack, then stretches, tilting the chair back against the wall. "Do you want to walk? I'm getting a cramp from sitting here."

"Considering that you were late…" The last sip of chicory tastes especially foul after the rare treat of coffee.

Mick crams his papers into the leather satchel that is his constant companion. "You're cute," he says, unfolding himself from the chair, "but you're a terrible nag."

My cheeks heat again but instead of hiding, I grin at him. "And yet you're asking me to walk with you."

"It must be shell shock."

He throws a handful of coins on the table and waves to Pascal, who is inside with the sour-faced owner. I wiggle my fingers in a separate farewell, hoping he understands my gratitude for the unearned pastry.

There is no discussion, but we head further into the St. Michel neigh-borhood, weaving through streets wide and narrow until we reach the wrought iron gates of the Jardin de Luxembourg and the cool green world within.

"I love it here." I turn around to take it all in.

"What's your favorite part?" He grabs my hand and pulls me out of my spin, so that I stumble against him.

"The fountain." I searched it out after receiving Aunt Claire's letter, and although I also located Leda's fountain on the other side, the Medici Fountain stole my heart. It is as old as my hotel, but far grander, a long, narrow pool that somehow pulls me back in time whenever I see it. We pass the Grand Bassin, surrounded by squealing children and patient or impatient mothers and nannies. "My cousin Teddy sailed his boat here when they lived in Paris before the war."

That sailboat, an impressive piece of shining wood, white sails, and brass fittings, returned to Philadelphia with him, only to look out of place in the shallow fountain at Rittenhouse Square. I was surprised he had such a clear memory of sailing, but after my first visit, I found a postcard of the fountain and sent it to him.

Mick grabs two green-painted metal chairs and settles them on the sandy grit common to all French parks.

"Tell me about your family." He angles his body forward, his expression alert and interested. He probably looks like that all the time, except when he's asleep. The thought of what he might look like sleeping almost makes me blush again.

"I'm one of six," I tell him. "Second oldest. Two younger brothers and two sisters. We grew up in a mining town near Scranton called Scovill Run." My grim birthplace is as unimaginable in Paris as Paris would have been to me when I was growing up there. "My father died in '32. After that, we moved to Philadelphia, I grew up, got an education, and became a teacher."

"Mining is a chump's game," he observes. "All that risk, and for what?"

The sun goes behind a cloud. My stomach tightens and I resist an urge to flee the park.

"My father wasn't a chump," I say, my fists clenching. "He wanted to feed his family. And he died in that mine. Unless you've been down there, I don't need to hear your opinions."

Mick blinks at the ferocity of my response. "I'm sorry," he says immediately. "That was thoughtless. I was only repeating what I've heard."

I accept his apology, but it's harder to accept that a man who makes a living with words can be so careless with them.

"What about you?" I ask, to keep from dwelling. It will come back to me later. "What's your family like?"

"Picture a handful of marbles dropped on the ground." He shrugs. "Scattered everywhere. I had two brothers, both in the Marines. One came home, one didn't."

It doesn't seem possible to speak so blithely of a dead brother. Perhaps men learn a certain distance, because they aren't supposed to show their feelings.

"Any sisters?"

"One." Mick's smile turns rapidly to something else. "Janey dropped out of school to get married. She's got a half dozen kids and she's barely thirty."

Not so different from my mother, but I'm not about to expose her choices to his harsh judgment. I say simply, "Her kids will never be lonely."

A trio of pretty students walk past, chattering excitedly. Mick watches them with frank interest, then turns back to me. "I'll never get used to hearing wooden shoes."

Even as I envy their youth and freshness, I am called to defend their footwear. "It's not as if they've been able to buy shoes for six years," I point out. "We're lucky to be American. No matter how poor we are back home, we have more than all these people."

His laughter makes heads turn all around. I shrink back, embarrassed to have drawn attention; every noisy conversation I've heard in Paris has involved Americans making their presence known.

"You can't bear to hear anything bad said about anyone, can you?" he asks. "How do you plan to write about the world if you can't think ill of any of it?"

"There's plenty of bad in the world." Hitler and the evils of fascism which have just been defeated. The everyday evils that face us all: poverty and hunger and cruelty. "People will prove themselves one way or the other. I choose to start on a more positive note than you."

Mick's eyes turn serious. "Perhaps you're what I've needed all this time. Someone to make me less of a cynic."

I push down my cynical thoughts. Mick was in the war; I know how my younger brothers came home. He deserves a little grace as he readjusts to civilian life.

"What are you working on now?" I ask. "Is it anything like the *Harper's* article??

"I've given up on all that," he says. "The world has had enough of war and I've had enough of being rejected by magazines who think they're better than me. I'm writing a novel, but it's not some fluff piece. It's about a man who fought in Spain and his search to find meaning when everything he held dear has been destroyed."

That not only sounded like war, it sounded more than a little like Ernest Hemingway. I bite my tongue. "It sounds fascinating. How does he find meaning?"

He spreads his hands. "I haven't gotten that far. What about you? More stories, or have you embarked on a novel?"

Someone is playing a violin on the far side of the bassin. I pause to listen before responding. "I'm not sure."

"Tell me." His large hand circles my wrist. My bangle presses into my flesh.

"Not now. It's not clear yet." I tug my hand free. "Let's go to the bookstore again, the student one we went to yesterday. There's something I want to buy."

I return home at five, which gives me time to take a nap before dinner. As high up as I am, the window delivers a breeze which isn't always felt on the lower floors.

Despite having written more in the last months than I ever have, these sustained hours with Mick are wearing. If Sartre and Beauvoir wrote like this every day, I understand why they drank to excess.

The story I refused to share with Mick is slightly out of reach, as if there are people on the other side of a door, having a conversation that I can only faintly hear. I know this feeling; if I wait, the door will dissolve and I'll learn what I need to know.

A faint headache begins at my temples. I get up and take two aspirin from the bottle on the shelf above the sink. The last time I checked, the pharmacy didn't have any, so I've been rationing myself. This small bottle will not last until next spring, not with all the reading and writing and staring at art and old buildings and interesting people I've been doing.

Lying down is uncomfortable, so I sit in my armchair, close my eyes, and wait for the aspirin to kick in.

"Mon dieu, you *must* have money to spend. Look at everything you've added to this room. When Yvette lived here, it looked like an attic."

"I don't want to live in an attic." And I don't think the small bits I've added—books and secondhand goods from the market—prove that I have money to spend. Then again, even the poorest American is flush with cash compared to the average French citizen.

On nights when Cécile has a date, Remy comes up and sits on my bed and we trade stories about our lives. She has five brothers and sisters, but as the youngest; her experience of growing up is far different than mine, and I listen to her, fascinated.

"What about cousins?" I have six, but we saw them infrequently even before moving to Philadelphia.

"So many." Remy falls back, rolling her eyes. "My mother had three sisters and they never learned to say no." She reels off names and ages until I am thoroughly confused, and concludes by saying, "And then there is Solange."

Her voice has gone flat.

"What about Solange?"

"She is no longer part of the family." Remy's usually merry face is solemn. "I miss her, but..."

"Did she move away?" This conversation appears to require more than a normal back and forth. I reach into my top drawer, pull out a pack of gum, and toss it onto the bed. She opens it immediately and folds a piece into her cheek.

"She is gone. I'm not sure where." Her eyes close for a moment, in reminiscence or simple enjoyment of teaberry gum. "The family made her leave."

What could Solange have done that her family drove her away? I can't imagine anything short of murder—and Mama would support her children even if they'd done something criminal, once they'd recovered from her punishment.

"Were you close to her?"

"Always." Remy slides off the bed and wanders to the window. "She watched me when I was a baby, so often that I thought she was my mother, even though she was only six years older."

That was enough time, though, to feel mothered. Grace called me Mama Pearl until I made her stop.

"What happened?" If it's painful, I don't want her to talk, but I've never seen her this solemn about anything. My writer brain needs to know what could quench her spirit. "If you want to tell me, that is."

"I can't speak of her to my family." She flung herself back down on the bed. "My father and uncles won't allow her name to be mentioned. I think it's worse with my mother. She held Solange up as an example, so she feels especially betrayed."

Remy has spoken before about the occupation, but this time she tells me about her village, not what happened in Paris. Soldiers everywhere, men being taken away, resistants being shot. Fuel shortages. Cold and darkness and lack of hope. Little food for anyone but the Germans.

"Solange's husband was one of the first to be taken," she says. "He left her with two babies."

"How terrible." I can see it: the open door, the dark car speeding away with a beloved man inside. The babies, crying. The woman, holding onto them. Holding on *for* them.

"She never gave up hope." Remy swipes at her eyes and takes another stick of gum.

"I understand," I say. "Until the war is over, you don't want to believe someone is really gone."

"But she had children." Her voice goes reedy with strain. "Antoinette, the baby, was colicky. You could hear her scream all over the village. And Thierry, he was two years older but a bag of bones."

My stomach knots. I don't want to know where this story is going.

"Solange took a job cleaning for the Nazis. That was bad enough for most people, that she would work for them, but then one of them took a liking to her." Remy licks her lips. "He came to her house after dark."

A sickening shame fills me for what Solange was forced to do—not by that specific German soldier, but by the war itself.

Remy's cheeks shine with tears. "That first winter, if Antoinette hadn't been sick so often, Solange might have been able to keep it a secret, but the German brought a doctor."

"Your family blamed her for saving her child's life?" I rub her thin shoulders, no longer afraid she will misinterpret my affection.

"She died, anyway. He said she was too malnourished to fight the fever."

I put my arms around her and let her cry.

After a minute, Remy gives a mighty sniff and sits up. "After that, Solange no longer cared what the family thought. When her father called her a putain, she said she had to keep Thierry alive. She wouldn't listen to anyone. She took the German as her lover, openly, and he fed her boy." Her throat works as she forms the rest of the story. "When the Germans left, my uncle dragged her into the square before the church with the other collaborators. He shaved her head himself, and the women stripped her bare and made her walk through the village." Her voice drops. "That was when we found out she was pregnant."

"Remy, I'm so sorry." I weave my fingers through hers; it is like touching a live wire. "And they made her go?"

"Why would she stay after that?" She takes a long, uneven breath. "That night, I went to her house. She wouldn't let me in, but Thierry opened the window, and I gave him some money I'd stolen from my grandmother. Two days later, they were gone."

The next day at the café, as I work on my latest story—which is not going well—my mind returns to Solange. I put myself in her place, in an occupied town with no husband and two children to feed, and wonder: would I have made the same choice? It is possible she never felt that there was a choice to be made. A German soldier could easily take what he wanted, so it seemed to me she made the best of a terrible situation.

And she still lost her child.

I remember those first weeks after Teddy's birth, before he was adopted by my aunt and uncle, when Mama was unable to care for him. His constant crying terrified me, though it was nothing more than normal infant behavior. Could I watch my child starve, knowing it could be prevented by an exchange of my body for food and medicine? Could I do it?

I could, I thought, even though the idea of being invaded in that way sickened me. But children, unable to defend themselves, have to come first. It is one of the reasons I don't want them; as the eldest daughter, I don't remember a time when I ever came first.

Mick snaps his fingers in my face. "Wake up, Pearl."

"I'm awake," I say, cranky at my thoughts being derailed when they were just going somewhere. "I'm thinking."

"You were a million miles away." Swinging his foot down, he tips his head back to let Pascal know that he requires attention. "You'll never take the world by storm if you spend your life daydreaming."

"Yes, sir." I sketch a salute. "Any other orders?"

When he laughs, the tension is broken. He takes my hand, drops it to my thigh and holds it. "I thought we could take the train out to Versailles this afternoon. I heard they're allowing rowing boats on the Grand Canal again."

"Not today." I promised to have lunch with Madeleine, and if I help her clean up, perhaps she'll agree to go for a walk and answer some of my questions about the occupation. "I already have plans."

When his lip juts out, he looks remarkably childlike. "But I made this plan yesterday."

"And you told me about it today." I raise my eyebrows. "I'm not always available."

"You should be." When Pascal comes to take his order, he shakes his head curtly, digs into his pocket and drops his money on the table. "Maybe I'll see you tomorrow."

June 10, 1946

Dear Mama,

I've added this extra page just for you (although you can show Dr. Max if you want) because I need to know what you think about something.

During the occupation there were men and women who collaborated with the Germans. They all had their reasons: belief, expediency, desperation. All are deemed equally bad, but Remy, my friend at the hotel, told me her cousin, Solange, was stripped publicly and had her head shaved (by her own father!) for what they called "collaboration horizontale."

Why does the world assume that women enter into these relationships for the same reasons as men? Solange's husband was taken away and she had young children to feed. Should patriotism trump keeping children alive? Remy said the family cast her cousin out. They were willing to keep her little boy, but they wanted her gone before she gave birth to the baby given to her by a German soldier.

Solange told them "Va te faire foutre" which is very rude and exactly what they deserved. She took her boy and got on a train and now no one knows where she is. Remy misses her but also blames her for giving in.

Am I wrong to think she had no choice? I can't imagine what she would have said to her husband, but would it be any easier to explain that she let their babies starve? Does a woman ever have a choice once there are children?

Also, does it make me a terrible person that I want to write about her? I can't think who would publish it since I can't find a publisher for my non-controversial stories, but it feels important.

Maybe I'll write it anyway, for me. And for Solange, who will never know. Thank you for listening, Mama, and for being the kind of mother who taught me to empathize instead of judging.

Pearl

On the iron railing outside my window, a mating pigeon cooed insistently. I threw my arm over my eyes and listened, as he could not be ignored. On the sturdy bolster beside me was the knowledge that I was here under false pretenses. A fraud. An imposter. Why did I think a year in Paris would turn me into a writer? All it had done thus far was to separate me from my family and cost me a job that I liked and was good at. Either I am a writer or I am not; living here, with my less-than-perfect French and my shaky grasp of when to kiss and when to shake hands, has done nothing to improve my confidence.

At breakfast, the girls saw my mood and Cécile made the surprising suggestion that I meet them at six and go with them for a bistro dinner, and perhaps on to a jazz club after that. I agreed, because I couldn't feel worse, and then spent the day trying to distract myself. I bought flowers for my room, then went to the Cluny to commune with the unicorn tapestries. I took a circuitous route, walking to the far end of the Île de la Cité, crossing the Seine and circling to the southeast to approach the museum from the point farthest from the Quai des Grand Augustins.

I can't face my story today. More importantly, I can't face Mick. His abundant energy and lack of care would be shattering in my current state. He makes me feel alive, but on a day when my flame burns low, his excess could torch me to cinders.

Our trip to Versailles was delayed for an additional day while he got over his sulk. Even then, he wasn't himself, which confounded me. I couldn't possibly mean so much that turning down an invitation would put him in such a state.

As we strolled the enormous palace and grounds, I understood how Marie Antoinette and her husband ended up on the scaffold. Poor people can only be kept down for so long before the knowledge of their situation boils up and sometimes blinds their better angels.

That is the kind of story he would want me to write, not the story of Remy's cousin. And I've tried, jotting notes about the disparity between ordinary people and the American and British military residing in the city, men in sleek uniforms who have access to everything the citizens of Paris do not, like hot water and fresh vegetables and cars. The words don't sound like me and I throw the pages aside in disgust and write letters to my sisters, who sometimes even answer.

Mama always answers, but I haven't waited for her response to begin Solange's story, which is so insistent that it wakes me up at night. Because Mick often looks at my pages, I use the time before dinner to sketch an outline and work out who my characters are. I've never written to a plan, preferring to let my stories bubble up on their own, but there is too much about her world that is unfamiliar.

A soothing hour of breathing in the same air as the exquisite medieval tapestries does much to restore me. It is difficult to feel my problems are at all significant in the face of the serene lady and her unicorn, who have withstood so much over the centuries.

My stomach rumbles. It is lunchtime. I bid a silent farewell to the lady and leave the Cluny's peaceful precincts for the bustling streets of the Latin Quarter. I find an inexpensive student café and order. The watery soup and stale bread stale taste like penance.

As I chew, I consider my situation. Self-pity is an insult to Uncle Harry. He was rarely wrong about what people needed, and he gave me this year. I would be ungrateful to not live every moment of it to the fullest. If I do not become a writer here, perhaps it will happen later; I'll certainly have more material.

I leave the chattering students behind and begin to walk. When I first arrived, I walked for miles every day, trying to learn every corner of the city. The Métro has its uses, but I prefer being above ground. Some of my best discoveries have been unplanned, like the odd, modern St. Odile, built in the 1930s to give work to unemployed laborers, or the tiny jewel box of a shop in the third which sold shocking underwear at even more shocking prices.

Since I began working with Mick, my explorations have been curtailed. It feels good to stretch my legs. I head west, knowing I can cross the river at any point and find Avenue Matignon. I choose the Pont Royal so I can walk through the Tuileries, treading the gritty tan paths, smiling at well-behaved children, dogs, and the plethora of statues scattered throughout the park.

I emerge at last at the Place de la Concorde, known as the Place de la Révolution when it was the execution site of Marie Antoinette, so recently in my thoughts. An obelisk looms, and I shiver in its chill shadow. I continue on until I reach the Champs-Élysées.

There is an abundance of shops and galleries to keep me occupied until it is time to meet the midinettes. I wonder if they can bring me inside the house. I would love to tell Mama that I visited a real French couturier. I had prepared, somewhat, for this opportunity, returning to my room after they left for work to change into my black suit, which I have not worn since my dinner with Julian Armitage. Made of lightweight wool, the fit is perhaps even better now that I have taken up daily mountain-climbing. If I'm fortunate enough to pass through the doors at Lelong, I will not be embarrassed.

I stop in front of a gallery with several small Picassos in the window. My heart beats a little faster, seeing them. He is not my favorite painter—I share Aunt's love of the impressionists, though I am Monet to her Renoir—but seeing his work available in a shop window reminds me, again, that despite the privations around me, Paris is a different world.

Inside the gallery, a tall, thin man makes a beckoning gesture with his head. I shake mine regretfully and move on.

"Mademoiselle Kimber!" A smooth voice at my shoulder makes me nearly jump out of my skin. I whirl around to see the Vicomte Luc Reynaud looking at me with the same expression my little brothers bestowed upon chocolate layer cake.

"Monsieur." For a moment, my mind darts about, panicked—do I offer the first *bise*, or does he?—but then he moves in, initiating the process of cheek kisses that I find so confusing. "It is very nice to see you."

"Enchanté." He is as beautiful as I remember, and he smells delicious. "I thought perhaps you had left Paris with Mademoiselle Gold."

"I had a note from her the other day." She invited me to stay for a week in the summer, promising hospitality and southern sunshine and as many parties as I could bear. *Bring a swimming costume!* she concluded—the one item of clothing I had not thought to pack.

"She is well?" He offers his arm. "And you, you are well?"

I place my hand lightly on his sleeve, registering almost unconsciously the quality of his suit. "She is very well," I say. "As am I."

The vicomte stops. Pedestrian traffic flows around us. "I think you do not tell me the truth," he says in that caramel-smooth voice. "I see sadness in those lovely blue eyes."

Is it that obvious?

"I am missing my family," I say. "It will pass."

"Will they join you for the summer?" He begins to walk again, his longer stride tempered to match mine.

I try to imagine my family organizing itself to travel anywhere, and then I stop trying, because it is ludicrous. After she married Dr. Max, Mama attempted every summer to get us to Atlantic City, but it never worked. Someone always got sick or disappeared or had other plans. Eventually she gave up and went with him and whichever of us were available.

"They don't travel," I say. "Nor have I, before this year. The farthest I've been from home is New York."

"Sometimes home is best. I have traveled extensively, but I cannot imagine anywhere I could love more than France."

"Paris, specifically?" He is taller than me. My eyes are the level of his jaw, the angle of which is sharp enough to cut paper.

"Paris, yes, and my family home near Anjou." His expression tightens, and if my eyes are sad, his are downright haunted. "My mother and sister lived there during the war. It needs much restoration."

"Was there fighting nearby?" I don't recall hearing about fighting in Anjou, but it was in the German zone, so it is entirely possible.

He shakes his head slowly. "The château has been neglected. It suffered further under the occupation. It is my dream to bring it back to life and spend the rest of my days there."

If I had a château, I imagine I would feel the same. "Do you have a house here in Paris?"

We have walked back the way that I came. As we reach the corner, I see the sign for Avenue Matignon which I had missed in my contemplation of Picasso's paintings.

"I do, Mademoiselle Kimber." The vicomte smiles, and if Mick Rafferty makes my stomach flutter, this man releases a flock of butterflies inside my rib cage. "It would give me great pleasure to invite you to a small gathering on Friday evening." He raises my hand to his lips. "Unless you require more notice?"

"No... not at all," I stammer. "What time? How do I find it?"

"I will expect you at eight," he says gravely, and hands me a card. "This has been a most unexpected pleasure. I look forward to spending time with you on Friday."

Another series of cheek kisses, three this time, and he strides away without looking back.

"A vicomte!" Remy says as I relate the story of my encounter over plates of steak frites in a dark restaurant not much bigger than a closet. "Where did you meet a vicomte?"

"We were introduced at a party," I tell her. "Remember the woman I stayed with when I first arrived, the friend of my aunt's? She knows him."

"Seduce him," Cécile advises, steepling her fingers under her chin. "We'll help you get ready. I have a drop of Chanel perfume left."

"He's already seen the only gown I have." I wonder if I should even wear a gown to a 'small gathering' and pose the question to the midinettes. Their shocked expressions make me understand that anything other than my most formal attire would be the equivalent of appearing in my underwear.

Remy's eyes light up. "Could we...?" she murmurs to her friend.

"Perhaps." Cécile looks skeptical. "It would be for a good cause."

"What are you talking about?" While the frites are golden and delicious, the steak is unexpectedly tough.

"Borrowing a dress," Remy says. "A few francs to the directrice would settle the matter."

"More than a few," Cécile corrects. "She has a crippled brother to support. She will want at least two hundred. Could you afford that?"

"Two hundred francs!" The amount they are proposing is the equivalent of four trips to the public baths. Then I look down at my solid figure in its black wool. "I'm not built like a mannequin. I doubt there would be anything that would fit."

"We certainly couldn't alter it and then bring it back." Cécile looks glum and stabs her knife into the meat. "This is going to give me stomach pains."

Remy reaches over and removes the remaining portion to her plate. "If you will not eat it, I will. Viande chevaline or not, I am hungry."

"Viande what?" I ask. "Isn't it beef?"

"It's horse," Remy says around a mouthful of meat. "Chevaline."

The piece of meat in my mouth grows bigger and bigger, like Alice in Wonderland. I cannot possibly swallow it, but I do, because I do not want to choke to death before I see Luc Reynaud again.

The subject of my lack of evening wear comes up as we make our way back to the hotel. The promised jazz club was exactly what I needed: smoky and loud enough to drown out every thought in my head. Despite my throbbing feet, I am happier than I've been all day—an untroubled happiness, not the tremulous butterflies of my conversation with the vicomte.

"Your mother, she teaches you to sew?" Remy weaves around a bollard; Parisian sidewalks are too narrow to walk three abreast, and Cécile is leaning heavily against my shoulder, a bit worse for wine.

"She and I made most of my wardrobe together."

She nods, and swerves again, this time around nothing. "We cannot borrow a dress," she concludes sadly. "It would never fit. But Madame has a sewing machine."

"Would she let us use it?" I ask. "Even if she did, we can't possibly make a gown by Friday evening."

Cécile lurches upright. "We are professionals," she says unsteadily. "If you can sew, we can help you."

A spark glows bright in my chest. I have missed conversations like this. "What about fabric?"

"Pas de probleme." Remy links arms with me as we enter the Place Dauphine. "If you can go to Montmartre in the morning, you can get everything you need, and we will help you cut it out."

"Madame will lend the machine," Cécile croaks, digging into her bag for the large key that opens the front door after hours. She always seems to have Madame's extra key. "Or I will tell Madeleine that Philippe patted my bottom."

Anyone passing in the street below might look up and see the small bright square that is my window. They might wonder who was up so late and smile, thinking perhaps it was two lovers, returning from a late walk along the Seine, having a final glass of wine before going to bed.

Instead, I am pacing the floor, stopping every so often to prop my elbows on the sill to look out over the darkened city. Am I mad to consider taking them up on their offer? Can we make an evening gown in one night, leaving me all day Friday to do the finish work? Will Madame loan her precious sewing machine to such a new resident? And if all these questions are not mad enough, am I capable of turning out a dress that would make my mother proud? Perhaps I should make adjustments to my green dress, enough that he doesn't immediately recognize it and assumes that all my evening dresses are the same color.

He doesn't strike me as the sort of man who would fail to notice these things. I could get away with wearing the same gown twice in front of Mick, who sees what suits him. Luc Reynaud is the sort of man who notices everything.

The fact that he noticed me at all brings a flush to my cheeks. I put my hand to my face, feeling the warmth, then let it slip down to my breast. I remember what his hand looked like, holding a glass of champagne that first night in Miss Gold's apartment and catch my breath.

Then I remember Pat O'Shaughnessy's rough workman's hands
and how he touched my breasts—and the rest of me—with something
akin to worship. The vicomte wouldn't touch me that way. Sinking
down on my desk chair, I wonder what it would feel like he did touch
me and realize I haven't thought of Mick all day.

Remy pushes her way in before I have finished dressing. "Cécile has a
headache," she tells me. "She should have shared some of that wine."

I wondered how she would feel. At the club, her blonde prettiness
earned her endless dance partners, along with a quantity of drinks.

"Would she like an aspirin?" The evening had been intended to
cheer me up; I should help to ease her pain.

"Madame will give her a tisane and a lecture," Remy says carelessly.

We go down for breakfast, picking up the unfortunate Cécile on the
way. She is pale, but when we reach the dining room, she takes a deep
breath and assumes vivaciousness like a mantle. "Bonjour, Madame!"
she cries, kissing our landlady on both cheeks. "We need your help."

As she explains my predicament, Remy and I gather round, trying
to add an occasional word when she stops for breath.

Finally, Madame holds up a hand. "He is a vicomte?"

"Vicomte Luc Reynaud."

"Reynaud?" She looks at me with dawning respect. "And he asks
you for dinner when?"

"Friday, Madame." It is impossible. She will never say yes, and I
can't construct a gown all on my own. If only I had Mama to help
me!

Her lips pinch. "A real man would either sweep you off your feet
at once or give you more warning. Even so"—she nods decisively—"I
will allow you to use my machine. But you should not attempt to
make something from nothing."

Gratitude surges through me even as I understand that she doesn't
think I should not make a dress. "What, then?"

Again, her hand raises and she shouts for Madeleine. Her daughter joins us and there is a harsh, whispered conversation. Madeleine
glances at me, then back to her mother. "I believe it would work," she
says. "I will retrieve it as soon as I am finished serving the breakfast."

Madame's unaccustomed smile tells us she has somehow won a contest which none of us realized was occurring.

"In these times, no woman who is not wealthy will have a brand new gown," she says. "And you would make what my husband would have called a hash if you tried to do it quickly."

"But her mother is a dressmaker," Remy says. "And she has us."

"Three little girls. No." She sits at the small table where she monitors the dining room. "Philippe will set up the machine in that corner. And Madeleine will bring you a black dress which was once mine." She looks me up and down. "We are the same height, and I wore that dress after my first child was born, so I was not as slender as I once was."

I accept the backhanded compliment, realizing she is giving me something from her wardrobe which has not been passed on to her daughter.

"Merci, Madame." I try to convey how much the offer means.

"An old dress?" Remy objects. "How will that help to catch the vicomte?"

"Mademoiselle Kimber has an eye," she states. "And you and your sickly friend have the skill to assist her."

Cécile has wilted into a chair by the window, her part in the proceedings at an end. She stares into her cup as if it contains the meaning of life.

"We were out late," I admit.

"I heard you come in," Madame says. "That one, she needs to learn that her looks won't last forever if she swallows every drink that is offered."

Madeleine's duties do not end until after the girls have left for work. Once the dishes are collected and put to soak, she ventures into the family quarters to root through her mother's things. I wait anxiously in the dining room, noting with relief that the sewing machine, when Philippe staggers in with it, is a treadle model very similar to the one my grandmother taught me to use.

Not long after, Madeleine's slow step pulls my attention from the machine. Her arms are full of black velvet, which she spills across the surface of the largest table with a sigh.

"Is that it?" I come to stand beside her. "Velvet, how lovely."

"It's the wrong season for velvet," she says. "You'll be warm."

"Black velvet always looks good." I shake out the dress and revise my estimate of Madame's age. Judging by the voluminous skirt and sleeves, full to the elbow and tight below, I realize it is from before the first war. I flatten it on the table and look at the waist. "She wore this after you were born?"

"My brother Michel was her first." Madeleine draws her finger along the sleeve. "He died in a German prison camp."

"I'm so sorry." Every time I think I've placed the war, it pops up closer. "I didn't know."

She meets my eyes, and I see the sorrow she keeps close. "Philippe was with him at the end," she says softly. "Maman would have preferred my brother to return instead of my husband."

"I wish they had both returned." I reach for her hand and she lets me take it. "Do you not want this for yourself?"

"When would I wear it?" she asks with a trace of bitterness. "To scrub the floors or to serve the breakfast?"

"You did not want to work here?" She never stops working, cleaning and cooking and dealing out plates.

She looks over her shoulder, but Madame has vanished to her station by the front door. "This hotel was my parents' dream, not mine."

"Why don't you leave?" Perhaps they can't; money is tight all over and I don't imagine our rent covers much more than the upkeep of such an ancient building.

"How?" Madeleine eases down into a chair. Her reddened hands knot together in her lap. "I am all she has left, and she has made a place for Philippe."

"Could he not return to his old job?" I have no idea what Philippe and Madeleine's life was like before the war turned everything upside down.

"No." She squeezes her eyes shut and wipes away tears. "He was a pompier—one who puts out fires, yes? His body can no longer do the work, and his mind..." She straightens her spine, under control again. "He has many bad dreams. Even if he was physically able, he could not do that work."

"I suppose not." I tell her that my younger brother is a fireman and that in his case, returning to the firehouse was the only thing that kept him from breaking apart after his experiences in the Pacific.

"This evil war," Madeleine says with surprising savagery. "Death is easier to accept than the half-life left behind. I mourn my brother. How do I mourn the man who sleeps beside me every night?"

I think about how my mother's life was cut off by my father's death; she changed, continued on, for us and because she couldn't conceive of giving in. No matter how happy she is with Dr. Max, she thinks about the life she and my father might have had. I do not tell Madeleine this—we are speaking of her family's tragedies, not mine—leaving it at, "Philippe is alive, and so are you, but you are different people in the same marriage. There is nothing wrong with mourning what you had together that was lost."

She rises, whipping a duster from her pocket and wiping the back of her chair. "Thank you, mademoiselle. Good luck with Maman's dress. May it bring you the vicomte's favor."

As she heads up the stairs to begin her duties, I turn her words over in my mind. Do I want the vicomte's favor? I have escaped the bonds of matrimony and even love until now, but Paris, throwing one man after another in my path, seems to have other plans.

The sewing kit in my room is insufficient for the project ahead of me; I hadn't come to France to make dresses, after all. But in a way that I understand in my bones, my family history has made this possible. I send my love to the invisible presence of my mother and grandmother and take the Métro to Montmartre to equip myself for the day ahead.

Having carefully looked over Madame's velvet, I know I need very little in the way of fabric, but I will purchase some muslin to firm up the interior and perhaps some black grosgrain to reinforce the neckline and the armholes, as I intend to do the unspeakable and remove the sleeves. A pair of sharp scissors, a packet of pins, and black thread complete my shopping list.

In no more than thirty minutes, I emerge onto the steep streets of Montmartre, all of which lead to the gleaming white domes of the basilica of Sacré-Cœur, which has been on my list of places to visit. I regret that my time is too limited to stop in and say a prayer for the angels on my shoulders. But saying a prayer for Mama in one of these shops is more appropriate than kneeling down in any church.

There are easily a half dozen stores on this street alone, wares spilling out onto the sidewalk. It is more than Fourth Street at home, more than the garment district in New York, which I visited with Mama and Aunt Claire to buy fabric for my college graduation dress.

It is not just that French is being spoken all around. It is the cloth itself, the colors and the way it offers itself to the Parisian sunshine. I will have to return here, too, when I have more time.

Ahead is a narrow shop, its front window blooming with spring florals in pink, blue, and yellow. A thin woman in a severe navy dress comes out the door with a bolt of fabric in her arms, which she slides carefully into a wooden box holding other, similar fabrics.

"Bonjour." The French custom of greeting a shopkeeper upon entry to their business is ingrained in me now.

"Bonjour." She turns to go in and holds the door. "May we be of assistance?"

Her dress shows its age along the seams, but the cut and construction is exquisite.

"I hope so," I say, and follow her inside.

By the time Remy and Cécile return, I have cleared away my work so the dining room can be readied for dinner. Madame's gown has been deconstructed and the skirt is cut down to a length that suits me. The bodice, bereft of sleeves, gapes open at the sides. Help will be required there; I have never been good at fitting myself. The process will go quickly with multiple hands.

"You did so much!" Remy says, as I hold the skirt against me. "Only the hem to bind after it is attached. The length is perfect."

Its velvet fullness ends at mid-calf; I decided, abruptly, to make a cocktail dress instead of a gown. It will get more wear in the long run, and it doesn't feel as made over this way.

Cécile is more interested in the bodice. "Will you adjust the neckline?"

"I can't raise it," I say. "And if it goes any lower my bosom will fall out."

"And that is bad?" Her eyelashes flutter. "I tell you, seduce the vicomte and take us to the Ritz to celebrate."

Folding the dress away until later, I say, "I'm not going to seduce him. For one thing, I wouldn't know how to go about it."

I hadn't seduced Pat O'Shaughnessy, only tipped him in the direction he wanted to go. But a man like Luc Reynaud! Just thinking about him—his elegant hands, the curve of his jaw, his dark eyes—makes a quiver run through me. It is inconceivable to show interest in such a man, only to reciprocate if interest is shown.

"I have some suggestions," she says archly. "And perhaps Madeleine will have others."

It is likely that Madame has more experience in the art of seduction than her tired, sad daughter, but I don't share what Madeleine has told me. It is not my story to tell.

By bedtime, we have restructured the bodice until it fits me like a glove. When I lay the pieces on my desk to wait for morning, the pins holding it together sparkle like tiny rhinestones. Cécile got her way with regard to the neckline, which has been squared, if not deepened, showing enough flesh to satisfy her. Remy helped with binding the armholes and produced from her bag, with a merry smile, a pair of long black gloves.

"From the storeroom," she said. "I doubt they will be missed, but if you feel bad about keeping them, I will take them back on Monday."

They are sleek and lovely, something Aunt would wear with diamond bracelets. I want to keep them, but I don't want my friend to get in trouble. I can always buy gloves.

Friday is spent sewing the the dress together and painstakingly inserting a side zip. I do not trust Madame's machine, made before the invention of the zipper, to do it properly, so I stitch it by hand. It is a slow process, as the velvet is slippery, but when I raise the pull under my arm, the closure is almost invisible.

"The dress is finished?" Madeleine asks as I tidy my things away. "May I see?"

It is impossible not to point out tiny flaws—a slightly uneven seam, a place on the left side where the velvet's nap is flattened from the heat of the iron—but she sees none of it.

"You will be stunning. May I do your hair?" She waves a vague hand at her mouse-colored locks, pulled severely back from her face. "I once had a talent for it."

At half-past seven, I climb carefully into the vélo-taxi, being careful not to catch my skirt on the rough wooden frame. When I told my friends that I intended to take the Métro, they broke out in protest.

Even Madame stopped lecturing the young men from the third floor and barked at Philippe to call for a taxi.

"How would it look, showing up on foot?" Cécile asked. "Rich men don't want poor women."

Sita is more practical. Straightening my neckline, she asks, "What if you break a heel? You'll never be able to fix it."

"My dress," proclaimed Madame, "will not take the Métro."

She had the final word and now I am whizzing over the bridge and along the uneven streets in a contraption that looks like something my brothers would have built when they were ten. The cab is no more than a box on wheels with a padded seat and a crackling cellophane windshield, attached to an aged bicycle with a red-faced driver standing on the pedals. It is nearly as expensive as a motor taxi, but far easier to come by as the few real taxis left in Paris rarely stray far from the high-end hotels.

My destination, the Reynaud hôtel particulier—defined by Cécile as a grand townhouse—is in the eighth arrondissement, not far from where I encountered the vicomte. When the bicycle's thin tires skid to a halt, the whole structure jounces forward and I grab the edge of the seat before I hit my head. My elbow strikes the door at the perfect angle and hot pain shoots down my arm.

"Four hundred," the driver says sullenly. "You want me to come back?"

"I don't know when I'll be leaving," I tell him, and he rattles away.

I stand on the sidewalk, gazing up at the house. Philadelphia has townhouses; this is a mansion. Constructed of the creamy limestone so often used in Parisian buildings, it stands three stories tall with a gray slate roof intersected by round-topped dormer windows. An elegant staircase leads to a dark red door with unlit gas lamps on either side. Climbing the steps, I press my lips together, wishing I'd thought to check my lipstick in the taxi. I can't whip out my compact now—what if the vicomte is watching? I raise the heavy brass knocker and let it fall.

In a matter of moments, the door is opened by a gray-haired man with the saddest mustache I've ever seen. "Bonsoir, Mademoiselle Kimber."

"Bonsoir." I surrender my small wrap, whipped together by Cécile from leftover velvet. "Am I the first to arrive?"

His eyes narrow. "No, mademoiselle. Monsieur le vicomte is waiting for you." He leads me through the echoing reception hall and knocks lightly before opening one side of a pair of gleaming double doors. "Mademoiselle Kimber."

I step through the door into another century—at the very least, the same decade as my made-over dress. In between tall windows obscured by layers of rich drapery and lace hang a series of gold-framed portraits. Two chairs with spindly legs and a carved table covered with a linen cloth are set before the hearth, where a small fire crackles.

"Mademoiselle Kimber." Luc Reynaud appears from the shadows to kiss me on both cheeks. "I am so glad you could come."

My inspection of the salon complete, I now notice its emptiness, along with the chill. Opening those enormous windows to the summer air would do a better job than a fire that size. "I thought you said this was a small gathering?"

He gestures that I should sit on a brocade settee. "Small was, perhaps, the wrong word. My English is not always clear. I meant intimate."

His English has been exceptional up to this point. I sit, then stand again. "Am I the only guest, monsieur le vicomte?"

"Please," he says. "I'd prefer that you call me Luc."

"I'd prefer to know when I'm being made a fool of." My voice is shaking with sudden fury. This beautiful man has lured me here because he thinks I'm a stupid little American eager to open my legs for nobility. My fantasies about his elegant hands evaporate.

"Mademoiselle Kimber. Pearl." He gestures again, his hands floating like birds. "I meant no disrespect. I was so pleased to see you that I simply said the first thing that came into my head."

The servant enters quietly. He looks at the vicomte, who in turn looks at me.

"I planned for us a nice dinner, if you will give me a chance." His tone turns pleading. "At least stay for champagne."

I couldn't leave this soon—I'd be back at the hotel before everyone had gone up for the night. They would see me creep in at nine o'clock and know I'd been taken for an idiot.

"One glass." As the servant eases the cork from the bottle, I wander to the fireplace, admiring the gold candlesticks on the mantel. Ornately worked, they look like museum pieces, not something I'd expect to find in a house. Even one like this.

Luc appears with a glass. "I am remiss. I have not told you how beautiful you look this evening."

Instead of thanking him, I take a sip of champagne, letting it drown my sarcastic response. I was a plain, awkward girl, and even with care and attention to my hair and clothes, I will never be beautiful.

"You do not believe me." There is a smile in his voice. "American men, are they all blind?"

"They do not flatter blindly." I take another sip, watching his reaction. I have unsettled him by not being as skittish as the newly arrived Pearl or even the lonely young woman of earlier this week. "You, monsieur le vicomte, are what my stepfather would call a bullshitter."

He puts his glass on the table and laughs, bending until his hands rest on his thighs and his black hair falls across his forehead. I feel that beastly tug of attraction again.

"You are surprising." He drains his glass, and it is immediately refilled.

I fold myself onto the settee, trying to arrange my skirt and my legs and keep him from getting a close look at my shoes, which are better than those of my friends but inferior to what a black velvet cocktail dress deserves.

Luc sits beside me, leaving as much space as can be left between two people on an antique piece of furniture. "Here's to surprises."

I touch my glass to his. "Are you going to tell me what's going on?"

His eyes are as dark as coffee, and equally warm. "After dinner?" he hazards. "There is vichyssoise and roast chicken…"

My mouth waters at the thought of roast chicken. Anything to erase the memory of that poor horse we ate the other night. "It *is* difficult to resist a good roast chicken."

"Exactly." Lucien nods and the servant vanishes. "Now, tell me, what do you do with yourself in Paris that I have not seen you before?"

"I write." I peel off Monsieur Lelong's gloves. I'm not sure if I should keep them on, but I can't eat properly while wearing them. It's hard enough, remembering to do everything in reverse of American table manners. "I walk. I go to museums and markets and cafés."

"And yet we have never met." Overripe sentimentality is creeping into his voice again; he needs to be punctured every so often, like a balloon. "It is tragic."

"Hardly tragic."

His man brings in a tray with two bowls of soup. He sets them on the table, then stands expectantly behind one chair. Against my better judgment, I sit, and he places the napkin across my lap with a flourish.

Another glass is filled, this time with white wine. The pale soup looks more substantial than the delicate bowl in which it is served. The silver is heavy, with monograms on the handles. Miss Gold's wealth was jarring in its abundance; this is the kind of understated old money found in books. I can almost smell it wafting from the damask walls.

Luc raises his glass. "To reunions."

"To vichyssoise." I set my wine down untouched and dip a tentative spoon into the bowl. It is delicious, light and rich at the same time. "There's real cream in this."

"Of course."

I force myself to eat slowly, though I would like to swallow the bowl and beg Monsieur Mustache to bring me the pot.

"Only the best for my lovely companion." He reaches across the table and puts his hand over mine. A frisson runs up my arm and lodges in my chest. "I hope you understand how pleased I am that you accepted my invitation."

Does the butterfly thrill as it is pinned? Something is happening here that I don't understand. A small part of me wants to bob along on the current, letting his perfect hand stroke mine. Letting myself be seduced with food, when, according to Cécile, I'm supposed to seduce him. Whatever this is, I wouldn't have to try very hard if that were what I wanted.

But why does *he* want it? Luc Reynaud is titled, wealthy, painfully handsome. I am none of those things.

As the bowls are cleared, I fold my hands and look at him. "What are you doing?"

"What do you mean?" He looks puzzled. "I am enjoying an excellent meal with a beautiful woman."

Now I need the wine. I finish half the glass before a platter of succulent roast chicken appears between us. The servant dismantles it rapidly, putting two slices on each plate, then adds a serving of asparagus with silver tongs.

When he has gone, I say, "You can cut the flattery. We met once and you're behaving as if it were some grand affair. I'm not beautiful. I'm not even particularly charming. And while I might go to bed with you, I don't think you need to try this hard with me—or any woman—for that to happen."

He sits back, dumbfounded. "Are all Americans so direct?"

"The ones raised by my mother are."

"Then I will return the favor." He tops up both our glasses. "You see my family home, Pearl?"

"Yes. It's lovely." The chicken is succulent and juicy, with crisp, flavorful skin. I want him to stop talking so I can enjoy it.

"All that I have left is in this room and one other, where I sleep. The rooms upstairs"—he waves his hand—"they are empty."

"What do you mean?" I look again at the salon's faded elegance. "Why are they empty?"

"Because we have no money." He puts down his fork. "My father gambled most of it away. Then the war came."

"You certainly know how to keep up appearances." His dinner jacket fits him beautifully, and the cufflinks peeping from his sleeves are gold. My monthly rent is likely equivalent to what he pays his barber.

"In France, appearance is everything," he says soberly. "I am expected to maintain a certain level of existence. Anything else is unthinkable."

As I eat my asparagus, I consider the level of existence at which my family lived for my entire childhood. Anything else was unthinkable for them, too, but because they had nothing, not because they lived beyond their means so as not to be judged by others.

"The château in Anjou," I say, "where your mother and sister live. Is it the same situation?"

He nods slowly. "It costs less for them to live in the country. I remain in Paris to do my duty as the head of the family."

Somehow, the asparagus is gone. I cast a glance at his plate, which holds food he cannot afford but has not eaten. "And what is your duty?"

"To marry a woman whose fortune can restore my family's honor." Luc takes my hand again.

"And that's me?" Is his palm slightly sweaty?

"I would like it to be." His voice drops. "We could be very good together, Pearl. I think I could make you happy."

"You might make me happy," I say drily, "but I wouldn't make you rich. Where did you get the idea that I have money?"

His seductively lowered lids fly open. "But you are friends with Mademoiselle Gold—"

"My aunt is friends with her." I stifle the giggles that are rising to the surface. "I am a very poor relation." I let him know how far astray his calculations have led him. "When I was a child, we didn't have an indoor toilet or electric light. I wore shoes only in the winter so they were good enough for my sister to wear them next."

I have shocked him—or rather, he is shocked by how he allowed himself to be misled. I expect to be asked to leave, so that he wastes no more time or money on me.

Instead, he smiles and shakes his head. "That is too bad. I would have enjoyed you."

I want to say that I would have enjoyed his enjoyment, but my outspokenness has subsided. "Do you want me to go?"

"Why?" he asks. "There is still wine, and I sent Montlaur for macarons. It would be a shame to waste them."

"Have you no other butterflies in your net?" I should be angry, but instead I can't wait to get home and write this down. Somewhere in our mutual humiliation there is a story.

"Alas, they have all fluttered away." Luc looks down, and the firelight gilds his profile. What little experience I have strains toward him, wanting to know more. "And now I have made a fool of myself with you."

"Not a fool," I say gently. "Though you did waste a considerable amount of money."

He spreads his hands. "An enamel and gold snuff box belonging to my great-grandfather. Among the many losses my family has suffered, it will not be missed."

There must be enough ornaments left in this house—even in its denuded state—to restore his château, but I know better than to suggest such a venture, even as I think of all the distinguished household goods on display at the street markets. If it were possible, it would have been done; a vicomte cannot be seen to be selling off his family heirlooms. Standards must be maintained.

Suddenly, I feel sorry for him.

"If you let me eat those macarons," I say, "I will write to Mademoiselle Gold and ask her to invite you to visit. She is bound to know a half dozen legitimate heiresses who might fit the bill."

"You would do that?" His eyes soften, going from coffee to melted chocolate.

"It all depends on the quality of those macarons."

Luc offered to see me home but I told him I was fine on my own. He knows I'm not rich, but it's unnecessary for him to see where I live. And I've don't feel unsafe, even as I descend the steps and wait for the last train of the night. Several minutes later, it clatters into the station. I climb on, grasping the pole as the car judders beneath my feet, and drop gratefully into a seat.

What can I tell the others? Madame will be disappointed that I have not snared a vicomte; Madeleine will smile her sad smile, the one that knows things never turn out as planned. Remy will laugh. And Cécile...

Do I tell Cécile how, after strong coffee and several feather-light macarons, I allowed Vicomte Luc Reynaud to show me the only other furnished room in the house? Do I tell her about the wide bed with its silken canopy? Do I tell her that while I was found lacking in funds, I was replete in other areas?

"I had intended this evening to end with a seduction," he said as he showed me over the rest of the house. "I am having a remarkably pleasant time despite the change of plan."

"I was advised to seduce *you*," I told him. "We have both failed."

"Or perhaps not." He lifted a brow and tilted his beautiful head toward the open door behind us. "There is yet time..."

Luc was surprised by my acquiescence, as I was surprised that he wanted me after finding I had nothing to offer but my body and an abundance of curiosity. He was more than happy to satisfy my curiosity, while I was pleased to discover my instincts had not steered me wrong. Once the game of courtship was over, Luc devoted himself to pleasure. He was thorough, attentive, and inventive—insofar as what I knew about the act of love.

I couldn't wait to start writing the story inspired by this evening. Even as I walk from the Métro to the hotel, words are already arranging themselves in my head. I manage to get up to my room without seeing anyone but Philippe, who is drowsing at the desk and woke only to exchange the spare key for my room key.

Should I set the tale in Paris? I think not, as I don't know the sort of intimate details of French daily life that would breathe life into my characters. It's the same problem I am having with Solange. I could set it in New York or even Philadelphia—the chasm between rich and poor is as vast, and a man fallen on hard times could make similar mistaken assumptions.

What if my main character didn't ask uncomfortable questions? How far would the relationship progress before the subject of money came up?

I am grateful to Luc for the inspiration he has provided. This idea is as exciting as anything I've come up with since arriving in Paris. Once it is done and polished to the best of my ability, I will type up a copy and send it to Grace, to see if she can find a home for it.

A faint chafe of beard burn on my thighs makes me shift in my chair. I flush with something that is neither shame nor embarrassment. Had we really—?

As Luc positioned himself over me in that grand eighteenth-century bed, he asked why I'd agreed to go to bed with him. I came to France for an education, I said; I would accept every lesson on offer.

June 24, 1946

Dear Hazel,

You'll be pleased to know that Paris has affected your normally staid and proper friend to an unexpected degree. On Friday evening, I went to dinner with a vicomte in his family mansion wearing a black velvet cocktail dress of my own making.

I drank champagne, ate vichyssoise, and negotiated the surrender of my virtue. Said vicomte looks like a film star and smells like a dream. He's also absolutely penniless and got the wrong end of the stick in that he thought I was rich and could save him!

Anyway, we had a very lovely evening of which I will say no more as you haven't seen fit to share any of your details with me.

Love,

Pearl

June 24, 1946

Dear Miss Gold,
I had an interesting dinner with Vicomte Reynaud on Friday. He is in need of a wife of substance. May I leave this matter in your capable hands?
Pearl Kimber

DARLING. I WILL EXTEND AN INVITATION TO GASSIN IMMEDIATELY. WOULD YOU VISIT AT THE SAME TIME OR DOES THAT DEFEAT THE PURPOSE? BISES, MJG

July 1946

The summer evenings stretch long. Darkness doesn't settle over Paris until almost ten o'clock. Some evenings I wander through the Île Saint-Louis alone or relax with a book on a bench near Notre Dame; other nights, I accompany Remy and Cécile for an evening drink or dancing at a club. On Wednesdays and Fridays, I meet up with Mick and we go to a concert or take a walk. I prefer walking; his abundant energy makes him twitch through most concerts.

"Stories for the *Post* and *Colliers* are all well and good," Mick says, continuing a lecture that began over dinner. "But you have a talent, Pearl. A real voice. You should be writing important pieces for magazines with substance, not fluff pieces for bored housewives."

"The *Saturday Evening Post* isn't for housewives," I protest, stung by the implicit criticism—not just of my writing but of me, someone who had aspired to be published in that magazine, and of my friends and relatives, all of whom waited each week for the *Post*'s arrival.

"Maybe not"—he stretches, almost knocking over his glass—"but I'd like to see you tackle something with some more weight to it."

"Like what?" Mick's authority as a newspaperman cannot be discounted, but I don't know where to start writing articles with weight;

all I've ever wanted was to write fiction. Solange's story nags at me like a sore tooth, but I have not yet found my way in.

That stumps him for a moment. He takes a sip of wine as he mulls over the problem of my future career. "It has to appeal to a broader audience," he says at last. "Something you've learned while in Paris…"

I think of the women of my hotel, the stories they've told as they've come to trust me. "There are things," I begin. "Some of the women I've met—"

"Women's stories," he says dismissively. "You need to think bigger."

Women's stories *are* big, I think rebelliously. We're half the population of the world—if our stories aren't important enough to tell, then do we even matter at all? It is a topic that drove Mama to frothing, how we are expected to birth and raise the next generation without being trusted to write a check or sign a lease or even, until far too recently, vote.

French women lag behind American women in that regard; they'd only been given the vote when the war was nearly over. Until the war turned everything upside down, most couldn't work a job without a man's permission, something that became impossible to enforce when all the men were either called up or imprisoned.

"Let's go," I say abruptly. It is nearly ten, and I am tired, both physically and from listening to his harangue about the important work I should be doing. If we are not Sartre and Beauvoir, he sees us as a younger version of Hemingway and Gelhorn. Even as I thrill at his assumption that we're a couple, seeds of doubt spring up in my mind, fertile as weeds in a garden

"Wait." He stops, and we nearly collide. "Listen."

Over the night sounds of the city—traffic, footsteps, the rush of the river—comes faint music. "It's over there, I think."

We follow the sound and discover, on the pedestrian bridge to the Île Saint-Louis, a trio of tuxedo-clad musicians. A small crowd has gathered to watch as a half dozen couples dance, swooping and ducking like swallows to the strains of a tango.

Mick's grip changes. "Come on, Pearl."

"I don't know how to tango," I say, at his heels, because what sane person can resist dancing along the Seine by moonlight?

He can't tango either, but he gets a solid grip on me and we follow the music. My breasts are crushed against his broad chest and the large hand at my waist is warm and possessive.

I close my eyes, dazzled by what is happening—that the grim black-and-white world I encountered on my arrival has blossomed into this moonlit evening by the river, being whirled and quick-stepped by a man who, despite my irritation at his high-handedness, I want very badly to kiss me.

"Still want to go back home?" he murmurs in my ear as he spins me around and brings me back against his body. Somehow, the musicians have altered their selections to keep up with Mick's dancing and we're now being serenaded with Benny Goodman on violin, cello, and upright bass.

"No." I gasp as his hand slides below my waist and across my bottom. It returns to its original position so quickly that I might have imagined it. "This is wonderful."

Eventually, the musicians cease their playing and bow to scattered applause. The crowd disperses and I turn to go.

"I'll walk with you." Mick tangles his fingers with mine. "I'm not letting you get away that easily."

The Place Dauphine is quiet, its few streetlamps shrouded in the thick greenery of the pollarded trees. There is no one to watch us walking hand-in-hand, shoulders brushing. An electric current flows between our palms; it might be the sole reason I am upright.

"This is me." The street door is unlocked. I will not have to ring and summon Philippe from the desk. Madame's chair is empty, but her vigilance hangs in the air like the smell of tonight's stew.

"No one around?" He follows me into the closet-sized entry. "This is cozy."

I turn and he's right there. His arms come up hard around me, trapping me against the rough plaster wall. The suddenness of his approach makes my heart leap to my throat, and I fight an urge to strike him, to flee, before I force myself to relax. My body has wanted this since he asked me to dance. I take a slow breath, then another.

Mick nuzzles my neck, and my nerve endings come to painful life. "I didn't expect to find a girl like you."

"I'm not that special." Never in my life have I been that girl for anyone.

He doesn't disagree, because his mouth is over mine and his hands are sliding down my body. It is too fast, and it feels good, and I am afraid Madame will look down the stairs and see me pinned next to her chair and I will have to move out in disgrace.

"Stop!" I drag myself away, my heart pounding and a familiar warmth burning low in my belly. "Someone might hear us."

"Only if you moan loudly." Mick cups my breasts with both hands. "I've wanted to do this since the day we met."

His fingers are warm through my dress and the brassiere beneath. I want him, I realize, quite badly, the way I wanted Luc. There is no way I can get him five flights up to my room, nor will I try, no matter what I want at this moment. My room is my refuge.

"Stop," I say again, more firmly. "It's too soon, and not here."

He backs away, hands raised in submission. "But later, and elsewhere," he says with a wicked grin. "I'll hold you to that."

July 3, 1946

I can't sleep. Every time I close my eyes, I think about that surge of panic when Mick cornered me in the doorway. I wanted him to touch me, and he did, so it's a stupid overreaction. He's pushy. That's his way.

We're together almost every day. I know him better than Pat or Luc, and I never stiffened up with them (and did far more with them). Why did I freeze when Mick touched me? It doesn't happen all the time. If he holds my hand or kisses me, I'm fine. Better than fine. And I liked how it felt when we danced together, even though it was too close and I could feel that he wanted more.

I'm giving myself a headache thinking about this. I'm going to bed.

Nope. Still awake. Now by candlelight, because when I turned the light on, nothing happened. Losing power in the middle of the night is better than in the evening, when we'd miss it. I'm maybe the only person awake in the building. On the whole island.

Mick isn't awake. I know for a fact that he doesn't stay up at night overthinking. And maybe that's part of it. Because he's thoughtless, maybe I don't completely trust him with me.

Or me with him. If I'm frank with myself (and that's the point of this book, after all), I feel the same things with Mick as I did with the others. The butterflies, the heat, the desire. I want to know what it would be like with him, except I also don't.

What I did with Pat and Luc (and whether it was good or bad), they wanted no more from me than I was willing to give. Giving in to Mick feels like it would give him power over me, and he's not the sort of man who would give it back.

The next morning, Remy is my sole breakfast companion. "Cécile was out later than you," she confides, gleeful. "She fell through the door after midnight and then spent fifteen minutes on her knees in the toilet. She'll be down soon."

"How will she go to work?" I'd heard doors banging downstairs long after I got in, but had assumed it was the young men.

"I don't know. I couldn't." Remy shakes her curly head. "And I don't understand how she's such a fine seamstress. If she's not blind drunk, she's exhausted."

I spread a thin layer of butter on my bread. "You never go out with her?"

"And her boyfriends?" Remy cackles. "Where would I fit there?"

For all the condemnation Remy leveled at her cousin, I wonder if it has ever occurred to her that Cécile—whom she loves and abuses in equal measure—would sell herself for a pair of stockings or a night out. She doesn't need the impetus of a hungry child to sway her.

"Don't you have a man of your own?" I have asked before, but despite Remy's talkative nature, I know very little about her personal life.

She ducks her head, paying close attention to the pot of strawberry jam sitting between us. "Men aren't what I like."

"Oh." I thought her gamine appearance was a different sort of French style, but apparently not. Then it occurs to me how many times we have been to the baths together and I grow hot all over. Which of us does she like?

"Don't look like that," she says, wrapping her fingers around my wrist. "There was someone at Lelong, late last year, but her landlady found out and she went back to Avignon. You are safe from the wicked lesbienne."

Lesbian doesn't sound as insulting as the names I've heard used about men like my brother, but I'm sure there are other words. There always are.

"It's not that," I say, half honestly. "I have a lot on my mind."

Her brows arch. "Is it your large American?"

"Mick. Yes." I tell her that I had trouble sleeping, not the cause of my sleeplessness.

"There is something more," she says. "You are upset. Did he hurt you?"

I shake my head. "No. He scared me a little, but it wasn't his fault. He didn't *do* anything. It's me."

"Ah." Remy finishes her bread, staring out the window. "You were, as my aunt would say, interfered with."

"Yes." There was a man named Nolan, who briefly rented a room in our house. He made a game of putting his hands on me and telling me what else he would do, given the chance. It never went further than that, but every once in a while, that feeling of powerlessness comes back. When Mick trapped me against the wall, I didn't remember that small, frightened girl; *I was her.* It wasn't until now, though, that I put the two incidents together.

I've never told anyone about Mr. Nolan; even thinking about him in the sunlit dining room is obscene. Not long after he left town, my father died, and we moved to Philadelphia. It was easier to put the memory of his stealthy touch someplace where I couldn't easily stumble over it.

"Do you like this Mick?" Remy turns as Madame greets Cécile.

"Yes…"

"Then you must tell him." She pushes the empty chair back and helps Cécile into it, gently, as if she were an invalid. "Not what happened, but what he did that you don't like." Her smile is crooked. "Find a way to tell him that makes it sound like a compliment to his lovemaking. *You are so strong, you startled me,*" she trills, and I have to laugh.

Cécile blinks at us and turns her face from the light. "Must you be so loud?"

I've started Solange's story five different ways, and each time I stop because I don't understand what happens next. Growing up in a small town, I thought I could write someone else's life in an equally small town, but her life is alien to me. It's frustrating. I need details that I can't get without questioning Remy further, and she's already suspicious that I'm writing about her cousin.

I can see why she'd be touchy; it is her family's tragedy, after all, but I think even if it were my family, I would want to use it. Writing is how I make sense of the world. If this happened to my cousin, I would write to understand how I felt or how she felt. Although I'm not sure I could write from the point of view of Solange's family, because I can't see them as anything but inhumane.

Thankfully, *A Match of Mistaken Identity*, the story based on my night with Luc, has come together quickly. I can't write exactly what happened, because magazines would never publish a story where an unmarried woman goes to bed, clear-eyed, with a man she has no intention of marrying.

I am mulling over these problems as I come in, passing by the reception desk without stopping until Philippe calls to me.

"Mademoiselle, stop. You have a letter."

"Another one?" The mail had come early; I took letters from Mama and Hazel to the café to read and digest, avoiding both conversation with Mick and thinking about Solange.

"This one was delivered by hand." He hands it over with a grin.

The envelope is made of thick, ivory paper; it feels expensive. My name is written neatly on the front in precise black ink.

Apologies for the lack of warning. I will be at Bistrot Romaire at seven o'clock this evening. If you are free, I would greatly enjoy your company.
Julian S.J. Armitage

I glance at Philippe, torn. Remy and Cécile and I had planned to go out after the meal, but they would shout at me if I turned down an invitation to a restaurant. "Do you know what Madame is making for dinner?"

Amusement flickers over his face. "Potage parmentier."

Potato leek soup. Again. It's not that it isn't tasty, but the monotony of our menu is beginning to wear. "Anything else?"

"I saw a basket of courgette on the table."

Squash is no more appealing, whereas a nice bistro dinner...
"Madame will be annoyed with me, I think."

"Is it the Englishman?"

"Yes." Bistrot Romaire was where we'd gone in the spring; is it a favorite restaurant, I wonder, or does he simply assume I will be able to find it?

"Belle-mère will forgive," he says. "She likes him."

I didn't think the prickly Madame liked anyone but her small dog and possibly Madeleine. How had Julian Armitage won her over?

"Will you tell her?"

His face falls. "If I must."

I name a price he will accept. "You can have one of my Hershey bars."

"Bon."

The church bells ring out as I cross the bridge and I pick up my pace. I'd misjudged the length of the walk, then stopped to exchange brief pleasantries with the flower seller. Before I knew it, I was running late.

A departing patron holds the door and I skid inside. Catching sight of my disheveled reflection in the mirror, I press a hand to my chest, as if that will improve my appearance. "Bonsoir," I say to the superior-looking man whose mouth quirks at my self-examination. "Is Monsieur Armitage here?"

"This way, mademoiselle."

Mr. Armitage rises when he sees me, holding out his hands in welcome. I kiss him on both cheeks to show how French I've become. "I'm sorry I'm so late."

He cocks his head. "It's just gone seven. And this is early for dinner in France."

I take my seat, then the menu, putting it to one side while I get situated.

"Two champagne cocktails," he says to the waiter. "We'll order when we're ready."

"How do you do that?" I ask.

"Do what?" His gray eyes survey me, and I swear that he doesn't notice my red cheeks or the damp patches along my hairline.

"Be so beautifully rude. He wasn't even offended that you told him to go away."

"It's called being British," he says with a disarming laugh. "It's how we built an empire."

The drinks arrive and the waiter stands unobtrusively to one side until we've looked over the menu. "Salade niçoise to start," he says. "Then the roast chicken with green beans, and the fresh fruit tart to finish." He glances at me. "Does that suit?"

"Perfectly." Even if the tuna is from a can, as is likely these days, the meal will be far better—and certainly more filling—than anything that graces the hotel's tables. Madame is an excellent cook, but even she can do only so much with what's available.

"I'm sorry about the short notice," he says, taking a sip of his cocktail. "But I thought you might like a treat."

I press my lips together, hoping my lipstick won't come off on the glass. "I thought you were going to let me know before you came to Paris, not after you'd arrived."

"Ah, yes. That." His expression undergoes a small change. "I wasn't certain you would wish to be reminded of your situation, or that you wouldn't have better things to do with your time."

"My situation, as you put it, is unavoidable." It sounds as if he'd been *afraid* to write, in case I turned him down. "And I have many things to do with my time, but I do not refuse dinner invitations on principle."

My friend Lenny always said that unless the man issuing the invitation was a troll who lived under a bridge, it was best to say yes and then make a hasty retreat if things weren't going well. "At least you'll run away well fed," she said. That was rich, coming from a girl who'd had not one but two fiancés—neither of them trolls—and was now happily married.

"I'm glad." He looks out the window at a knot of people passing in the square. "I've wondered how you were getting on. You didn't respond to my letter."

"I didn't think it was necessary." He'd been one of the few people I wanted to tell when I'd heard about my *Post* story. Telling him now will sound like bragging. Instead, I talk about the friends I've made at the hotel and the café where I write each day. I do not mention Mick. "At first it was hard. I'm used to being busy. But I've got the hang of it now."

We trade information more easily this time, growing less shy with each other. I tell him to call me Pearl, and he counters by asking that I use his first name. In this manner, we make our way through the salad and the chicken.

"This is delicious," I say. "I wish I could order a portion to take back to the hotel to give to my friends."

"Then do it." Julian places his knife and fork across the plate. "I'm not foolish enough to tell you how to spend your money, but you take very little advantage."

"How much advantage *should* I take?" There is a puddle of golden, buttery juices that all but demands to be sopped up with bread. I look resolutely away.

"You understand that a significant amount was put aside for your use," he continues gamely, having the grace to look abashed. "You don't need to live like a student. Even living in your hotel, you could treat your friends to restaurant meals instead of waiting to be invited."

I give in to the siren call of the sauce and tear off one last piece of bread, then say, "I wouldn't be comfortable doing that. You wouldn't understand."

"I wasn't raised with wealth, either, Pearl." Julian cocks his head. "My father was a younger son and lived on his wits, joining the bank when he left university and returning, as I did, when his war was over."

The waiter clears our plates. Julian removes a silver cigarette case from his jacket pocket, offering it to me. I nod, even though I try not to smoke very often, and watch his hands as he lights two cigarettes. "My uncle Jasper was the eldest son, but he never married. He died of a heart attack at the end of the war. My brother Jeremy inherited his title."

"Your brother has a title." English cigarettes don't have the same bitterness in the back of my throat as the Gitanes I occasionally buy at the café.

"He does." Julian exhales a plume of smoke. "Does that bother you?"

"No." I knew he came from a good family; those manners are generational. "I just hadn't realized."

His pinstriped shoulders rise slightly. "It's not something I speak about with clients—" His expression shows that he thinks I am offended by being called a client. "I meant only that I don't talk about my family. Jeremy and I aren't close."

"I thought you weren't close to your sister?" It is unimaginable: even when I want to throttle my siblings, I love them to death. You don't choose your family; often you *wouldn't* choose them. But they are a fact of life; my memories are contained in them.

"I'm not." Stubbing out his cigarette, he looks over his shoulder for the waiter. "Do you want dessert?"

What I want is for him to explain why he doesn't get on with his brother and sister, but I don't think he'll tell me—and not just because I'm a client. There is a deep well of reserve in Julian that will not allow him to discuss his troubles with someone he barely knows.

The room swims. The noise and the wine and his expectations suddenly too much for me. I take a deep breath and speak rapidly.

"I was afraid to get an apartment. Living in a hotel means I can't hide from the world."

Julian gives me his complete attention and the waiter, lingering, turns to fuss with our wine bottle. "Why would you hide?"

I twist the napkin, waiting until our glasses have been refilled and the waiter has departed. "Because when I got here, I was scared to death. I knew if I didn't force myself, I would hunker down and waste this opportunity."

"You've made a nice recovery," he says drily. "I couldn't tell, even then. You were so obdurate about the Grand Hôtel Dauphine, I didn't know how to change your mind."

Knowing I'd managed to conceal my fear was gratifying. "I'm glad you didn't. It's shabby and run down and the plumbing is a disaster, but it was exactly what I needed."

"Good."

The fruit tart arrives—fresh berries in syrup with cream drizzled over top. I stop myself from inhaling it in one bite and wonder instead if I could convince Remy to come here for wine and dessert.

"Would you tell me about your wife?" I dig my fork into the flaky pastry. "Unless that's too personal."

His eyes flick up, away from his plate. "What do you want to know?"

"Never mind." I can feel the stain of embarrassment on my cheeks. "I shouldn't ask such personal questions."

"It's not that I mind telling you. I'm simply not used to people being interested in my life." He leans back, pushing away his empty plate. "We first met when I was at university. Her older sister, Felicity, was in my class. After that, we ran into each other times at house parties or in London. One day, a few years later, I was back at Cambridge visiting my tutor and bumped into her. We traveled back to London on the same train, and by the time I put her into a cab, we'd made plans to meet for lunch the following day."

"So, love at first sight, slightly delayed?"

"More or less. We married in 1934 and set up housekeeping near Kensington Gardens." He lights another cigarette. "She was caught out at the shops during a rare daytime raid. They never found her body."

The six years between their marriage and her death, along with his calm retelling of the tragedy, reminds me of how Mama tamped down her grief over Daddy so we wouldn't worry about her.

"Were you in London when it happened? Or in the army?"

"London."

There is nothing more to say, and then I think of something. "You had no children?"

Julian's lips twitch; I've hit a nerve.

"No," he says at last. "Helen's mother died when she was very young. She found the idea of childbirth terrifying, so much so that when we married, she made me promise I would never ask her for children."

In the seconds it takes him to complete that sentence, I revisit every conversation I ever had with Cliff about marriage. Helen Armitage's reason for not wanting children wasn't the same as mine, but she made the same request, and received, from as traditional a man as I have ever met, a far different response.

"You didn't mind?" I ask tentatively. "That you wouldn't be a father?"

His sigh this time is louder. "It's a little late to ask that question now."

There is so much pain behind his words that I abruptly ask if we can have coffee at a different café nearby, to get us moving and change the subject. Once Julian has settled the bill and we are outside in the balmy air, he begins to relax. I find a likely-looking café with tables clustered under golden lanterns and lead us to a seat by a flowering plant in a gleaming ceramic pot.

"Gardenia!" I close my eyes. "Isn't it lovely?"

"Is that your favorite flower?"

"Lilacs are my favorite." I tell the waiter we would like two coffees. "But gardenia is harder to find."

Julian draws the ashtray close and lights a cigarette. "You were very kind back there."

How was it kind to have dragged the painful details of his life from him against his will? "What do you mean?"

"You saw that I was struggling." He hands me a cigarette. "Is it the writer in you that asks questions, or are you just curious?"

"It's the same thing." I hold the smoke in my lungs, then release it slowly. "I've always been interested in people. It makes me ask too many questions. I'm sorry."

"Don't be." His eyes crinkle. "Am I going to find myself in a story one of these days?"

"No!" I say quickly, then amend, "Not in a way that you'd recognize, anyway."

July 7, 1946

Dear Pearl,

London is a dreary place after Paris. Perhaps it is the company that is dreary. My own and those around me.

My apologies for any awkwardness during our evening together. As I said, I'm not accustomed to talking about myself. I hope your new friends are more open and do not make you feel uncomfortable for asking perfectly reasonable questions.

If you are willing to risk it, I will strive to do better next time.
Sincerely,

Julian

July 9, 1946

Dear Julian,

It's for me to apologize. I always ask too many questions and sometimes it comes back to bite me. In your case, I don't know enough about you to judge until I've overstepped. I'm now keeping a list of topics so we can either check them off one by one or avoid them completely. I leave that up to you.

Maybe we could choose a question in advance, so we have time to prepare a response? This may fall into the 'too personal' category, but I would like to know why you agreed to your wife's request not to have children. Don't go into detail if you don't want to, it's only that I've never known a man who didn't want them.

To prove this is not a wholly one-sided conversation, I'll share a story you would probably rather not hear. I was engaged once, or almost. I broke it off when the boy who wanted to marry me insisted that I could find time to write, even after we had kids. Having helped to raise my little brothers and sisters, I knew what would happen, and how little it would bother him when it did. And it turned out I loved writing more than him. Though I think I knew that from the start. I thought I might be able to have both.

There. That should be uncomfortably personal enough to even the playing field.

I look forward to your reply, if I haven't offended you into your next lifetime.

Pearl

Walking along the river at night, below street level, makes Paris feel very far away. When Mick takes my hand, a spark runs up my arm. Again, I am equally drawn to and scared of him.

We come up to a bridge and pass into its shadow. He puts his other hand on my waist and spins me into the darkness with him. "Very handy, all these bridges."

"I'm sure that's why they built them, just for you." I try to keep moving, but he maneuvers me toward the wall. "Mick."

"What, baby?" He lowers his lips to my neck. "You enjoy this, right?"

A chill runs over me. I push lightly at his chest, then harder until he looks at me. "I do." Remy's advice rings in my ears. "But I don't like being manhandled."

His expression goes defensive. "I'm not manhandling you."

"That's not your call to make." I step away from him. "It's not that I don't like it. Sometimes you move too fast and I feel surrounded."

I walk to the edge of the promenade and look out over the slow-moving river. "When I was a kid, there was a man. He used to touch me."

"He raped you?" Mick's voice is too loud and that word—*rape*—echoes over the water.

"No." I think he would have, in time. He was playing cat and mouse games, waiting for the fear to break me down entirely. "But when you grab me too hard, or I don't realize you're going to do it, it makes me remember." He doesn't understand, and I give him a tentative smile. "It doesn't feel romantic."

Mick nods slowly, beginning to get it. "So, can I kiss you?"

"I don't know." The teacher in me comes out. "*Can* you?"

His eyes glint. "*May* I kiss you, Miss Kimber?"

"Try me." I curl my fingers, beckoning him to come closer.

He crowds in immediately and we stumble back into the shadows. Even though I asked for this, the sheer bulk of him and the speed at which he moves stops my breath for a moment, but when he kisses me, I don't freeze up. I melt, the warmth in my belly flooding upward into my chest. Not for the first time, I wonder what it would be like to go to bed with him. I won't, not tonight, not when this feeling is so new, but it's a change for the better.

"How's that?" he gasps against my mouth. "Not too rough?"

"Mmm." I lock my hands behind his neck and draw his head down again. "Just right."

The door closed quietly. Solange stood at the table, facing away, waiting. Knowing where he was in the room by how the boards sounded under his boots. When his hands came down on her shoulders, she stopped breathing.

"This is good?" he murmured, his ugly accent soft as his lips touched her neck. "You like this?"

She thought of Nina in her cradle, of Thierry—so thin, and with that worrying cough—and nodded wordlessly. Hans turned her around and looked at her, reaching behind to untie her apron. He brushed the top button of her dress with his fingertip.

"Undress now, yes?"

Solange nodded. "Yes."

He left before dawn, before the children woke up crying. His space in the bed was still warm. For a moment, Solange closed her eyes and remembered

Raymond, how he was warm all the time, even in the depths of winter. Then she sprang from the bed and vomited on the floor.

When she went to get a rag to clean up her mess, she found a basket of eggs on the kitchen table, along with a tidy pile of francs.

He would come back. And she would let him.

The day before Bastille Day, Mick tells me that his roommate, known only as Conroy, is having a party that night. "Bring your friends, if you want," he adds. "We can always use more girls."

I pass along the invitation, expecting them to refuse—Remy had organized an entire day out—but they accept with alacrity and immediately begin planning what they will wear.

"What about going up to Montmartre to watch the fireworks and dance?" I'd been looking forward to it; it felt like a very French thing to do.

Remy rolls her eyes. "An American party will have better drinks."

"And more men!" Cécile adds. "What is your man's friend like?"

"I've never met him." There is no point in mourning a canceled plan, so I get into the spirit of the new one. "What are you wearing, Remy? Cécile, I assume you're wearing your pink dress?"

Behind her glasses, her blue eyes widen. "But of course! I made some chiffon flowers for the bodice. It will look totally new."

It will not, but after years of rationing, new ornaments are as good as a new dress.

"What should I wear?" The midinettes have much better instincts about these things than I do. "The black or the green?"

"The green," Remy says decidedly, as Cécile says, "The black."

I go with the green: with Cécile in pink and Remy in yellow, we will look like a bouquet of flowers. We dress together in their larger room, laughing and chattering like the girls we so recently were. It reminds me of my high school friendship with Peggy, Hazel, and Lenny, and I suddenly miss them so much it hurts. I will write to them all in the morning.

We take the Métro to save money for the ride home. Our footsteps are hardly audible over the music and conversation that pours from every open window. The streets are filled with people, celebrating as if the war has just ended. One young man, already drunk, tries to kiss Remy. When she pulls away, he loses his balance and falls flat on the sidewalk, causing laughter all around.

The concierge calls upstairs to announce our arrival. As Remy draws the elevator gate, we hear a shout, and a breathless couple crams in with us. "Fourth floor?" the woman asks.

"Yes," I say. "Conroy's party?"

The man jiggles the gate until it closes properly. "Great fellow, Conroy," he says. "Have you been to one of his bashes before?"

I shake my head. "We're friends of a friend. Michael Rafferty?"

"Oh, I adore Mick!" the woman gushes. "Isn't he a darling?"

Remy pokes me in the ribs. "Is he, Pearl?"

When we spill out into the carpeted hall, one door at the end is propped open. Strains of Dizzy Gillespie draw us in. Cécile is dancing by the time we enter the apartment.

Mick is nowhere to be seen, but a dark-haired man with horn-rimmed glasses pushes his way through a crush of dancers to shout a greeting. He points to the dining room, where a bar has been set up. I assume he is our host and smile my thanks. All this will be easier once I've had a glass of champagne.

Cécile manages to immediately find a man to pour a drink for her, then carry her off to the other room to drink by the window. I raise my eyebrows at Remy. "She's incorrigible."

"She likes her fun." Remy accepts a martini and gulps it down with more enthusiasm than she usually shows for alcohol. "I'm going to find someone to dance with while you look for your boyfriend."

It takes a while to find him. Drink in hand, I wander through the rest of the apartment. He is not in the kitchen, on the balcony, or in the large room with the dancers. There are several doors along the hall, which I assume are bedrooms. I knock on the first and call his name. When no one responds, I push it open. There is a squeal and a sense of movement in the dark; I have intruded on a couple seeking privacy.

"Pardon," I say. "You should lock the door."

I knock at the next closed door. Eventually Mick opens it. His shirt is unbuttoned at the neck and his hair looks as if he's been running his fingers through it. "Pearl," he says, startled. "You're here already?"

"It's after eight." I kiss his cheek, smell the whiskey on his breath. "Were you writing?"

"Trying to finish something. Come in." He steps back and I follow, curious to see where he spends his time. "Do you want a drink?"

"Already have one." I wave my champagne glass. "Are you going to join the party?"

"I suppose I should." He looks me up and down with an appreciative smile. "Though I'm not fit to be seen with the likes of you. You look great."

"Thank you." The room's only light is a small desk lamp, casting its yellow glow over a typewriter and messy stacks of paper: his café table, on a larger scale. Beyond is an unmade bed, a tall dresser, and a bookshelf with more volumes missing than on its shelves. "You could change."

His mouth quirks. "Into what?"

"A gentleman?"

"Don't suppose you'd help me?"

"I don't think so." I back away as he tugs his shirt loose and undoes another button, giving me a shadowed glimpse of his chest.

"Pearl." His hand curls like iron around my wrist.

I go stiff as he pulls me close and kisses me.

"Let me guess—too rough?" His hand slides down to gather a handful of crepe. I shiver at the touch of his fingers on my thigh.

I can't keep letting my past get in the way of my future. Or my present, as Mick would have it. Closing my eyes, I let him walk me toward the bed. When my legs touch the edge of the mattress, I tip backward and Mick collapses heavily on top of me, one hand under my skirt.

As he strokes the skin above my stocking top, I don't fight him, but I can't encourage him either. I've broken apart and am floating somewhere, watching a girl in a green dress and a man in a rumpled white shirt. He pushes her skirt up to her waist and rests his big hands on her thighs.

The door bangs open and Mick springs to his feet. "Christ!!"

I yank my skirt down and scramble off the bed. "I knew that would happen," I say, skinning past him. "I'll see you out there."

My heart is racing. I make my way back to the main room, pick up the first glass I see and throw back the contents. Why didn't I push him away? Why didn't I scream or fight back? He knows how I hate being handled.

But I know why. Though it isn't the same at all, when he pushed me toward the bed, all I could think of was Mr. Nolan and his sly, creeping fingers.

The crowd has grown, while the tempo of the music has slowed. Everyone has either a drink or a cigarette, or both. Smoke hangs heavy, clouding the corners of the already dim room. I steady my breathing and look for my friends, locate Cécile dancing with our host. Remy is huddled with a tall blonde woman in a well-tailored tuxedo.

Hmm. It would be nice if my friend could find someone.

An arm snakes around my waist and I squeak in surprise.

"I've changed," Mick's voice says in my ear. "Is this better or worse?"

My skin prickles where his breath touches me. In the time it took me to remember how to breathe, he has managed to change into an unfamiliar dark suit. His damp hair shows tracks from a comb, something that always strikes me as boyish and weakens my defenses.

"Drink or dance?" He maneuvers me in the direction of the bar, one hand sliding below my waist.

"We've been drinking," I point out, turning before he can reach the table and placing his hand back where it belongs. "Dance with me."

The problem with dancing in a crowd is that we're pressed together, my skirt bunching between our legs as we move. Before long, his grip grows tighter. I know he's wondering how to get me back to his room. It comes to me, suddenly and far too late, the difference between Mick and the other men I've been with.

I felt safe with them because I felt respected.

"I need air." I break away and make a beeline for an open window. Though it isn't much cooler outside, I hope for a breeze. "Can you get me something cold—without alcohol?"

Mick goes off and I lean against the sill, trying to catch my breath as the party goes on around me. I could slink away and no one would notice. But why would they? I've been introduced to no one, not even our host; we were left to fend for ourselves.

I shouldn't have to constantly hunt Mick down, I think, growing annoyed when he doesn't return. For all the company he's been, I might as well be here alone. I exhale with frustration, debating whether to wrest the girls from their partners and see if they want to leave.

"Did you ask for this?" It's the man with the horn-rimmed glasses. He holds a sweating glass, several precious ice cubes clinking against the sides.

"Thank you." I take a quick sip and squeeze my eyes shut as the cold goes straight to my head. "Oww."

An arm goes around my shoulders, and he leads me to the corner. "Move, Jackson," he says sharply, then presses me into a chair. "Are you all right?"

"Just drank too fast." I see the warm sympathy in his gaze and want suddenly to cry. "Where's Mick?"

"In the kitchen, talking." He shrugs and leans over the arm of the chair, offering his hand. "I'm Conroy, by the way. Jason Conroy."

"Pearl Kimber." We shake hands awkwardly. "Are your parties always this... disorganized?"

"Usually." Conroy slides a flask from his pocket and offers it to me. When I refuse, he tilts his head back and drains it. "I'll regret it tomorrow, when ten people are sleeping off their hangovers under my table." He laughs. "I don't know half of them, and they'll be the ones to stay."

"Why do you do it?" A shriek cuts through the general noise. Cécile, giggling madly, is being dipped by a man in a purple velvet smoking jacket. "If you don't enjoy it?"

Conroy slides down the wall until we're at the same level. "Because when the war ended, I promised myself that I would never turn away from pleasure, not ever again. We're not promised a set amount of time, Miss Kimber. I'm going to live."

"You sound like Mick."

His laugh turns into a cough. "We had very different wars."

When we finally leave, my head is aching from the combination of wine and noise. Conroy somehow finds a cab and bundles the limp Cécile into the back seat. She giggles and tries to kiss him, but he darts away, wishing us a good night.

"I hope there is no one under your table tomorrow," I say.

He kisses my hand. "One can hope."

Remy crackles with energy, as wide awake as when we set out. She cranes her neck out the window as the cab pulls away.

"Did you have a good time?" I don't look back. I haven't seen Mick for the last hour. When he returned to find me in conversation with Conroy, he pushed in between us, as if he hadn't been the one to disappear in the first place. Conroy backed away with a faint, embarrassed smile and I didn't see him again until we left. Mick vanished long before, sulking when I refused to go back to his room.

"I had a *lovely* time." Remy is smiling enormously, making her smeared lipstick more obvious. "Did you see her? Isn't she magnificent?"

"Tell me everything." Cécile starts to slide down the seat and I prop her up with my elbow.

Breathless, Remy tells me about Vera Mathis: thirty-one, a photographer from Chicago on extended assignment in Paris. They are going out Friday night.

"There is a bar in Montmartre," she says, her eyes gleaming. "Where we can dance and no one will care."

"No one cared tonight." There were a few curious glances but overall, the reaction was mild. "I'm glad you've met someone."

She reaches across Cécile's crumpled pink skirt to take my hand. "Did *you* have a good time? I saw you having words with your man."

I rub my temples, wincing as the cab hits a pothole. "He was being an ass," I say honestly. "He kept going off to talk to other people and getting annoyed when I did the same."

She makes a dismissive noise. "He is attractive, but perhaps not the best choice for you."

"I like him!" Cécile chirps, then slides into Remy. "Are we home yet?"

"Almost, cherie." Remy settles her friend's head on her shoulder, then turns her attention back to me. "You are very presentable now, Pearl. You could easily find someone more suitable."

"I know." As the cab crosses the Pont Neuf, I rummage in my bag for coins to pay the driver.

The driver helps get Cécile to the door and accepts the tip I press into his hand when I discover that Conroy has paid our fare. We let ourselves in and call up the stairs until Philippe comes to our aid. He hoists Cécile over his shoulder and carries her to her room.

June 28, 1946

Pearl,

I am glad you wrote to me about your friend's cousin. I am proud of the woman you have become that you can sympathize with her plight and not judge her. But you have always seen people clearly, and with grace and kindness.

What I write here is not known to the family, even Claire. You remember Trudy, our old neighbor? She told me once that after my father died, your granny did something she was ashamed of. I can't say she was right, but I know for certain that the agent didn't throw us out when we were behind on rent and even fixed the roof on one occasion. Mama did what was necessary, being without money or support, to save her family.

So yes, I think you should write Solange's story, even if it doesn't find a place right now. It's a story worth telling, and you are the person to write it.

Mama

It is very late when someone scratches at my door. I am curled in the armchair by the window, unable to sleep, and call quietly, "Who is it?"

"Me." Remy sounds as bubbly as Cécile. "Let me in."

I open the door, and she spins through, wearing one of Cécile's dresses which had been hastily altered to fit her smaller frame. She kisses me on both cheeks and collapses across the foot of my bed, managing to bang her elbow on the edge of the armoire on the way. "Merde," she says absently, rubbing it. "Why are you awake?"

"Because I was waiting for you." It is as good an answer as any, and I am curious about how her evening went. "Did you and Vera have a good time?"

She sits up and falls back again, as if all the stuffing has been taken from her. "Do you believe in love at first night?"

Dropping back into my chair, I lean forward, elbows on my knees. "I suppose it's possible."

I am treated to a recitation of their evening—dinner at Bofinger, where Remy ate an obscene number of oysters, then a walk through the twilit streets to Montmartre to a bar she'd never heard of, a magical place filled with women who were there to drink and dance with each other.

"It was amazing, Pearl." Her eyes are huge, tears gathered at the corners. "I have never seen anything like it."

"And was Vera everything you expected?" I fold myself up against the headboard so she doesn't have to move. Her smile tells me all I need to know.

"I'm seeing her again tomorrow, and then again on Tuesday." She sits up. "Oh. We were talking about the party. She knows your Mick."

"I assumed she would, if she's a friend of Conroy's."

"Not from Conroy," Remy says. "From the war. She said they worked together on something called *Stripes and Stars*."

Stars and Stripes? Mick had never told me that he'd written for the military newspaper during his stint in the army. Perhaps it wasn't a good experience. It was like him to neglect to mention something if it hadn't been entirely successful.

"Did she say when?"

Her face scrunches. "Forty-three or four. Italy. She'd come from London, attached to a British general, and he'd just arrived."

"But Mick was in France, not Italy." It didn't make any sense. "Are you sure she's got the right man?"

"She knew his name, and that he was a journalist in uniform, not a soldier," Remy says, her chin jutting at any slight to her new beloved. "She said he came from a place called New Jersey."

When Mick joins me at the café the following morning, I don't immediately bring up what Vera said, knowing he won't react well to being the topic of such a conversation.

Every day, we reach a point where we stop at almost the same time, drink another cup of chicory, and talk before going for another hour. I wait until then to say, "Conroy's party was interesting."

"You liked him?"

"I liked that he was sober enough to make certain we got home okay."

He huffs. "I was in the kitchen, talking to an old army buddy."

That's always his excuse when he disappears, whether from a party or from the city entirely.

"The French don't want to talk about the war," I say, "and we Americans never stop."

"For some of us, it was the biggest adventure we'll ever have." His lips curve in a reminiscent smile. "On the front lines, life is very stripped down. A man whose name you don't know would give his life for you, and you'd do the same for him." It's the same tone he always uses, but I listen differently now. "It's not something you could even conceive of, little Pearl."

His world-weariness irritates me, as does his assumption that I can't imagine a soldier's existence.

"I suppose that made it hard to come back to real life."

"This isn't real," he says, tossing back the rest of his chicory. "That was real. This is like theater—artificial, everyone speaking lines they know are bullshit."

"And yet you participate." He is too convincing; Vera must have it wrong.

"And yet I do." Mick picks up my hand and brushes his lips over my palm, sending a surge of heat to my core. "What else am I supposed to do?"

"Remy made a friend at the party," I say, when he seems unable to remove his focus from my hand. "Vera Mathis. Do you know her?"

His fingers tighten. "Did she say she knew me?"

"I just asked if you knew her." I tug my hand free and pick up my cup. "She and Remy have hit it off, that's all."

"Vera Mathis is a dyke," he says with sudden violence. "A man-hater who preys on young girls. Your friend should be careful around her."

His crude language makes me feel cold all over. I've never told him about Dan, and after this, I never will.

"Remy is a grown woman," I say stiffly. "She knows what she's doing."

"And I know who she's doing it with." His lip curls with disgust. "Why do you and Cécile bother with her?"

"Because we're friends." I close my notebook with a snap. "I'm done for the day."

I don't go back to my room. My thoughts will be too loud there.

Why do I tolerate Mick when I find so many of his opinions repulsive? And why does he want me? In his eyes, I've never been enough. I write stories for women, about women; I am not serious like Martha Gelhorn or Simone de Beauvoir. My attachment to the midinettes and my interest in fashion are superficial. Why, then, have I wasted so much of my precious year on Mick Rafferty?

He has made me angry, he has made me melt. But he has not made me into the sort of girl he wants. For that I thank the strong women in my family, who have shown me, all my life, that we do not have to turn ourselves inside out to be loved.

If we'd met in Philadelphia, I wouldn't likely have accepted a second date. Is it simply wanting the familiarity of an American voice? His is not a voice I would have listened to at home; he is more like my younger brothers than a man I would choose to be with. Yet here, while I have friends like Remy and Cécile and even Madeleine, I have allowed Mick to weave himself into my life. Is this city, even in its shattered state, so romantic that I must have a man?

Julian Armitage flashes through my mind, and I push him away. He is a man, but not like that.

Something I've actively avoided thinking about is what Mama would have to say about Mick. She would understand his appeal, but equally, she would say that looks aren't everything. More concerning to her would be his manners and the way he speaks to people, neither of which are up to her standards, and thus, should not be up to mine.

Perhaps that's another reason I've kept him at arm's length. Denying him keeps me in control of my thoughts; giving in might make me more forgiving of his irregularities. I'd seen it happen before and always wondered that my friends could dissolve so easily into another person, but Mick is a force I'm not sure I can withstand.

A shout jerks me back to the present and I step hastily out of the street, where a vélo-taxi has come dangerously close to clipping my toes.

Without having noticed, I have come to the Tuileries. My feet knew what I needed, even as my head is still wrapped in the puzzle of Mick Rafferty. I head for a bench and pull Dan's most recent letter from my bag.

It is undated and has no salutation; it is exactly like him.

So Grace told you about Tommy. He was wounded pretty bad at Monte-cassino. Better now, other than a bad ankle and a limp. Got his old job

*back at Baldwin and thinks he found us someplace to live down in the Neck
where they won't care if we're cousins or not.*

Everybody is fine. Miss you. Don't forget to come home.

Dan

Where is the Neck? Not that it matters; the important thing is that Dan
and Tommy are together. Whether or not they masquerade as cousins,
at least they're together.

I miss my brother. There is pressure over my eyes, and I close them
against the bright sky and the coming headache. Dan calls them responsibility headaches, pointing out that they happen when I am too hard on
myself. But what else am I supposed to do? I put his letter away and rise
from the bench.

If I have come, unconsciously, to the Tuileries, I will find peace at the
Orangerie.

When I come back from the museum, a letter from Mary Jayne Gold is
waiting. I rip it open and pull out a scented blue sheet with an invitation
to Gassin, promising sun and companionship and, should I choose not
to go to the nearby beach, a pool the color of the sky.

"Only a week, I'm afraid," reads her careless scrawl, "as absolutely
everyone wants to come and I don't have bedrooms sufficient for you
all. Unless you'd be willing to share with a certain devastating vicomte?
Alas, there has been a change in his situation. I found a slightly boring
but enormously rich American as eager to accept his proposal as he is to
acquire her money."

I snort with laughter, hoping the American isn't too boring; in exchange for the resurrection of his family fortune, Luc would be faithful,
but he is only human.

Miss Gold's letter continues, "I know you've come here to work,
darling, but I would be remiss in my duty to your aunt if I didn't offer
you a bit of fun and perhaps the chance of a summer romance."

And I would be remiss in my duty to myself if I didn't take Miss Gold
up on her offer. I don't require romance—I have enough of that here,

should I want it—but a week in the south of France, pretending to be a Fitzgerald, has a certain appeal.

Until I think of my personal Hemingway. Mick isn't going to want to lose me for a week, and I can't bring him along without an invitation. He'll make cutting remarks about my rich friend and accuse me of wanting to live in luxury. Which I normally do not, but Miss Gold's slightly scatty charm and the abundance of champagne in her world is a potent combination. Throw in the Mediterranean and it sounds like paradise.

We meet for dinner the next evening at a tiny, smoky student bistro that he favors. I've put on a dress with a full skirt, an indication that I want to go dancing later; dancing always puts him in a good mood because he can put his hands on me.

"Babe," he says as our meals arrive. "Remember the fellow I ran into at Conroy's party?"

"The one you abandoned me to talk to?"

"That's the one," he says. "He invited me to catch up with him and some of the other boys."

I take a sip of wine to hide the gleeful smile that rises unbidden to my lips. "Really? When?"

"The first week in August. You could sole shoes with this," he says, throwing down his knife. The card said steak, but after the horse incident, I look askance at all red meat. "Come with me?"

Miss Gold's invitation was for the last week of July, but I will send a cable in the morning asking if I can come later and hope that I don't ruin her arrangements.

"Your buddies wouldn't appreciate that." I do my best to sound disappointed. "Having a girl around when they want to drink and carouse and tell stories?"

His hand slips under the table and his fingertips trail along my thigh. "But then I'd have a girl around to carouse with after the drinking and the storytelling."

A girl to help him upstairs and watch him fall into bed, more likely. If I'm not willing to be his lover on the French Riviera, I'm certainly not going to give in at a cheap hotel surrounded by a group of hard-drinking ex-soldiers.

"I'd feel very out of place. All those men." I allow his fingers to wander as high as my stocking top. When they begin to fiddle with my garter, I put my hand over his. "It might do you good to get away from me. Think of all the work you'll get done if I'm not there to distract you."

Mick laughs good-naturedly and his hand emerges to pick up his glass. "I think you want a break from *me* distracting *you*."

"Maybe just a little."

After dinner, we spend two hours locked in each other's arms on a packed dance floor, then return to the hotel where any chance of intimacy in the entryway is forestalled by Cécile, who is already there, grappling unsuccessfully with a short but determined Frenchman.

"Leave off!" Mick demands.

The man whirls, angry at being interrupted, and then his eyes go up Mick's length—he is a solid foot taller—and he slinks off, muttering. I kiss Mick goodnight and escape up the stairs with Cécile.

"He is powerful, your man," she comments, pausing on the landing at her floor. "You are fortunate."

"Some days, yes," I tell her. "Some days, I'm not so sure."

August 1946

By the time we reach Fréjus, I'm simultaneously exhausted and energized, stiff from hours of sitting in one position and excited to have seen more of France—and it feels like I've seen all of it. The train left the Gare de Lyon in the early morning and now, after stops both planned and unplanned, it is nearly six; if it were winter, I'd be arriving in the dark. As it is, when I step down onto the platform, I am so happy to see Gaston that I nearly embarrass us both by hugging him.

"You look well, mademoiselle," he says, gesturing for the porter to follow us outside. "The journey was long, yes?"

"Yes." I slide into the cushioned luxury of the back seat, wondering if he'd notice if I slipped off my shoes. "How far to Miss Gold's?"

"Thirty minutes." Gaston eases the car smoothly into the road. "Close your eyes. We will be there soon."

But I don't want to close my eyes. I want to see *everything*. As we glide along the road from Fréjus, glimpses of brilliant blue water are visible in between buildings and dark, spiky trees. The Mediterranean.

Before I leave, I must swim in the Mediterranean. To do that, I must acquire a swimsuit. It's just as well that it never occurred to me to bring one to Paris, as my old blue and white suit with its flared skirt is dreadfully out of style. Despite the assistance of Remy and Cécile, a decent suit could not be located in time. I am optimistic that Miss Gold will have a spare, or better yet, know where I can purchase one.

I sent a short letter to Julian last week, telling him of my plans, and he forwarded an extra payment from the trust to cover what he called "incidentals." Is a new swimsuit a justifiable expense or an incidental? Either way, I can afford one, even if the shops here are more expensive than those in Paris.

I will send him a postcard. It makes me smile to think of him receiving the card at his office, turning it over and seeing my name.

The road turns away from the coast and begins to climb. We pass through small villages of sand-colored houses set in long stretches of forest. The air is crisp and cool, and I can smell the salt-brine scent of the sea. Against my will, my eyes drift closed.

"Pearl!"

The car is stopped on a circular gravel drive and my hostess leans in the window. Clad in white shorts and a red halter top, possessed of an enviable tan, Miss Gold is somehow more elegant dressed like this than she was when wearing diamonds and satin.

I emerge from the car into her welcoming embrace. The sky has lost its daytime brilliance and is the tremulous, enameled turquoise of a Maxfield Parrish illustration. I want to stay and admire it, but I'm also in desperate need of the toilet.

"Come, darling," Miss Gold says, taking my arm and hauling me along. "Gaston will bring your things into the house and Nina is waiting to get you settled."

The house, as she so airily refers to it, is a large, rambling structure in the native stone, with blue shutters and balconies and the starts of green vines—wisteria?—beginning to trail up the walls. If not for the freshness of the paint on the shutters, I would assume it to be a much older house.

"It's beautiful."

"Isn't it?" She waves a thin arm, decorated with two inches of narrow gold bracelets. "I've always loved this area. Back in my flying days I would zip down for a long weekend and think nothing of it."

"I didn't know you flew." The door cuts off the light and I stumble in the interior's sudden darkness. Pausing until my eyes adjust, I say, "I'd love to hear about it, but first, can you point me toward the bathroom?"

As I make my way towards sweet relief, I hear the clink of glasses being brought out.

My room has a floor of honey-colored tile and French windows hidden behind airy linen curtains. The bed is soft, the sheets crisp. It's as if the war never existed. After my previous stay with Miss Gold, I should have expected it, but I've had months of Parisian austerity since then and the comparison is sharp.

Miss Gold—who insists that I call her Mary Jayne—ordered me to sleep as late as I wanted. "We're all on our own schedules here," she said last night, after I joined her and her other guests on the patio for a glass of champagne. "Come down whenever you're ready. One of the servants will scare you up something to eat."

I wake at dawn, the unusual silence and the quality of the light dragging me from sleep as surely as an alarm clock. Instead of going in search of food or coffee, I shrug on a watercolor-flowered silk dressing gown and open the doors to the balcony.

Directly below is the patio where we gathered the night before, and just beyond a low stone wall is the sparkling pool, lit golden by the rising sun. The property meanders until it reaches a line of tall cypress trees, on the other side of which is a golf course.

The beach, Mary Jane assured me, is but a few miles away. When I told her I didn't drive, she immediately volunteered Gaston, but I asked instead if there was a bicycle I could use. There will be plenty of time for socializing, but the purpose of this visit is to take advantage of the quiet and get as much writing done as I can before it is time to return to Paris.

Much of yesterday's journey was spent mulling over what I'd written so far, and the seemingly insurmountable problem of understanding Solange's life. I understood *her* just fine, but no matter how hard I tried, or how many questions I asked, the story wouldn't come right because I couldn't comprehend where she came from.

Somewhere around Marseille—nearly the end of the journey—it occurred to me that I could tell Solange's story, but through a lens I absolutely understood.

My grandmother, Lillie, came to Pennsylvania from Ireland in 1880. While Scovill Run was never occupied by a hostile force, she faced opposition and oppression from every direction, not to mention similar difficult choices. Mama's letter, which is tucked into my bag, was the deciding factor. Granny was one of the most moral people I'd ever known, a woman with a strong Catholic faith but an equally strong streak of pragmatism. She did what had to be done to protect her children.

After breakfast, equipped with a creaking pre-war bicycle and scribbled directions, I set off for the beach. According to Nina, whose smile has grown even brighter, there are several nearby, the smallest and closest of which is the Plage de Cogolin.

"The beaches are all open now," she assures me, handing over a bottle of lemonade and two sandwiches, which I stow into my bag along with my notebook and several pencils. "You needn't worry."

"Why were they closed?" Had the Germans ordered them blocked off? This part of France had been Vichy to begin with, but eventually the occupation had spread south.

"Ordnance," she says with a shrug. "But it is cleared now. Mademoiselle's guests will not be blown to bits!"

Mary Jayne's guests are unlikely to be blown to bits on the beach because they appear unwilling to leave the house and its environs, as everything they need is here. There had been talk, the night before, of visiting the golf course or driving into St. Tropez, but Nina said such plans rarely came to fruition as it took until afternoon before everyone assembled. By then, they were more likely to retreat to the patio with a cocktail or to swim in the pool.

Because of the pool, Mary Jayne had a collection of swimsuits in varying sizes. She insisted I borrow one or more for the duration of my visit. I chose a modest dark red suit with a fitted skirt and a halter neck and wore over top a pair of linen shorts and a simple blue-and-white striped top, also from her wardrobe.

"Your things won't do, pet," she said, looking them over after breakfast and squinting at the sunlight pouring through the window. "The Riviera demands light fabrics, or else you'll sweat to death."

Summers in Philadelphia were meltingly humid; I thought that the Riviera had nothing to teach me about sweating. I humored her and allowed her to choose my clothes. Once I was pedaling down the dusty road from the house, I saw how right she was. The shorts gave me freedom of movement while protecting my bottom from the hot seat, and the mild breeze cut right through the loosely woven linen.

Gassin's medieval town looks like something out of a fairy tale. As I follow the road around the town, I decide that I will visit tomorrow—unless the ocean casts its spell and I am incapable of going anywhere but back to the beach. Through the town and the outskirts, then past small cottages and deep stands of trees, I finally come to a rise and stop to rest my legs. Ahead of me, the road falls dramatically. I can see now that it winds around another small settlement before reaching the turquoise sea, which sparkles like a drift of sequins in the sun.

I coast down the hill, my hair blowing out behind me, the salt air already loosening my hard-won curls. What did I care? There were palm trees—palm trees!—ahead of me, and pale golden sand and the brilliant, smooth water beyond.

August 6, 1946

Things about the beach that I didn't notice while standing on top of that hill:

1. It was crowded. Packed as Atlantic City in the middle of summer except without so many shrieking children, and with the negro people not confined to Chicken Bone Beach.

2. It might not have been boiling hot, but the sun was blazing. Even with Mary Jayne's sunglasses, my eyes were stinging from the glare.

3. I didn't know how to do this.

I took a deep breath, rode down, and figured it out. I handed someone a few francs to rent an umbrella. He offered to watch my bicycle at no extra charge, but I kept it with me. Mary Jayne wouldn't have cared if it was stolen, but it would have been a long walk back.

A man from a nearby family helped me set up the umbrella and spread the blanket, after which I discreetly took off my shorts and top and folded them into my bag.

The sounds of voices and music were constant, but I lay down and closed my eyes so the sun was no more than a red glow against my eyelids. Only then could I focus on the sound of the waves and the feeling of the air as it moved over my body. That much was like the beaches at home; sometimes I have to block everything out to be able to catch the part of the day that I need.

By afternoon, a lot of the families were gone. A woman can only spend so much time trying to keep her children from drowning before she can't take any more. I moved my things closer to the water, so that the most ambitious waves lapped at my feet, propped myself on my elbows and stared across at the green hills and whatever towns existed across the Gulf of St. Tropez.

I didn't get back until nearly five, my legs like jelly from riding in the sun. Mary Jayne said she was about to send out the cavalry to find me, but I assured her that I was fine, that the heat had got to me a bit. I don't want Gaston ferrying me to the beach tomorrow.

She hugged me, and that's when I noticed how sore my shoulders were. I went off to take a cool shower, and now I'm sitting on the bed, relaxing before dinner, and listening to the voices in my head.

I'm going to do it. I'm going to tell Granny's story.

I'm excited.

I'm also scared.

The days in Gassin pass in a blur of writing by the pool before the others are up, solo rides to the beach, where I choose to trust the umbrella man and stop sharing my blanket with a bicycle, and evening meals on the patio with Mary Jayne and her friends. They are an interesting lot: French and English and American—several with no occupation beyond wealth. Currently there is a lawyer, an actor, and a journalist. His presence made me glad that Mick hadn't come with me.

Each night I choose one of Mary Jayne's featherweight dresses and descend the stairs with my heart in my throat, and each night I go to bed understanding that I am far more capable than I imagined. My French isn't flawless, but I can converse easily enough. The American actor is handsomer in person, but it's his everyman persona I find charismatic. He spends a considerable bit of time trying to convince me to turn my hand to film scripts.

"Never!" I wave him off, all the while thinking how unreal this whole situation is—being flirted with by a man who I've watched on screen for more than a decade. "I want to tell stories. A script is nothing but dialogue and stage directions."

"But if you did that, what would I do with my face?" His dark brows lift slightly, and his sleepy eyes widen—*deepen*—somehow. It's an expression I've seen in countless movies, and other than the thrill of having it directed at *me*, it does nothing to make me want to write something for him, and he knows it.

"He likes you," Mary Jayne whispers later, when we give up and leave the men to play poker and drink her excellent whiskey. "Aren't you tempted?"

I shake my head. "I'm flattered, but no. What about you?" Mary Jayne is closer to him in age, but like so many men, he likely prefers his ladies on the young side.

"He's a dear," she says lightly, "but rough around the edges." She spins in a slow circle on the tiled floor. "Anyway, this is enough. A house. A life of my own choosing."

Not so different from me, then, minus the house. Although Aunt Claire told me that Mary Jayne's name had been linked with many men, she'd never chosen to marry or have children, and no one thought less of her for her choice. I certainly don't.

On the last day, I finally visit the old town and fall into a fairytale. The streets are steep and cobbled, winding without any particular plan other than to delight. Bougainvillea spills over windowsills and high balconies; the air smells of jasmine.

I stop at a café for a glass of wine and to flip through my notebook. In six days, I have filled pages with notes and snippets of dialogue, and while I don't look forward to the morning's train journey, I can't wait to get back to my routine and see what becomes of the story.

The wine is cool and crisp; the sun is high—bright but not too hot. I tip my head back to soak it in.

Strangely, the sunlight isn't just on my face and my shoulders, but inside me. I feel lit up, and it has nothing to do with the sun and everything to do with my grandmother's alter ego, Brigid Malloy. Plain old Pearl Kimber couldn't attract a lanky, drawling movie star, but the Pearl who fizzes with inspiration, so filled with words that I wake up with them in my mouth? She is capable of that, and more.

I stare at the blank page so hard the lines begin to blur. There's a pressure building in my head that aspirin cannot cure; I should wait until I get back to the villa, but the words don't understand patience.

Colliers Forge, Pennsylvania, 1880, I write at the top of the page. The words look back at me, waiting. I chew my lip and continue.

Three weeks ago, she left a village so small it was known only by the name of its church: St. Brigid, for whom she was named. Following her husband, she traveled by donkey cart and train and steamship, then a second, longer train journey, before arriving in another town so small as to be almost nameless. The ticket agent in New York, after he scratched his head at her brogue, took a full ten minutes to locate it on his map of Pennsylvania.

She stepped down from the third-class carriage, a sleeping Liam in one arm and her worldly goods, such as they were, in a carpet bag clutched tight in her other hand. Her hat was askew from sleeping against the window, but she didn't have time to straighten it when the conductor called out, "Colliers Forge!"

She'd asked him to wake her, but he hadn't. Now he stood at the door, a wide grin on his well-fed American face as she scrambled to gather their things and pushed past him. "Welcome to America!" he called after her.

Brigid muttered something in her granny's Gaelic and quickened her step in case he understood.

Sitting back, I read what I've written, surprised by the words that flowed through my fingers. I don't even remember thinking some of them; they just came, like a flood. Brigid is fully alive. Feisty and strong-willed, as much like Mama as Granny, not afraid to speak her mind, unwilling to show fear when she learns that the man she's traveled thousands of miles to rejoin is dead.

I drain my glass, suddenly excited to get back to Paris and throw myself into this world that is both unknown and totally familiar.

Mick is still away. I take advantage of his absence to continue my head-long drafting of Brigid's story, tentatively named *The Choices We Make.*

Cécile is seeing someone she met at Conroy's party. She passes on word that Mick won't be back for another week. There has been no such message for me. I decide to think later about whether that is worrisome; right now, I have words enough without having to make space for his. It occurs to me that I should be more upset about his disappearance, but I put that thought aside, as well, more interested in creating a past for Brigid: happy in spite of her poverty, so it will hurt more when it all comes crashing down.

Writers are strange creatures. In our ordinary lives, we want everything to run smoothly, but in our stories, there is nothing better than tragedy. Drama, at the very least.

Francis, I call her husband. Frankie Malloy. He's black-haired and merry and charming, and he leaves their impoverished village when they learn Brigid is pregnant, to go to America. Once the baby is born and he's sent enough money home, she will follow him. There are scenes with his family and hers, both calling him foolish for trying to build a better life. Only Brigid supports him.

His letters are short and infrequent; he's embarrassed by his lack of schooling. "The work is hard, but the mines pay well," he wrote. "Soon you'll come to me."

The mines did pay well, for a while. Even when I was small, after the first war, things weren't too bad, but by the time my brothers were born, it was worse. Then my father got involved with union organizers. From then on, we were never more than one step from losing our home. I felt my parents' worry as a girl, and now I know how bad it must have been that I even caught wind of it, because there's no one like Mama for hiding her fear.

I'm content to have this time to work, seeing Remy and Cécile at meals, talking with Sita or Madeleine in the afternoons, retreating to the café or my room to write or to the streets if I need to walk until the words come clear. When I receive a note from Julian that he's in town, it strikes me: I haven't spoken to anyone outside the hotel in nearly a week.

Using Madame's telephone, I leave a message at his hotel that I will be available tomorrow after one. I want to see him, but I won't give up my morning writing session; I might start scribbling notes on my napkin, and that would be rude in the sort of restaurants he likes.

By the time he arrives, I've written two good scenes and made a quick solo trip to the public baths, so I'm scrubbed and smelling of lavender bath salts.

"Your gentleman is here, mademoiselle." Philippe appears in the dining room doorway.

"Thank you." I catch up my gloves and bag and follow him to the front desk, where Julian is perusing Philippe's copy of *Combat*, the resistance newspaper. At my approach, he looks up, a smile brightening his face. No pinstripes this time, but a double-breasted summer suit with a white shirt and a tie of sky blue and white stripes.

"Pearl!" He drops the paper and extends his hands. "Don't you look a picture? The south obviously agreed with you."

His praise makes me warm, but my tan disguises any blush. "It did," I say. "And you look like something out of *Casablanca*."

"It's warm," Julian says, as uncomfortable being noticed as I am. "Shall we?"

"Where are we going?" The stairwell is dim and muggy, clogged with hot air from the street. I am glad of my light dress and bare legs, even if they aren't appropriate now that the war is over.

"Lunch, I thought." He fans himself with his hat, then settles it on his head. "After that, I wonder if you might show me your favorite parts of Paris."

"Me?" My mind stutters to a stop at the thought of showing this cosmopolitan man anything—what can I possibly know about this city that he hasn't seen?

"Why not?" he asks. "You've been here five months now. You must have some places that are special to you. I'd like to see them."

"You probably know them already." I trip over a cobblestone, and he catches my elbow. "You've been coming here for years."

"Please don't remind me." His gray eyes are teasing. "And even if I've been there before, I don't know it through your eyes. That will make it different."

Lunch takes place in a snug bistro beneath a lazily turning fan. We have leeks in vinaigrette, chicken with tarragon, and a bottle of white wine, while I mull over where to take him.

"I do enjoy these meals," I say, clearing the last of my plate and wondering if he will want dessert. "You always feed me so well."

He puts down his fork. "Have you not started treating yourself better?"

"I won't make my friends feel poor by treating them." I tried to take Remy out for her birthday; she not only refused but did not speak to me for two days.

"Then I will continue to appear like Father Christmas and give you your treats," he says. "But I'll let you buy the ice cream since you're a wealthy woman."

"You have a deal." It occurs to me then where I want to take him. "Are you up for a walk?"

Julian raises a finger to catch the waiter's attention. "In Paris? Always."

We stroll along the river, stopping frequently to peruse the bookstalls. "These are one of my favorite things," I tell him, pausing to look at a particularly lovely etching of Notre Dame.

"Mine, too." He flips through a worn leather bound volume and nods to the stallholder. "I always find something."

"What's that?" I put the etching aside to peer at his book while he transacts his business. "I haven't read Proust."

"Neither have I," he admits. "But I have a friend who's read him multiple times, and she has a birthday coming up."

I note that the friend is female. It's none of my business if Julian Armitage has a special friend; his self-effacing manner does him no favors, but there is something beneath the ordinariness of Julian's looks that makes me want to keep looking at him.

"Let's go." I don't like thinking about Julian this way. "We have a good distance to walk."

He steps away agreeably, the wrapped book tucked under his arm. "I don't suppose you're ready to tell me where we're going?"

"Not yet." I remain silent as we cross the Pont des Arts. The Louvre and the Tuileries loom ahead, but we are going to neither. As we enter the gardens, our pace slows. August is the traditional vacation month for Europeans, but as not everyone is able to travel, Parisians of all ages and classes are out enjoying the weather. Most are sitting on benches, but some sprawl on the grass, their faces turned to the sun. It is tempting to join them, but I want to keep moving.

"The Orangerie?" he says when we at last reach the museum. "I haven't been here since university."

"You've seen them, then?" I am disappointed, even though I knew it was unlikely he hadn't been here before. "We can go somewhere else."

"Absolutely not." He takes my arm and leads me into the building. "Today you're my guide. I want to see what you love about this city."

Monet's glorious water lily panels are displayed in two long, oval rooms lit by skylights. The paintings wrap the walls, giving the feeling of bobbing in a boat in the middle of a pond. A line of benches runs down the center of each room. While they are usually crowded with tourists and Parisians alike, the weather has drawn most people outdoors, and we have the second room to ourselves.

Julian moves slowly along, looking at each painting, then turning to view the one across the room at a proper distance. When he is done, he sits on the bench, shaking his head. "Thank you."

"For what?" I sit beside him, putting my bag between us. "You've seen them before."

"It was years ago. I'm a different person now." He tilts his head. "I believe the war has made me better appreciate their peace."

I understand how after years of gray, these vibrant blues, greens, and lavenders must seem like a new world. "Spring come again?"

"Something like that."

It's easy to sit with him, not talking. I lift my gaze toward the painting opposite and let my eyes unfocus so the colors blur together even more.

"How is the writing coming along?" His quiet gentleness is appealing after a steady diet of Mick's ebullience. "Is Paris working its magic?"

"I had a story in the *Saturday Evening Post* back in July," I tell him. "It's not going to take over for the trust in paying my expenses, but it was nice."

He leans forward. "Wasn't that one of your goals?"

"It was." It had been for years—how quickly I had forgotten. "But it was a piece of fluff. Not real writing."

"All writing is real writing, I would say." His brow creases. "But who am I to offer my opinion? It sounds like you've taken counsel from someone who knows more about the business than I do."

As I hasten to say that his words are welcome, it occurs to me: I'm forever telling some man that his opinions about my life and work are valid. First Mick, now Julian. Even with Luc, I ended up feeling bad for him rather than being insulted that he wanted me for my non-existent fortune.

"I have one question," he says, "before you explain yourself out of existence. Even if you were to write more substantive work in the future, what problem could there possibly be with beginning as you have? You've worked hard, submitted stories, and been accepted. By that definition alone, you've succeeded." His sober smile is encouraging. "You should be proud of yourself, Pearl. Have goals. Have ambitions. But don't discount what you've accomplished because of them."

Bowing my head, I take in his unquestioning support and wonder why that support—and that sort of relationship—doesn't seem to be in the cards for me. I've tried on men like Aunt tries on hats, seeing what suits me. Pat showed me I could have feelings for someone without falling head over heels; Luc proved that emotions didn't need to be involved in matters of sex; and Mick has made me examine my past in a way that is not entirely comfortable.

Both he and Luc could have stepped out of the pages of a romance novel. Different novels, by very different authors. Julian Armitage could also be a character in a book, but not the one the heroine loses her head over. At least not at first. He's the steady, caring man who's always there, the rock she discovers when it's almost too late.

Like my Uncle Harry.

"What do you like to do?" I ask abruptly as a cold realization touches my spine. "When you're not... banking."

"I used to sail, before the war." His eyes go distant. "I had a small motor launch, the *Fair Rosaline*, moored at Hammersmith. It was my grandfather's. He gave it to me when I left Cambridge, and I brought it to London after I took the job at the bank. Perhaps if I'd left it with him, I'd still have it."

"You don't anymore?"

"No." Julian hesitates. "It was sunk. I couldn't replace it, with the war, and then I... never got around to it."

There is a sadness in his voice that I don't understand; surely the bank doesn't keep him so busy he can't take a weekend to mess about in boats.

"How was it sunk?" I think of the Blitz and the bombs that rained down over London.

"You've heard of Dunkirk?" He gets up from the bench and begins slowly to circle the room.

While I had seen *Mrs. Miniver* and, with the rest of the theater, cried over Vin's bride and thrilled at the plucky British housewife capturing a German in her very own home, the Dunkirk evacuation was only part of it. The movie's focus had been on the domestic side of the war—which was dangerous enough.

"I'd registered with the Small Vessels Pool when the call came over the BBC. We all did. We hadn't a clue at the time that it would come to anything, but then..."

But then the British Expeditionary Force, along with Belgian and French soldiers, were cut off, trapped along the French coast. After making their way to the port of Dunkirk, thousands of them were rescued and taken across the Channel by a flotilla of small boats sent from England for that purpose.

Julian gives me more details, including the fact that wooden-hulled boats like the *Fair Rosaline* were preferred because there was less risk of attracting mines.

"Were you scared?" As soon as the question leaves my lips, I realize how stupid I sound.

He stops, looks around as if noticing we are still in the museum. "Do you mind if we leave?"

Once outside, Julian lights a cigarette. His hand is shaking and he does not offer it to me, which tells me the depth of his distress.

I fish in my bag for my pack of Gitanes, which are so much easier to find than American cigarettes. They are a part of this life, a few moments of doing nothing but focusing on my thoughts and the taste of tobacco, the sensation of smoke in my lungs. I will stop before I go home.

"To answer your question," he says, exhaling, "yes. We were scared, all of us. Terrified. We also couldn't conceive of *not* going. We thought we were the only thing standing between Hitler and the invasion of England."

I start down the path back into the Tuileries. "You said we. Did you have friends with you or are you referring to the whole group?"

"Both." He is calmer in the open air, his stride opening up until I have to trot to keep pace with him. "Ronald Briers was a friend from school. He worked in London. We often sailed or played cricket at weekends."

He plays cricket. I file this information away for later. "And he was with you?"

"Yes." He tells me how they set off, a long line of small craft in the darkness, eventually meeting up with more boats, and still more, until when the sun rose, the water was covered as far as he could see.

"Then we saw the smoke of the ships burning in the port. Soldiers wading out into the water, trying to get to us, while the Luftwaffe flew overhead, shooting at anything and anyone that moved. Because our boats were small, we were able to get closer than the destroyers moored in the Channel.

"We were hit, but not badly. Ronald got the worst of it patched, and we made two trips before being sent back with a final load. Halfway home, the bilge pump gave out. There were ten soldiers on board. The ones who were able bailed almost all the way into Dover. We sank a half mile offshore and had to be picked up."

I have a strange urge to put my arms around him, but he wouldn't stand for it, not in public and not from what he would see as pity. But it's not; it's a form of awe, that an ordinary person could have done something so heroic and then tell me about it as blandly as if he were recounting a trip to the grocery store.

"Would you like a drink?" I say instead, and he looks at me with gratitude. "There's a café right over there."

We don't return to the hotel until nearly seven, having sat over our drinks for an hour and then walked slowly down the Boulevard Raspail until we reached the Montparnasse cemetery. Julian had a love of old graveyards, he told me. Had I ever been to Père-Lachaise?

I had not, but promised I would go as soon as the weather cooled, to walk the green lanes and visit Heloise and Abelard's tomb.

Despite the apparent ghoulishness of walking in a cemetery, it was a pleasant way to end the day. The ghosts of Dunkirk were banished among the precise rows of above-ground tombs and tidy French planting. By the time we emerge from our taxi in the Place Dauphine, Julian is as relaxed as he is capable of being.

"Well, this has been an interesting day." He is on the sidewalk while I stand on the hotel's shallow front step, bringing me almost to his eye level.

"Interesting good?" I ask, stalling so he doesn't leave yet, then wondering if I truly want him to stay. "Or interesting bad?"

He hadn't expected to tell me about Dunkirk, nor had he expected to walk miles through a cemetery of France's glorious dead.

"Interesting good." His smile tips sideways. "For the most part. The company was excellent."

Something fizzes in my veins, the way it does when I find a perfect turn of phrase or how to convey something tricky in a few words.

"I would say the same." My throat is tight. "Do you go back tomorrow?"

An errant car rumbles past, an unusual enough occurrence that it draws our attention. It continues down the street and stops.

"I have a meeting at nine," he says. "I'll be on my way after that."

And then we will be relegated to letters again. Letters for which there is no purpose other than that I enjoy writing to him almost as much as to Mama.

"When will you come back?" The door opens behind me, and I step down, brushing against him as Antoine Trier slips past.

"Are you angling for another lunch?" Julian looks delighted. "I'll write and let you know."

"Next time, you must show me *your* favorite place." I smooth my skirt, worried that I sound demanding, or coquettish. "If you like."

"We'll do that." His hand brushes my arm, fingers sliding lightly down to my wrist. "And thank you again for the water lilies. I hadn't expected to have such a response to them."

"I always do," I say. "They make me feel like I'm floating."

When I move back on the step, tacitly giving him permission to leave, I see that the car is idling a short way down the street. Mick leans on the hood, watching us, a cigarette in his fingers.

"I don't want to keep you," I say brightly, stepping back against the door. "You must have things to do—to get ready for tomorrow."

I'm babbling, unsure how to proceed with him in front of me and Mick a hundred feet away. His presence draws my eyes like a magnet. He's close enough to see that we're speaking but not to hear our conversation. Close enough to interrupt, if he chose. I do not want that to happen.

Julian fiddles with the knot in his tie. "I was going to ask if you'd like to change your dress and come out for an early dinner. We could make an evening of it."

"Ah. Um, no. I can't." My mind races, searching for a reason, and snags on my landlady. "Madame doesn't like it if we miss a meal without warning her first."

"Someone could have seconds," he suggests as disappointment, quickly masked, flickers over his face. "No, you're right. I'll see you on my next trip."

I hadn't expected him to be disappointed. My eyes raise. Mick is still watching. Why did he have to come back *now*?

"I'm sorry," I say inadequately, and hold out my hands. "You'll write and let me know your plans?"

"I will." His equilibrium is seemingly restored. "And you'll remember that *all* writing is writing and stop being so hard on yourself?"

"I will." His hand is smooth. I lean forward and kiss his cheeks. "Thank you."

Julian walks past Mick without a second glance. Once he is out of sight, Mick straightens and lopes over to me. He's wearing his grubby army jacket and no tie and is badly in need of a haircut.

"I leave town for a few days, and you replace me with an old man?" He folds me into an embrace, backing me up against the door. "I thought we had an understanding."

Squirming out of his grasp—why can he not remember that I don't like being mauled?—I say, "It was two weeks, not a few days, and that was my trustee, you idiot."

And he's not old, I add silently, as Mick maneuvers me so my back is resting against his chest. One arm comes around my waist, holding me in place.

"Maybe he's *not* so old," he says reflectively. "He was looking at you like he wanted to gobble you up."

"Don't be ridiculous." It's too warm to be this close. I don't want to wriggle free because I'm almost certain I can feel him against my bottom and I don't want to inflame the situation.

He kisses my neck. "What about welcoming me back and going to dinner?"

How many invitations can a girl turn down in one day?

"Madame doesn't like us to miss meals," I remind him. "I pay for this."

"A girl with a trustee can afford to waste a little money." Mick lets go abruptly and I stumble forward. "I thought you would have missed me, but you look like you've had a fine time." He grabs my bare arm. "You didn't get a tan like that in Paris. Are you sure your *trustee* didn't take you away for a little fun in the sun?"

I whirl around, filled with sudden fury. "Since you weren't here," I spit, "I went to visit a friend in the south. Julian Armitage had nothing to do with it, other than advancing the money for my train fare."

"Ah, Julian," he drawls. "The perfect name for that gray old stick. It's a shame there's no place for him in my novel. I'd kill him off."

"Well, you're not the only one who writes fiction." I reach past him for the doorknob, grateful that Madame has not been downstairs to witness all this. "I might kill off a rude American in my next story."

August 19, 1946

Dear Pearl,

Thank you again for coming to lunch with me last week, and for generously sharing your water lilies.

I apologize if I overstepped by asking you to dinner. After having already spent your afternoon with a tiresome old man, I can understand your reticence in agreeing to extend what must have been an extremely long day.

Congratulations again on having a story accepted by the Saturday Evening Post. *Your uncle would be proud of your achievement. If it matters at all, I am proud of you, as well.*

I will be in Paris again in early October, should you wish to subject yourself to another meal with your trustee.

Julian Armitage

August 22, 1946

Julian,

You are ridiculous. I was tired, but not of you. I needed to eat my dinner at the hotel so as not to disappoint Madame and ended up disappointing you instead.

Honestly, even though I'm afraid of her, I am sad that I let you leave thinking I didn't want to spend more time with you. Please give me another chance in October. I offer a resounding yes to any invitation.

And you are not old. You are older, which is not the same thing at all.

Pearl

When I see him next, Mick is over his petulance. Because I am more interested in writing than rehashing his bad behavior, I let it go, focusing on my notebook. When he sees how intent I am, he asks what I am working on.

"I don't want to talk about it yet," I tell him. "I'm afraid I'll jinx it."

The story is going surprisingly well. It already had been, but somehow, my conversation with Julian made the words flow even more easily. There is no one in the manuscript who resembles him, but I fully intend to take out my frustration with Mick on the character of my grandfather.

"Are you going to tell me where you were?" He turns his cup in the saucer. "I told you where I was going."

"My friend has a house in Gassin," I say with a shrug.

His eyes widen. "So while I was drinking cheap whiskey and refighting the war with my buddies, you were gallivanting around the Riviera?"

I smile tightly. "That's about the size of it. It's a shame you'd already left, she told me I could have brought a friend."

There was no need for him to know that she hadn't, only to realize what he had missed.

With a snort, he puts his head down, paying attention to his writing instead of mine. I'm not working on *The Choices We Make* today; I'm putting the finishing touches on *A Match of Mistaken Identity*, the story inspired by my night with Luc. Unless I am wrong, it's good. Possibly very good—pointed and sharp and drawing attention to all the ways men and women mislead each other. Very possibly no one will touch it, but I feel better for having written it down.

August 26, 1946

Darling Grace

Here's a new one for you. I was going to hold it until I came home, but I think it might be too good to wait that long. Let's see if your magic works. Start with the Post *this time, and if it gets rejected, then send it to the rest of the list. Maybe they'll accidentally say yes again.*

Christmas is coming, little sister. There will be something extra in my box for you.

P

September 1946

Autumn arrives in a ballerina swirl of leaves and crisp mornings. The air smells of smoke, although it is too early to build fires and waste wood, which will undoubtedly be in short supply as soon as everyone remembers that winter follows fall.

On chilly days, I wrap a red scarf around my neck, thrust my hands in my pockets, and walk the streets as I haven't since I first arrived, discovering new neighborhoods without seeing anything beyond the tale being enacted inside my head.

Brigid's story pours out of me, at the café and when I return to the hotel, the pile of sheets beside Mona growing each day. When I go to bed, the light from the window falls across the pages and I drift off thinking of the scenes I will write the next day, after several miles of walking.

I write to Mama, telling her I've found a way to tell Solange's story *and* her mother's, and that I can't wait for her to read it.

My departure is scheduled for mid-April. If I keep up my current pace, I will have a completed draft by then. It won't be perfect, but it will be done. I've never attempted a novel before, and it still surprises me that I've apparently managed to write one. Or most of one.

Afternoons are the best time to type, but I can write any time. I come in, kick my shoes under the chair and settle on the bed, the pillow between my back and the headboard. My notebook braced on my knees, I review what I've written to decide if it is worth transcribing, and then I type like a madwoman until people start coming home from work. In the afternoon, no one but the old couple on the second floor is around to be bothered by the noise, which, according to Madeleine, echoes down the spiral stairs like machine gun fire.

I have gotten as far as the breakdown of Brigid's second marriage. Never having met my grandfather, I give him Mick's magnetism and controlling personality, along with a weakness for drink that is accurate to them both.

The babies kept coming. They both knew how to prevent them, but Mart didn't want that, even as Brigid told him how hard it was to keep up with a baby on her hip and two more clinging to her skirts. They fought often. Occasionally he struck her, and then she apologized and let him back into her bed. It was too hard, otherwise, to have a man in the house like a glowering thundercloud, waiting always for the next rumble or flash of violence.

He wasn't that different from her father, who'd been the reason she married Frankie. There hadn't been a sweeter boy in her village, and Brigid knew from childhood she wanted a husband who would never hit her. And he hadn't, but her instincts misled her the second time around. Or rather, she'd let her instincts lead her instead of her common sense, so maybe she deserved what she got.

The priest intervened on her behalf; she'd asked him not to, because Mart didn't like anyone meddling in what was his. On the rare occasions that her husband went to church, he came home in a filthy mood. Brigid put herself in his way, so his rage wouldn't reach the children first.

"You have to stop trying to talk to him," she said in the confessional the following week, one hand pressed to her sore ribs. "What's broken in him is too far gone even for God. All you do is make him angry."

"No one is beyond God's help," the priest's musical voice chided. "Let me try a different tack, Brigid."

What then, she wondered? Would Mart try a different tack? Would he strike her face instead of her body? Would he hurt her babies?

"Don't bother," she said shortly. "I made this bed, and in it I shall lie. You talk to him much more, it'll be a coffin I'll be lying in."

Mick hasn't mentioned Remy or Vera since our argument. I've given him little opportunity, varying my arrivals at the café so we're not always there at the same time. I don't give up going entirely—my creativity appreciates a routine—but my tolerance for his company has decreased.

If I spend time with him, I would rather it be in the evenings, when I've finished writing for the day and am in need of some kind of distraction. That distraction is provided by either dinner or dancing, almost always with others. Frequently we go out with Cécile and her current beau; that way I'm almost guaranteed to avoid a wrestling match on the front step. Mick hasn't pushed the subject of my avoidance, for which I'm grateful. There is enough in my life right now that the idea of negotiating with him over my body or my time is exhausting.

It's something new for me, examining my family under the lens of story. I've written things based on real life before—my evening with Luc, a story Dan brought back from his hobo summer—but this is personal. It is uncomfortable to think about Granny like this, but I also feel that it's necessary.

She was an important part of my childhood. Mama worked outside when I was small, until the babies started coming steadily, and Granny raised me in the kitchen as she did chores. She never taught me anything so much as she let me absorb what she did, correcting me gently when I forgot to punch down the dough or failed to add enough salt to the soup. We cleaned the house together, top to bottom, a never-ending task in a mining town. I can hear the songs she sang as she polished the floors and washed the windows, hymns and Irish songs like *The Parting Glass* and *The Wild Rover*.

Granny taught me one more thing: after God and the Holy Roman Catholic Church, family is the most important thing in the world. Honoring them meant taking care of my brothers and sisters, being a help to my mother by learning to sew, and being a bright light for my father, who spent his days in darkness.

All good lessons, but a heavy burden for a little girl. I'm beginning to learn how much those lessons have weighed on me.

I was eleven when she died. Up until then, none of us knew she'd been married before. A few more years and we might have questioned how someone named Kovaleski had come from Ireland. It makes me wonder how many of her stories were misinterpreted because we were too young to understand. I walk and think and remember things that she told me, memories I thought were lost, and I come back and write them down.

Brigid—and Granny—come to life on the page. Brigid has her petite build, which made people wrongly assume she was weak. I give her dark hair and blue eyes and a whip-smart intelligence, along with a sharp tongue that gets her into trouble. And I give her a big heart, to love her people, and toughness to withstand all the pain in her life, often caused by the people she loved.

After some thought, I give her another love, one whose existence I can only speculate is true. Father Thomas, I call him, the town priest, based on our Father Dennis. Mama told me that Granny once said the one man who took her fancy was the one she couldn't have, and so she chose my grandfather instead.

Though I'm not writing a romance, I feel that this unrequited-love-turned-lifelong-friendship was even more important than her marriages, and I rework the scenes between Brigid and Tom to show that. Father Dennis was there for Granny whenever she needed him, for baptisms and funerals, confession and companionship. He'd prayed with her not long before she died, and at her funeral, his voice was thick with tears.

I remember sitting on his knee in the kitchen while they drank tea and talked over the state of the world. None of their conversation remains—I was too small—but I felt warm and safe. Children's instincts are rarely wrong.

Brigid meets Father Tom in the church, where she immediately goes upon learning of her husband's death. He takes the baby from her and lets her pray, and once she's off her knees, he feeds her tea and sandwiches in his office and tells her about a job at the hotel. She spends the night with his housekeeper, a suspicious woman who is rightly protective of the priest. If left to his own devices, he would help everyone and leave himself without a crumb and the church without a penny.

She gets the job, as Granny did. It comes with a tiny room off the kitchen for her and her son. It's not much, but it will do until she saves enough to return to Ireland, even though Father Tom tells her there's no going back, that her path lies forward.

Then the men start coming around. One after another, smiling as she brings out the food, giving her compliments, trying to make her smile when she feels she'll never smile again. No more Irishmen, Brigid decides, if she ever takes another husband. Frankie is dead, and the only other man who appeals is married to the church. So much for Irish luck.

She makes it six months before Martin Finley swaggers into the dining room and sits at the single men's table. There's some dark magic to this man; she can feel it rolling off him as she brings the tray around. Brigid lasts a week before they go out walking, and it's barely a month later when they stand up in front of Father Tom. Their first child is born nine months from the day of the wedding.

I drop the pencil and shake out my cramped fingers. It's only notes that I've written, but the story will flow more easily for having it all down on paper, and a part of my brain feels lighter for having explored this slice of my family's past.

If I could ask for anything, it would be for Mama to appear at my door so I could get her opinion about what I'm writing. I've considered sending her a copy of what's already written, but she has so little free time. She responds to my letters as quickly as the mail allows, but that's different from reading a manuscript and telling me where I've gone wrong.

That conversation can wait until I get home. For now, I need to do this on my own. I'm beginning to believe that my future depends on my ability to examine and deal with not only my past, but that of the women who came before me.

September 5, 1946

Dear Julian,

I must thank you again for all your encouragement. It means more than you can possibly know.

We did not talk much about my trip over lunch, as I was too busy asking questions, but I want to tell you now. Gassin was wonderful, not only because of the sea and the sun (though I enjoyed those greatly, along with Miss Gold's hospitality), but because I finally figured out how to write the book I've had in mind for months now.

Originally, it was based on something one of my French friends told me, but I could live here for fifty years and not be French enough to write about a French person. I've taken the bare bones of that story and found a way to fit it around characters I do know—my mother and grandmother. It's been very hard but also rewarding.

Why am I telling you? Because you've been so supportive about my writing, but also there is no one here who will understand. Madeleine, Madame's daughter, would be closest, but she's so busy that I don't want to bother her. Also, she's not a reader, so when I told her that people appear in my head and talk and I write things down, she looked at me like I was a crazy person.

I'm not crazy. Or not very. When I'm writing, I feel like I'm at my most normal, because I don't question myself until I look up from the page. Then I wonder if it's all foolishness, but I keep going anyway, because I can't be certain until it's done.

It's been interesting, turning over my grandmother's life and wondering who she would have been if her first husband had lived. I wouldn't be here to write this story, obviously, but I'm thinking purely about Granny. Would she have been as careful, always assuming that something was going to go wrong, because it always had? Yesterday I remembered that I'd once found dollar bills pasted into her Bible against emergencies. As my father was away and there was no money coming in, they were a blessing. Would a woman who hadn't been on the verge of losing everything all her life have done something like that?

Enough. You're a busy man and you don't need to hear about all this. I started this letter to tell you about my book, which has consumed nearly all my waking thoughts, and to thank you for the spending money for my trip. (I definitely should have done that in person). Miss Gold loaned me everything I needed, but I did treat myself to several café lunches as I rode to and from the beach every day. I know. I should be more extravagant, but I don't think it's in me. (See above about the dollar bills).

When will you next appear like Father Christmas and take me to dinner? I've been very busy and am in desperate need of a treat.

Pearl

The rain caught me on my way back from the café. Madame is tucked into her alcove, safe from the damp, and she and Pepe exchange glances as I trot past, my hair in my eyes and my ever-present notebook tucked under my sweater to protect it.

I run up the first flight and lean in the door to check for mail. Once I'm upstairs and in dry clothes, I won't want to move again until dinnertime.

"Pearl!" Madeleine is behind the desk for a change. She waves a white envelope to catch my attention. "Look at this!"

She hands over the square white envelope as if it were an invitation from the King of England. Tearing it open, I see something nearly as impressive.

THE HONOR OF YOUR PRESENCE
IS REQUESTED AT THE MARRIAGE OF
MISS BONNIE JOYCE EVERLY
TO
VICOMTE LUC OLIVIER REYNAUD
ON
SATURDAY, NOVEMBER 23 AT 10:00
ÉGLISE SAINT-SULPICE, 6ÈME ARRONDISSEMENT, PARIS
FOLLOWED BY A RECEPTION AT
HÔTEL PLAZA ATHÉNÉE
25 AVENUE MONTAIGNE, 8ÈME ARRONDISSEMENT, PARIS
HOSTED BY MR. AND MRS. RONALD EVERLY

"He's sent me an invitation to his wedding," I say, stunned.

"Who?" Madeleine reaches for the card, running her fingernail over the raised calligraphy. "Who has time to write invitations like this?"

"The vicomte. The one I made the dress for."

"The one you failed to seduce?" She leans her elbows on the desk, smiling as she recalls the story that I gave them all the next morning.

I look around to make sure the room is empty. "Come over here."

Once we are at the window table, I tell her, my voice lowered, "It wasn't that I failed to seduce him. He failed, as well."

"How?" Her brows raise. "He is a vicomte."

Apparently, a title is all that it takes to be considered a success. I want to ask what happened to the French spirit of revolution that had cut off the heads of so many titled men, but I do not, choosing to instead enjoy the warmth that has grown between us. I understand it, I think; her life, such as it is, is confined to the hotel, her husband, her mother. Their American resident, with all her questions, is an amusement for Madeleine.

"He was under the impression that I was rich." I fish a pack of Gitanes from my bag, shake one out and offer it to her. After a quick glance at the door, she accepts. "When he found out I was not, he lost interest."

I tell her of his family's lost fortune and that I sent him south to my friend Mary Jayne in order to find a properly-funded wife. She weeps with laughter, choking on her cigarette, until Madame's voice echoes up the stairwell, inquiring as to our health. We cling to each other, laughing, until it is time to set the tables.

While I am very fond of Remy and Cécile, sometimes they strike me as a different species entirely. Talking to Madeleine isn't the same as having Mama or Hazel or Peggy, but we understand each other; raised in France, I might very well have *been* Madeleine, tied to my mother and her choices until death did us part.

I tuck the invitation into my bag and look at my bedraggled reflection in the window. "I don't look like someone invited to such a fancy wedding, do I?"

September 13, 1946

Yesterday, while talking to Madeleine, I learned something that makes me look at her and Madame in an entirely different way. I was keeping her company while she cleaned, trying to help and asking questions (as usual). We were talking about the Occupation and for some reason I asked about the roundups. Since I'm not writing about Solange any longer, it doesn't matter. But like I told Julian, I'm curious, especially about things that could never happen at home.

At least I hope they couldn't happen. But I'm sure the French never expected the Nazis to do what they did, either. Never to say never.

She paused in her endless polishing, then asked why I wanted to know things they all preferred to forget.

They might prefer, but they aren't successful; most of the Parisians I've spoken to are haunted.

"They happened," she said finally. "Jews, yes, but not always. Trouble-makers, students, communists. People stupid enough to protest." She leaned on the table, her eyes far from the dining room. "The roundups were bad, but the arrests were worse, because they came at any time, for any reason."

She has suffered so much. Her brother in a camp, her husband damaged (beyond repair? I don't know). Her demanding mother. Trying to keep the hotel afloat until the war ended.

Madeleine told me Philippe was in a café when a party of German soldiers entered. He threw down his money and walked out. They came after him. Such a small act of resistance, for which he'd been sent to a prison camp for three years.

I made the mistake of asking if it had been the same for her brother. No one will say more than that he is dead.

"Marcel was not sent to a prison camp," she told me. "That is the story Maman wishes us to tell."

Such a conversation required more than a sympathetic ear. I dug into my bag and produced my last Hershey bar, kept against such an emergency.

She unwrapped the bar and snapped off a piece of chocolate before saying, "He was arrested, that much is true. But it was the Gestapo, not the police." Her eyes are closed in unwilling pleasure at the rare taste of chocolate. "They came here, to the hotel, hammering on the door in the middle of the night. All the guests were dragged from their beds and forced to show their papers."

I try to imagine the scene: the scared residents, mostly women, fumbling down the stairs in the dark, the harsh German voices driving them on. The scent of fear in the air.

"We were assembled in this room," she goes on, her voice as even as the tale is horrific. "Maman, me, Marcel's wife, Vivi. Six guests, including the Fauchers."

The elderly couple from the second floor chose to remain at the hotel after such an experience! No wonder Madame is kind to them.

Marcel was their target. He was not there, though he should have been. The Gestapo held everyone at gunpoint until he returned in the early morning. My stomach turned over at the thought of being trapped in this room... waiting.

Madeleine covered her face with her hands, then lowered them slowly. Her eyes were dry. She has no tears left. "Marcel opened the door, saw them, and turned to run. Vivi screamed. One of the Germans struck her in the face. Instead of escaping, Marcel threw himself on them in her defense." A tiny shake of her head. "They beat him, put him in handcuffs, and dragged him down the stairs."

There had been no mention of Vivi before this. I asked what happened to her.

"She followed them down the stairs, screaming to let him go. They shot her." Madeleine's voice was completely flat. "In the morning, Maman scrubbed her blood from the front step and sat in her chair as she always has."

I don't even know what to say. How to look at Madame or Philippe or anyone who ever again. I will never be capable of writing about this. I've known hard times, but I have never, as they have, known true evil.

The invitation is propped on my dresser, where I can see it every time I enter the room. There was a second, smaller card tucked inside, along with a stamped envelope. It begs a response, which I have not yet given. I have written to Mary Jayne, asking if she has received a similar invitation, and if she intends to come to Paris for the wedding. It will be easier to attend if I have company; we can sit in the back of the church and snicker, if it comes to that.

I wonder about Bonnie Joyce Everly and her proud parents, Ronald and Jean. Will they drive Luc mad, or will he be so happy to have his fortunes restored by their money that he will put up with their ways? His mother, I think, will be a challenge for a young American girl. Without having met Madame Reynaud, I know that any woman who forced her son to maintain a pretense of wealth in order to snare a rich bride will be a less than forgiving belle-mère, a title that sounds far more pleasant than mother-in-law.

It had to have been Luc who put me on the guest list. How do I RSVP to such an invitation? It is a social situation as complex as anything in a Jane Austen novel, had Miss Austen's characters ever been so vulgar as to make love before being united in holy matrimony by the local vicar. Although I do have my suspicions about Lydia Bennet.

What would Miss Austen's recommendation be in such a situation? I cannot ask Miss Austen, but there is someone who will be able to advise me.

September 20, 1946

Dear Aunt Claire,

You have always been my ideal as far as how to behave in society, and boy, do I have a puzzle for you.

When I first came to Paris, I was introduced to a vicomte at one of Miss Gold's parties. He was DASHING. That's the only word for it until I can think of a better one. Tall, dark, dreamy. The kind of eyes that make your knees weak.

Anyway, we met once, and then, months later, ran into each other on the street. He invited me to dinner at his home (I thought it was a party. It wasn't) and it turned out he got the complete wrong end of the stick in that he thought I was as rich as she was, and he was desperately in need of a rich wife.

Me, rich! Me, married to a vicomte!

Obviously, there is no ring on my finger, and that's fine. I could never marry a man who is prettier than me. But I sent him to Miss Gold and asked her to find him an American bride, which she has done. And now I've got an invitation to his wedding!

Do I go? What does one wear to the union of a French noble with an American girl named Bonnie Joyce? Do I attend the wedding and not the reception? It's at the Plaza Athénée, which terrifies me as much as the Ritz. I won't know a soul except the groom and possibly Miss Gold, and there will be enough silverware to paralyze me with confusion.

Help? I don't know if this will get to you in time for you to reply. It should, as the mail seems to be running more smoothly, but anyway, I look forward to receiving any advice that will make me feel less like an idiot.

Love,

Pearl

October 1946

"How long are you planning to stay in Paris, anyway?" Mick leans forward in his chair, one elbow on the table, his fingers spiked through his shaggy hair. "We've never talked about it."

"I'm leaving in April." We *had* talked about it, but it was so long ago that he's forgotten. "I have a year."

"That's not long enough to accomplish anything."

"It is for me." My dreams of home, of my sisters and brothers, have become increasingly frequent. Once I woke abruptly, thinking I'd heard Mama's voice. "I miss my family."

"I'm never going back to the States." He shovels the last of his croque monsieur into his mouth. "The army taught me that much."

"Why didn't you stay in, if you liked it so much?" I've never bothered to investigate Vera's claims that he wasn't in the army at all; at this point, I'd prefer not to know if he's been lying to me, and everyone else.

"I did my time," he said, pushing the plate away. "I didn't want to be part of the occupation forces, helping the Germans rebuild what we bombed into oblivion, and I sure as hell didn't want to be a target for every fraulein who wants food she can turn around and sell on the black market."

"They're hungry," I say, thinking of Solange, of Brigid. "The same as the French were." I have no sympathy for Nazis or even most Germans who took the path of least resistance, but he is talking about girls like Remy, who grew up during the war and have known little else.

"Then let them prey on the Russkis." He tips back the last of his wine. His ink-stained hands are too big for the delicate glass. "There're enough of them to keep every German skirt busy from now until 1950."

I busy myself with a piece of bread, so I don't have to look at him. Mick is attractive and full of life and he talks about all the things I should care about—art and literature and culture—but there is a hardness in him that I can't get past. The solution is to ignore it until the sensation passes.

Realizing that I've stopped listening, he takes my hand, turning it palm up. Tracing the veins of my wrist with a fingertip, he says, "I thought we'd go into the country this weekend. Conroy is getting married. The poor bastard is off to meet the fiancée's family, and so long as his car's back by Sunday night, he won't even know it was gone."

I sink into the feeling of his rough fingers on that delicate area of skin. It makes my stomach flip in a way not unlike how I felt my first night at sea. And I am at sea now, drowning in something I don't want to feel, though every time I've forgiven Mick, it has led me farther down this path.

If I go with him... I can see it, like that flashback scene from *Casablanca*: the two of us in a rickety French car, speeding down a dusty country road, my hair blowing in the breeze. Mick will sign the hotel register *Mr. and Mrs. Rafferty* and we will eat a delicious supper at a café on the edge of a sandy boules court filled with old men who look up from their game to watch the American couple who are so much in love.

Except that we aren't.

"I can't." The regret in my voice isn't wholly feigned. "I'm meeting my trustee on Friday."

Julian's letter arrived three days ago. As I haven't found time to answer yet, he will be in Paris before my response can reach him. Still, I had flat-out asked him in my last letter to take me to dinner, so I can hardly refuse, nor do I want to.

"Tell the old man to find some other girl to wine and dine." Mick stops doing distracting things to my wrist and picks up his cigarettes instead.

"You've got a previous engagement." He draws out the word as if being engaged is somehow worthy of mockery. "Don't you, babe?"

"I'm sorry. I really am." I lick my lips. "But I promised. You never mentioned anything about going away."

His hand crashes on the table, making the glasses jump. "I couldn't, could I? I didn't know the car would be available until today."

"I'm sorry." My voice gets smaller each time I apologize.

Mick's eyes narrow. He gestures to the waiter for more wine. "If you were really sorry, you'd change your plans. You can't put this off forever, Pearl, no matter what you think happened to you as a kid. And now"—he covers my glass to prevent it from being refilled—"you'll have the whole weekend to spend with your trustee! Do you think he'll treat you any better than I would? Afterward, you can go back to your hotel and write a pretty story about it. Maybe you'll be able to sell that one. I hear the ladies' magazines can't get enough of girls being rescued by rich old men."

"That's unkind." I slip my jacket over my shoulders and pick up my bag. If I don't leave, I'll either shout at him or cry, neither of which I want to do, and certainly not in public. "I've done nothing to deserve that."

My voice doesn't wobble. I won't think about the way he touched my wrist or the times he kissed me in the stairwell and turned my knees to jelly or what might happen in a battered iron bedstead in a village twenty miles outside Paris. Instead, I think of Julian—steadfast, kind Julian—who would never behave so crudely.

"Haven't you?" Mick raises his glass. "Then like our taste in literature, darling, we'll have to agree to disagree."

October 8, 1946

Why does he keep doing this? Inviting me places at the last minute and then getting angry because I have other plans? I hate that about him. The fact that almost every time I've said no to him has been because of Julian really winds him up and I either end up defending him (he's not old) or I say nothing, which makes me feel terrible, because of all the people I've met since leaving home, Julian is the kindest. He certainly wouldn't throw a tantrum and say vile things if I turned down a date. As a matter of fact,

I turned him down and he was as polite as could be. I can't imagine him banging on tables and saying the kind of things that Mick said.

Why have I put up with him? That's a better question than why he does things. I don't control him, only myself. And I've allowed this relationship to drag on when I should have ended it months ago, because when he's not being cruel, I enjoy his company. But that's not enough. Mama raised me better than to allow myself to be treated like this. She would certainly never allow it.

Did Granny ever want more for Mama? Or was she satisfied that her daughter married for love? Granny understood Mama's choices, unlike Aunt Claire, who not only married up, but away. She never talked much about Aunt as an adult, though she told me so many stories about her as the sweetest yellow-haired little girl. When she talked about Mama, it was as if she were a grownup, no matter how far back the stories went. And Mama wasn't even the eldest daughter. But she was the one who stayed.

Mama always made a point of thanking me when I helped her. She treated me like her daughter, not as another adult, and I see now what a difference that makes.

My mind is going in circles. How did I get from Mick to Mama? I shouldn't ask that, because the answer is obvious.

Three days later, as I dress for my dinner with Julian, I'm still angry. The rational part of my brain knows I made the right decision. Not only do I want to see Julian, but I've begun to fear the power I've given Mick. His careless cruelty proved me right, but it's difficult to remember that when I wake up from a dream of his hands on my body. It's good I never allowed that to happen; it would be harder to break up with him if we'd made love.

And that is what I've decided to do. Tomorrow, on the strength of an enjoyable night out with Julian, I will meet Mick at the café and tell him things are over between us. I dread it, but it must be done.

To cheer myself up, I put on the red flowered dress which proved lucky aboard the *S.S. Oregon*. I've barely worn it since, out of some misplaced sentimentality. It's one of my most flattering dresses, aside from the green crepe and black velvet, neither of which are suitable for a bistro dinner.

Why shouldn't I wear it for Julian? He's bound to take me somewhere nice.

I take my hair out of its pins, loosen the curls, and screw on the gold earrings that were Aunt's bon voyage present. I take more trouble over my makeup than usual, patting on light foundation and a touch of rouge, then covering my lashes with the black mascara Remy insisted I purchase. It suits me surprisingly well to have dark lashes around my pale eyes. The final touch is a coat of my cherished Elizabeth Arden lipstick.

At seven, a bell echoes up the stairs: five distinct clangs. A visitor for me. I catch up my coat and gloves and slowly make my way down, not wanting to twist an ankle or arrive on the landing in a tangle of arms and legs.

Julian waits in the reception room, a beautiful Chesterfield coat folded over one arm. We exchange kisses. He smells of cold air and a light, leathery cologne.

"Are you ready?" he asks. "I have a taxi waiting downstairs."

Madame's indrawn breath at such extravagance is audible. I give her a sidelong glance as I place my hand on his arm.

When the taxi turns into the Place Vendôme, I look questioningly at Julian.

"You deserve a treat." Which is his unspoken way of saying he knows I eat nothing but cheap café food and whatever Madame puts on the table.

"I've never eaten at the Ritz." Mary Jayne had taken me to the bar during my first week so I could experience the Paris she knew and loved. It had been intimidating enough; now I wish I'd worn one of my nicer dresses, as the restaurant will likely scare me to death.

"It's a treat for me, as well. The shortages are as bad in London. Only the rationing system makes it feel less chaotic."

The French black market is far more organized than their rationing system; I have no idea how Madame does what she does with the tickets we hand her each week. The few times I have ventured into grocery stores, the shelves were nearly empty, and more than once I've seen French housewives arguing outside a boulangerie over an extra baguette.

He offers his arm and as we pass through the wide front doors into the hotel, I can't stifle a gasp. Time has stood still here, the privations of the war invisible in the rich appointments and fine clothing of not only the guests but even the Ritz staff in their crisp uniforms and shining buttons.

The dining room is a world away from the austerity of my life at the Grand Hôtel Dauphine. Tables covered in crisp white linen dot the room, adorned with silver, crystal and fragrant fresh flowers. A low hum of conversation fills the space, punctuated by the clinking of glasses and the soft murmur of waiters. The mingled scents of perfume and expensive tobacco make for a heady mix.

Sconces and discreetly hidden lights cast a soft glow on the silk wallpaper and reflect off the polished marble floor. I try to walk quietly so as not to draw attention to myself, wishing instead that I could sink through its smooth, pond-like surface.

We are guided to a table with a clear view of the door, and my estimation of Julian's influence goes up. No one will be interested in us, but I can't resist such an opportunity to people watch, filing away my observations until I can write them in my diary before bed.

"Do you see over there," he murmurs, tilting his head slightly to the right. "The couple by the window?"

The man is fair, with fading blond hair and a dinner suit that I can tell, even from this distance, is of excellent quality. He is accompanied by a thin, sharp-featured woman with severely parted black hair and enough diamonds to decorate every woman in the Ritz dining room.

"Is that—?"

"The Duke and Duchess of Windsor," he confirms. "Haven't you run across them before?"

"We don't travel in the same circles." I try to imagine that attenuated, elegant couple at the Café des Grand Augustins and lower my face so he can't see my laughter.

Unfurling his napkin, he says under his breath, "The French are welcome to them."

The abdication, and the former king's marriage to an American divorcee made headlines even in Philadelphia, but it hadn't occurred to me how an Englishman would feel, watching his king shrug off his re-sponsibilities when it was clear that war loomed on the horizon. I didn't understand why he had been prevented from marrying whomever he wished, but I'd also been brought up not to leave a job unfinished.

"She doesn't look very American." I would never acquire that sort of polish with the company I kept. Millionaires versus midinettes. Royalty versus a man like Mick Rafferty.

I stop there, having vowed not to think about him tonight. Julian has brought me here; he deserves my attention. It's not just that, I *want* to pay attention to him. I enjoy his company, although he's never made me come alive with a glance or set me to trembling with a touch of his fingers. Then again, why would he? A man like him, older, well bred, wouldn't pay that sort of attention to a raw American girl whose emotional growth had been stunted by the war.

"She doesn't," he agrees. "All that money has taken the life out of her. When she first hit British society, she was a firecracker." As the waiter approaches, Julian raises his eyebrows. "Champagne?"

"Yes, please." Anything to get the everlasting tastes of chicory and cheap red wine out of my mouth.

The waiter returns with two brimming coupes, which is a disappointment. I want to watch him open the bottle, to see if he eases the cork out or lets it pop joyfully, like in the movies, with champagne flowing everywhere. I pick up my glass, inhaling the sharp, sweet scent, which to me always smells like luxury. "What do we drink to?"

Julian raises his glass. "To my being sent to Paris, so I have an opportunity to see you? Or something more aspirational, like the end of rationing?"

"We both know that won't happen anytime soon." I clink my glass against his and take a sip. "Here's to you visiting Paris."

With champagne to bolster my courage, I open the menu. It contains a vast list of dishes I've never had the opportunity to taste. I chew my lip, then swipe my finger discreetly across my teeth in case I've smeared them with Montezuma Red.

"Shall I order for us both?" He knows my discomfort with menus by now. "Is there anything you particularly don't like?"

I put the menu down gratefully. "I have no idea. I've never tried most of this."

"Then I'll order, and if you don't like it, we'll order something else." He lifts his chin and, with the sixth sense common to good waiters in any setting, ours appears.

As the men confer, I look discreetly around the room. I recognize no one other than the Windsors, but there are enough couture dresses and expensive jewels to finance the recovery of the French economy. But like the rich at home, the French are more concerned with their personal economies. It reminds me of Remy, her optimistic talk of communism and what it could do for France. From listening to Uncle and Dr. Max, I understand that communism also seemed like a good idea to the Russians, until it turned into the old system with a new name.

The first course arrives, to be eaten with the champagne: scallop mousseline with tiny ebony beads of caviar. I've never tasted caviar and I'm not sure what I think, but the dish is delicious all the same.

The rest of the meal is a parade of astonishments. Oysters—which I adore as soon as I understand how to eat them—with a white burgundy, followed by tender blanquette de veau. The veal is bathed in a sauce with so much real cream that I pause after the first taste because it isn't fair that anyone can eat like this if they have the money. There are buttery potatoes and braised leeks and more of the burgundy, which I like as much as the champagne.

Miniature souffles appear. The waiter calls them entremets, which Julian explains, after he has gone, is something served between courses.

"How much do they think we can eat?" I am almost uncomfortably full, but I can't bear to leave anything on my plate; it would be an insult to both the chef and those under rationing, who wouldn't get the scraps if I left them. I think of Hazel, who always ate before going out for dinner dates, so as not to appear to have an appetite. It's too late for that here. Julian has watched me wolf down three days' worth of food with an indulgent smile, while doing similar damage to his own meal.

Our conversation has been pleasant and somewhat scattered, as we have been as interested in the food as each other, but as Julian sits back to allow for the delivery of a selection of cheeses and crusty bread, he says, "We won't have time to see any of my favorite places this visit. I leave again in the morning."

"You're here for the day?" I think what a long journey it is for a meeting. No wonder he wants to have a nice dinner at the end of it.

"That's it." He nods at the plate. "Aren't you going to have any?"

I give in to the call of the brie, then the camembert. Eventually I say, "Stop me before the waiters have to carry me out." I blot my lips with the snowy linen, knowing that my lipstick is long gone. "That would be embarrassing, in front of royalty."

"The Duke and Duchess have left." Julian pushes aside his plate, having laid waste to his portion of the cheese. "And I would quite like to see that."

"Well, you won't." I flap my napkin at him. "Just for that, I won't eat another bite."

The waiter arrives and there is a quiet discussion, at the end of which a bill is tendered. Julian produces his wallet and counts out a stack of notes. He checks his watch.

"It's not ten yet. Do you want to have a drink at the bar? They make an excellent champagne cocktail."

"I think I've had enough champagne." My head is buzzing.

He rises obligingly to pull out my chair. "Would you prefer to go straight back or would you like to go somewhere else?"

Club Montez immediately springs to mind, but he would hate a jazz club. "Not really," I say reluctantly, as we head toward the door. "It's not something you'd enjoy."

"I think we've already established that we don't know each other as well as all that," he chides. "Where would you like to go?"

Taking a deep breath, I look at him. His gray eyes are clear as water, and there is no judgment in them. "A jazz club."

"You think I wouldn't enjoy that?" His eyes crinkle when he smiles. "I'm old. I'm not dead. Take me to your jazz club."

"Could you get my coat while I powder my nose?" Club Montez has one of those appalling Turkish toilets and I've had sufficient wine to not want to risk balancing over a hole in the floor.

The hotel in whose basement the club is located is no better than where I live, only in a livelier Left Bank location. We file down the steep staircase into a dark room filled with the reek of tobacco and inadequately washed bodies. Music washes over us like a wave and a smile breaks across my face before I can hide it.

Julian catches my hand and leads me to a miraculous empty table. "I saw that, you know."

"Saw what?" I slip my coat off; the room is warm and will grow warmer when the dancing starts.

"That smile." He removes his coat and hat, gesturing toward the club's sole waiter. "You haven't smiled like that all evening, not even when you tried your first oyster."

"I was afraid to, in there." I push back my hair. My hair is wilting from the heat. "No one else looked like they were enjoying themselves."

"They dine there so often, they don't remember that it's special." He accepts two glasses of red wine and passes one to me. "I didn't order this."

"It's all they serve," I tell him apologetically. "It's not bad."

He takes a sip. "It's not good, either. But the music makes up for it."

We listen without speaking. While his attention is occupied by the band, I watch him. Julian continues to surprise me—I was certain he would never agree to come to a place like this, yet he is listening with every evidence of enjoyment, his hand beating time on the tabletop, a neglected cigarette in his fingertips.

The tempo changes, and around us, people abandon their seats for the tiny dance floor. When I come here with Remy and Cécile, we dance with each other if there aren't enough men. I look around but see no familiar faces.

"Dance?" He crushes out his cigarette. "If we can fit."

I remember how I danced in this red flowered dress. "I'd love to."

We push through the crowd, making space for ourselves on the floor, and when he puts his arm around my waist, his palm is warm. I blink in confusion. It must be the wine, the way I can feel each separate finger through the fabric.

He's a good dancer, understanding within minutes the limitations of the space we are in, holding me closer so we don't get stepped on. I give myself over to the sensation of being held, my head resting against his cheek, my nostrils filled with the scent of his cologne, somehow still there through the club's abundant other smells.

"What are you doing for Christmas?" I feel the words as much as I hear them.

"Nothing special." I am trying not to think too much about the holidays and how much I will miss my family. "You?"

Julian pulls back enough so I can see his face. "My friend Felici-ty—Helen's sister—is having what she calls Orphans' Christmas," he says. "Not orphans, obviously, but friends whose spouses haven't been demobbed or who can't get away to their family homes for some reason. Waifs and strays, it's what she's good at." He cocks his head. "I thought you might like to join me."

"Join you?" I try to decipher his meaning. Is he asking me to spend Christmas with him—and his sister-in-law—because he feels sorry for me? Is this another aspect of his work? "I don't know..."

The music changes and he stops, holding my hand. "Let's reclaim our table before it's gone forever, shall we?"

Tucked into the corner, he turns so his back is facing the room, giving me all his attention. "What is it?" he asks. "If you have plans, you should tell me."

"It's not that." I turn the stem of the glass in my fingers. "I don't like people feeling sorry for me."

"Well, that's good, because I don't." He laughs quietly. "Pearl, while I invited you to come to London because I thought you might be spending the holiday alone, it's also because it makes me very happy to spend time with you." His hand covers mine on the table. "In case you hadn't realized that."

The warmth of his hand races up my arm. The noise level in the room rises with my heartbeat and I look over his shoulder toward the stairs, where two very familiar faces have entered the fray. Cécile is in the lead, wearing a dress I helped to alter. Looming behind her, his hands on her shoulders, is Mick.

"I need to leave." The words surprise me, but I can't be here, not with them. "My head aches."

Because the room is small and life is not fair, we pass so close on the way out that Mick sees Julian holding my hand and I see traces of Cécile's lipstick on Mick's mouth.

We are quiet in the taxi. I sit stiffly, holding back tears, my hands folded in my lap where they can't get me into any trouble. Julian knows something is wrong, but I don't know how much, if anything, he saw at the club.

"The young man back there," he says quietly. "The one whom it upset you to see. Wasn't he the man who was waiting for me to leave the last time I was in Paris, the night you wouldn't go to dinner?"

I hadn't realized he'd noticed Mick then. "Yes."

"Did my presence cause a problem?"

I press my lips together and take a deep breath, then tell him the truth. "No. He caused the problem. Not tonight, but other times. I'd decided to tell him I didn't want to see him anymore, but I think I've been saved that conversation."

He takes my hand. There is nothing possessive in the gesture this time, only an attempt to comfort. "Relationships are messy." After a pause, he says, "Since you appear to think I'm some sort of paragon, it might help to know that Helen and I were having problems before she died."

"What sort of problems?" He is so easygoing; it is difficult to imagine something a woman could find fault with.

"My work, for one." He rubs his eyes. "Not the bank, my war work. It took me away from her too often, though I pointed out we would have been apart much more if I'd joined up."

Julian has never said what he did during the war, and I've begun to think he can't. With his family connections, it isn't a stretch to think he'd been pulled into something confidential. "She thought you should have come home every night?"

"I did when I could." A pause. "Most of the time. There were nights when it was easier to sleep at the office than go back to the flat and have the same argument."

"I'm sorry." Whatever his war work, I think it has little to do with why he is so self-contained. That must stem from his upbringing, or perhaps his perceived failures with Helen.

The cab stops in front of my hotel, and I move toward the door. This night will end in tears, whether over Mick or whatever it is that Julian wants to say. "I should go."

"Wait, please," Julian says to the driver. "I'll be right back."

He walks me to the door, his hand light on my upper arm. "I'm sorry the evening didn't go as smoothly as I'd planned," he says. "But I do hope you'll keep Christmas in mind."

"I will." When he leans in to kiss my cheek, I turn and our lips touch. I open the door before anything else can happen and run straight up to my room without stopping for breath.

The thought of facing Cécile in the dining room is unbearable. In the morning, I slip past the door and down the stairs. I can't go to the café, either, in case Mick is early. But when I walk to the tiny park at the tip of the island, he is *there*, leaning against the base of the statue of Henri IV. When he sees me, he springs to his feet.

"Pearl!"

I look at the calm space of trees and benches that, until now, has been one of my sanctuaries. "I don't want to talk to you."

"Pearl, you have to listen." Mick comes closer, grasping my arm.

"I have nothing to say to you." I twist away.

He walks backward in front of me, his expression pleading. "I went out with her because you made me mad. I came to the hotel to ask you to change your mind. She said you'd gone out, but that she was free. It's *her* fault."

That sounded like Cécile. "And no isn't a word in your vocabulary?"

"Not as much as it is in yours." His tone is suddenly spiteful. "You put me off and put me off and then go out with someone else. Cécile doesn't have your high standards."

Does he realize how that sounds? Unexpected laughter wars with my hurt feelings. I circle around him, showing neither.

Mick catches up, jogging alongside. "So I went to bed with her—so what? It didn't mean anything. The whole time, I was thinking of you."

"Then I feel bad for both of you. She deserves better than that."

By the time I reach the Pont Neuf, his steps have faded. His words take longer. Cécile could no sooner stop flirting than my sister could stop dancing; it isn't in her. I am angry, but the blame lands on Mick, who didn't have to ask her out. He certainly didn't have to sleep with her. And to blame us—me for not canceling my plans and Cécile for a bit of innocent flirting!

Enough, I think, ducking down into the nearest Métro station and purchasing a ticket. It doesn't matter where the train takes me. I need to get away.

October 1, 1946

Dear Pearl,

I've received your letter. Intrigue on intrigue—I'm sure there's more to this story than you've shared, and I hope you'll consider telling me everything when you come home. My sister's children have always been a joy, but to have you grow into a woman with whom I can exchange confidences is a pleasure I never anticipated.

Sofie was never a sharer. She still isn't. I suppose you know she's on her way home? I can only assume the trip was unsuccessful and she will tell me in due course. Has she written to you about it?

As far that invitation, if you haven't already responded, my suggestion depends entirely upon your relationship with the vicomte and how comfortable you will be in the presence of his wife and her family. Another consideration is whether or not you will have an escort to blunt the effects of the day. To be perfectly honest, I don't know if I'd have the courage to go by myself, or if I would need to. Is it necessary to see the door closed or is it enough to know that it is?

Anyway, St. Sulpice has a large square out front, and unless something has changed, at least two cafés where you could watch the wedding party emerge.

Just my two cents, darling. You will, I'm sure, do what's best for you.

Claire

Remy knocks on my door before dinner. "You are coming down to eat?" she asks directly. "Or are you scared of Cécile?"

"I'm not scared of her," I say, letting her in. "If anything, I'm hurt."

"Why?" She sits on the bed, her feet hanging above the floor like a child's.

Facing her in the armchair, I say, "Do you know what happened?"

"It is who she is," she says with a shrug.

"It is not who I am to forgive that."

"You are too intellectual. Too cold. You do not feel."

Stung, I say, "I feel plenty. Especially right now."

"Do you? You are angry with Cécile for taking your man, but she would not have been able to take him if you let him know that you felt love for him."

I think of Mick's expression when he saw me with Julian. But if he cared for me, would he have strayed? Perhaps I shouldn't have chosen to have dinner with Julian over seeing him, but it wasn't insecurity about my feelings that caused Mick to turn to my friend, it was a childish response to being thwarted.

During the long years of the war, when all my friends were falling in love, I kept apart, realizing that most young men would be like Cliff, wanting a quick marriage before going off to war. I think of Pat and Luc, both of whom enlarged my experience of love without touching my heart. What is wrong with me that I could go to bed with two men I barely knew, but kept the man I was dating at arm's length for months?

The problem is, despite my hurt feelings, that I don't love Mick. He's fascinated me, but I've begun to realize that fascination was almost like hypnosis. Because I was lonely, because he was American and a writer, I convinced myself that I enjoyed his company and his conversation. But he is not the only man whose company I enjoy. And conversation with Julian is less combative and far more interesting. He is a gentle, intelligent, and kind man, and he can discuss books and current events and the small moments of absurdity which make up our days without ever making me feel that I'm not enough.

Remy's bright eyes rest challengingly on my face. "Do you want him back? He doesn't have enough money to keep her for long."

"My vanity wants him," I say slowly. "But my heart doesn't."

"Why?" She cocks her head like a bird. "You've known him since when—June?"

"May." If I close my eyes, I can almost feel the impact of his arrival at the café. I've been off balance ever since, but lately I've started to feel the ground beneath my feet again. It happens every time I see Julian. "We want different things."

She laughs. "Well, he and Cécile want the same things."

I don't want to think about that. Just because I don't want him doesn't mean he should slot someone else into my place so easily.

"Doesn't it ever bother you?" I ask. "That she lets you play at lady in waiting, but she'll never love you back?"

"I have Vera." Remy folds her arms over her chest. "Or I will, when she comes back to Paris. And we were talking about you."

It is rare to get the upper hand with Remy. I can't hide my smile. "And now we are talking about you."

October 13, 1946

Dear Pearl,
As always, thank you for the pleasure of your company on Friday
evening. I hope that whatever distress you felt has faded and that you will
consider my invitation.

Julian

The weeks after my breakup with Mick are a mixed bag. I sometimes miss his company, but not how he made me feel about myself; I miss the café, but I'm not ready to share space with him; I miss my undemanding friendship with Cécile, but I can't bring myself to forgive her. Though why should I hold her to a higher standard than him?

Remy goes on as if nothing has happened. She sits between me and Cécile at the table and comes to my room most nights after dinner to sit on the bed, where we work on remaking a dress for her to wear out with Vera.

In late October, Remy brings news that both she and Cécile are leaving Lucien Lelong for a new house being opened by one of his assistant designers.

"He claims he is reinventing French couture." She leans back on her elbows, staring at the water stain on the ceiling.

"Is he?"

"I have no idea," she says with a laugh, "but the pay is better. And the directrice at Lelong said if he fails, we are welcome to return." Rolling over onto her stomach, she makes a pad from my quilt and rests her head on it. "I believe she expects him to fail."

The part of me that is my mother's daughter is fascinated by the idea of starting a couture house. I would like to question Remy endlessly about the atelier, the designer, and his plans, but I hold back, afraid of distracting myself.

I let *A Match of Mistaken Identity* go off to my sister without another thought, so when I received a letter with another check, it barely raised my head from Brigid. I took the check—sixty dollars this time, with an invitation to submit future stories—to the bank and deposited it, dashed off a letter to Grace, and fell back into my pages.

Being away from Mick's very specific ambitions for me has opened a door in my head. Words are flowing, nearly effortlessly, and the hours I spend alone in my room each day account for a growing stack of pages on the desk. I go over the manuscript again and again, making notes in the margins of ways to deepen the emotional moments of the story. The news of Frankie's death becomes more poignant, while Martin Finley takes on even more of Mick's attributes, both good and bad. I keep going until I run out of paper and then waste an entire afternoon scouring Paris for typing paper so I can continue working.

My plan—and I cannot believe my audacity—is to finish the book before the end of the year, perhaps before I go to England in December.

If I decide to go. I never gave Julian an answer that night, nor have I answered his brief note. He hasn't written again; he is, of course, waiting for me to respond, so I don't feel pressured.

What if Mick had thought of my feelings before his own? If he'd behaved that way, I'd likely have fallen in love with him, because it is astonishingly nice to have someone act as though you're the most important person in the world.

I wouldn't know what to do if it were genuine. Without my noticing, Julian has become embedded in my life, second only in importance to my family. But caring for him is as impossible as caring for Mick. I tick off the reasons: his position as my trustee; our age difference, which seems to bother him; the fact that he lives in London and I can't wait to go home.

Rubbing my eyes with the heels of my hands, I wonder why I'm even thinking about him this way. Just because he's said some things that could be interpreted to show interest doesn't mean that he's actually interested in me. I'm very fond of him, but that's the extent of it. I will miss him when I leave. Perhaps we'll exchange letters for a few months, but soon this period of being linked by Uncle Harry's bequest will be over and our connection will be severed.

Cécile catches me on the stairs on the way to breakfast. "Pearl."

I stop, cautious now of this beautiful girl whom I'd never taken seriously until she stole Mick away. "Yes?"

"You are angry with me." It is a statement, not a question. If she's not bright enough to figure it out, Remy will have enlightened her by now.

"I hadn't expected Mick to find someone so quickly after we fought," I say, trying not to notice the red marks of passion on her neck. "Or that it would be someone I thought of as a friend."

"And you expected what?" She exhales a laugh. "Men have needs."

"I hate that excuse," I say bluntly. "Men have needs and women give in to keep the peace. Well, I won't."

"It is not just them." Her voice is coy, the inflection I imagine her using with Mick. "There is much to be savored for us, as well. You should not hold your virtue so tightly. You will miss out on much in this life."

It wasn't that I had such a tight grip on my virtue—Cécile would be shocked to learn that her prim American friend had had two lovers, for no reason other than curiosity—it was the thought of surrendering specifically to Mick.

"Well," I say, since it appears she is waiting for me to respond, "you are welcome to him."

She looks up through her lashes. "I have a date tonight."

My nails dig into my palms. "I'm happy for you."

"Not with Michael." She winds a golden curl around her finger. "He told me I was stupid."

That is cruel even for him. "I'm sorry."

"C'est bon." She shrugs again. "In bed he is very selfish, thinking of his own pleasure before mine." Her red lips purse. "We can both do better."

I smile against my better judgment. "Thank you for saving me the trouble of discovering that for myself."

Her laughter echoes as she continues down the stairs. I remain on the landing, thinking, astonished, that in mere days she allowed him more leeway than I granted in months. If I'd given in sooner, he would have never gone with Cécile. But he took up too much of my mind and exercised too much control over my work. I am better off without him. I didn't come to Paris to find a man, especially one who doesn't take my writing seriously because it doesn't fit into the role he's constructed for me.

I will consider Julian's invitation again. I don't want to pass up an opportunity to see London, or him. After a few days of Orphans' Christmas, I can retreat to the city and go to the British Museum or Oxford or any number of other places: travel in England cannot be as terrifying as it was when I first arrived in France.

October 26, 1946

Dear Julian,

I'm sorry to have kept you waiting. If the invitation stands, I'll come to England for Christmas. I should have accepted immediately, instead of dithering.

And if you're certain my presence will be welcome. I don't know your friends and they don't know me, and I don't know if waltzing into their celebration (despite the whole Orphans' Christmas theme) is going to be comfortable for any of us. You have told them, haven't you? Warned them that I'm gauche and American and spend time in my head with imaginary people?

I don't mind being alone on the holiday. If I can't be with my family, it doesn't matter if I'm in Paris or London or the surface of the moon. And that doesn't mean I'm not grateful for your invitation, only that it's been a long time, and I miss them so much. I can stay here at the hotel if you prefer. Madame will cook for her family anyway and I can eat in the dining room.

That sounds pathetic, but it's progress. Once upon a time, I would have started my letter over with a plain yes or no.

So, which is it? Yes, I suppose. A nervous yes, so long as you convince me it won't be a terrible mistake.

Pearl

October 29, 1946

Pearl,

You are very much wanted here. If it were possible, I would transport your entire family to England, but as I cannot do that, I will transport you instead. On December 20, take the early train to Le Bourget. A friend will be waiting to deliver you to England, where plans have been made to distract you from your tristesse.

Please come. It will not be Christmas without you.

Julian

November 1946

When I slide into my chair, Remy is already at the table. "Is Cécile running late?" Generally, she is the earlier of the two, unless she's dressing for a date.

"She's in bed." Remy gestures with her fork. "Our employment with Monsieur Dior doesn't start until next week. Until then, Cécile intends to divide her time between dancing and sleeping."

"How does Madame feel about that?"

"We've told her it's temporary. The atelier opens on Monday." Remy takes a bite of bread and chews energetically. "I would still be at Lelong, if not for Cécile."

"What do you mean?" From everything they've said, Lelong was a good job, even though it didn't pay well enough for them to have separate rooms.

"When Monsieur Dior offered her a position, she refused to accept unless they took me, as well."

"Tell me about this Monsieur Dior." I spread butter on my bread and wait for her to finish chewing.

"He was an assistant designer," she says. "But he found backing for his own house, and he's been pinching the best workers from all the houses of Paris. Midinettes, mannequins, everything."

It is a testament to Cécile's skill—and her kindness—that she was able to wangle a position for her friend.

"I can't wait to hear about it." I have always assumed my creativity came from my mother, who can take fabric and stitch it into a dream of a dress, but she swears that sewing is a skill, nothing more. It is a skill, I think, as writing well is a skill, and one made better by practice. But Mama doesn't always follow patterns, and there is something in her that knows what best suits the wearer, even when it's not what they've asked for. It is a form of magic, that sort of knowing, and it's the same magic that finds me when a story is going well.

"I want to know everything—what it's like to set up a couture house, what your workrooms look like. Everything." My life here in Paris may have become all about writing, but I've never lost my interest in fashion, and it will give me something new to tell Mama.

Remy grins at me, childlike. "Maybe we can sneak you in. It was impossible at Lelong, but I'll try again."

I imagine the letter I will write if that occurs and cross my fingers under the table that Remy can make it happen.

I'M SO SORRY BUT I CAN'T COME TO THE WEDDING. DO ATTEND IN MY PLACE AND TELL ME EVERY RIDICULOUSLY AMERICAN DETAIL. HAVING MET HER PARENTS, I EXPECT NOTHING SHORT OF RINGLING BROS.

BISES,

MJG

I send my regrets to the Everlys without regret. If Mary Jayne had come to Paris, we could have gone together, but without her, I do not feel comfortable attending. What business Luc and I had is over; having instigated the matchmaking that brought it about, I do not need to witness his marriage.

Madeleine, who was personally invested in the vicomte, is disappointed by my decision. "I wanted to hear all about it," she laments as she delivers my breakfast. "You describe things so well."

"There's no real reason for me to go," I tell her. "Aside from curiosity. And I don't want to go to the reception alone."

"What about the church?" She puts her hand on the back of my chair, unwilling to let go of the issue that easily.

I think of Aunt Claire's advice. "What are you doing on November 23?"

I wait impatiently for Remy and Cécile to get home from their first day at Maison Dior. They trail in later than usual, both looking slightly stunned.

"How was it?" I hand them each a small glass of wine from the bottle I purchased that afternoon to celebrate their new positions. "You look tired."

"He is a madman," Remy says, at the same time Cécile says, "He's a genius."

The midinettes drink quickly, with Cécile looking expectantly at the bottle, as if to say that I must pay for my stories. I pour more wine all round and we carry the glasses over to our usual table.

"Remy first," I say. "Why is he mad?"

She slides down in her chair and tips her head back, looking like an exhausted child. "He wants to present the collection in February. At this moment, it is no more than a pile of sketches that we were not shown."

"They are amazing." Cécile is alert despite her obvious tiredness. "I have never seen such gowns."

Both girls' exposure to couture, even while working at Lelong, has been during the years of cloth rationing. This has, judging by Cécile's dazed smile, come to an end.

"How did you see them?" Remy's eyes snap open.

"Because I am above you." Cécile's smile is catlike; I can almost hear her purring. "We will no longer be in the same part of the atelier. I will be upstairs with the more skilled hands."

Remy makes a rude sound. "I'm not sure we weren't better off where we were."

"You, maybe." Cécile finishes her wine. "I like the money Monsieur Dior will pay me, and I like the challenge of these more complex designs. If I do well enough, perhaps someday I will have Madame's job."

Such ambitions are, perhaps, at odds with Cécile's habits, but I remind myself that she is only twenty-three. She has time to mend her ways before wine and late hours begin to show on her face. If she has landed a job that can make better use of her talents, she might not even mind.

"We'll see about that." Remy is skeptical. "When it gets in the way of your little love affairs, let's see how dedicated you are."

"At least I *have* love affairs." She pushes her chair away from the table. "Thank you for the wine, Pearl. I'm going to change."

Remy stays behind. "I have love affairs," she grumbles. "But Vera's away again, and it's not as easy for me as it is for her—or for you."

"Don't drag me into this." She needs no encouragement to poke her nose into my business.

"What happened with your Englishman?" she asks, right on cue. "Have you seen him since your break with the large American?"

I do appreciate that she rarely bothers to use their names. "Julian has invited me to England for Christmas," I say. "I said yes, but I'm not sure if I should."

"If you do not go, you will have lost your mind," she declares. "We are being given four days for Christmas, but Monsieur Dior says they are the last days off we will see until the collection is launched." She shakes her head. "I was better off at Lelong."

"You followed because she is your friend." I pat her arm. "Have you heard from Vera? Will she be back soon?"

My question does not put her off in the least. She drags an envelope from her bag and regales me with the contents of Vera's latest letter. By the time she reaches the part that makes her blush and fold the paper away, she has forgotten my love life entirely and I am able to read my letters from home.

October 15, 1946

Dear Pearl,

So... I have news. I'm pregnant! We're pregnant, that is. We weren't trying to be, not this soon, but accidents happen, right?

Press is over the moon, and I guess I will be once I'm done throwing up. Did your mom puke every morning for 30 minutes straight, whether or not she'd eaten anything? I thought I was supposed to gain weight but I'm getting skinnier because I'm sick all the time.

Everyone says pregnant women glow. I'm not glowing either. I have pimples and my hair won't behave, and I have to pee <u>all the time</u>.

But when all this is done there will be a baby, and he will be perfect, and maybe Press will stop having nightmares about the war and being grumpy all the time. I don't know if or when I'll ever get back to Dad's office, but we did want a baby eventually, so this is just a change of plan.

When are you coming home? My baby needs a godmother.

Hazel

The rain, which has drummed on the window and over my head for three days, has finally stopped. I lie still beneath the blankets, not eager to get up and wash at the sink. The stove is cold; I light it when I'm working, spending the time after dinner in the common room where the lack of coal is offset by the number of bodies.

It's been days since I've left the hotel; I've left my room only to eat and use the toilet. Hazel's letter, coming right before the gray skies and rain, put a pall over everything. I should be happy for her—and I am—but it just feels like one more bit of proof that everyone is getting on with their lives but me. I knew we'd never spend another night gossiping in my room about boys and dresses and dreams, but it never occurred to me that she would become a mother so soon.

I didn't want to think too much about how it felt to be left behind, so I threw myself into my writing until the mood passed. My story was no more uplifting, but it kept my thoughts from circling between all the complications my life has suddenly assumed.

Granny's story, as well as what Mama went through to keep us together after my father died, makes me realize the desperate lengths a woman will go to in order to protect her children. Even if it's something immoral, as in my grandmother's case, if it served the greater good of her family, she did what she had to do, prayed for forgiveness, and moved on.

I've decided to end my story with a wedding. Brigid can rest, knowing that her daughter's husband will assume the lease on the house and Kathleen will be taken care of. Should I foreshadow the tragedy to come or end on a happier note, knowing that attentive readers will understand that Kathleen is living her mother's life over again?

Enough. I sit up and throw back the covers, letting the cold air shock me awake. This clearing in the weather is perfectly timed: it is Luc's wedding day.

I dress carefully, brushing my dark coat and putting on my beret before going downstairs. The reception area is empty, but Madeleine's raised voice echoes from the family quarters. A moment later, Philippe scuttles out, looking shaken.

Madame's words are not as clear as her daughter's, but she has the edge on volume. Philippe leans on the counter, his hands over his ears.

"You can manage without me for one hour, Maman. I am going out."

I look inquiringly at Philippe. "Will Madame hold a grudge?"

"When does she not?" He looks worried but brightens as Madeleine walks calmly into the room, buttoned into a brown coat with a brilliant blue scarf tied around her neck. "Enjoy yourself, Madi."

"I shall." Rouge highlights her usually sallow cheeks, and as we leave, she snaps open a compact and carefully draws on a dark red mouth.

"You are a different woman," I say, looking at her.

Madeleine shakes her head. "I am who I always was, I just need to remember her. Now let us go before Maman chases me with a broom."

We walk to the Place St. Sulpice and take seats at an outdoor table directly across from the church doors. When the waiter comes, I tell Madeleine to order whatever she likes, as today is my treat in exchange for her company. She hesitates, then nods briskly, and tells the waiter to bring her coffee and a pain au chocolat. I order the same.

It is some time before the bells begin their joyous peal. I lean forward and wait for the doors to open. When they do, people in formal dress spill out into the square, some with cameras, others weeping into large white handkerchiefs.

"Why do they cry?" Madeleine murmurs. "No one has died."

At last, the bridal couple emerges. Luc is stunning in morning coat and striped trousers, a gleaming top hat resting on his equally shining hair. His eyes roam the square, looking for something. When he sees me, a slow smile spreads across his face. He raises two fingers to his brow in salute.

Beside me, Madeleine gasps. "He is so beautiful."

I lift my cup, then turn my attention to the bride. Awash in a billow of white satin, Bonnie Joyce Everly Reynaud is a brown-haired, pink-cheeked girl who does not look long out of the schoolroom. She clings to Luc's arm like a life preserver. Her doting parents, right behind her, could be a magazine ad for something wholesome and Midwestern, although if they have money enough to purchase a vicomte, appearances may be deceiving.

Off to one side, in stark contrast to the bride and ten young women in rose-pink gowns, is a tall, thin, staggeringly fashionable woman in black. The widowed mother, to whom this corn-fed American princess will be given over for training in the ways of the vicomtesse.

"Good luck to you both," I murmur, watching as the bridal party piles into a line of long black cars and glides off toward a financially secure future.

I order more coffee, drink it quickly, and walk back to the hotel with Madeleine. As we cross the bridge, it begins to rain. We run inside laughing, our hair wilting from the moisture, to find a florist's box on the desk.

White roses, carnations, and baby's breath, with trailing strands of miniature ivy. It is identical to the bouquet carried by Bonnie Joyce. The attached card reads simply "Merci."

November 24, 1946

I was glad to have Madeleine with me yesterday. It was a surprising blow to see them come out of the church. Not because I'm in love with Luc myself, but because it is one more example of everyone moving on.

Hazel's letter really bothered me. I wonder if she's quite so blasé about this pregnancy. Her mention at the end of not going into her father's office tells me that a small part of her regrets it or perhaps regrets the seven years she spent in college and law school, experience that will now be wasted as she changes diapers and comforts her husband.

Not that those things aren't worthwhile. I can't even explain myself to myself. But of all my friends, she was the one with real ambitions. Even though she always had boyfriends, we planned futures around what we were going to do, not what we were going to do with someone else. Now she's married and pregnant. Lenny's married, too, but she's working. Like me, she can't imagine not *working. Peggy's married to God and working harder than any of us.*

Not that many years ago, the four of us were inseparable. Now they're all scattered and married and I'm likely going to be an old maid. Please, God, let me be an old maid with a career as a successful novelist. Is that too much to ask?

December 1946

Despite shortages and rationing, Paris does its best to prepare for the festive season. Boughs of greenery appear on fences and in shop windows, although the merchandise displayed is not very festive. Madame skimps on meals in order to save up for a special dinner to be served the week before Christmas, as most of the residents will be returning to their families for the day itself.

I have purchased what presents I could and sent them off by Thanksgiving—a holiday not known in France, and which I observed privately by taking myself to dinner at Bistrot Romaire. I sent Julian a note afterward to let him know I'd finally begun to spend Uncle's money on more than the bare necessities.

His response contained congratulations and detailed instructions for my journey to England. Upon reaching Le Bourget, I should make my way to hangar number three, where I will be *flown* to London by a friend named Mel Baxter. "Don't worry," he wrote. "It's a short hop, and Mel is a capable pilot."

I am nervous about flying, but when I tell the girls, Remy and Cécile bounce in their chairs like excited children, and Madeleine, who has come out of her shell even more since the conflict with her mother, orders me to pay attention to every detail so that I can tell her everything upon my return in January.

"Every detail," she repeats. "What it feels like to be up in the air. How Paris looks from above."

"Oui, madame," I say with a salute. "Do you also want to know every detail about England?"

"Yes, of course!" She looks shocked. "And I want to hear all about how special your English gentleman made you feel."

I try not to think too much about my English gentleman and what this trip may or may not mean. There are less than four months before I return home, and I will not allow myself to get entangled, especially with a man who cannot be taken lightly. Julian deserves more than that; I will have to find a tactful way to discourage him, if indeed he needs discouraging. It may simply be his manner and I've taken him too seriously because of my own feelings.

I don't want to feel that way about him, any more than I wanted to be in love with Mick. They are very different men, but for me, getting involved with either would give the same result: I would be far away from my family.

As the holiday break approaches, the midinettes come home later and later each evening, hollow-eyed and exhausted, but also excited by the work they are doing.

"The whole house hums," Cécile says animatedly. "Not just the sewing machines. Monsieur Dior's genius has a motor, as well."

I laugh, thinking of the plump, shy man I saw sidling from the atelier when I met them after work one day. "Can you tell me more about the collection?"

"Not yet." Remy looks glum. "I see pieces, not dresses. Cécile gets to go in with the mannequin when a model is presented to Monsieur Dior, and he tears apart all the work that's been done and shows Madame Marguerite and the premier where they've gone wrong with his precious designs."

"You are too hard." Cécile plucks my pencil from the table and sketches a rough shape on a blank page in my notebook. "These dresses, Pearl, they are like nothing I've seen. It is why they are so hard to translate. The shapes, the fabrics... it is wondrous. There are two models. Not models, but shapes. *Corolle* is tiny in the waist"—her hands make a circle no bigger than my thigh—"and *Huit* is more fitted."

The wasp-waisted shape she has drawn has a voluminous, calf-length skirt. I turn the book toward me and study it, wondering if it is his design that is unusual or if Cécile simply cannot draw very well.

"Tell me what Remy means."

"Remy has not seen it," she says. "I have. Dresses are made in the workrooms, by many different hands. Some stitch sleeves, others, bodices. No one sees the entire dress except the premier, who heads the workroom, and Madame Marguerite, who stands as Monsieur Dior's technical directrice. She is the one to judge whether a design has been interpreted correctly. After much fashioning and refashioning, a dress is ready to be presented to Monsieur Dior.

"Sometimes it is as Remy says. He tears the design apart. Not literally," she hurries to add, "but he will say such cutting things that the premier is often in tears by the end. That is where Madame Marguerite's genius comes in, because she will elicit from Monsieur Dior precisely what it is that he does not like." She is standing by now, in the position of the mannequin who is being worked on as if she were a tailor's dummy. "Often it is something as small as the fit of a shoulder or an inch of sleeve length, and with the application of a few pins, all is resolved."

"What about the girls?" I ask. "The mannequins. How do they handle this barrage of criticism?"

"They hear nothing," Remy says with a laugh. "They are all busy planning their next night out or what they will cook for dinner. They're so shallow, if Cécile wasn't such a brilliant seamstress, she would have made an excellent mannequin."

Cécile elbows her friend, and they dissolve into laughter. I envy their bond, but I also envy their access to the wonderland of Monsieur Dior's atelier.

"My mother will be fascinated," I say. "Can I send her your sketch? I am going to write to her tonight. But first—what should I take as a gift for my hostess at Christmas?"

Their mirth ceases immediately as the serious question of a gift is considered.

"She is rich?" Cécile asks.

"I don't know." Julian said Felicity has a house in the country, but that could be anything from a mansion to a four-bedroom house not unlike where my parents live. "Possibly."

"Food or drink," Remy says. "The English are also rationed. Perhaps a nice cheese, one that won't stink up your luggage."

"I can't have that." I imagine the horror of arriving with all my clothes reeking of camembert. What an impression that would make!

I take the thorny question of the gift to Philippe; it is common knowledge that he has contacts in the black market. After listening to what I want, he considers for a moment, then writes an address on a slip of paper and gives it to me. The location is in the eighteenth, not far from the street market. I decide to make a day of it and see if I can find a gift for Julian while I am out.

The wine merchant is on a narrow, winding street. The front window is dirty and there is very little stock on the shelves. I wait at the counter, looking at the few unexceptional bottles of wine, until the proprietor appears. He is a whip-thin man with black hair and a drooping mustache.

"Bonjour, mademoiselle," he says, dusting his hands on his trousers. "How may I be of assistance?"

"I am looking for something special." Placing Philippe's paper on the counter, I say, "A friend gave me your name."

"Ah, Philippe." He touches his nose with one finger and his smile widens. "What is it that you require?"

I look around the empty shelves again, not certain what I want but equally certain it is not here. "I am visiting friends in England," I say. "I need a gift to... ease my entry into their society."

"I believe I have what you require." Disappearing behind a curtain into the back of the shop, he returns with a dusty, long-necked bottle with a bulbous base. "Armagnac. Distilled in Gascony in 1936."

"How is it here?" I examine the label. "I thought the Germans took everything."

"That could not be permitted." He grins, looking suddenly piratical. "We bricked up our best stock behind a false wall in the cellar."

"May I have this, please?" It doesn't matter what he's charging; I want to share this magical survivor with people who will appreciate its history. "And a gift for our mutual friend. Do you know what he likes?"

I leave the shop with two carefully wrapped bottles, one of the Armagnac and the other a narrow bottle of eau de vie de marc for Philippe. According to the merchant, it is form of brandy, made from pomace, the grapes left after winemaking. It was considerably less expensive than the Armagnac.

Back on the windy streets, I venture into the market, hoping it will be as easy to find something for Julian. I have no idea where his interests lie beyond food, wine, and sailing.

I browse books and prints and fountain pens, ashtrays made of marble and crystal and ceramic, cigarette cases and lighters and clever knives for cutting cigars. But he has a silver cigarette case and lighter already, and I don't know if he smokes cigars. I move on to a covered stall crammed with men's clothing, some of it new, the rest exquisitely old. Neckties and mufflers and gloves are laid out for my inspection. I purchase a particularly heinous paisley tie for my stepfather, whose terrible taste in neckwear is a running joke in the family.

Secondhand is fine for Dr. Max—he appreciates everything given to him—but I can't imagine giving something to Julian that has been previously worn. Unless... I glanced up at the elderly stallholder.

"Do you have any watches?"

"Oui, mademoiselle." He bends to a low shelf and presents a wooden tray, where six watches in varied condition are displayed on black velvet. Two are pocket watches, and I eliminate them from consideration; Julian's manner of dress is traditional but not archaic. The rest are wrist watches with leather or linked bands.

Leather, I think, because his cologne reminds me of leather. There are two watches marked Gruen, which the old man tells me is a Swiss company, and another which, when I squint, reads Fleurier.

"French?" The watch has a rectangular bronze face with small, neat numbers. Unlike the others, it does not need to announce its value by being showy.

"Also Swiss," he says. "From the early 1920s."

It is a lovely piece. I would wear it myself if it were smaller.

"How much?" I blink when he names a price far above what I expected. "Is that the best you can do?"

He cocks his head, weighing my taste against my wardrobe, and arrives at an estimate of the contents of my wallet. "For you, mademoiselle—"

Have I made a mistake? I wonder, riding back on the Métro with a neat leather case tucked into my coat pocket. Should I have spent almost two months' rent on a gift for a man I hardly know, even though I consider him to be a dear friend, if not more? I hear his amused voice telling me that my uncle's money is intended to be spent, and it tickles me to think that some has been spent on him. And after all, my rent is quite low.

Dazed by what I'd done, before I left the market I found a pretty scarf for Madeleine, millinery trimmings for Remy, and a peony-pink lipstick for Cécile. After an internal debate, I purchased a leather collar and leash for Pepe, knowing there was nothing in all of St. Ouen that would satisfy his mistress, but a gift for her dog might touch her heart.

December 12, 1946

Dear Mama,

I hope my gifts have arrived. I sent them in November, but now I worry that I should have mailed them sooner. If I can't be there, I want everyone to have something from me and know that I'm thinking about them.

It's hard, being away at Christmas. I won't lie and say that I'm not thinking of you all at every moment. I hope Grace takes my place and reads Little Women *as I used to. That book was one of the best gifts Aunt ever gave.*

You mustn't worry about me. I was going to stay at the hotel for Christmas and get more writing done, but Julian Armitage, the trustee from Uncle's bank, has invited me to come to England for a house party. He's become a good friend, appearing every few months to take me to dinner when he's in Paris for work, and he insists that he's asked me for Christmas not just because he feels bad that I'm going to be alone. I do want to see England, and the idea of a house party, of whatever sort, is intriguing. I'll be sure to write and tell you all about it.

The most interesting part, so far, is that I'm FLYING to England. You'll have to tell Toby. He won't be as impressed as he would have been before the war, but maybe he'll smile at his stick-in-the-mud sister in an airplane. Julian has a friend who's a pilot and I will be flying over with him before Christmas. I'm a bit nervous, but mostly I'm worried about whether my luggage (and Mona) will fit in the plane.

I purchased a tiny calendar for 1947, and as soon as the year turns, I'll start marking the days until it's time to come home. Paris has been wonderful, but I miss you all so much.

Merry Christmas.

Pearl

Mel, as it turns out when I reach the airfield at Le Bourget, is short for Melinda. She stands at the counter in hangar no. 3, wearing a padded flight suit and drinking a steaming cup of what smells like chicory. When I introduce myself, she shakes my hand with a firm grip.

"Jules told me all about you!" she says with enthusiasm. "You haven't flown before?"

I shake my head. *Jules*? "How long have you been flying?"

"Since I was fifteen." She grabs my larger bag and leaves me with the small one and my typewriter case. "When the war came, I joined the Air Transport Auxiliary."

"What did you do?" I can imagine Mel being fierce enough to fight. "In the Air Transport?"

"Ferried planes, mostly," she says laconically, striding across the airfield to a silvery open biplane that looks too insubstantial to carry us across the Channel. "If a pilot came down at the wrong airfield, I'd fly his plane back. Then I'd pick up another that'd been repaired and fly *it* where it needed to go."

"It sounds fascinating."

It was more interesting than the work my friends and I did. There had been articles in the newspapers about the United States's women's flying unit, but they were disbanded in 1944, and I didn't know anyone who'd actually been in it.

As we approach the plane, a man comes around the side. He has a cigarette wedged in one corner of his mouth and wears a leather jacket similar to the one Mel wears over her suit. Nodding to me, he slings my bags into the plane before conferring with her in a low voice.

"Weather's clear but cold," she tells me. "Jake, do you have kit for my passenger?"

Jake goes behind the plane and returns with an armload of clothing, which he offers to me. I look down at my heavy wool trousers and winter coat. "I'm quite warm."

"You won't be." Mel's grin is cheeky. "Once we're up you'll be praying for a blanket. Put it on."

I obey, removing my coat and stepping into a padded khaki flight suit with multiple pockets. Mel helps me with the zip and then holds out the fleece-lined leather jacket, folding my coat while I put it on.

"Thank you for doing this."

"Not a problem." She looks me up and down, then wraps my scarf tighter around my neck. "Flight time will be about four hours. Do you have gloves?"

"Yes." I hold up my hands, clad in my best leather gloves. It is difficult to move in all these unfamiliar layers. "Will these do?"

"Not in the slightest." She turns. "Jake, run back and borrow a pair. And bring a helmet while you're at it."

He takes off at an uneven lope toward the hangar, the cigarette unwavering in the corner of his mouth.

"I don't mean to be an inconvenience." Why has Julian done this? I could have easily taken the train and then the ferry. "I must be putting you behind."

Mel leans against the side of the plane and rubs her forehead, leaving a faint smudge. "Don't worry. He knew I'd be flying back empty, so he asked me to bring you along."

"Do you come to France often?" I feel no discomfort speaking with her, other than the strangeness of the situation. Her easy shortening of Julian's name makes me wonder about their history. "For Julian, I mean?"

She looks over my shoulder and I turn. Jake is jogging in our direction.

"Not too often, but he knows I'll take any excuse to fly. When the bank has to send someone over, he always calls me." She grins again. "You're the first Christmas present I've ever delivered, though. Don't fall out or anything—there'll be hell to pay if you arrive damaged."

My cheeks heat as she buckles the leather helmet under my chin. My hair will never survive; I hope there will be time to tidy myself before Julian sees me in this ridiculous getup. The leather gloves are also fleece-lined, making my hands thick and clumsy, but frostbite would be even worse.

"In you go," Mel says, tipping her chin up at the plane.

I look from my place on the grass to the rear seat, high above me. "How?"

"Jake!"

He comes around and helps me onto the wing, then boosts me, with one enormous hand on my bottom, into the front seat. "You step over," he says helpfully. "Into the back."

Steadying myself in the front, I try to work out how to make it over the separation and into the back without damaging any of the instruments or breaking a leg. I take a deep breath, close my eyes, and step over, landing hard—but successfully—in the seat.

"That's the worst part." Mel follows quickly and without Jake's assistance. "Can you buckle yourself in?"

"I think so." I fit my arms through the shoulder straps and fasten the belt across my lap. "Is this right?"

She looks me over. "Perfect. Now you sit tight until we're off the ground. Once we're up, if you have any questions, lean forward and shout. I'll hear you."

Lean forward? The straps pin me back against the seat; with all the extra clothing, I can barely move. But I grew up in a full house; I can shout with the best of them.

Mel busies herself in the cockpit, leaning over the side to have another call-and-response conversation with Jake. At the end, he trots to the front of the aircraft and spins the propeller. The engine roars to life.

I close my eyes as the plane bumps across the grass like a toy car over an uneven carpet. My stomach is in knots and my chest is so tight that I'm having trouble breathing. I can't last four hours like this. I struggle forward to tell her that I've changed my mind but suddenly we're up, skimming above the grass, rising slowly until we clear first hedges and then a row of trees at the edge of the airfield.

Once we are airborne, my heart returns to its normal location, though my stomach isn't certain about having been brought along on this trip. I lean to the right and look out over the landscape as Mel brings the plane around. There is the smudge of Paris in the distance—not a long train ride at all, yet seemingly so far away.

"All right back there?" The plane climbs beyond any ground obstructions and Mel is able to turn her head to look at me.

"I think so."

I thought I'd be terrified, but now that we're up, I want to bounce in my seat like a child, pointing and calling her attention to every steeple, every town as we fly over. Four hours of this will not be enough. When we reach the Channel, the air grows abruptly colder. My teeth start to chatter, and I flex my fingers inside the fleece gloves; despite the thickness, they are freezing.

"This is the worst part!" Mel shouts above the sound of the engine. "Once we're over England it won't be so cold, and we'll be at Sculthorpe before you know it."

"Where?" I ease forward to hear her more easily.

"RAF Sculthorpe, in Norfolk. They allow some civilian traffic."

I hope Julian's sister-in-law's house isn't too far from the airfield. Flying is faster than train travel, but I will be worn out simply from the novelty of flying and that surge of fear at takeoff.

It is easier to call to Mel now. "How do you know Julian?"

"I flew him around a few times," comes her response. "We became friends."

"You didn't know him before the war?" Friends sounds safe; I don't want her to tell me they are engaged or something like that.

Mel hoots. "Someone like him? Not bloody likely."

Before it seems possible, we are touching down at another airfield, this one larger and with military planes in ranks outside numerous hangars. Although there are visible long concrete runways, Mel sets the plane down on the grass and we roll toward the nearest hangar. My stomach makes itself known again.

"I like flying," I call to her. "It's taking off and landing that I don't like."

"You did grand."

She jumps down and I recreate my journey from back seat to front and then down to the ground with no more grace than in France. A young man comes to retrieve my bags, and I remove my helmet and hand it to Mel.

"Thank you," I say, patting at my hair. "This was wonderful."

Mel slings an arm over my shoulder. "Look," she says, pointing. "Someone's come to greet you."

Julian stands at the edge of the airfield. Beneath the brim of his hat is a blazing smile. At his raised hand, an answering smile breaks across my face, even as I realize how ridiculous I must look. How did he even recognize me in this billowing flight suit?

"Help! Is there somewhere I can change?"

Her eyes crinkle as she grins at me. "Don't worry, he won't even notice what you're wearing." At my alarmed expression, she adds, "Right through that door there. I'll keep him occupied while you change your kit and freshen your lipstick."

I sprint toward the door as she saunters in his direction. "Jules! Playing the country gentleman, I see."

His response is lost in the slam of the door. I wrestle free of the suit, smoothing my slightly squashed outfit. My compact shows curls that are both flattened and tumbled. I do the best I can, hoping I will have time to tidy myself properly before meeting his friends. A dash of lipstick brings my confidence back up, and I bundle the borrowed finery under my arm and emerge, shivering, into air that feels even colder after the protective clothing.

The air is moist and smells of the sea. Despite my eagerness, I stop to gaze across the airfield to the flat land beyond, green despite the winter cold. This is not an area of England familiar to me from the movies; I want to take it all in, but most of all, I want to take in Julian, whose back is toward me as he talks to Mel. While part of me admires the set of his shoulders beneath his tweed jacket, the rest of me just wants to look at him, to acknowledge that I survived the flight and my reward—ten days in his company—is worth any lingering discomfort.

"Julian." He spins around, hands outstretched, clasps my upper arms and draws me in. Just then, Mel says something. I turn my head to catch it, and his lips brush mine. She grins.

"You're here," he says, sounding pleased. "How was your flight?"

"Interesting." I meet Mel's dancing eyes. "I hope the rest of my visit will be slightly less—"

"Eventful?" She reaches into her flight suit and pulls out a packet of cigarettes. "She handled it beautifully, Jules, once we got her into the plane."

He raises his shoulders. "That's the most difficult part."

"Personally, I'd say takeoff was the worst." I think of the dizzying feeling of the earth dropping away beneath us and shudder. "Also landing, but I knew what to expect by then."

Julian picks up my bags and eyes Mona's case. "A working holiday?"

"I don't like leaving her behind." Shrugging back into my coat and picking up the typewriter, I bid farewell to my pilot and follow Julian around the building, where a horse and cart wait by the roadside. When I realize the cart is for us, I laugh. The horse blows, tossing his head. "From an airplane to a horse and buggy, all in one day!"

"Sorry about this." He puts my things in the back and hands me up onto the seat. "I arrived yesterday, but most of the party is coming today. Felicity went to retrieve them from the railway station, and as I didn't know precisely what time you'd arrive, it seemed easier this way."

I haven't ridden behind a horse since I left Scovill Run, and it wasn't something that happened often, even then. Squinting against the bright, watery sun, I wrap my scarf higher and ask, "How far is it to the house?"

"About an hour's ride." He gives me a sidelong look "Will you be warm enough?"

My fingers are numb, but I nod anyway. "I'm mostly cold from the flight. And I assume it's warm in Felicity's house?"

"In a manner of speaking." He flicks the reins, and the horse starts off at a brisk trot. The cart rumbles over the rough verge and then the road evens. "It was selfish of me to put you through this. I should have left word to wait and come to get you when the car was available, but"—his glance is almost boyish—"I wanted you to myself before the rest of them get hold of you."

"That sounds rather dire. Are you sure the natives are friendly?"

Julian's laughter is genuine and surprises us both. "Almost certainly. Fliss's bark is worse than her bite."

"Do you always spend Christmas with her?" His description isn't encouraging.

"Often, before the war," he says. "She and Helen were very close. I was here last year, and '42 and '43. The other years, no."

I wonder how he spent that first Christmas without his wife, whether she'd died in the early months of the Blitz or later, in 1941. I don't want to ask; he's answered every personal question I've thrown at him, but other than telling me that he and Helen were having problems, he's never volunteered information.

When it comes down to it, I know so little about him—when and where he was born, where he went to college, that his wife and parents are dead. I know that he sails and plays cricket and is a good dancer, but I don't know who his favorite author is or what kind of music he likes. But while my brain wants to know that information, my heart doesn't appear to care. Something inside eases when I see his handwriting on an envelope and speeds up, as it has now, when I'm in his company.

"I hope they like me." I'm more nervous about meeting his people than I was at Mary Jayne's party; not only are they *his* people, but I will be spending more than a week in their company and if it doesn't go well, it will be uncomfortable for everyone. Particularly Julian, caught in the middle. I vow to do my best to fit in and be the easiest houseguest Felicity Shawcross has ever had.

We travel in companionable silence, Julian occasionally pointing out a circling bird of prey or a big house set back from the road. Finally, we turn onto another road, less well paved, and he says, "The Grange is beyond the trees there."

Felicity's house has a name? "Julian, are they... fancy?"

He slows the horse to a walk and turns to look at me. "Does it matter?" he asks. "You're as good as any one of them. Likely better. So don't worry."

December 20, 1946

This is going to be the longest trip in the history of the world.

The others weren't back when we arrived, so Julian gave me a quick tour, including the drawing and dining rooms, so I won't get lost later. It's a rambling barn of a house, beautiful but run down, and very *damp. My room is nice enough, though the fireplace was cold and, according to the maid who appeared to take my clothes away to be pressed, likely to stay that way. "Mrs. Shawcross prefers to use the public rooms," she said. "She doesn't like waste."*

It looks like I won't be getting a lot of writing done, because my teeth will be chattering louder than Mona's keys.

I was waiting for the maid to return so I could ask her useful ques-tions like how they dress for dinner when I heard female voices in the hall. I started to open the door but stopped when I realized they were talking about ME.

"Imagine how desperately lonely he must be," a woman drawled. "A dumpy little American. Can't one of you find someone for him?"

"He's apparently made *his choice." A different voice, younger.*

"I hope not. How could he do this to us? Bring this tragic little thing to Christmas? She won't even know how to dress!"

The other women (there had to be 3-4 of them) join in the laughter.

I wanted to fling the door open and confront them, but while writer Pearl loves a scene, real Pearl gets sweaty-palmed and sick to her stom-ach at the thought.

For now, I've decided to act like I didn't hear them. Mama always said no good came from eavesdropping. Maybe they'll change their tune when they find out I'm not everything they're afraid of. Julian doesn't think of me like that. At least, I hope he doesn't. When we met at the airfield, it looked like he felt the way I do, but without the fear of showing it.

What it must be like to be a man, free to do or say whatever you want.

I spent a solid thirty minutes hiding in the large hall bathroom, soaking in a hot tub and stewing over how to present myself when so little was expected of me. Dumpy! It was insulting to both me and Julian, but I couldn't repeat what I'd heard—I wouldn't say such things about his friends.

Emerging from the bath, I dress quickly and retreat to my chilly room to deal with my hair and put on a fresh face. When I come downstairs, the bottle of Armagnac in one hand, the hall swarms with people, though when I stop to count, there are ten. Julian is off to one side, but he notices me immediately and beckons me to him.

"Fliss," he says, guiding me over to a tall woman with dark blonde hair pulled severely back from her face. "This is Pearl Kimber. Pearl, this is my sister-in-law, Felicity Shawcross."

"Thank you for including me," I say, as she shakes my hand. Her grip is limp and disinterested. "I brought this for you."

"You certainly qualify as a waif and a stray," Felicity says in a clear and perfect voice, the voice which had called me tragic. She takes the bottle without acknowledgement and puts it on the nearest flat surface. "When poor Julian asked if he could invite you, he made it sound like you were quite alone in the world."

"Not in the world," I say, my hackles rising. Had his wife been like this? "Just in Europe."

Felicity's laughter is like glass shattering. Her eyes rake me from my shoes to the top of my head. "He spends so much time worrying about his responsibilities for that dreadful bank, I volunteered to help. And here you are."

I take a shaky breath as she turns to speak to someone else. Julian shakes his head slightly, as if her behavior is distressing but not worthy of comment, and brings me around to everyone himself, introducing me not as a client but as his friend and a writer. By the time he is done, I feel much better. There are several people who are far more pleasant than my hostess. Still, unless I manage to win Felicity over, it will be slow going until the new year.

Dinner is a formal affair, occurring in a vast paneled room with candles and flowers on a long table and two maids bringing out platter after platter of obviously black market food. Despite the quantity, it all strikes me as insufficiently seasoned after months of Madame's cooking. There is an abundance of wine, which makes all the conversations in which I'm not included easier to bear.

Julian is seated to my left. He gives me much of his attention, but I don't want to feel like a charity case, needing him because the others are ignoring me. I attempt to make small talk with the man on my right. He eyes me over the roast beef and says, "Fliss says you're one of Julian's clients."

"I'm a friend." Am I to be downgraded to a needy client? I resist the urge to push back my chair and run up to the safety of my bedroom. Most of the time, I think twenty-six is old and that life passed me by while I waited out the war. With these people, I feel all of twelve, babyish and afraid to speak up for myself.

After dinner, it gets better. Everyone moves to the drawing room, where a crackling fire heats an area ten feet around. I stand close to the flames, thawing my fingers, and one of the women comes over to me.

"So you're Julian's waif." She makes it sound as if he produces a different one each year, and I wonder if he has. "I'm Geneva, in case you were so overwhelmed earlier that it didn't stick. Meeting the lot of us at once must have been a bit much."

"It was." I rub my hands together. "Have you known Julian long?"

Geneva shrugs. "Since Fliss started collecting us for Christmas," she says. "I assume he exists the rest of the year."

She tells me this is the second time they've gathered at the Grange, which Felicity rents from the neighboring estate. "Before that, during the war, we were in Devon twice, and once she took a place up in Scotland." Leaning close, she says, "It was colder than a witch's tit, and not everyone could make the journey. Or wanted to."

"Is Felicity married?" I saw a stunning sapphire on her left hand, but there appears to be no man in attendance who belongs strictly to her.

"More or less." Geneva looks around before adding, "They don't get on. I don't think they ever did, but the war exacerbated things. Everyone lived for the moment and in Gerald's case that meant setting up housekeeping with a tart in Wandsworth, of all places."

Well done, Gerald, I think. "Is he still with her?"

Geneva shakes her head. "But neither is he with Felicity. Her anger is something to behold."

I would believe that. When Geneva moves off to talk to her husband, I track Julian down, standing at his side until he finishes his conversation with a short, tweedy man with bristling eyebrows.

"Are you all right?" he asks immediately.

"Fine," I say, although I'm not. "Would anyone mind if I went up early?"

"Of course not." He takes a breath that could almost be a yawn. "I'm not too bright myself, and I didn't fly the Channel today. I'll say my good night as well, and we can skulk out together."

There are raised eyebrows from Felicity and two of the other women as we exit together. I don't care. I've reached the level of exhaustion where tears are possible, and I don't want to show that kind of emotion in front of these people. Perhaps it's tiredness, after all; if I have a good night's sleep, maybe Felicity will be a different person in the morning. Or maybe I will.

At the top of the stairs, Julian pauses. "I'm in the other wing," he says. "I'll say goodnight."

"Good night." I kiss his cheek properly, not in the French way, remembering his kiss at the airfield. Kissing is permitted now within the bounds of our relationship. "Thank you again for asking me."

He smiles briefly. "I hope you say that when it's over. Sleep well, Pearl."

When I wake, it is cold enough that I can see my breath. Bundling into my robe, I go to the window and part the damask drapes with their heavy linings. Shreds of mist cover everything, masking the overgrown garden I'd seen the day before, as well as the road we'd traveled from the airfield. I shiver, grab my diary, and dive back beneath the covers. There is no point in getting up until I hear someone else moving around.

I had wanted to write about the flight and my impressions of the countryside, but I only had the energy to put my pajamas on and rub cream onto my face before falling asleep. The day had been exhausting even before my chilly welcome: the early train, the stress of the flight, my anticipation of seeing Julian on his home ground. The disappointment, after the initial pleasure of his company. Are these people really his friends?

Behind the drapes, a gust of wind makes the windowpanes rattle. I am drawn back to my childhood, when there was never enough coal and the windows leaked air so badly that it wouldn't have mattered anyway. I pull the robe closer around my neck as the draft reaches the bed and concentrate on getting my thoughts down on paper.

Two pages later, there is a light knock on the door and the maid pops her head in. "You're awake," she says, surprised. "Would you like me to light the fire?"

"Please." I manage to keep my teeth from chattering. "Is it always this cold?"

She kneels, busying herself with the fire tools. "It's the damp, miss, more than the cold. It gets into your bones."

It has; when I get up fifteen minutes later, my joints are stiff. That could be from being crammed into the rear seat of the Tiger Moth, but I would rather blame Felicity for my discomfort than Mel. Dressed again in my wool trousers, with a blouse and a different sweater, I make my way down to the dining room where breakfast is set out. I fill a cup with scalding tea and warm my hands with it while I evaluate my options.

Eggs. And bacon. How long has it been since I've had bacon? Is it greedy to help myself to a few sausages, as well? As no one else is in the room, I fork two onto my plate and quickly eat them with my fingers, disposing of the evidence.

"Good morning." A couple—I have no idea of their names—enters the room and begins to peruse the buffet. "Frigid, isn't it?"

"It is," I say, after returning their greeting. "I didn't realize England was this cold."

"It's the damp," the wife says. "I do wish Fliss had taken a house in London this year."

I take a chair far away from the windows. "Wouldn't it be as cold?"

The husband sits beside me. "Yes," he says, "but there would be more places to get warm. In Norfolk, we can stay in or go out. Bloody miserable, either way."

It's comforting that at least two other guests are as unhappy as I am. I devote myself to my food and desultory conversation. When Julian appears, I sag with relief.

"There you are." He takes a plate from the stack on the sideboard. "Did you sleep well?"

"I slept." I get up and refill my tea. "You?"

"Fine, except for the wind." He sits on my other side. "It's better today. I've already been out."

He's never struck me as an outdoorsy type, but he's a sailor: dampness and wind will be nothing to him. I have apparently become a hothouse flower.

"What's on today?" he asks the man to my left. "You and Cora have plans?"

The woman—Cora—leans past him. "I'm thinking of taking to my bed with a hot water bottle," she says. "Does Fliss organize these occasions for maximum unpleasantness?"

Julian laughs without responding. "What about you, Pearl? Would you like a walk after breakfast?"

While I would like to spend time with him, the thought of being out in the wind isn't appealing. "Which is colder," I ask. "Outside or in?"

"Outside you'll be moving, if that's any comfort." He touches my sleeve. "There are some nice walks, and a fourteenth century church in the town that I think you'll like."

"Then I'll go." I'll add another layer or two to protect me from the cold; what do I do to protect me from feeling like he touched my bare skin instead of my sweater?

Felicity's swooping voice reaches us before she enters. She pauses in the doorway until her presence is acknowledged, then works her way along the table, kissing Cora and her husband on their cheeks and bending down to whisper to them. I scarcely merit a greeting before she slips her hands around Julian's neck and rests her cheek against his. "Don't get up, you silly man! It's as much your house as mine."

"Hardly, Fliss." His shoulders hunch and she steps back, brushing a finger against his neck. "Did you have any plans for us today? Otherwise, I was going to show Pearl the church. And maybe before we leave, we could visit the shrine at Walsingham." Julian looks at me questioningly. "It's not far, if Fliss will allow us the use of her car."

"You said she was a writer." Felicity's laughter is both sharp and shrill. "Is she writing a guidebook on the most tedious aspects of Norfolk? The poor child will be bored senseless."

"If you're referring to me, I'm very much looking forward to it." I am unable to keep the edge from my voice.

There is a momentary silence, and then Cora's husband says, "Brava."

After breakfast, Julian sends a servant to locate a pair of high rubber boots and a waxed jacket for me. "You'll be more comfortable now." He is dressed in similar fashion. "I'm sorry it's so cold."

"You can't control the weather." I'd rather he acknowledged our hostess's coldness. Perhaps she thought he wouldn't actually bring someone.

The heavy front door closes behind us. I take a deep breath and feel my spirits rise.

"Are you and Felicity close?"

"I knew her before I knew Helen," he says, which is not an answer. "We don't meet often, though. Gerald's in the navy, so she followed him to all his postings. When the war began, she took a house in Gloucestershire with friends. She was terrified of bombs, even before the Blitz. Even before Helen."

It's nice to know something scares this woman. I'm sorry her sister is dead, but I'm sorrier on Julian's behalf, even though otherwise he'd be a married man now and I'd be spending Christmas alone. At least I wouldn't have this tightness in my chest every time he gets close to me; I would never have allowed myself to form an attachment, and he would naturally have been less attentive—very likely he wouldn't have thought to see me each time he came over.

The road rises and falls beneath our boots. Julian tells me about the small houses that we pass—estate cottages, some with their original tenants, others occupied by those who fled London and decided to stay on. As we continue walking, the houses grow closer together until I look up and see that we're now surrounded by buildings.

"This is Fakenham," he says. "It's a medieval market town."

It looks medieval. It looks like a storybook illustration or a movie set, all tidy brick houses and bow-windowed shops. "It's lovely."

"I was at school not far from here," he says. "Gresham's."

"Can we go there?" I'm curious about his early life.

"It's not *that* close." He points to a looming church ahead of us. "That's our destination. St. Peter and St. Paul."

There are more churches in Norfolk than any other part of England, he tells me. Something to do with the wool trade and merchants proving their love of God by building enormous houses of worship. "I could take you to a different one every day," he says. "But Felicity is right, you'd die of boredom."

"More likely frostbite." We circle the church and admire the tower and the golden stone. "Does the tour include the inside or are we going to stand here, shivering?"

The interior is dim. It feels old; I can almost taste the dust of centuries. Julian leads me to an octagonal font covered all over with intricate carving.

"Fifteenth century," he says reverently. "Not all the church is that old. There was a lot of reconstruction during the Victorian era. But some of the original windows are still here, and a few memorial brasses that you might find interesting."

I admire everything, particularly the breadth of his knowledge and his enthusiasm. It also gives my hands and feet time to thaw, so that by the time he asks if I want tea, I accept without mentioning the cold at all.

December 22, 1946

Another day, another walk. I wonder if he's deliberately keeping me out of the house, and if so, for whose sake (mine or Felicity's)? Maybe he's simply trying to freeze me to death.

It's Sunday, so we walked back to Fakenham to go to church. Church of England makes me nostalgic for mass at Notre Dame with my friends. Julian and I are the only members of the house party who bothered to attend, though he assures me they'll go on Christmas Eve. More for the carols than anything else, but it counts.

Does it, though? I'm not willing to cut Felicity that much slack. Is he sure the ceiling won't fall in?

There's something about the way she behaves with him that sets my teeth on edge. As if she has rights to him. Was there ever something more to their relationship? Did they date, perhaps, before he met Helen? While I find her terrifying and unappealing in the extreme, a man might see differently. She is attractive and wealthy, with an absentee husband. It might be convenient for both of them.

There's nothing I can do or say that will make that woman like me. I'll never see her again after this hideous week, so I don't care, but for Julian's sake, I'd like things to be better. Today I thought he would bring it up (he seemed on the verge of talking about something important) but instead he veered off and started telling me about rooks and how he'll take me to see the marshes if we have time.

All we have here is time. I get up early to miss the breakfast crowd, and we get tea and sandwiches out. Then I stay in my room, wearing two sweaters over my dinner dress, until I hear the dinner gong.

Because they dress for dinner, and here I am without the right sort of clothes, wearing my black velvet every night. Julian was kind about it and whispered that he thought she'd gotten over formal dinners, but apparently not. Mama's green dress is hanging in the wardrobe, but they don't deserve it. And anyway, if I showed up in a gown, it would be the night they decided to wear pajamas as a lark.

I should be able to handle this. I survived a week on the Riviera and talked to a movie star, for Pete's sake. These are only English people, not particularly rich nor, in my opinion, particularly well bred.

If only Julian would speak up. Say to Felicity that, like it or lump it, I'm here as his guest. It's been so lovely spending long stretches of time with him, even if we're outside for most of it. It's not helping me feel less attached to him when he's the one person in the house, aside from the dogs, who takes any pleasure in my existence. For all that this group of 'orphans' is supposed to provide support and company over the holiday, I might as well be alone with him. And I wish I was.

On Sunday evening, the drawing room conversation devolves into stories about wartime Christmases. Felicity regales us with a tale of 1940, when her husband was briefly in London and she took the train to be with him. Due to a jammed door, they spent the whole day stuck in a bomb shelter.

"By the time we were released, we couldn't stand each other!" She tosses back her martini and runs a finger along the rim of the glass, wiping away traces of lipstick. "I got on the next train and fled back to the country."

"Have you seen him since?" This from Roger, Cora's husband, who shares my jaundiced view of Felicity.

She tucks her chin and looks at him from beneath blackened lashes. "As often as I need to," she says. "What about you, Rog? What's your wartime Christmas story?"

"Well, it doesn't involve being locked in with Cora," he says to general laughter. "Although I'm sure we'd have come out of it in a much different state than you and Gerald. I was stationed up in Scotland for much of the war, and in '43 I got three days' leave. We agreed to meet in York and *both* of us got stuck on trains. When we finally arrived, we had two hours in the station café before we had to start back."

Felicity lounges back in her chair, looking like a liquor advertisement. "What about you, Pearl? We already know that Julian doesn't talk about himself."

"Not much to tell," he says, clearing his throat. "Go on, Pearl."

It is difficult to know what to share—or what I am willing to share with them. Britain had been at war for years before we were even drawn into it.

"Christmas of '41 was probably the worst," I say. "We knew we'd be in it eventually, but Pearl Harbor was so shocking that no one felt very festive."

"But it was an island," Felicity says, with a scarlet smile. "Not even part of the United States."

"All those sailors were part of the United States." I hate her suddenly, Julian's sister-in-law, with her veiled barbs and casual cruelty. "And it was our naval base."

"War is hardly a competition." Geneva stirs in her seat, looking for a way to ease the tension. "It was terrible everywhere."

Felicity raises her glass. "I wasn't being competitive, darling. I'm not sure our young friend comprehends what it was like for *us*. Last Christmas it didn't feel real. No one was home yet—" She glances at Julian and looks away. "Even those who weren't in the services weren't around."

"Fliss," he says mildly. "Perhaps you should choose one or the other."

"Hmm?" She cocks her head.

"Talking or drinking." He taps his cigarette on the edge of the silver ashtray, sending a cylinder of ash into its shining bowl. "They don't mix."

"Have I summoned your protective instincts by not cosseting your little friend?" She sticks her tongue out like a child, an action made all the more ridiculous by her gold satin gown. "I'm sorry, but you said she was a grown woman. I assumed that meant she could hold her own."

"And so I can," I say, stung. "But Julian told me this was a gathering of friends, and I feel more like I've been thrown to the lions." I drink the last of my sherry and push the glass away. "I'll say goodnight now and leave you to your fun."

"Good girl!" Roger's palms touch in silent applause.

"Pearl—"

Julian rises but I cut him off. "I'm perfectly fine. Just a headache. I'll be better in the morning."

The only way I will be better is if Felicity Shawcross vanishes overnight in a puff of smoke, or perhaps chokes on the olive in her martini. Falls off a horse, face first into the mud? The violence of my thoughts is cheering.

By the time I reach the second floor and shut the door behind me, my headache has begun to ease.

Throwing my formal clothes on the bed, I pull on flannel pajamas and add my bathrobe for good measure. The fire is laid for morning, and despite what I know will be the maid's deep disapproval, I kneel down and light it now, sick to death of being miserable *and* cold. Perhaps she'll throw me out for wasting firewood. I hope so.

They're still downstairs talking. How could Julian not have come to my defense? He obviously didn't expect his sister-in-law to behave this way, but he hasn't stopped her, either. I was looking forward to this time with him so much, but for every good moment with Julian, there was one with Felicity that negated it.

I don't even want to go down in the morning and face Felicity's sly, knowing eyes. Or Julian's lack of spine.

I make one more circuit of the patterned carpet before it comes to me. *I don't have to put up with this.* Felicity can be as rude as she wants, but I don't have to tolerate it. I can leave. I'll go downstairs in the morning, all right—with my suitcases.

The decision gives me renewed energy. I fling open the wardrobe and pile clothes on the bed, putting aside my gray trousers and a sweater for the journey. I am so involved in packing that at first, I don't hear the quiet knock on the door. I open it cautiously and find Julian on the other side.

"May I come in?"

"Why?" I block the opening. "So you can say everything you didn't say down there?"

"Please, Pearl." His face crumples.

I open the door wider, wondering why I should give him another chance. For all my silly, hopeful thoughts, he's no better than Mick.

He looks at the open suitcase with dismay. "You're leaving?"

"Why should I stay?" I swerve past him to the table and snap Mona into her case. "There hasn't been a moment since I arrived where she's treated me as anything other than an imposition. And that's being kind."

"I know." He looks at me for permission before sitting in the armchair. "Fliss is protective."

"What is she protecting?" I turn away; even covered, cold radiates through the glass. "Her precious Christmas tradition? Or her plans for you that she thinks I'm disrupting?"

"Sit, please?" Julian waits until I perch on the edge of the bed, leaning against the carved post. "This isn't a tradition," he says. "It's something she came up with to fill the house with people because the only family she has left is a husband who can't be bothered to come home."

I roll my eyes. "I wonder why?"

"She wasn't always like this." Pausing, he says carefully, "She was never very nice, but she wasn't like this. I generally ignore her when she gets this way."

I bend to pick up one of my stockings, roll it into a ball and tuck it in the suitcase. "By ignoring her, you gave her permission to treat me like garbage. And you told *me* it was all right." Tears prick and I close my eyes to drive them back. I will not cry in front of him. "That's why I'm leaving. Not because of her, but because of you. Because you watched her and said nothing."

His expression goes very still. Have I shocked him? I don't care—although I do, or I would have simply left without saying a word.

"I am sorry." He takes my hand. "I should have stood up for you. You deserve better. It's no excuse, but mine was not a happy family, Pearl, nor a close one. Keeping silent to get along is an old habit. It's never served me well, but in this case, it's done damage to someone I care for."

The touch of his hand, as well as his words, lowers the volume of my anger. I squeeze his fingers, and he squeezes back.

"I won't change my mind." I accept his apology, understand how patterns of behavior in a family can go on for years without being challenged. "But I'll miss spending Christmas with you."

"Then I'll come with you, if you'll have me."

"You can't."

"Why not?" When Julian lets go of my hand, I feel bereft. "You were my guest. You were made to feel unwelcome. If you go, I go."

"She'll never forgive you." My voice wobbles but I'm near laughter. "And she'll hate me even more."

"We'll have to live with it," he says gravely, one hand on the door-knob. "I'll let you get on with your packing. The train from Fakenham leaves at nine. We'll have time for breakfast." An impish smile crosses his face. "Fliss isn't an early starter. We might miss her entirely."

I put my hands on his shoulder and kiss his cheek, inhaling his clean scent. "Wouldn't it be a shame if she came down and found we'd eaten all the bacon?"

Paris's war damage is shown in shabby wardrobes and empty shelves, but as soon as we emerge from the train station into the gray drizzle, I can see that London is different. It's proud of its survivor status. *Keep calm and carry on*, I think, gazing up at the boarded-up windows across the street. I stand on the curb with our bags, wide-eyed, while Julian summons a black cab.

He pauses to light a cigarette and sees my expression. "It looked much worse this time last year."

"Where you live," I say. "Is it like this?"

"Some of it." Julian hands me into the cab, then gets in beside me. "And some is worse."

As we pass through streets of neat brick houses with sudden, shocking gaps, it reminds me of sitting in darkened theaters with my friends and my sisters, watching the flickering, unreal news footage, and the shattered church at the end of *Mrs. Miniver*. But the hope I felt at the end of the movie drains away when I see how widespread and horrific the damage is.

"We were so sheltered from the war."

"Bloomsbury had its share of raids," his quiet voice continues, as if I hadn't spoken. "Not like the East End, but enough. Bedford Place. Woburn Place. The British Museum was hit three times."

"It's still there?" How much history has been lost?

"Do you want to visit? We'll have time before you go back."

"Yes, please." He puts his hand absently on mine and something turns over in my chest. I swallow hard and move my hand away. "Do you go there often? To the museum?"

"Not since the war."

The way he says it makes me realize he's had enough of talking about the past. Did my pulling away make him shut down? I don't *want* to pull away; I realized when we accidentally kissed at the airfield that coming to England might have been a mistake. Despite my attraction to Mick, I recovered quickly from our breakup. There is something about

Julian that is harder to resist. He has somehow, stealthily, become very important—and thus very dangerous.

The taxi circles around a green square and turns into a street of narrow brick houses with white-framed windows and high doors with fanlights above.

Julian raps on the barrier separating us from the driver. "Here."

"This is lovely." It looks exactly like I imagined London would look—barring the three missing houses near the end of the block.

"It's a family flat," he says shortly, handing me out and counting the bags that emerge from the trunk. "My parents kept it for when they came up to town."

"It's not the whole house?" I wrap my scarf more closely; the wind is barreling down the street.

"Just the ground floor," he says, "and a kitchen in the basement. A sitting room, a small breakfast room, two bedrooms and a bathroom. And a boxroom that I've turned into a library." He touches my arm. "Careful there."

I circle around him to the front step, looking down the precipitous stairs to the basement, which, before the war, would have been protected by an iron railing; square holes in the paving show where it was sheared off to be melted down.

Julian unlocks the door and ushers me into a wide front hall. He stops, checks the mail spread on a shining console table, then wields his key on the next door we come to.

"Welcome," he says, shutting it behind us. "There's a room ready for you. I had hoped you would have time to visit before returning to Paris. Since neither of us slept much, you might like to rest for a bit. We can find something to do later."

I follow him into a small, cheerful room overlooking the back garden. Papered in a muted floral stripe, the room contains a bed with a rosy spread, a high dresser, and a table and chair before the window. I hasten to the table and put Mona in pride of place.

"Will this do? If there's anything you need—"

"It's perfect," I assure him. "Don't let me keep you if there's anything you need to do." Despite the lack of sleep, suddenly I am itching to pull out my manuscript; without the hostile atmosphere of Felicity's house, my creative energies have returned.

He lingers at the door. "I have a few calls to make. Do you think you'll want lunch?"

We ate breakfast in Norfolk and then sandwiches on the train. "I'm quite full."

"Then I'll leave you. We'll go out for dinner later—could you be ready by half six?"

At five, I emerge to search out the bathroom and then my host, eventually locating him in a tidy, book-lined room across the hall from my bedroom. Ensconced in a tweedy armchair, he has his feet on the fender of a small coal fire and a newspaper open on his lap.

"Pearl." The paper crackles as he puts it aside. "Have you been resting? I thought I heard the typewriter."

"I meant to rest," I admit sheepishly. "It's a very inspiring room."

"The garden's not at its best in December, but if you're writing, I suppose the view isn't important." He shifts his chair and makes room for me in front of the fire. "Can I get you anything?"

"I'm fine." I toast myself, turning slowly. "I wanted to know our plan for the evening, so I know what to wear. I don't suppose you have an iron?"

"I don't believe I do." He looks as though he's trying to remember. "I send my things out to be cleaned and pressed."

"That isn't helpful." I'll have to wear my black velvet, which I am heartily sick of, but my green crepe is hopelessly wrinkled. "Where are we going?"

"To the Albert Hall," he says. "I thought we could have a quick bite here and then a late supper after the performance."

"Are we going to a concert?"

"You mentioned once that you liked opera." Julian looks immensely pleased with himself. "I was able to get tickets to tonight's show."

"Who's singing?" My black velvet will be fine for a concert. With the gloves I bought to replace the ones Remy borrowed and my best jewelry, I can stand up to anyone but Felicity Shawcross.

Julian opens the paper and shows it to me. "Renate Steiner. Have you ever heard her sing?"

A joyous laugh bubbles up as my disastrous Christmas takes a comic turn. "Many times. She's a friend of the family."

As we climb out of the cab onto the sidewalk, my gaze darts from one fantastical structure to the next: first, the brick-and-terracotta Royal Albert Hall, then the ornate but slightly ridiculous Albert Memorial across the street. The concert hall's glass dome, topped with a gilded statue, glows from the inside.

We approach the entrance, flanked by towering columns, and Julian offers me his arm. "Happy?"

"Yes." Happy, but with a nervous fluttering in my chest because of how close we are and anticipation of sitting beside him in the dark for the next few hours. "Thank you for this."

He removes two tickets from his overcoat pocket. The smile he directs at me feels like a secret. I suppress a shiver and follow him to our seats.

The vast auditorium reminds me of Philadelphia's Academy of Music, where we'd seen Renate perform several times. The decoration is put on so thickly it feels like a stage set of a concert hall. We are seated in the stalls, slightly left of center, and I crane my neck to look around, taking in the more expensive boxes above us with their velvet curtains and gold chairs, along with the well-dressed crowd. There is a muted buzz of conversation that matches the hum of excitement running under my skin.

When I'd come into the sitting room in my tired black velvet, Julian turned from the fire and looked at me with frank appreciation. "You look splendid," he said. "I shall bask in the glow of your elegance all evening."

At intermission, I want to stay in my seat, but Julian leads me out to the bar for a glass of champagne. "To continue your Christmas treat," he explains.

Sipping the bubbling liquid, I play the concert back in my head. Renate's voice is so much richer in person; there is a warmth that doesn't translate onto a shellac disc. I wrap myself in the music, waiting impatiently for it to be time to go back inside.

"Would you mind if I stepped away for a moment?" Julian looks at me inquiringly. "I'll be right back."

I'm glad I went before we left; at events like this, there is always a line for the ladies' toilet, and I don't want to risk missing a second of her performance. I shift to the side, leaning against a pillar while I wait for him. He returns quickly.

"Another gift for you," he says, his voice tinged with muted glee. "I sent word backstage. We've been invited back after the show to see Miss Steiner."

Listening to her was a joy; getting to speak to her after all this time is as thrilling as the music itself. I can't help it: I lean over and kiss his cheek and watch, flustered, as he raises his hand to the spot.

When the final applause fades, I almost hate to ruin the concert's spell with conversation, even with Renate, but Julian went to a lot of trouble to secure tickets and arrange a meeting. I won't disappoint him, not after dragging him from Norfolk and upsetting his friends. And I *am* eager to see Renate, it's only that my response to music is to block out other distractions and let it play in my head until I fall asleep, or until it wanders away on its own. I've been to concerts of familiar music where it's kept up for days on end, like the background score in a movie.

A crowd lingers outside her dressing room, elegant people—mostly male—with their arms full of flowers. I remember Aunt telling me that Renate and her husband are divorced, which seems a shame after all they'd been through.

I hang back but Julian takes my hand and tows me resolutely forward.

"Miss Steiner." His low voice cuts through the din. "Here's an old friend to see you."

The room is heavy with scent—both from the bouquets already gathered on the dressing table and from Renate herself. Gold-tinged bulbs around the mirror cast liquid light over several costumes laid out to air. She is seated at the dressing table, wiping cold cream from her face. When she sees me, her eyes light up.

"Pearl!" She opens her arms, looking like a tropical bird in her blue and gold kimono. "Claire said you were in Paris, not here."

"I'm here for a visit." Her embrace feels like home. "Do you have an engagement in Paris?"

"Sit down, my dear." She waves at a nearby sofa, including Julian in the gesture. "Yes, next month. I believe it's the eighteenth, but I'll have to check."

"It's the twenty-second, ma'am." A young woman comes forward to collect Renate's concert gowns. "At the Théâtre des Champs-Élysées."

Renate resumes her application of cold cream. "Thank you, Danielle." When the door closes, she turns to me with a stage grimace. "She's not Katie, but I'm trying to be patient."

"Where is she?" Katie had been my aunt's maid, but Renate stole her away, offering as inducement the opportunity of traveling traveling to places more tolerant of her dark skin. "I was hoping to see her."

"She sailed for New York three weeks ago," Renate says, "with her husband."

Husband! The word hits me like a blow—Katie and I had sworn we would never marry and be trapped into our mothers' lives of men and children and unending housework. Even though her existence at that point consisted of doing housework for my aunt and uncle, it was paid labor, not what she did each day after she finished her other work. It is disappointing to have another friend fall into the trap of marital bliss.

"I didn't know," is all I can manage. Beside me, I feel Julian's interest, and add, "Is he a good man?"

Renate unpins her black hair and drags a brush through it. The unflattering light deepens the creases at the corners of her eyes. The lines bracketing her mouth make her look severe until she smiles.

"Would you expect anything less?" Mirth edges her voice. "She met him while we were on tour last year, and he followed us everywhere. The flowers he sent her were more expensive than the ones I received. All she did was lecture him on his extravagance until he appeared in Edinburgh with an enormous bouquet of silk roses which he said would last until they were old. That finally did it. She carried them as her bridal bouquet."

Katie was raised to be thrifty, and while grand gestures might be appealing, she would prefer to know a man wasn't going to waste his money on frivolous things before she committed herself.

"I wish I'd been able to see her."

"They'll be in Philadelphia when you get home." Renate disappears behind a screen and her silk kimono floats up and over the top edge. "She promised her parents they would stay for a year, but he wants to move to California."

If that happened, I would never see my friend again; she wasn't much of a correspondent, and when the babies came, she would stop writing entirely.

"Could we interest you in a late supper, Miss Steiner?"

I'd almost forgotten Julian was here. "I don't imagine she has time."

Renate emerges in a neat black dress with a froth of lace at the throat. "I wish I did," she says, sounding genuinely regretful. "But my manager is waiting. He's organized a supper with some people I should meet. I'd much rather dine with the two of you."

As we turn to go, her dark eyes light on Julian. "Speaking of Katie's happy situation, what ever happened to Clifford?"

"He's dead." The words fall like stones.

"I'm sorry." She draws on a red mouth and runs a matching scarlet-tipped finger over her brows. "He was an excellent accompanist, but not exactly husband material."

It had rained while we were inside. The streets shine with wet, but I am warm through.

"All right?" Julian asks quietly.

"Just thinking." My mind is whirling—the music, Renate's news about Katie, and especially the way Julian folded himself protectively around me in the crush backstage and remained silent while we caught up. Mick would never have tolerated so much conversation in which he was not the center of attention. "It was good to see her again."

"Harry and I saw her perform once when he was in London on business." He removes his gloves and lays them over his knee. "He never mentioned that he had anything to do with getting her out of Europe."

The car turns and I slide on the seat, my shoulder brushing his.

"He wouldn't."

"He was a good man." It sounds like the highest compliment Julian can bestow, and how I've always thought of my uncle.

I tell him that my year in Paris wasn't Uncle Harry's most surprising bequest. When the lawyer read out his will, there was a long silence when we learned that he'd purchased my family's home almost ten years ago and used our rent to pay it off; my mother and stepfather were handed the deed and told that the house was theirs. Mama hasn't recovered yet from the shock.

"Amazing," he says, shaking his head. "And Miss Steiner stayed with them when they arrived in America?"

"For a few months. When they first came, she wouldn't even listen to her recordings. But then my stepfather found someone to accompany her, and my aunt engineered a meeting with the conductor of the Philadelphia Orchestra, and she was back on stage before the end of the year."

"Your family is good at managing people."

I've never had that talent; almost every time I've involved myself in the lives of others, it has fallen flat. That's why I'm shocked that Julian chose to come to London with me.

"I don't have to stay for Christmas, you know."

"Why would you say that?" The cab stops and the driver comes around to open the door. Julian pays him and we walk up the front steps, navigating by the dim light of a nearby streetlamp. There is no moon.

A turn of the key and we are inside. He takes my coat and hangs it up, then removes his own. Returning to my side, he asks, "Do you want to leave?"

"No..." My eyes sting. "But I've disrupted your holiday. If I start back in the morning, you could be in Norfolk for Christmas."

Julian cups my elbow and guides me down the hall, switching on the lights as we go. "And you would be back in your hotel, all alone. What sort of Christmas is that?"

"The sort of Christmas I would have had if you hadn't invited me."

Down a short flight of steps is the kitchen, a dusky room that flares into unsteady brightness as he turns on the overhead light. Freestanding cabinets stacked with dishes loom out of the shadows and a polished black range is hunched against the wall like a beast.

"Sit." He points me to a long, scrubbed table. "I'll make tea."

He puts the kettle on before sitting across from me, waiting for more of an explanation.

"I felt like a fish out of water," I confess. "I finally got the hang of Paris, but Felicity's house—the way she lives—I don't belong in places like that."

"You belong wherever you are, Pearl." He takes my hands. "I'm sorry Fliss was so unwelcoming, and sorrier still that I didn't take her to task as I should have, but that has nothing to do with the fact that I wanted you there. Very much."

His words warm me almost as much as his hands. I draw back before I have a chance to enjoy it too much. "That's easy for you to say. Your life is as foreign to me as Paris."

The kettle begins to shriek. Julian moves smoothly to turn off the burner and transfers the water into a china pot to which he has already added tea. He brings it, along with a knitted cozy, to the table and sets it between us.

"As your life is foreign to me," he says. "That's what getting to know people is all about. Our lives grow bigger as the distance between us grows smaller."

Decreasing the distance between us is something I've spent too much time thinking about over the last few days, but to what purpose? It's a ridiculous preoccupation brought about by loneliness. Julian is a far better man than Mick, but no better for me. If anything, he inspires the kind of complicated feelings I've been trying to avoid. Getting involved with him would disrupt my writing—the reason I'm away from my family for Christmas to begin with. He deserves better than that.

"Hello?" He slides a cup and saucer in front of me. "You're far away."

My face flames, hoping he can't see the future that I mapped out and discarded in those few seconds. "I'm tired, and a bit overwhelmed."

"It must have been a shock to see your friend again." He is kind to pretend that my distress is caused by Renate. "You'll be better after a good night's sleep. I thought tomorrow I could show you the city. Perhaps we could go to the carol service at Westminster Abbey in the evening."

"I'd like that." I wrap my hands around the cup, letting the warmth seep through the delicate porcelain and into my palms. "You're going to a lot of trouble for me. I'm sure the bank would say this was unnecessary."

"Blast the bank." Julian meets my eyes across the table. "I thought you understood, this has nothing to do with my duties as trustee. I invited you to London because I wanted to spend the holiday with you. Not because we're both at loose ends, but because spending time with you makes me deeply happy."

I choke on my tea. Sputtering, eyes streaming, face red, I hide behind a napkin until I can face him. And when I can, what I say is, "I should go to bed."

Safe behind a closed door, I toss my dress aside and climb into my pajamas. I'm drained, but between the music and Julian's words, my brain is on fire. I won't be able to sleep for hours.

Instead of focusing on Julian's words, I think of Renate's offhand mention of Cliff. Because of his position as her accompanist, he became a part of Aunt Claire's regular Friday night dinners. Tall, blond, and talented, he seemed almost perfect, at least until the first time he had dinner alone with my family. Without my aunt's calming influence over my brothers, Cliff escaped looking like he'd been dragged through the mail slot. I should have known then: if he couldn't handle my family, he wasn't the right man for me.

The last time I saw Cliff was when he appeared on our doorstep in a crisp Army uniform, hat in hand and another proposal on his lips. "I might not come back, Pearl. Don't you ever think about how happy we would have been?"

It was more accurate that when I thought of us, I congratulated myself on a narrow escape from a marriage that would have made us both unhappy. But there was no point in sending him off to war thinking the worst of me.

"It wouldn't have worked. You'll come home and find the right girl. If you even remember my name by then, send me an invitation and I'll come and dance at your wedding."

But I didn't dance at his wedding; I didn't even find out that he'd been killed until the war was over. Part of me feels guilty; I could have married him and made him happy, but at what cost? I preferred to think of him as being somewhere else, with a sweet girl who didn't mind staying home to raise his babies while he went off and had an interesting life.

Thinking of Cliff—or Julian—is pointless. I take my tea and sit down at the table where I've set up Mona and retrieve the stack of typewritten pages from the drawer. It strikes me, looking at how the room is arranged, that Julian must have moved the table in here deliberately so I would have a place to write. My throat tightens at his thoughtfulness.

Putting my complications aside, I pick up the first page of chapter 6, where I'd left off revising. Brigid's problems, for the moment, have priority.

When she walked into the hotel with the baby on her hip, every head turned ~~toward her~~ to look at them. Brigid took a deep breath and prayed that her fear didn't show on her face. She approached the desk. "I'm here about the job," she said. "The priest told me that you're wanting a cook."

The man behind the counter was ~~perhaps~~ near forty, with a raw, sunburned face and a withered left hand.

That explained why he wasn't in the mines, she thought.

"You can't bring your baby in here," he said, staring at her.

Brigid rounded on him, not caring that her temper might cost her this necessary job. "And where would you like me to put him?" she spat. "In the ground with his father? Or maybe I should ~~send~~ be sending him back to the old country on the next boat?"

A laugh ~~ran~~ rippled along the line of men at the bar. The clerk shook his head. "It'll be up to the manager. Wait here."

The clock on the bedside table reads half-past four. I have fallen asleep at the desk. Standing, I stretch the kinks from my back and turn my head, feeling my neck pop. Julian advised a good night's sleep; perhaps I can catch a few hours before it is time to face the day. And him.

The situation doesn't feel so dire in the morning. I tidy away the manuscript and dress for a day of sightseeing outdoors. There is no sound from Julian's room, so I go down to the kitchen, put the kettle on, and poke around to see what there is for breakfast.

By the time his step sounds on the stairs, the sausages are browned and set to one side and eggs are frying in the pan.

"You're bright-eyed," he observes, coming over to sniff the sausages and kissing my cheek. "Sleep well?"

"Not really." I dish up the eggs and shove two thick slices of bread into the toaster. Gesturing at the sausages, I say, "I hope these weren't being kept for a special occasion. I found them in the icebox and couldn't resist."

Julian looks surprised. "Mrs. Haynes must have got them. I called before we left Fliss, to tell her I was returning early with a guest. I asked if she'd pop in to make sure the boiler was on."

"I'm honored." I'm also hungry; the sight of the sausages in their stained paper wrapper woke something in the vicinity of my stomach. If he hadn't come downstairs, I would have eaten them all myself.

He pours the tea and fetches a jug of cream. "Tired of bread and jam?"

"I miss eggs." I dig in, poking the fragile yolk with the end of a sausage and watching as the golden yellow spreads across the plate. "And sausage, for that matter."

"Has it been difficult?" he asks. "Adjusting to Paris as it is instead of what you assumed it would be?"

He understands. Of course he does.

"At first. But there's so much good that shortages aren't that important." I blot my lips. "I've seen so many wonderful things. I've made friends. And I've done work I didn't know I was capable of."

"Harry would be so pleased." He leans over and retrieves the toast and puts one slice on my plate. "I read your *Post* story, by the way. It was excellent."

"You read it?" I say around a mouthful of toast.

"I asked my newsagent to hunt up a copy." Julian smiles. "It's in my desk upstairs, if you don't believe me."

"I believe you," I say. "I just don't understand why."

Julian takes his plate to the sink and runs water over it. "You don't seem to grasp that my interest in you extends beyond the professional."

My breath catches. Every time I'm convinced that my feelings are one-sided, he says something that makes me question myself. I can still feel his kiss of greeting on my cheek.

"Perhaps it shouldn't," I mutter, reaching for the dishrag.

"Leave it," he says peremptorily, his expression darkening. "Mrs. Haynes will be in later."

"On Christmas Eve?" I place my dish on top of his and cross to bask in the stove's warmth.

"She insisted." Shrugging, he says, "She won't be back until after Boxing Day, so don't worry."

We leave the kitchen and its tensions behind and go upstairs.

"Still up for sightseeing?" There is something brittle in his tone, which is my fault.

"If you like." I lean my forehead against his shoulder and he tenses. "I'm not good at this, Julian. Be patient with me."

His hands grasp my shoulders, and he presses his lips to my hair. "Of course."

The day is pleasantly spent seeing the sights of London—most of them from the outside, as it is Christmas Eve and only Julian's cleaner chooses to work. I admire the houses of Parliament, and a shiver runs through me when Big Ben chimes the hour.

Hearing it, I whisper, "*This is London.*"

"I know. We only heard the chimes on the BBC or at the pictures. It's lovely to have it back."

We have a pub dinner and walk slowly back to his flat. The wind slices through my coat and when I shiver, Julian wraps his scarf around my neck and takes my hand. It feels too good not to let him, and we walk that way until he stops to unlock the door.

It's after ten. We're worn out from the cold and playing tourist. When he asks if I'd like tea, I shake my head. "I think I'll turn in. I should be able to sleep tonight."

He disposes of our coats and hats and follows me down the hall, leaving a lamp burning by the front door.

"I want you to know how happy I am that you agreed to come to England." Before I can speak, he forestalls me with a finger placed gently over my mouth. There are scant inches between us. "I know it didn't go as planned, but I'm not sorry to have you to myself."

"I feel the same." My lip tingles where he's touched it. The air is heavy with possibility.

"Good night, Pearl." Julian brushes his lips against mine. It is more than the tickle of his mustache that sets every nerve alight. I gasp and his mouth draws closer, our lips meeting in a proper kiss this time—something I've been thinking about since the airfield. Fire traces its way down my spine and settles in my low belly. I wrap my arms around his neck, and he gives a momentary start of surprise, then kisses me again, thoroughly and with surprising mastery.

His chest is firm and warm, and the wool-clad shoulders under my hands are sturdy. He raises his head, and I feel an immediate loss, but then he lowers his lips to a spot on my throat, below my jaw, and my skin comes to singing life. His hands are braced on either side of me, not holding me down, not imprisoning me, but lightly keeping me where I have no desire to leave.

I want to tell him this—I want to tell him many things—but for all my love of words, they seem to have drained from my brain and pooled in a place which does not need words to make its feelings known.

After our early meetings and from reading his letters, I felt warm affection for Julian, but over time that has changed to something more, something I'm not willing to name. Wanting him causes a physical ache in my chest. I slide one hand through his hair. Julian makes a small sound of appreciation as his lips continue their journey along my neck.

"Julian."

"Hmm?" His cheek rests against my collarbone. I can feel the beginning of stubble along his jaw, and I want to rub myself against him like a cat.

"What are we—?" It is difficult for me to believe he wants me, despite all evidence to the contrary.

He straightens, one hand going immediately to his tie, the other to smooth the hair which I have disarranged. His pupils are wide, making his eyes nearly black.

"What I would like to do right now," he says, and his careful language is gone, "is take you to bed. What I will do is what I intended, which is to say good night and wish you a happy Christmas."

I can no longer see the man who rendered me nearly insensible by kissing me. I want him back. I want him. "But I—"

"Goodnight, Pearl." A muscle twitches by his left eye, the only proof that he feels anything. "Happy Christmas."

I lurch forward, losing what little grace I possess as I throw my arms around his neck and kiss him. For a moment, he doesn't react, then his arms go around me and his lips part. The first sweep of his tongue strikes deep in my core. My legs tremble and I clutch him harder to stay upright.

"I don't need your pity, you know," he says against my mouth. "I was perfectly fine before you came into my life."

"I don't pity you," I say unevenly. "I want you to take me to bed."

Julian's expression changes—surprise?—and he leans in. I stumble back against the door. He reaches past me to turn the knob, and we are in his room. Light spills in from the hall and from between a narrow gap in the curtains, illuminating the bed.

Should we do this? *Are* we doing this? My mind whirls with questions even as we come together again to sink onto the bed. His hands glide slowly down the outsides of my arms, making my skin prickle. I splay my fingers on his chest, feeling the warmth of his skin through his fine cotton shirt, and wait for him to touch more of me.

"Pearl." He's removed his hands entirely. It is as if a cold breeze has entered the room. "Is this—?"

Interesting question, coming from a man who, moments before, had his hand on my breast.

"Don't you want me?" His tie has gone, and I hook my index finger into his collar and work the button free. The pulse in his throat thunders beneath my fingers. "Julian?"

"God, yes."

He shifts to one side, reaching for the pull chain of a bedside lamp. It glows into brightness and we both blink. With a scrape of metal, he pulls it again and the darkness returns.

"I wanted to see your face." He brushes my cheek with the backs of his fingers.

I capture his hand and bring it to my lips. His fingers, I notice, are bare; at some point he's removed his wedding band. My stomach tightens for a second, but then he places his other hand on my breast, and I think my heart will stop from wanting him.

From there, I rapidly lose track of what happens, whose hands are whose, and where my underwear has gone. Julian's skin is warm against mine, his breathing labored. When I shiver—from too much feeling, not from cold—he pulls a blanket over us and lowers his head to my breast.

It occurs to me that he might expect me to be a virgin and will be disappointed. "Julian, I'm not—"

He silences me with a kiss. "We're both adults," he says. "We've had lives before this moment."

My relief is so deep that I want him from sheer gratitude, but there's more to it than that; I feel cherished and protected and desired in a way that is totally new. I want to offer that same gift to him.

When he rolls over in his sleep and kisses my bare shoulder, I understand what I have done.

I'd worried Mick would trap me in a false love, but what has happened with Julian is far worse—I've trapped myself in something genuine, as solid and comforting as what Aunt had with Uncle Harry but with the same spark that makes Mama and Dr. Max laugh behind closed doors until they go quiet.

This trip was supposed to be about finding myself and building a future, not finding love and turning my life upside down. There is no room for a man in my plans, especially a man like Julian, who is good and kind, and who will understand that I can't stay here. I can't bear to hear him say it, though, to tell me that he understands, and that he will be better off without me in his quiet life with his job and his friends who don't like me. That his feelings are an aberration brought on by the losses of war.

Everything can be blamed on the war; it is so convenient.

At some point it begins to rain. For the second time in as many days, I try to find a reason to stay in a house where I should not be.

I shift toward the edge of the bed and Julian makes a questioning sound.

"Toilet," I whisper. He buries his face in the pillow while I, like a coward, creep naked around the room picking up the clothing we had flung off in our haste to devour each other.

Back in my room, I pack my bags haphazardly, then write a brief note and leave it on the bedside table. I tiptoe down the corridor, my shoes in my coat pocket, trying not to make a sound until I'm outside the flat in the entry hall.

The heavy front door closes behind me with a quiet thud. I stand on the marble steps, fighting to remain upright in a sudden gale. The rain has slacked off, but it is pitch dark, except where streetlights glow ominously through the fog.

I have no idea how to find the train station, much less how to get back to Paris. Gathering my courage along with my bags, I set off down the wet street. Passing the hulk of the shuttered British Museum, I remember there is an underground station close by. After a false start, I find the sign for the Russell Square station and descend the steps.

At the ticket window, I explain my need to get to Paris. An ancient man with an impenetrable accent tells me—twice—what to do. Finally, I ask him to write it down, blaming the earliness of the hour instead of my stupidity and jangled nerves. I make my way to the platform, waiting with a handful of sleepy people for the first train of the day

From the underground to a train to Dover, then a ferry to Calais to catch another train, my Christmas is sodden and steeped in misery. My feet are wet, my beret has slumped into a sad woolen mess, and my coat feels like a blanket that's been left in the rain. The monotonous sound of the wheels does nothing to lull my frantic brain into silence. Instead, my thoughts pick up their rhythm: *Julian, Julian, Julian*, over and over until I want to scream.

The already slow trains are further disrupted by the festive season. No one wants to be traveling. Station employees, porters, and conductors are uniformly surly; the few passengers keep their eyes on their newspapers or attempt to sleep. I pull my damp journal from my bag and try to set down my thoughts, but the lines blur and I fish out a handkerchief to blot my tears.

Writing deemed impossible, I attempt to distract myself by thinking about my family, who, when they wake up, will gather in the living room and open presents under a tree strewn with silver tinsel and colorful glass balls. I wonder what they will have for breakfast, whether they will go to mass or if they went on Christmas Eve, whether they will like the gifts I sent. If Mama is sitting somewhere with a cup of coffee, thinking about me.

I have never felt so alone in my life.


```
                                    DECEMBER 26, 1946
        LEFT MANUSCRIPT IN DESK. PLEASE FORWARD AT
EARLIEST CONVENIENCE. HAPPY CHRISTMAS. PEARL
```


```
                                      26 DECEMBER 1946
        MANUSCRIPT WILL ARRIVE BY COURIER PARIS
OFFICE 2 JANUARY.  HAPPY NEW YEAR. JA
```

January 1947

The new year closed in with freezing days and even colder nights. Once my manuscript is back in my hands, I devote myself to edits with the knowledge that the finished book must be good enough to justify what has been thrown away for its sake. I work in the dining room after everyone has left for work or wait until mid-afternoon to walk to a café close to the hotel. When the midinettes come home, their cheeks red with cold and their fingers painfully stiff, we eat and then sit in the reception room, talking about Monsieur Dior, until they grow sleepy.

When Madeleine asks about my holiday, I say it was not meant to be. Remy is harder to put off, but when she sees that I'm on the verge of tears, she bows to my request to keep talking about dresses. I am grateful to Monsieur Dior for the distraction he provides. My fascination with his work has grown now that I need something to think about that is not Julian.

Once the girls have gone up, there is little else to do but climb into my bed in a sweater and two pairs of socks and work or write letters. I write by hand because the desk, placed to take advantage of the window, is the coldest spot in the room and I can't type with Mona balanced on my knees. Madeleine distributed rags to wedge into the leaky windows and while the drafts are reduced, the glass itself is so cold that it burns to touch it.

Remy and Cécile invite me to sleep with them, and to bring my coal allotment. It may yet come to that, but for now I cherish my privacy—when I can hear my thoughts over the chattering of my teeth.

January 3, 1947

How could I have been so careless? With Pat and then Luc, I was playing at being the kind of girl who could sleep with a man and not lose her heart. It was pleasurable but not personal. A part of me watched from a distance, waiting to be swept away and vaguely disappointed that when it was over, I was still Pearl. With Julian, it was different, and it terrifies me.

Sneaking out while he was asleep was a terrible thing to do. If he truly does care (and I don't think he would have allowed himself to touch me otherwise), I don't see how he could ever forgive me. I wouldn't. And maybe that's for the best. How could I have let myself fall in love with him? I came away this year to prove I needed neither man nor marriage to be successful and content. Am I giving in to expectations or is he really what I want?

Hearing that Katie was married was a blow. She was the last of my friends to give in. Do I want to come home alone and disappear into my old life with all of my married friends and be the one they have to constantly find an extra man for at their dinner tables? Will writing be too hard then? I can see myself going back to teaching because it pays consistently and I'm good at it, but that would be giving up on my dreams after so much hard work.

If I wanted a man, Mick would have been a better choice. He wouldn't have allowed me to go back to teaching. The problem was, he also wouldn't have allowed me to write what I wanted. He had too many opinions. And who's to say that someday he wouldn't wake up and want kids? I could see him wanting a legacy. He would be the kind of father who would devote endless time and energy for a few days or hours, then be absent or drunk or busy and everything would fall on me.

That's what is so hard about walking away from Julian. He's everything I wanted, if I want a man at all. He's kind. He respects my work. He respects me. He doesn't want children, although I think he could be swayed by the right woman. Is it fair to deprive him of something he'd end up loving, just because I'm selfish?

There's no point in even thinking about it. I'll never see him again.

It's supposed to snow again tomorrow. If it's not too heavy, I'll go to the Louvre; it's not that far and public buildings have better heat. Parisians have abandoned cafés and adopted culture as a way to keep warm. The last time I went to the museum, there were jostling crowds around the vents and a near-riot when a rumor went around that there was real coffee in the café. The rumor turned out to be false and we returned disconsolately to stamping our feet and contemplating the art.

My Christmas package from home was waiting when I returned from London. It was the only thing that could possibly brighten that bleak time. Mama came through with everything I asked for—aspirin and wool socks and another pair of trousers, which are warm but too big, as exercise and lack of food have caused me to lose weight. Dan's contribution was a pack of typing paper, which I could have used sooner but am happy to have.

The best part of the gift was two whole pounds of coffee! Everything in the box was fragrant with it, which was good because I gave the coffee to Madame. She got downright misty-eyed, and I think I've been forgiven for any misstep over the past months because of it. Madeleine brought up a small pot the other day when it was sleeting and after she left, I poured a cup, then slid the tray under the blanket so the pot could warm my feet.

In addition to coffee, there was a tube of my favorite lipstick from Thelma and six Hershey bars from Grace. I gave one each to Madeleine, Remy, and Cécile, and kept the remainder for the time of the month when homesickness gets the better of me.

January 6, 1947

Dear Miss Kimber,

Please allow this letter to serve as notice that I have replaced Mr. Julian Armitage as trustee for the remaining months of the trust established in your name by Harrison Warriner.

Mr. Armitage has advised that you understand the terms of the trust. Funds will continue to be deposited in your account on the same schedule. It is unlikely that we shall meet as the Paris office does not require assistance from London in handling your affairs. Should circumstances warrant, I may be contacted at the address above or, for emergent matters, through Monsieur Delaune in the Paris office.

Yours faithfully,

Townsend Petrie, Jr.
Assistant Manager - Trusts and Estates

I drop the letter on the bed and want to drop down beside it. When Julian returned my manuscript, there had been no cover letter, and thus no mention of stepping down as my trustee. He must have come to that decision after I disappeared with no explanation beyond the note I left in my room.

I'm sorry. I can't.

As if that said anything. If I was honest, it said everything—sorry that I'd led him on, sorry to have gone to bed with him as if he were someone who didn't matter. Sorry that I'd agreed to come for Christmas at all, since his relationship with Felicity was likely irreparably damaged. Sorry that I'd fallen in love with him, considering the impossibility of anything beyond a professional relationship.

"...the Paris office does not require assistance from London in handling your affairs."

That made it sound as if Julian's visits were personal, rather than business-related, but that can't be true; he and this Mr. Petrie must have different clients.

I slump wearily into the armchair, rubbing my temples. My head is throbbing—from staring for too long at Brigid's pages in the dim light or from guilt at what I have done to Julian?

It doesn't matter. I take two aspirin from my replenished supply, then roll a clean sheet of paper into the typewriter. But the words won't come; I don't often write letters on Mona, and it doesn't feel right to try, especially such an important letter. I take a blank envelope from my case and write Julian's name and Bloomsbury address on it; this isn't a letter to my former trustee.

January 9, 1947

Julian,

I just received a letter from Mr. Petrie. I'm sorry that you are uncomfortable with continuing as my trustee, but I understand. Thank you for everything you did on my uncle's behalf.

Thank you also for returning my manuscript. It was very kind, considering.

Pearl

Despite the cold, I can't stand being inside where I can't escape my thoughts. Buttoning my coat over two sweaters, I wrap a scarf around my neck and head out. In my pocket is the chapter I'm currently revising. I battle my way across the bridge, head down against the scouring wind, to the Café des Grand Augustins. If Mick is there, and bothered by my presence, then he can leave. The café is mine as much as his.

The windows are fogged, likely with the heat of bodies more than actual heat. I will take either, I decide, pushing open the door and catching Pascal's eye. He nods toward an empty table in the back, but it is close to where Mick is holding court to a rapt audience. All their voices are animated, but his voice is the loudest, his gestures the most expansive.

I shake my head and approach a seat by the front window, asking the woman sitting there if she minds sharing her table.

Pascal brings me a cup of real coffee. I raise a grateful face and he smiles sympathetically. I inhale the rich, bitter scent before I take my first sip, then I push the saucer to one side and fan my papers across my half of the table, looking studiously down so I won't be tempted to see if Mick is watching.

What he thinks doesn't matter. I'm not here for him. He would hate what I'm writing, anyway—it is the exact sort of women's novel he always derided and the exact sort I've always wanted to write.

I've reached the point in the story that I've been circling, unable to see clearly how to make it come right: the mine disaster that kills

Brigid's second husband, leaving her with a house full of daughters and a surviving son who will soon run away. The plot mirrors my family's sad history a little too closely, but every time I try to change the story, it stalls.

Granny wants her story told.

Writing about the collapse sends me back to a dark place in my childhood. I wake up thinking about the night when I held my squirming, sobbing brothers and watched as the adults of the town tore at the blocked-off mine entrance with picks and shovels and, in many instances, their bare hands, trying to reach the men trapped underground. Two of whom were my father and my brother Dan.

It had been twenty-odd years since my mother stood with her sisters and waited for the result of a similar rescue effort. A few years after that, she married my father and watched as he went underground every day. Not for the first time, I wonder how she has survived her life.

My eyes are hot. I blink hard and take another sip of coffee. I can't cry here—if Mick sees, he'll think it's because of him. I feign a sneeze to have an excuse to wipe my eyes.

Boisterous laughter erupts from the back table. The woman sitting across from me makes a judgmental noise and gets up, wishing me a good day. I spread my papers wider and try to ignore the noise.

"Teddy, you have to tell her!" Mick shouts.

The name pierces me like an arrow. I haven't included the original Teddy in my story, because I thought that, before losing her husband, it was too heartbreaking that my grandmother also lost her youngest boy. Teddy's death is a tragedy my family will carry for generations. It took four sons before Mama could bring herself to name one after her brother. Aunt Claire once speculated that she waited until Granny was gone, because it would have been too painful.

Should I include Teddy? I've seen enough movies where tragedy is used as a cheap way to manipulate emotions. My family deserves more than that. I'm just not certain I have the skill to tell their story in the way it should be told. But even if I fail, I have to make the attempt. If my mother and grandmother could live through those sorrows and somehow come out the other side, the least I can do is to find a way to honor their bravery.

I drag myself back to the hotel at five, exhausted by my labors and several hours' studied avoidance of Mick. He finally left an hour ago, pausing at the open door to look at me and letting in such a blast of cold air that several patrons spoke sharply to him. He turned and walked away without saying anything.

Though I would never tell him, part of me is now grateful that he went with Cécile. Would I otherwise have had the strength to break free? What if he'd had his way and turned me, somehow, into a serious journalist and I looked up at fifty and saw him for what he was and regretted the books I'd left unwritten?

Reaching the reception area and its bleak warmth, I forget my frozen toes when Philippe smilingly brandishes three envelopes. One is from Mama, the second from Aunt Claire, and the third bears a London postmark.

Julian.

"Would you like a coffee?" he asks softly. "Belle-mère would not mind if you had a cup."

"Thank you," I say, putting my hand on his arm. Philippe has come a long way since my arrival. He barely spoke then, but now he's almost conversational, though I think he is wisely frightened of his mother-in-law. "I'm going to go and read my letters, and maybe write a bit more before everyone comes in."

The stairs creak as I climb but I barely hear them. Julian has written! Even if it is to say good riddance and may Mr. Petrie have better luck than he did—although I don't believe Julian could be that rude.

I throw off my coat and peel my gloves from my frozen fingers. The air in my room is glacial, so I resettle the scarf around my neck, take off my shoes, and crawl into bed to read.

Mama first. Her letter is short, filled with my sisters' doings and a story about Dr. Max acquiring a new car, his old Model T having finally fallen to pieces. She ends with words that make my eyes brim.

"It's hard to believe that in less than four months you'll be home. I'm glad you found your wings, but the nest has been empty without you."

What have I done with my wings? I wonder bitterly. Nothing but blunder about like a lightning bug, banging into things, trying to find my way. Soon I'll be home, and I will have learned nothing.

Aunt Claire's letter is easier. Teddy is doing well at school; she's found a new charity to help with resettling war refugees; and Sofie is home—but of course I know all about that. I do not, because other than a one-line letter informing me of her arrival in Berlin, my cousin has not written once. I'm not surprised. She is as single-minded as Thelma, and I always felt that she looked on my trip as a vacation.

Only Julian's letter remains. I sigh and touch the tiny gold cross at my neck. "Don't let him hate me," I murmur. "Please."

January 13, 1947

Dear Pearl,

I apologize for not writing personally to inform you of Petrie's appointment. It seemed the right course after overstepping the boundaries of my position. After such a lapse in judgment, for me to continue as your trustee would have been highly inappropriate.

I'm glad you have been reunited with your manuscript. I must make a confession, in addition to an apology. When I packaged your book for the courier, I gave in to curiosity and began reading. His departure was delayed for several hours as a result.

You have written something very special. I hope you understand that. I realize it is not complete, but I would suggest you copy off the first few chapters and send them to several publishers to gauge their interest in the project. I believe you will be pleasantly surprised by their response.

Affectionately,

Julian

The paper trembles in my hands as relief floods through me. He doesn't hate me—of all things, *he* feels guilty about what happened on Christmas Eve!

I move from that astonishing thought to his other comments. My initial reaction to learning that he's read the book is embarrassment; it is private. Mine. But is it? If I am lucky enough to have the book published, it will cease to be mine. All Julian has done is push me further toward that goal.

I choose to ignore my discomfort and take his advice. As far as our feelings—mine and his—there is nothing to be done about them. As Mama would say, least said, soonest mended.

Although it seems impossible, the temperature continues to drop. The miniscule coal ration makes such a small fire that its heat scarcely reaches beyond the stove. I'm cold, even in bed, and it reminds me of my stay at the Grange and its sad aftermath. When I can no longer comfortably hold a pencil, I pack my blankets and pillow and knock on the midinettes' door, so we can combine our coal and stay reasonably comfortable.

Being in their cluttered, perfumed space makes me homesick. Even though I had my own room, many evenings were spent sprawled on the bed with my sisters, talking over our days or doing homework. If I was not with them, I was with Mama or Hazel or Peggy. Remy and Cécile are not family, but feminine companionship feels like home. When their conversation shifts to Monsieur Dior, I recall quiet evenings with Mama, working on one sewing project or another. I'm happy not to have to sew for a living, but their excitement about his designs and the thought of bolts and bolts of shining new fabric make me reminiscent.

Maybe Mama has the right idea, to work with her hands. Maybe writing is too hard. Even though I intend to send my manuscript to publishers, as Julian advised, I should start thinking about where I want to teach when I return to Philadelphia. I broach this thought aloud and, surprisingly, the girls shout me down.

"No!" Remy throws back her blanket, shaking her black curls. "You're a writer, Pearl."

"Not much of one." I am sitting on the floor, legs outstretched so my feet are near the stove. "I've only had two stories accepted in the time I've been here."

"That means nothing," Cécile argues. "You are not there to send out your stories. You cannot count on a little sister to do that work. She is probably out chasing boys."

With Grace, that is unlikely, unless her intent is to strike terror. Growing up as the youngest of six, she is fearless in ways I cannot imagine.

"Maybe," I say. "But I haven't finished editing my book, either."

Remy tosses a pillow at me. "Because your fingers are frozen, imbecile. Now come and get into bed so we can go to sleep."

January 25, 1947

Dear Mama,

Ever since the new year, it has been some combination of cold, gray, or snowy. Most days, it's all three. When it's like this, Paris reminds me of Scovill Run. The only part of the war that ever truly ended here is the shooting. Rationing is bad enough, but the shortages are worse. Right now, it's coal, and it's hard not to be angry knowing there are people whose houses are warm as Turkish baths when I can see my breath in my bedroom.

I can hear you worrying, and you shouldn't. I've got warm clothes (thank you for my new trousers!) and plenty of bedding. Madame brews a tisane in the evenings that she swears will prevent us from catching cold and Madeleine makes soup with enough garlic to kill a vampire. Between one thing and the other, I may not smell nice, but I'm healthy.

I haven't talked much about my trip to England, and that's because it was disappointing. The people I stayed with weren't up for having an American and I left early, spent two nights in London (and saw Renate perform!) and then came back to Paris. She told me about Katie. How exciting! Is she home yet? Give her a big hug for me and tell her she's not allowed to leave before I get back.

Christmas being a disappointment was okay in the end, because between my short holiday and the cold weather, I've done so much writing. I can't wait for you to read this, Mama. I hope I've done Granny proud. And you, as well.

I'm counting the days until I see you all again.

Pearl

February 1947

The stillness in the air tells me that more snow fell overnight. Pushing aside the curtains, I peer through the frosted glass. The square and the sidewalks below are solidly white, while the streets show faint marks of bicycle tires and the footprints of early risers.

Of whom I am not one: my alarm says it's nearly seven. I dress hastily, forgoing my customary wash at the basin when water fails to flow from the faucet. I arrive in the dining room just in time for Madeleine to deposit the breakfast trays and apologize for the lack of water. Cécile is at the table, a blue scarf knotted under her chin. When Remy joins us a few minutes later, she is wearing woolen gloves with the fingertips cut away. We share rueful smiles and dig into our breakfast; inadequate though it may be, the bread is warm, while the jam is strawberry and tastes of summer.

"Are you working today?" I wrap both hands around my cup. "Does the Métro run in this weather?"

"The Métro did not stop for the Nazis, and a little snow will definitely not stop Monsieur Dior," Remy says with an emphatic eyeroll. "I don't believe he sees anything beyond the fantasies in his head."

They are beautiful fantasies, if the descriptions the girls have given me are anything to go by. I've listened to their conversation in the evenings about the resurgence of couture and their employer's extravagant designs, meant to prove to the world that the war was over and Paris is once again the center of the world of fashion. I wonder, though: when most Parisian women are making do with pre-war dresses, is it appropriate for Monsieur Dior to use such obscene amounts of fabric, no matter how beautiful the design? Is the impression of prosperity worth rubbing the noses of one's countrywomen in the dirt?

Although that is a woman's story which might carry enough weight to be taken seriously by one of Mick's important magazines, I'm not the one to write it; while I disapprove, I would rather slip into the atelier and have a look around than pass judgment upon it. Cécile says security is tighter than at Lelong; Monsieur Dior does not wish his designs to be stolen before they are shown to the public for the first time.

I hadn't planned to leave the hotel today, but the snow lures me as surely as a child. Once dressed in my heaviest layers, I slip my diary and a pencil into my pocket and venture out. Flakes drift lazily from a white sky, stinging my cheeks, then melting to ice water. I wipe my face with my mitten. Soon I will be so cold that the snow won't melt.

Trudging awkwardly through the quiet streets, I call a good morning to the shopkeepers in their doorways, and eventually make my way to Notre Dame, standing in the open plaza out front until my feet are frozen through. In this light, with snow covering all its peaks and gargoyles and every stone outcropping, I can almost believe myself transported back in time, were it not for some ragged children throwing snow at each other with thoroughly modern shouted insults.

Circling around the cathedral, I peer into the garden. The walkways are frosted with white, the hedges humped like polar bears. I continue on to the pedestrian bridge to the Île Saint-Louis.

The first time I crossed this bridge, I'd been with Julian—after our very first dinner, when he was Mr. Armitage and I was Miss Kimber. It feels like long ago, but it is only that so much has happened in nine short months. My life is completely transformed, but inside I'm the same Pearl, wanting the world, afraid that I might get it.

Here it is easier to believe I've fallen through time; even on an ordinary day, the narrow lanes have a medieval aspect. I walk and walk, ending up on the Right Bank in an unfamiliar but well-heated café, where I take a seat and let the ice on my hair melt and drip onto the table. I will spend an hour here with my thoughts, which are always clearer once I've written them down.

They are becoming repetitive, though; it is just as well there is no one to whom I can talk about Julian. By now they would have told me to either throw myself at his feet or buy an early ticket home. Neither option appeals. I haven't found one that does.

It is likely that London is also blanketed with snow. I think of him walking to the underground station, going to work at the bank, staring out the window, thinking of—what? The stupid American girl who asked him to make love to her and then escaped before dawn like a burglar?

I close my eyes at the memory of the bare finger on his left hand. He will forget me soon enough. And if I can't forget, I will be back in Philadelphia before long and the distance between us will make yearning impractical. The thought of him in my world is impossible; he is so very British.

Aunt Claire would adore him.

My brain throws the thought mercilessly before me, and I can't ignore it. He is so like my uncle, both in his unruffled exterior and in his gentleness.

My non-exhaustive knowledge of men, gained from studying my mother and aunt at close range over the years, tells me there are three kinds: ones like my father, intense, often difficult, apparently worth it. When he and Mama looked at each other, the air crackled between them. I understand that now.

Dr. Max proved that a man didn't have to be handsome to be attractive; his abundant energy and charm made up for any lacks. And he had mastered the difficult task of seeing my mother clearly, while also loving her without reservation.

But the relationship I'd always envied was the one between Aunt Claire and Uncle Harry. It was a quieter love, but no one who knew them questioned the depth of their feelings. Until his health began to fail, I also had no doubt that their physical relationship was strong.

Truthfully though, part of what I found so attractive about their marriage was its stability. Perhaps it came from being so unsettled as a girl, worrying always about the roof over our head or whether we would have enough to eat—worries unfit for children, but which all poor children suffer from—but I want more than fireworks and feelings. What Aunt and Uncle had was a *safe* love. Feelings were involved, but not the dangerous variety. And that, I had decided years ago, was the love for me.

And that is what I found, and what I walked away from.

I open my diary again and begin to write—not to myself, but to the one person who always knows my heart.

Dan,

This year has been spent exchanging letters with everyone I know, but only once or twice with you. I understand. I got all the words, and sometimes I think you got all the feelings. You just don't talk about them, so people don't realize. The same way they think I know what I'm doing because I can write a coherent sentence.

But I'm in a mess, big brother, and you're the only person I want to talk to right now. I know you'll see all these words and think I've lost my mind, wanting you to read them and then answer, but that's what I need you to do.

You know why I left home. What I want. So, tell me how I've managed to mess everything up and fall in love with someone who is absolutely perfect for me but that I can't possibly have.

His name is Julian Armitage. Uncle Harry selected him to be my trustee, and I feel like he's Uncle's final gift.

Before you ask, Julian isn't like Cliff. He doesn't want to turn me into someone else, and he doesn't think I'm unnatural for not wanting kids. He read my Post *story and the novel I'm writing, and he thinks I'm a good writer. He thinks I'm enough.*

I was trying so hard not to fall for him. Then he invited me to England over Christmas. Everything was going well. We even saw Renate in concert. And I ruined it all by going to bed with him and then panicking and running back to Paris before he was even awake. To make it worse, it was Christmas Day. He's written to me since, but I've been handed off to someone else at the bank, so he doesn't want to see me.

I haven't told Mama because I'm embarrassed to say that after all my carrying on about not wanting a man, I came to France and found one. But he lives in England, and I can't be that far away from you all for the rest of my life. I'm not sure how I've lasted this long.

That's it. Please give me some common sense à la Dandy. That's fancy French for I need your advice, brother. Tell me I haven't done something so dumb that I'll regret it forever.

Love,

Pearl

I come in, brushing flakes from my shoulders and hair. "Any letters?" I ask Philippe.

"Not today." He gives me a sad face around his ever-present cigarette. "I am sorry."

Instead of going upstairs, I sit in the chair nearest the tiny stove, letting its feeble heat thaw my hands and feet. The café was only a few blocks away, but I was as cold as if I'd spent the entire day outdoors.

Soft-footed Madeleine sits across from me. "You should not walk in such weather," she scolds. "You will take a chill."

"I don't get sick easily." I rub my hands together, flexing my fingers. They are stiff in the mornings now, making it difficult to write. "Don't worry about me."

She clicks her tongue. "You have not been yourself since you came home early from England. If you are sad, it is easier to get sick."

"I'm not sad." Is it that obvious? I've done my best to act normally, laughing with the girls and going to the café. "I'm fine."

"You are not." She reaches across, takes my hand. "You are sad."

I shrug. "Homesick, I guess."

"This is not homesickness." Madeleine looks at me critically. "If I had to guess, you are heartsick."

Tears flood my eyes and spill over before I can stop them, hot on my cold cheeks. "No."

Madeleine drops my hand and sits back, shaking her head. In that moment, she looks very like her mother.

"Why do you keep your troubles to yourself? You will feel better if you tell someone." She tilts her head. "You have not told Remy?"

"No." I've never found the right time. "She would... well, she might understand, but Cécile would not, and they are always together."

"For all they have lived through, they are children." She rises and holds out her hand. "Come with me."

I follow her into the family quarters, through the dark, cluttered kitchen and into a small sitting room. It is unheated, but the late afternoon sun strikes the window, making it almost bearable. She points to the sofa, and while she goes to a narrow wooden cabinet and retrieves a bottle and two glasses, I attempt to make myself comfortable on its uniformly lumpy surface. Madeleine pours an inch of liquid into two glasses, gives one to me, and raises the other.

"Sante."

To your health.

"Sante," I echo, and drink. The liquid turns to fire in my throat, and I cough until my eyes are streaming again.

Madeleine pounds me helpfully on the back, then draws a handkerchief from her sleeve and hands it to me.

"Dry your eyes," she says. "Then tell me what is wrong."

It is a relief to have someone else take charge. I fold my hands on my knee and say, "You remember my English visitor? My trustee?"

"Monsieur Armitage?" She smiles fondly. "A very fine gentleman. Is he why your heart aches?"

Ache is not the right word; my heart feels raw. "I didn't mean for it to happen. I didn't mean to fall in love with him."

"But love is a good thing!" Her cheeks flush with pleasure for me. "It is all we could cling to during the war—we could die, but they could not take our love."

"The war is over," I say bleakly. "And I must choose either him or my family, because I can't have both." It bubbles up again and I sob. "I can't lose them, Madeleine. I need my family."

She puts her arms around me, patting my back in soothing fashion. "You would not lose them, cherie. You would not be in the same city, perhaps, but they would want you to be happy."

But I wouldn't be happy without them, no matter how much I love him. I don't know how to make her understand how close we are, that I don't feel whole without my people. Writing to Dan wasn't the same as being with him, but even that tiny sliver of contact made me feel better while I was doing it.

"It won't work." I wipe my eyes one last time and tuck her handkerchief into my pocket to send out with the rest of my laundry. "I'll be all right. Once I'm home again, I'll forget."

There was no point, Brigid thought, in pining after a man she couldn't have. It only made it hurt worse, and she had things to accomplish. She would do what generations of women had done: put her head down and get on with it.

I stare at the lines, wondering what hidden corner of my brain had produced them. I was revising a difficult scene after the death of Brigid's husband, where she faces the fact that she's alone again, this time with four mouths to feed. Thinking about the priest won't help; he'd be there for her, but not in the way of a proper man. Not in her bed, at her table, helping her with the many decisions that lay ahead.

It's too late to rewrite this section again, but how can I not, when these words ring so true? Thinking about it, adding this won't change the arc of the story, and as I continue working, I can weave in that bright thread of loss to make her future choices more poignant.

I have taken Julian's advice and prepared submissions to several New York publishers. The sample chapters aren't yet completed to my satisfaction, but I've written three cover letters, asking in each that they send any response to my Philadelphia address. The worst they can say is no. With the way I'm feeling—and will no doubt still be feeling when I get home—I'll be no worse off.

At least my heartache is providing good emotional fodder for Brigid. I try to think of it that way, instead of lingering on how alone I feel, and how, in those brief days with him in England, I'd finally understood all the fuss and bother of wanting to spend my life with someone.

"It will make me a better writer," I say, my breath clouding before me. "And that's what I wanted."

For all that it hurts, I decide to behave as if I'd never gone to England. I can't pretend that we never met, but I can pretend that I hadn't behaved like an idiot and broke my own heart. Julian will mend; he is a man, and strong. He's already lost a wife—what was I, after such a tragedy? Just a little American mistake, soon forgotten.

Continuing distraction is provided by Monsieur Dior's upcoming collection. The girls' excitement is contagious, and I have become obsessed with the idea of seeing these magnificent creations. Each evening, Madeleine and I wait for them, listening raptly as they detail their labors.

"*How* much fabric?" Madeleine asks incredulously, when Cécile describes the skirt she'd worked on that day.

"Fifteen yards," she says. "Pleated, very fine. The hem is here"—she touches one foot to mid-calf—"and some dresses are longer."

"Monsieur Dior wishes to hide women's legs," Remy says, stretching. "He wants us to look like grandmothers."

"Elegant grandmothers," I say. "What else? Oh, I wish I could see the collection when it is shown."

Cécile slips off her shoes and rubs her feet. "I don't even know if *we'll* be able to see it."

"Not at all?" I ask. "Can you not even be in the room when the models are dressing?"

She shakes her head, and a blonde curl slips loose from her elaborate coiffure. "It is too crowded."

"I am so tired," Remy murmurs, leaning against me. "He is a genius, Pearl, but a madman all the same. We are only human. We cannot go and go and go like he does with no rest and no time for fun."

"Fun?" Cécile raises her eyes to the ceiling. "What I would not give right now for a night of dancing, even with the two of you."

"But better with a man." I grin at her.

"Of course! A man will have money for champagne and American cigarettes and steak."

Her normal activities have become a far-fetched dream. Work at Dior has curtailed Cécile's social life to a single Saturday night date, and even that has fallen away as the collection nears completion.

She pushes her glasses up and rubs her eyes, smearing the last vestiges of her makeup. "I am going to bed," she announces. "Before I fall down and embarrass myself."

"It wouldn't be the first time." Remy pokes her. "You don't remember because you were drunk."

"I wish I was drunk." Cécile gets to her feet. "Then I wouldn't know how tired I was."

January 31, 1947

Dear Pearl,

I was looking through some boxes in the basement yesterday and I found the costume Aunt Claire brought me from Paris. The spangles are tarnished but its ruffles are as bright as ever. What was she thinking, giving a cancan skirt to a little girl? I can't imagine what I could have liked more, but remember Mama's reaction when she described how the dancers kicked and flipped their skirts up?

Have you ever seen them do it for real? You've never written about any of the shows you've seen, which means you haven't seen any. How can you be in Paris for so long and not want to experience everything? I hope you've had some other fun and not spent all your time with Darling Mona.

Things are well here. I've got a small part in a show at the Forrest, but it's a speaking part, not dancing, so I don't care all that much. They needed a pretty girl to say a few lines and I was in the right place at the right time.

It will be good to have you home again. Sofie is back but no fun at all and Grace is too young. I guess I should have made a bunch of girlfriends at school, like you did, but it never seemed important.

Mama has a calendar on the wall counting down the days until you're back. Don't tell her I told you.

Thelma

February 12, the day the collection is scheduled to be shown, is brutally cold but dry. I wait impatiently for the midinettes to get home, having promised myself the reward of a long, chatty letter to Mama, telling her all about it.

According to the invitation, a draft of which they brought home for me to see, the show was set to start mid-morning. An hour before, the grand salon—described by Remy as a bland expanse of white and gray, and by Cécile as a calm oasis of dove-gray satin curtains and white walls intended to let the dresses shine—will be packed with press and the many wealthy women whom Monsieur Dior hopes will want to buy his dresses, all seated on gold chairs.

I imagine the expectant hush, then the appearance of the first mannequin in one of the dresses I've heard described. More than anything I wish I could be there.

Dinner is over. Sita and I helped Madeleine clear the tables and do the dishes, over Madame's objections, because we need to keep busy until they come in.

"How can they not be done?" Sita moans, drying the last plate and stacking it with the others. She runs a hand through her wispy dark hair. "They left before dawn—I heard them stumbling past on the stairs."

"And why so early?" Madeleine removes her apron and hangs it over the back of a chair. "The water pipes are right next to our room. Cécile Ménard, out of bed at four."

Polishing soup spoons with a cloth, I say, "The show might have been scheduled for half-past ten, but there are always things which need to be finished and last-minute miracles to accomplish."

"They will be exhausted." Looking around the kitchen, hands on her hips, Madeleine says, "Pearl, do you have any chocolate left from Christmas? I could melt it down with milk so they can have a hot drink when they come in."

Up in my room, I rummage through my drawers until I find my last two bars of chocolate—a low price to pay for what they have given me—and I am all right until my fingers touch the flat wrapped package holding Julian's gift.

I almost left it behind with my note, but somehow it seemed worse to leave a Christmas present while running away. I take it from the drawer, turn it over in my hands, hear the slight sound as the watch shifts in its leather case. What will I do with it? He would have liked it, I'm sure. Should I give it to Dr Max? Dan would never wear it—he abhors anything fancy—and I'm not close enough to either of my younger brothers to give them something like this.

Teddy can have it. My nephew was fifteen at Christmas: a good age for a nice watch, so long as Aunt hasn't gotten there first.

Tucking the chocolate bars into my trouser pocket, I go back downstairs and arrive as the girls are coming up from the ground floor.

"You're back!"

"It's my ghost," Remy says, throwing her hat on the reception desk and falling heavily into an armchair. "I am dead."

Madeleine snatches the chocolate and disappears, while Sita and I take their coats and Philippe throws more coal into the stove.

"How was it?" It is hard to tell their boneless postures and closed eyes.

"Transcendent." Cécile lifts her head slightly. "A word I learned today. Madame Raymonde told me it means surpassing the ordinary."

Remy opens one eye. "Our work surpassed the ordinary. I don't know about the dresses, since I didn't push my way into the staircase."

"Rita Hayworth was there," Cécile says. "Alas, I did not see her. I was at the very top of the stairs."

"Here, everyone." Madeleine returns with a tray of tiny cups filled with fragrant liquid.

Silence falls as we address the small miracle of hot chocolate.

"It is as good as Angelina," Sita murmurs, naming the tea shop on the Rue de Rivoli, whose chocolate is famous far beyond Paris.

"I added a bit of brandy," Madeleine confesses, taking a sip. "It is a celebration, after all."

Sitting up, Remy holds the cup beneath her nose. "We have two days off," she says. "With the weekend, that is four days. I intend not to move for three of them."

"You have a message from Vera." Philippe comes out from behind the desk, handing Remy a folded slip of paper and taking a sip from his wife's cup.

"She is returned!" Remy's eyes open wide. "Cécile, do you want to go to the baths with me in the morning?"

"No." She places her empty cup on the table and rises slowly. "I am going to sleep."

"I'll go with you." I have been thwarted in my desire for couture description; perhaps she'll be more conversational when immersed in hot water.

"Merci, my friend." She raises her glass, downs it in one swallow, and picks up her shoes. "And now, to bed."

February 20, 1947

Dear Mama,

By the time you receive this, Monsieur Dior's collection will undoubtedly be in all the fashion magazines. If it isn't, it should be.

My friends, Remy and Cécile, moved from their old jobs at Lelong to work for him in the autumn. Since he began preparing the collection I've barely seen them except at meals. The collection premiered last Wednesday, but it took a few days for the girls to have enough energy to talk because they've been sewing flat out. Cécile is one of the fine finishers, so she was working up until the time the models entered the salon.

I thought it was unfair that the women who sewed the dresses weren't allowed to see them shown, but apparently there is only so much room. Of course, space had to be given to the people who will buy the clothes, and the press who will write about them. Cécile did manage to get onto the top of the staircase, but she said she mostly saw the tops of heads and the fullness of skirts moving through the crowded room.

The applause for each dress, she said, gusted up the stairs, thick as cigarette smoke. That made me think of how you wouldn't allow anyone to smoke in the house when we lived on Ringgold Place, so your dresses didn't end up smelling of Lucky Strikes. Monsieur Dior either has no such concern or he is more worried about his customers' comforts.

The dresses, Mama. He has done something that hasn't been seen since before the war. Immensely full skirts and tiny waists and bodices sculpted to look like flowers. Remy says he wished to bring back joy after the dark years of the war, and he's certainly done that. Cécile's drawings are not very good, but her descriptions make up for them.

I don't have the money to even pretend to be a customer, so I won't see the dresses in person, but I'm looking out for articles in the papers here so I can save them for you. Aunt will go absolutely mad for these clothes—she'll be booking a trip to Paris as soon as the French Line is running again.

As for me, I've had enough of traveling. I'm looking forward to coming back to the good old USA and my family.

I love you,

Pearl

March 1947

Early on Saturday morning, I walk to the post office and deposit three substantial packets into the mail, all bound for New York. By the time anyone reads them, I will be in Philadelphia, and the inevitable rejection will not be as painful.

When I return, Remy is waiting. "I was going to ask if you felt well enough to go out in the rain, but you already have."

"I'm not sick," I say. "Just tired. What is it?"

"A magazine is going to photograph some of Monsieur Dior's dresses up in Montmartre today. Do you want to watch?"

She was right; I wasn't feeling particularly well, but I would get up off my deathbed to see a Dior dress in person. "What time?"

"Around two, at the Rue Lepic." She looks at me sideways. "I thought I could invite Vera along, and we could have lunch at a café there before. Will you come?"

"I'd like to see Vera again." I will dress warmly, if we're going to be outdoors for any significant length of time. I can always go to bed with a hot water bottle and one of Madame's vile tisanes if I feel unwell when I get in.

The afternoon is cold and clear, with puddles beginning to dry on the streets. As we settle into seats on the Métro, Remy says, "Vera was right, you know. About your American. He wasn't a soldier."

The question of Mick's military status is something I've chosen not to think about since we broke up. Could he have lied to so many people? I remember how convincing his war stories were, and all his high-flown thoughts on isolationism and everything else.

"I never said she was lying," I say at last, swaying with the car's movement. "I find it hard to believe he would have lied about his service."

But I've met Vera several times now. There's no bluster or artifice to her; she is, simply, who she is. As well, she appears to have fallen in love with my friend, which is a point in her favor.

"It no longer matters. I should have finished with him long before I did."

"Excellent." Remy squeezes my shoulder. "I understood the attraction, as well as I can, but he was never good enough."

"Did you say that to Cécile?" I will never tire of teasing her about how she fusses over her friend.

"I knew he would not last. They never do." She shrugs. "The war taught Cécile to look out for herself. If a man cannot give her what she needs, he is gone."

Huddled in a man's overcoat, Vera waits for us at the Blanche station. The wind has picked up. Montmartre's elevation makes it impossible to ignore. We walk quickly until we find a café with a clear view of the market. It is crowded, an ordinary day. I have seen fashion magazines use unconventional locations, but I can't imagine why they would choose to photograph Dior's dresses here.

"Will we be able to see them coming, do you think?" I nurse a hot drink in my hands. My head is aching, and there is a tickle in my nose; perhaps I *am* getting a cold.

"Absolutely," Vera says. "Photos in fashion magazines may look like one or two lonely girls wandering about in fancy dress, but when you take into account the photographer, his assistant, someone to touch up hair and makeup, someone to make sure the dresses look right, someone to hold coats so the girls don't freeze to death, and a driver or two, it turns into an army."

"They'll never even notice someone else taking pictures." Remy smiles slyly at Vera. "You did bring your camera, didn't you?"

Her big hand cups my friend's cheek. "You never have to ask me, pet."

Remy told me on the train that Vera had offered to take photos for me to bring home to Mama.

Our drinks are finished, and we are sitting and smoking when the first black car arrives. Vera perks up, easing her camera from its leather bag. "Here they are. Let's go."

Two more large cars pull up and park along the street. People grudgingly get out of the way, casting dark looks as they block the entrance to the market. Several men get out, talking loudly and pointing at various locations before waving for the girls to join them. The doors open and four young women step hesitantly into the street, wrapped in thick coats and scarves. Another young woman, less warmly dressed, follows on their heels, while yet another comes to fuss with their hair.

"Poor things," Vera mutters, leaning against the café wall, her camera at the ready. "Beauty knows no pain, I suppose."

"But it does know frostbite." Remy blows on her hands and tucks them into her pockets. "I'll watch from inside."

I move closer to Vera. At a nod from the photographer, the models are relieved of their coats and begin to arrange themselves in various poses along the market. Skirts billow and snap as they are caught by the breeze, exposing layers of petticoat. They look like upside-down flowers.

I have no words for how these dresses make me feel. If Monsieur Dior's aim was to bring joy, he has succeeded beyond his wildest dreams. My throat tightens and tears prick my eyes at the sheer loveliness of the colors ranged against the dingy grays, browns, and blacks of the mostly female shoppers and stallholders.

A dress of pale, smoky blue catches my eye. The model is tall and dark-haired, turning in a graceful arc so the skirt spins around her. I want this dress. I want it so badly that my knees go weak, but the glories of Dior are not for my middling height, thicker waist, and smaller bust.

"They're not happy." Vera shifts, clicking the shutter as two models pretend to browse a bin of cabbages. "Look at them."

She means the market women, not the models. Their faces are puckered and scowling as they stand, heads together, speaking emphatically.

When one model's skirts brush the legs of an old woman, I hear what she says.

"Putain."

For a moment, the model's mask shatters, then it is resumed, smoother than before. She drifts away, one arm trailing behind her, as if to say farewell to the crude woman in the headscarf.

"Salope."

A different voice this time, another woman bundled into a thread-bare coat. She holds a bottle in one hand. "No one wants you here."

"Ladies, please." The photographer's assistant steps before the growing crowd of women. "We will be gone in a few minutes. Please, stand back."

They shuffle back, then the woman with the bottle comes to a decision. She steps forward and throws it at the assistant. The bottle shatters on the cobbles, spraying a chunky liquid all over him and over the blue dress of the girl standing behind him.

There is a gasp. From the models or the women? Certainly from me as my dream outfit is spoiled with what appears to be vegetable soup.

"God, this is marvelous." Staying low, Vera scoots forward, still shooting. I follow numbly, knowing what is coming and yet shocked when the first woman takes hold of the model. She pulls away with a cry and her sleeve separates from the bodice with an audible sound of ripping stitches. The women swarm, shouting insults and obsceni-ties, tearing at her dress, her hair. All the tamped down rage, hunger, and exhaustion is directed at Dior's hapless model. She screams and drops to her knees, while the photographer's assistant hovers, shouting for the women to stop.

At a bellowed order from the photographer, he dives in, hauling a woman away from the model and catching a blow to the ear that sends him staggering.

The model is on her feet now, her dark hair hanging around her face, shivering with more than cold Her dress is unzipped partway, showing the white straps of her brassiere. Slowly she bends, covering her breasts with the torn bodice, and picks up her shoes. Too late, a man runs from the first car and offers a coat, which she settles over her shoulders.

As the entire party moves toward the cars, the model looks back at the market women, who stand in a knot, seemingly stunned by their actions. She nods graciously to them and ducks into the car.

I brace myself, suddenly dizzy. Vera turns to me with a smile. "This was more than either of us bargained for. You wanted pretty pictures, but you know what we've got here?"

"What?" All I want is to be away from all this ugliness and in my warm bed.

"A story."

The wind strikes the window and rattles the loose pane at the top. I twitch the curtain over it, blow on my fingers, and keep typing. Vera has made an appointment for us to meet her contact at *Life* magazine in the morning. My story must be word perfect by then, and not one word too long.

If only my head would stop hurting. I'd sneezed earlier, so hard that my ears rang, and now I have the stuffy, out-of-body feeling that heralds the start of a bad cold.

"Tomorrow," I mutter, moving the lamp closer. "I'll be sick tomorrow."

The words come obediently, describing the fragile beauty of Dior's dresses set against the gray streets, the comments of the market women—sarcastic at first, then increasingly angry as they were ignored—and finally a description of the event which led to the photo that Vera submitted tot illustrate the article, the model with her disheveled hair and torn dress, picking herself up like a queen and walking away from the women who attacked her.

She could no more afford those dresses than the angry mesdames, but at least she got to wear them, leaning languidly against a stall as if a March wind weren't blowing straight through to her underwear. That was a talent, to look blandly beautiful and unbothered by the world when you had frostbite on your bottom.

But she had been bothered, in the end. She shrieked like a teakettle when they laid hands on her, even though it was obvious that their fury was directed at the dress and Monsieur Dior, not necessarily in that order.

To a population who hadn't seen new clothes since 1939, and for whom rationing was a grim fact of life, that fresh-faced, pretty girl wearing a dress made of enough fabric to outfit five people was too much. I was shocked at what happened but not surprised.

Monsieur Dior wanted to celebrate the end of the dark days of austerity and war, and he had done just that. His dresses were breathtaking. While part of my brain was trying to work out how they were constructed, a larger part wanted to own one. Which was no more likely to happen than the market mesdames getting to wear them. Dior's dresses were priced for rich women, and no matter what my friends thought, I didn't have that kind of money.

I imagine asking Mr. Townsend Petrie, Jr. for an advance to buy a couture dress, and then I put the thought aside; it reminds me too much of Julian's advance for "incidentals" when I went to Gassin. I am trying very hard not to think about Julian.

It is difficult, finding a way to make the mesdames sympathetic; readers will feel sorry for the humiliated model, the couturier, even the dress, before they take pity on the boiling frustration of a group of usually invisible women.

Young people will riot and protest, and it is understood. They are young, easily led, and prone to dramatic displays. But a respectable woman in her fifties? All that is expected of her is to stand patiently in queues and turn a blind eye to a display of excess that makes a mockery of how she's been forced to live her life. There is only so much that can be borne.

Maybe it is the fever, but I tear the paper from the typewriter and begin again, this time relating not just what I'd seen, but how those women felt, and why their reaction was wrong but understandable. If *Life* doesn't like it, I can pitch it elsewhere. And no matter what becomes of it, I will send it to Mama, because she's the one who taught me to see beyond the surface of those ordinary women.

Astonishingly, Vera's friend likes the piece. "A bit personal," she says, "but strongly written, and quite a different point of view." She smiles broadly. "We'll get some letters about this, I can assure you."

I thank her and Vera and send grateful thoughts in Remy's direction. She is back at work at Avenue Montaigne, stitching away on the custom orders which have flooded in since the collection was shown two weeks ago.

"Celebratory drink?" Vera asks, striding ahead of me through the shining glass doors.

"No, thanks. I feel rotten." I am lightheaded with exhaustion and sickness. "I'm going to go home and go to bed."

The bell clangs five times in the stairwell. I do not budge from my bed. This pocket of warmth has taken too long to build; if I venture from beneath the covers, even for a moment, the cold will sneak in and I'll have to start all over. I sneeze three times in quick succession and duck under the blanket.

A few minutes later, there is a knock on the door. When I don't respond, the knob rattles and Madeleine pokes her head in. "You are still sick?"

"Yes," I croak. "Was there a call for me?"

"It was Monsieur Armitage," she says. "I tell him that you are sick in bed, and I would let you know of his call."

If I could have chosen to hear from one person, it would have been him, yet he is also the last person I should speak to. My feelings are under control—or I pretend that they are. The weather has prevented Julian from coming to Paris, and that has prevented me from having to decide whether I would see him if he does.

"Was there a message?" I pull myself up on my elbows.

"He says to feel better and that he will write soon. I'm sorry, petite."

"That's good." I close my eyes. "I don't want to see him. I don't want to see anyone when I feel like this."

A light touch, then water splashes in the basin

"You are feverish." A cool cloth is pressed to my forehead. "Do you have any of those pills that you like?"

"On the shelf over the sink." My voice sounds like I've been chewing gravel. "Thank you."

She returns with two aspirin and a glass of water. "I will come later with another blanket. You need to sweat this out. For now, sleep."

That is all I have wanted to do, but apparently, Madeleine has the power to make it happen. When I wake later, there is another, thicker blanket on top of the ones I already have, and the room is lit only by the glow of the coal stove.

The next day I am slightly better, but my head aches and my bones weigh more than they should. It exhausts me to get up, so I retreat to my bed with a book and another of Madame's tisanes.

"I am becoming worried," Madeleine says. She has been very attentive, bringing me hot tea and keeping Remy and Cécile away so they don't catch my cold. "You should be better by now. Would you like me to call the doctor?"

"No." I lean forward so she can adjust my pillow. "I'm better, really. Another day or two and I'll be fine."

She looks at me skeptically. "If you are not better by this evening, I will call the doctor."

In the late afternoon, there is a quiet rap at the door.

"Come in." It is not Madeleine's usual knock; it must be one of the girls.

Instead, the door opens to Julian Armitage, wearing his beautiful Chesterfield coat, and clutching a tray in one hand. He pauses just inside the door to catch his breath from the climb.

"What are you doing here?" I sit up hastily and my head throbs. "Madame will—"

"The fierce madame has given special dispensation, as I have brought soup for the patient."

"Soup?" I shift again, more carefully this time, wondering how awful I must look in my flannel pajamas with a scarf wrapped around my neck.

"Aigo bouido," he says. "Peasant garlic soup, guaranteed to cure whatever ails you." He puts the tray down on the tiny bedside table and fetches a spoon, napkin, and a half stick of bread from his pockets. "Voilà!"

I lean to the side and the steam from the bowl bathes my face. "I'm sure it smells wonderful, but my nose hasn't worked in days."

"It does." Julian drapes his coat over the back of the desk chair and drags it over to sit beside me. "Do you need me to feed you or are you strong enough to lift a spoon?"

To prove myself capable, I bring a spoonful of soup to my mouth and swallow. It feels good against my raw throat, and I imagine I can taste a hint of garlic.

"Why are you here?" I ask again. "Did the Paris branch need you so badly that you had to travel in this weather?"

"I'm not here on business." He gives me a one-sided smile. "Madeleine told me that you needed cheering up, so I decided to bring you soup. Mel sends her regards, by the way."

I try to make sense of his words. "You brought soup?"

"Not from London," he says. "From my hotel."

The spoon clatters into the bowl—which is somehow nearly empty. *You flew to Paris to bring me soup.*

"I did. You've described your room very well," Julian observes, looking around. "I recognize nearly everything." He leans on the desk and peers out the window. "Though I think your statement that you can see the Seine is stretching the truth."

"You can," I say, "if you put your head out and look to the left."

"I'll take your word for it."

The silence stretches. I finish the soup and throw the covers aside, sitting on the edge of the bed in my candy-striped pajamas and wool socks. My hair must be a fright, but I'm afraid to look in the mirror.

"Thank you," I say finally, shrugging into my robe. "I'm sure I'll feel better soon."

He sits beside me. "I hope so. You have a month left. It would be a shame to miss springtime in Paris by being sick."

A month! I've been trying not to think about it. Four weeks and I will be gone, back to my old life. There is enough of Uncle Harry's money left to see me through the summer, if I'm careful; if I don't go back to work until September, I should be done with editing the book by then. Will any of those publishers I contacted take an interest in it?

"Oh," he says, getting up and taking something from his coat pocket. "Philippe asked me to give you this."

An envelope. I glance at it briefly, then look more closely at the untidy scrawl on the front.

"Do you mind if I open it now?"

"Go ahead." He sits on the edge of the desk chair with the utmost patience as I tear open Dan's letter.

Sis,
You might only have the one chance. Don't waste it. You'll never lose
us, no matter where you are.

Dan

I drop back against the pillow, my eyes filling. It is as if Paris and the postal systems of two countries have conspired against me. And to have Julian, of all people, deliver this letter!

"Bad news?"

"No." I tuck it under the pillow. "A note from my brother. He doesn't write often enough."

"Men aren't natural letter writers," he says, making an excuse for his sex. "Most of us, anyway."

"You seem to manage." How are we having this conversation, when I am torn between wanting to hide under the covers and throw myself into his arms? But he is calm, rational; here from concern for my well-being, nothing more, even if he did fly the Channel to see me.

"I'm sorry about what happened on Christmas Eve," I say, illness taking away my fear of offending. "I woke up and you were there, and you were so warm and... I got scared."

He looks down at his hands, then back up, his gaze direct. "Scared of what, exactly?"

"You. Myself. I don't know." I get up and make my bed to keep from looking at him. "You'd never shown that kind of interest before and I wasn't sure if it was holiday sentiment or if we'd had too much to drink or if you were angry with Felicity."

"Or it could have been that I like you far too much for my comfort," he says. "And I mistakenly acted upon it."

Warmth burns in the center of my chest. "Why mistakenly?"

"Because I was legally responsible for you." He sighs. "As your trustee, I was, technically, in a position of power. It was an uncomfortable place to be when my thoughts tended more toward the romantic."

"Romantic." The heat spreads further, making me feel like my fever has returned. "Wouldn't Mr. Petrie disapprove?"

"Very much so." He captures my hand and I let him hold it, wishing I could rest my head on his shoulder until I feel better, or for the next ten or twenty years. But that is impossible.

"I want to go home," I whisper, my stuffy nose making the words almost inaudible. "I want my family."

A ragged breath, and then Julian puts his arms around me, firm and comforting. "You'll be home before you know it," he murmurs. "Back with your family and everything will be all right."

His gray eyes are cool. Dispassionate. Except that a tiny muscle is twitching by his left eye, the same as it was before we'd kissed outside his room. Julian's feelings, whatever they may be, are locked away so he can tell me what I need to hear.

"No, it won't." My head feels like it's going to fall off. "Because they're in Philadelphia and you're in London, and I can't be in two places."

There it is: the truth that I've locked away since Christmas, distracting myself with writing and fashion shows and suffering through the terrible weather.

I want Julian. I want him as much as I want my family. I want his solid, dependable care, his intelligent conversation, his support of my writing. His lovely hands, preferably somewhere on me. A surge of love rises up like sickness and I drop my head against his chest, creasing his his immaculate shirt.

"And you want that? Truly?"

I nod, wishing I could gather my thoughts—more scattered than usual by his presence—and tell him I'd left London not because I didn't care, but because I did. "Yes."

"It feels selfish to love you," he says quietly.

"What?" I don't know if I'm asking for confirmation of his feelings or the reason he thinks it's selfish to offer me what I most want.

"I thought I'd made it clear. I'm in love with you. I know, it's ridiculous. You're a vibrant young woman with your entire future ahead of you, and I'm a stuffy, gray-haired banker who hasn't progressed beyond the end of the war."

"You're not stuffy."

"But you don't debate the gray hair." Julian's smile is less strained. "Do you?"

I put a fingertip to the silver at his temples. He goes very still at my touch. "The proof is right here."

"Don't do that." His hands knot on his thighs. "Please."

"Why?" I run my finger down his sideburn to his jaw. "You're no longer my trustee."

"You're so young," he says, spreading his hands. "I'm nearly forty. What do I have to offer?"

"Yourself." I take the hand nearest to me and squeeze it. "But I can't live in London. I can't." I take a breath which turns into a cough. "I miss them too much."

His lips press briefly against my hair, and he pulls me close again. "Would New York be close enough?"

"New York?" I blink up at him; the words don't make sense. Perhaps my fever has returned—it's hard to tell when I'm this close to him. I wriggle closer.

"Stop it. I can't think straight when you do that, and there are things that need to be said." He leads me to the velvet armchair and pushes me gently into it, then sits on the desk chair facing me. "I know it was wrong to have done this without asking, but I had to see first if it was possible—after Christmas, I asked the bank if there were any jobs going in the New York office."

"And?" I lean forward. All the fluid in my head follows and I press my fingers to my temples.

"There is a job, if I want it. Assistant manager, with responsibilities similar to those I have here." Julian pauses, his eyes searching mine. "We could live in the city or on Long Island if you'd prefer."

He gets up, only to kneel before my chair. "Your family would be a train ride away. And all of American publishing is in New York City."

"You would be willing to turn your whole life upside down for me?"

"Darling," he says, and his face lights up in a way I find most irresistible, "you turned my life upside down a year ago. As far as I'm concerned, this is putting it right."

I reach out and catch his hands. "What are you saying, Julian?"

"That I want to marry you, my daft darling, if only to get off my knees." His laughter is reassuring; I want to relax into him like a warm bath. "Isn't it enough that you've probably given me your cold? Do you want to wreck my body as well?"

Tears run down my cheeks. My nose is blocked, my throat feels terrible, and I've never been so happy in my life.

"I don't want to wreck any part of you," I say, and my voice catches. "I want to keep you just the way you are until you're older and grayer and frighteningly distinguished."

Julian stands, grimacing, and draws me up and into his arms. "I'm going to kiss you now," he says. "Let me know when you can't breathe, and I'll stop."

His mustache brushes my upper lip. I whisper, "Don't stop."

Epilogue – April 1947

The breeze off the water is sharp and my neck prickles with the chill. I turn my fur collar up to my chin, grateful that Julian had convinced me to spend a little of the trust's remaining funds on myself, and not only on gifts for my family—though there are so many of those that I required a new suitcase to bring them all home.

From high on deck, with the shimmer of New York Harbor at our backs, I look down at the crowds milling about on the pier and wish that I'd asked someone to meet me.

To meet *us*. But I hadn't written to tell them that Julian and I were traveling together, or that we'd had a quiet registry office wedding in London before we left, so we could share a cabin aboard ship.

I'd had a tearful farewell with Remy and Madeleine before we set out. Julian surprised me by paying for them to come over to London on the boat train to attend the wedding. They found the British endlessly amusing, and dissolved any last-minute nerves I might have had. Philippe had to stay behind to manage Madame, and Monsieur Dior claimed he could not do without Cécile, even for two days.

"He's so much nicer than the large American," Remy had whispered, pressing her cheek to mine. "Be happy, Pearl."

"Write to me from America," Madeleine begged. "And send a copy of your book when it is published. I promise, I'll read it straight through."

"What will Madame say if you waste that much time?" I teased, holding her roughened hands.

"She may say what she likes." Madeleine tossed her head. "I am her daughter, not her servant. It is time we both remember that."

"I'll miss them," I say now to Julian. "My friends."

"We'll visit," he says. "Though we'll stay elsewhere, if you don't mind. I don't think I could cope with those stairs. I'm not as young as you are."

There will be another wedding when we get home, he promised, so all my family and friends can be there for me, as his family and friends came to the registry office. Jeremy and Camilla and a half-dozen suited men from the bank, including Mr. Petrie, who was as stiff as his letter led me to expect. A few others with posh accents, who scrutinized me and left before the wedding lunch. Also a somewhat squashed Felicity, at my particular invitation, so she would understand her part in driving us together.

Mama will want to make my dress and I will let her. My Dior dress—a gift from Julian—cowed both Felicity and Camilla, but it isn't appropriate for Philadelphia; only someone like Aunt Claire could carry it off successfully. In the life Julian and I will build together in New York, there will be occasions to wear it and remember my year in Paris, twelve months that changed my life in unimaginable ways.

If Julian is right and a publisher accepts my book, I will wear it for interviews and engagements and let it speak for me.

"There are so many people," I murmur, feeling momentarily like the scared girl who had departed from this same pier.

His arm tightens reflexively around me. "New York will be our home," he says in my ear. "Do you think you can learn to love it?"

I lean back against him, knowing that wherever he is, I will be safe and supported. And loved. "I can," I say, feeling the upcoming adventure of our life together surround me like a bubble. "What about you? It won't be too different from London?"

"That's the point," he says, his laugh a rumble against my back. "A new beginning for both of us, keeping only those parts of our old lives that we want."

His job, I thought. My writing. My family.

"I'm looking forward to introducing you to everyone," I say. "My mother, especially. I would have asked them to come to New York, but they're all so busy, they'd never have managed."

It would have hurt to ask and be told no, or for Aunt and Teddy to have come alone, or with Grace; I would have been looking for the faces of the missing.

The crew swarms busily over the deck. Soon the gangplank will be lowered, and we will pass into the vast terminal, present our passports, and collect our luggage. Our first night will be spent in New York, and we'll travel to Philadelphia in the morning.

Now, it is a matter of waiting until we can move. It is the hardest part of traveling—the space between, not on sea, not on land, not permitted to go anywhere.

Leaning on the rail, I stare down at the crowd, imagining the lives of all these strangers. My eye is caught by a tall, rangy man standing next to where the gangplank will be placed. His black hair is uncovered, and when he leans down to talk to the woman by his side, it flops across his forehead. He looks exactly like my father.

Dan!

And Mama, I realize, with Dr. Max beside her. Aunt is there, too, and Teddy and Grace and even—I blink in astonishment—Thelma and my younger brothers. The only one missing is my uncle, the man responsible for this magical year.

I close my eyes, thank him one last time, and turn. Through my tears, Julian's smile is blurred. "Did you do this?"

"The bank had their information on file in case of emergency," he says. "I couldn't think of anything more important than having them here to welcome you home."

I kiss him soundly, in front of the other passengers and the crew, some of whom hoot in appreciation. Turning back to the rail, I wave both arms until finally Grace sees me and points and then all of my people are waving. Mama and Aunt are wiping their eyes, and I sob with joy, knowing that soon I will be in their arms, and I can introduce them to this man I love so much.

"I can't wait for you to meet my family." I press my wet cheek to his and feel the comforting brush of his mustache. "They're going to love you."

Author's Note

This was unexpected. But I always seem to say that.

When I finished *Coming Together*, the final book in my *Ava & Claire* series, I thought I was done. Except what I apparently finished was the *Ava & Claire Trilogy*, which will be followed by a trilogy of books about Ava's daughters. Thelma has ideas about her story, and Grace... well, Grace has been giving me an earful ever since she wrote to Pearl in Paris. Get in line, kid.

Paris is one of my favorite places, and I gave Pearl the desire to go there in part because *I* wanted a trip to Paris, but I wrote that book during Covid, so it wasn't likely to happen. As my frustration grew, so did hers, and yet the more I researched, the more I realized that the Paris that Pearl had in mind bore very little resemblance to the city she would find when she stepped down from the train.

Just because the city wasn't bombed didn't mean that it was untouched by war. Four years of Nazi occupation, rationing, shortages, the loss of so many, whether they were soldiers, resistants, or unlucky citizens—it left a deep mark on the people of Paris. It occurred to me while writing that her reaction would be somewhat the reverse of Dorothy's in *The Wizard of Oz*—she's expecting glorious technicolor, but she opens the door to a black-and-white world. Because that's a reference Pearl would have, I gave it to her in the book.

Some parts of her Paris are mine, as well. When I first went there with a friend, in the late 90s, we stayed at a cheap and rundown hotel on the Île de la Cité very like the Grand Hôtel Dauphine. We were on the top floor, in a tiny room with a huge wardrobe, and the toilet was across a balcony over an airshaft. The tub and shower were downstairs, for an additional fee, and most days of our trip we took turns washing at the sink rather than facing those hideous circular stairs one extra time.

I do my best, in all my books, to stick to an actual historical timeline. Here, however, I have allowed myself an inaccuracy for the sake of the story. The attack on the Dior model by market women on the Rue Lepic did happen, but it was in October 1947, not March 1947. Years ago, when I first saw photos of the incident taken by Walter Carone for *Paris Match*, I tried to imagine how it felt, both as the model and the women who tore her dress. As I've learned more about postwar France (and become a semi-invisible woman of a certain age myself), I've come to understand the rage of those women much better. There is speculation—unproven—that it might have been a publicity stunt, but even if that were the case, it did something historically, beyond drawing attention to Dior's work. And personally, I think the model looks scared, but maybe as an author I just want it to be true.

As always, thank you for reading. If you have thoughts about the book, please feel free to reach out and let me know. You can sign up for my newsletter below, where you'll hear about what I'm working on next (possibly Thelma, probably something Tudor-related), and you can always hit reply and I'll respond.

Bises.

About the Author

As an only child, Karen Heenan learned young that boredom was the ultimate enemy. Shortly after, she discovered perpetual motion and since then, she has rarely been seen holding still.

Since discovering books, she has rarely been without one in her hand and several more in her head. Her first series, *The Tudor Court*, stemmed from a lifelong interest in British history, but she's now turned her focus closer to home and is writing stories set in her native Philadelphia.

She lives in Lansdowne, PA, just outside Philadelphia, where she grows much of her own food, makes her own clothes, and generally confuses the neighbors. She is accompanied on her quest for self-sufficiency by a very patient husband and an ever-changing number of cats.

One constant: she is always writing her next book.

Follow her online at karenheenan.com and sign up for her newsletter to receive a free novella and updates on what's next.